A Matter Of Revenge

Richard D. Thielmann

Copyright © 2006 by Richard D. Thielmann

All rights reserved. No part of this book shall be reproduced or transmitted in any form or by any means, electronic, mechanical, magnetic, photographic including photocopying, recording or by any information storage and retrieval system, without prior written permission of the publisher. No patent liability is assumed with respect to the use of the information contained herein. Although every precaution has been taken in the preparation of this book, the publisher and author assume no responsibility for errors or omissions. Neither is any liability assumed for damages resulting from the use of the information contained herein.

This is a work of fiction. Names, characters, places, and incidents either are the product of the author's imagination or are used fictitiously. Any resemblance to actual events or locales or persons, living or dead, is entirely coincidental.

ISBN 0-7414-2967-5

Published by:

PUBLISHING.COM

1094 New DeHaven Street, Suite 100
West Conshohocken, PA 19428-2713
Info@buybooksontheweb.com
www.buybooksontheweb.com
Toll-free (877) BUY BOOK
Local Phone (610) 941-9999
Fax (610) 941-9959

Printed in the United States of America
Printed on Recycled Paper
Published March 2006

1.

Heat rose in shimmering brightness from the asphalt parking lot of the Commodore Perry rest stop along the Ohio Turnpike. Late morning summer sun baked the black surface and bounced that heat at the services building it surrounded. The searing heat cooked the adjacent farmland and anything that moved through it. The temperature was increasing by the hour, a benefit for all of the corn and soybeans in the nearby fields. July in the heartland was just beginning. Tourists were streaming by on I-80, the main east-west artery running across the northern edge of the state, close to Lake Erie, moving on west to Indiana, Chicago, and the plains. Around here in this region near the small lakeside towns of Port Clinton and Sandusky, near what Ohioans like to call their North Coast, it would turn out to be a very different kind of summer.

The busy plaza parking lot was congested with a jumble of cars, vans, pickup trucks, long haul rigs, and motorcycles. The throng of people who had stopped there crowded the restrooms and fast food concessions, were two or three deep at the pay phones, and all of them grateful for the temporary relief the air conditioned building provided. Outside, those walking their pets or just stretching their legs sought what little shade was available. The lines for the gas pumps at the service station stacked up two dozen cars. The plaza was a welcome oasis for travelers on the move, a brief haven for the weary, and a God awful mix of humanity.

It was only eleven in the morning, but the entire parking lot area already looked trashed. There was a faintly recognizable smell permeating the air that greeted travelers, most likely a mixture of greasy cooking odors from the fast food spots and the main restaurant, gasoline fumes, and a multitude of food and drink spills on hot asphalt. The humid, oppressive air intensified the odor and made the morning feel hotter than it really was.

Away from the general crush of people moving through the plaza, toward the back of the parking lot, about two hundred feet from the main plaza building, a dark, late model sedan was parked. The sedan was far enough away from the main action of the plaza so that it would hardly be noticed. A young man sat behind the wheel watching people come and go, watching the rear of Nicky's, the restaurant serving the plaza. He had been there more than an hour, watching and waiting. It was the same way he had positioned himself four times so far in the last two weeks. He parked in a different spot each time he had come, but made sure he could observe the deliveries that Nicky's received. He kept a notepad and pen, binoculars, and a camera on the seat beside him, items he believed in a naive and inexperienced way he should have with him, items he had not used much. He had, in fact, taken no pictures and made only a few relatively meaningless notes. The binoculars he had deemed unnecessary for viewing what he wanted to see. Nonetheless, he felt better about having them with him each time.

He sipped on the last bit of the large coffee he had picked up at a McDonalds before he got on the Turnpike to head for the plaza. He had rationed it to himself so that it would last longer. Now, as he finished the cool coffee, he hoped he would not have to wait long for the day's delivery to Nicky's. He wished he could get another hot coffee, but that was out of the question. He would cope.

Jerry Bowen had been with the Highway Patrol ten years before he was picked to handle special investigations. He was selected because of an outstanding record as a trooper. He had also exhibited a sense for what the command had thought of as insight into criminal behavior. Whatever that meant, he wasn't sure, but it had helped him get the advancement he wanted. Attending classes at Owens Tech off and on for several years had gained him an Associates Degree in criminal justice and had helped somewhat in his work. Struggling for the degree showed his initiative. Within the Patrol he had been politically astute, rising steadily in rank and position by accepting assignments without complaint and by getting himself recognized as a team player.

Truck should be here soon, he figured, eyes scanning back over the service drive that entered the plaza from the Turnpike. Damn, there's nothing more boring than just sitting and waiting. Uncomfortable, too, because you can't move around a lot. The thing is you don't want to draw attention to yourself by getting out of the car to stretch or walk around a little bit. It was a matter of staying cool to see what was going on here. Regardless of what information command had, there wasn't much to be seen here although his suspicions had been aroused.

Jerry knew something strange was happening because boxes went back on the truck after boxes were unloaded. Command said a couple more days of surveillance before we'd pull back to let the Feds make a decision for what comes next. Jerry had enjoyed the two previous investigations he had been on, but this one didn't seem to mean much, nor did it seem to be going anywhere. He was not experienced enough to sense any of the subtleties and his instincts about the situation, beyond a basic thought that something unusual might be happening here, were of no help.

Situated nearby was a beat up van that showed the signs of severe wear and tear. Jerry saw the van when he pulled in, but he thought it must belong to one of the workers at Nicky's. Inside the old van, behind the dark tinted windows, sat two men. A tall, lanky fellow slouched back in his seat behind the steering wheel, while the other, heavy set, leaned forward in concentration.

Jerry slumped down on the seat somewhat, pushed his legs around trying to get more comfortable, before turning his head lazily toward the traffic flying by in both directions on the Turnpike. The steady drone from the vehicles on pavement was an insistent, penetrating rhythm that pulled at him. Who are all these people, he wondered, where are they going? The thought of people on the move made him reflect on his own vacation due next month. Vacations with Pam were different the last few years, difficult to arrange, a struggle to coordinate work schedules. Not having as much fun as they used to have. It bothered him. This year they were going to the Outer Banks, camp on the beach in their tent, enjoy the surf and sun, be away from the stress that each of them survived every day. He wondered why they did not have as much fun anymore.

Jerry and Pam had been married a little more than seven years and Pam seemed to have the itch. They met right after high school while Jerry was working construction and Pam was ready to start college. She finished her degree and became a paralegal with a good job in one of the better law firms in the area. Jerry eventually got into the Highway Patrol training program and became a trooper. He felt lucky that he was no longer a day laborer. Now, he had a career he was happy with, something meaningful for him.

They had no children, but not having children didn't matter until recently when Pam began to talk of being a mother, of having a baby. He shuddered now at the thought of kids. Not for me, he stated to himself, not the way our life is going, and for the first time he wondered consciously if his relationship with Pam was failing. Was he failing? He thought that probably he was, but had no idea how or why.

The short, compact man got out of the passenger side of the van parked nearby and walked at an even pace to Jerry's dark sedan. He opened the right side front door, said good morning, and got in. Once inside the sedan, he turned to face Jerry who had only slightly turned towards him because it had happened so quickly. Jerry realized the danger, but there was not enough time to do anything about it. He thought of the gun nestled in the shoulder holster under his left arm knowing he could not get it out quickly enough to deal with this man. There was fleeting eye contact and the visitor struck without warning in silent, deadly fury. He drove an ice pick into the young man's chest, piercing his heart, causing almost instant death. A second blow for insurance was struck, but it was not necessary. The short, stocky man knew it probably wasn't needed, but he wasn't taking any chances.

Using an ice pick in this manner took considerable skill and strength, and the man was proud of his ability, pleased with the efficiency of the weapon. Close in, he preferred the pick because he knew how effective it could be. He knew his victim was dead without ever looking at him or checking for pulse. He had supreme confidence in what he could do.

The tall fellow came from the van and together he and the ice pick wielder moved the body to the passenger side of the sedan. The tall man pushed in behind the wheel, started the car, and drove slowly out of the plaza and onto the Turnpike. The man who had used the ice pick got back in the van, drove it out of the plaza parking lot, and followed the sedan. It had seemed so routine, so ordinary, that their actions and the circumstances of their actions were part and parcel of the plaza activity. They had done their job matter-of-factly, and had casually looked around to see if they had been noticed. They felt secure in believing that no one paid any attention to what they had done.

They were wrong. Cuzo Mosca saw them. He was sitting in his dark blue Lincoln Continental parked in a line of cars in front of Nicky's. He could not see exactly what happened, but he had a pretty good idea what took place. He had been using small powerful binoculars, being careful to cover them with his hand when he raised them to his eyes. His view had been blocked part of the time by other cars and people walking through the lot, but still, he knew the young man who had been keeping Nicky's under surveillance was now dead.

Cuzo laughed to himself realizing that these Frangeletti guys must be getting real nervous to take somebody out right here in the parking lot in broad daylight with lots of people around. Very nervous. Must be very nervous. He had been watching the Frangeletti operation for about a month and the young guy showed up week before last. He figured the young man was some kind of law, but he hadn't had time yet to find out what kind. Cuzo knew the man was inexperienced, probably this was his first or second investigation. Made too many rookie mistakes, didn't know the Frangeletti guys had gotten wise to him, and didn't know Cuzo was watching. But then Cuzo didn't think the Frangeletti guys knew he was watching them.

Cuzo was the strategist and front man for an Hispanic group that was headed by Victor Padillo and was called Los Tigres. They were not at all serious about the name, but that is how they were identified on the street, so they accepted it. Padillo owned a series of self-serve car wash outlets around northwestern Ohio, probably 35 or so units, as Padillo Development Corporation, and each member of the Tigres was an employee. The Corporation also had a vending machine operation based in Ashland, Ohio, south of Cleveland. Padillo Development used both businesses as efficient cover for what the group did best: bring drugs into the Midwest from Mexico. They were direct competitors of the Frangelettis.

Cuzo was Padillo's problem solver. He understood the world around them better than anyone else in the group. He viewed their operation as a serious business professional would, although he had never worked for any company. He had the right instincts, a gut level comprehension of supply, secondary processing, transportation, pricing, and sales. He had a feeling for employee motivation, customer service, and long range planning. He was able to handle the business in very sophisticated ways without being educated in these sophisticated techniques. He might well have been able to manage many types of businesses, but he just happened to be part of a drug operation. It was running well, making Padillo and the Tigres a lot of money.

Early in May, Ramon Nieve was making a pickup from the coin boxes of a car wash in Clyde when someone put an ice pick in his heart. Padillo Development was under attack and Victor knew it, and he knew that probably the Frangeletti guys were the enemy. He assigned Cuzo to find out, make sure, and figure a way to neutralize Frangeletti. There was no such thing as defeating them and he was well aware of that, but he also knew there had to be a way to keep them at bay, keep them out of his business. There was enough for us both, he thought. The black guys screw around too much and don't matter because they're all freelancers, not organized, he figured, and they can't really hurt us. But Frangeletti could do damage.

Cuzo had good contacts on the street and a better contact, low level, close to the Frangeletti operation, so it only took three days to learn that someone from the Frangelettis stuck Ramon and another week to confirm the name and connection to Frangeletti. Then he started to investigate in depth. For that, too, he had an innate sense of what to do, where to go, who to talk to, who not to talk to, and what to observe. Somehow he also knew to use the legal records in various county courthouses to learn even more information. He began to stalk his prey and that is what got him to the Turnpike plazas on a regular basis in recent weeks.

Cuzo had seen the van move into position even before Jerry arrived; saw enough of what happened with the two men and Jerry. His attention was now caught by the unmarked semi slowly approaching Nicky's. As he watched, the truck made a U turn and backed up to the rear door of the building. Out jumped the driver and his helper, opened the rear swinging doors of the trailer, and began to unload, placing boxes on a two wheeled cart.

It clicked for Cuzo. Bingo. This is what the young law guy was watching - the deliveries to Nicky's. Cuzo thought about his discovery last week that someone else was watching Nicky's and what a meaningful piece of chance it was. Only chance, because he was covering all of the Frangeletti operation by himself and he and the young man happened to be at this plaza at the same time. Maybe not so much chance, he thought further, maybe the young law guy found out what I found out, that this Nicky's restaurant got more deliveries each week than any of the other Nicky's. This place was getting extra.

He made a careful mental note of the size and shape of the boxes, their color and packaging, and the way in which the men handled them. It appeared to be a normal delivery to a restaurant. Nothing to arouse suspicion, nothing to hint that it was anything but the usual supplies.

Cuzo did not wait for the delivery to get completed and backed out of his parking spot. He eased through the flood of vehicles that had descended on the plaza as it got closer to lunch time, exited slowly by the cars stacked up at the gas pumps, and merged with the easterly flow of Turnpike traffic. Those Frangeletti guys wouldn't try to get the car off the Turnpike, Cuzo reasoned, so they'll dump it east of here, by an overpass probably, so it won't be discovered for awhile. It will be found early this afternoon, he figured, and these plazas will be crawling with State troopers. Best to get off the Turnpike now.

He set the speed control of the Continental right at the posted limit and checked the rear view mirror to see if he were being followed. He saw nothing to alert him, so settled back for the drive to Exit 110 which was the next exit east of the Perry Plaza. From there he would head north toward the lake. Cuzo now began to reflect on what he had seen today in context with all that he had observed over the last month as he covered the Frangeletti business. The pieces were beginning to come together in his mind, but they didn't make complete sense yet.

He thought about the Padillo organization and the differences with the enemy. We are a lot smaller, but a lot more closely knit. We're not as strong, but we're careful, we've got a low profile so the law isn't aiming for us the way they probably are for the Frangelettis. We're fast on our feet, we're smart, and the black boys aren't trying to shoot our asses off the way they do the Frangelettis. We're going to be okay, he thought, we just have to find a way to keep them off of us. He could not put the pieces together yet, so he was frustrated. He started to sweat, turned the air conditioning control so it would get cooler, and ran his hand through his black, straight hair. Ordinarily he'd have it put together by now. That bothered him. What the hell is the matter with this thing, he agonized. Diós mio, shit.

He could not go to Victor and admit that so far he was stymied. He needed to talk to someone, someone who would listen and maybe help. At least listen so he could say things out loud to see how they seemed, hear some meaning in the words, feel some picture start to form. He called Luis Alazar on his cellular phone asking him to meet. Luis is a good listener and sometimes he has a good idea. Importantly, he can be trusted.

2.

Cuzo sat down to relax and wait for Luis. He positioning himself in the shade, back against a tree, some distance from the main lodge at Maumee Bay State Park on Lake Erie. Being here was a calm retreat for him as his mind ran through what he had witnessed at the Turnpike plaza. This place made him feel refreshed and he liked to come here by himself to think and plan. He enjoyed being close to the lake, to see its expanse to the horizon, to savor a peacefulness in the open space, and to relish the sound of the water constantly pushing at the rocks along the shore. Whenever he was here by the lake, he had the full sense of how far away he was from where he grew up in Mexico. Most of the time he didn't think about the distance and the differences, but when he was here it made him think about those things. He wondered, at times when he sat in solitude by the lake, if Mexico could ever be his home again. The way the Frangelettis were starting to put the pressure on the Tigres, the possibility of returning to Mexico might become real. It could be sooner than he ever had thought it would happen. When I get older and want out of the drug business, that is when I will go back. Take my money back to Guadalajara and settle down. The choice could get made for me quickly, he thought, the way things are going.

He scanned the shore line from right to left, keenly aware of what a beautiful location the Park was on the bay. Just west of the Park, the Maumee River emptied into Lake Erie. In springtime, some of the finest walleye fishing in the world took place around here as well as up the Maumee, and delicious yellow perch could be pulled from the Lake all summer long. Cuzo had wanted to go fishing sometime, but never got around to it.

Yes, I might have to go back to Mexico soon, he said to himself. If there is war with the Frangelettis, we will lose. It was a frank assessment he made to himself, unsettled by what that outcome would mean to him, to Victor, and to the rest of the Tigres. The realization of what such a result might be had come to him as he monitored the Frangeletti operation. They have had their way for a long time....many years. They have a rich, thriving business, they have political contacts, they have many men, they have a sure supply of drugs...probably from Columbia and other places. They don't want that messed with. It surely is only a matter of time. The question will be for us: how will Victor react to being squeezed out? We have done well here, it may be wise to move on. Besides it is only a matter of time before the Feds come after us...they're probably working on Los Tigres right now. One wonders why they don't go after the Frangelettis. Yes, it is for sure that the Frangelettis have connections.

In spite of the day's intense heat and stifling humidity, it was a perfect summer day by the lake, with gentle breezes keeping the leaves on the nearby trees in steady movement. Out on the water, twenty or so sailboats were seen hulls laid over at full sail and dozens of fishermen were bobbing at anchor enjoying the clear sky and pleasant warmth. It was a gorgeous picture for Cuzo as he looked with envy out over the steel blue water. He thought that it would be nice to have enough money and no cares so you could sail and fish and not think about anything else. He didn't realize that some of the people he was watching had problems, some with unthinkable problems. Sailing or fishing was their escape. For Cuzo, who could never relate to those activities as escape, the word escape meant being with a woman. With a woman you moved to a new world, a new level of being, you were a new and different person. With a woman, your sense of being as a man reached full reality, to pleasure and excitement found nowhere else. With a woman, the right woman, there was great escape.

Luis approached the spot where Cuzo was sitting. He walked at a leisurely pace carrying a leather briefcase large enough to hold a laptop computer. With his blue blazer and dress shirt open at the collar, he appeared to be just another casually dressed young businessman on the move with his computer. He sat down next to Cuzo without saying anything. He stared out over the water as his friend was doing. They both sat without speaking for several minutes. Luis unzipped the case. Inside, nestled in melting crushed ice were six cans of beer. Luis offered one to Cuzo, who nodded agreement, took the can and popped it open. Luis also opened a can and immediately took a long, steady drink. They sat there drinking and staring for several minutes without speaking, without looking at each other, until Cuzo finally turned to Luis and said: "Graciás, amigo." They rarely spoke Spanish to each other, but there were times when it seemed appropriate to do so to communicate the sincerity they wanted to express.

Cuzo carried a subtle tinge of envy for Luis that he had not allowed to interfere with their friendship. It was because Luis had been born in the U.S. His parents had come from a small town several miles north of Mexico City to settle in San Antonio, Texas. When Luis was still a small boy, the family relocated to Detroit, where he attended Catholic school in the Hispanic neighborhood in the southwestern section of the city. Cuzo secretly wished he had been born in the States. It was of little consequence to him that the circumstances of his well-to-do family had given him advantages early in life, with those times and his birth having been in Mexico. He had been well schooled and privileged, protected from the harshness of the poverty-plagued world around him, his father's gorgeous marble and tile mansion was a sanctuary of luxury and refinement. As a banker's son, Cuzo had not endured the hardships that followed Luis as he was raised. This faint envy was denied by Cuzo with disquieting uneasiness that still edged into his consciousness from time to time, but he was able to put it out of his mind.

Luis had been the first man he and Victor recruited and the best of all the men they brought into the organization. The friendship that developed with Luis had great value for him.

It spoke to the trust he felt, trust that Luis would not betray him, trust that Luis could always be counted on no matter what happened. It was a trust that Cuzo did not have for anyone else, not even Victor. Cuzo believed that Victor could be trusted only so far, there must be caution. Victor's background made for no other belief.

"Luis," Cuzo began, "I need to talk to you. I need you to listen and think clearly about what I am saying, about what I am telling you. There is an answer here in all of what I have seen, and heard...and read in the legal files. I think I have all the pieces, but I can't get them to fit right. Oh, I know most of what is going on, I think I know what else is going on, but I need a key to getting the Frangelettis under control and off our back. They will destroy us if we let them. They're a big organization, they have connections, they have power. Our power is limited."

"They understand death and pain," Luis said quietly. He continued to suck on his beer and look at Cuzo.

Cuzo nodded. "Yes they do...and are used to inflicting both death and pain. However, I am not so sure they fear them. I think they may be too sure of themselves."

He was silent for a minute before continuing.

"At first, I didn't think they would use their restaurants to cover what they were doing in drugs. I thought they were too smart for that. But I found out fast that they were using the restaurant operation to move stuff. Taking a big chance, but they had a reason. I've had to be real careful. I don't think they know who I am, but I couldn't get too close or I'd be nailed. They don't know too much about us yet, but they found out about the car washes and decided to send a message that was telling us to stay out of their business. Ramon was careless...he was not as careful as he should have been. It cost him. Killing Ramon was a signal to us to back off...get out of their territory...this is where they sell drugs and they don't want any competition. They're on the watch for us now because we are worse for them than the law.

They're not afraid of the law, the law is like a pesky fly that buzzes around once in a while. This is why they keep shooting the black boys who are dealing and mess in their territory...and get away with it. Besides, the black boys aren't organized. But even our organization won't help in the long run, I don't think. Anyway, I just don't know what the answer is to dealing with them."

"They will not back off," Luis stated in a simple, yet deliberate manner, "and they cannot be neutralized. The Frangelettis...they will not tolerate us...they won't back off."

He pulled out a pack of cigarettes and lighted one with a snap of his thumb on a lighter. He blew the smoke out and away from Cuzo, coughed, sucked at his beer.

Cuzo continued. "The stuff comes up I-75 from the south, but it does not go on into Toledo, it moves east onto the Turnpike to one of the turn outs where you stop for gas and get something to eat...a plaza. They have warehouses in Toledo, but they don't do it that way. They keep it on the move, always moving, changing the stops, changing the targets, but the general flow is up I-75, across the Turnpike. They use unmarked semis to haul their restaurant supplies and the trucks moving north are unmarked. Just a lot of unmarked trucks coming and going. My guess is that shipments get dropped at Nicky's restaurants along the Turnpike for distribution. The thing I found out watching those restaurants was that once their delivery guys had the truck unloaded they put boxes back on the truck."

"Moving it on to dealers?" Luis asked.

"Probably," Cuzo answered. "Different restaurants probably supply different dealers who are close by. It's a plain kind of operation, nothing fancy, mixed in with their normal business. It would not draw any attention because its part of their thing and it's almost out in the open; it's going on around lots of people all the time. They don't even do it at night because the normal deliveries to Nicky's are during the day. That's why they had to do this guy this morning before he could report what he knew. He was some kind of law in plain clothes, unmarked car. There must have been a tip, probably from the FBI or DEA...or maybe...maybe one of the black guys. We know the Highway Patrol would not have discovered this on their own. It's only a matter of time until the Frangeletti guys change the operation because there's heat on this one. They're not stupid."

"How did they take him?" Luis asked.

"From where I was...the best I could tell...Cappeletti got in the car and stabbed him," Cuzo replied.

Luis raised his eyebrows and looked at Cuzo. "Maybe with an ice pick," he proposed.

"Maybe. We won't know till they find the body," Cuzo affirmed.

Luis stared back at the lake. "It was an ice pick," he said softly.

"You are probably right." Cuzo admired the simple assurance Luis had, uncomplicated by complex intellectual thought, but rather secure in an innate ability to sense and feel the way things were. Luis brought all of his street wisdom to bear when a problem was posed to him. He was usually correct, forming a conclusion that matched the circumstances that proved to be right.

Luis looked at Cuzo, sensing something else bothering him.

"What else?"

Cuzo looked at him and took a long swig from his beer. He looked out at the water and wondered whether or not he should talk about what was bothering him. Finally, he said, "It's getting complex...the Frangelettis are going to keep up the pressure. I think you are right...the Frangelettis can't be neutralized and they won't back off. Isn't that what you said?"

Luis nodded yes.

"Maybe our days are short around here. We also might have to leave quickly."

"We would not do well in a war with the Frangelettis," Luis affirmed, we would do better to pack up our money and move on. An easy way to keep it simple. Do you think Victor could tolerate running away from a fight?"

"A planned, organized retreat is not running away from a fight. Smart businessmen know when to get out of a business...when to move on to do something else. It becomes a strategic decision. Strategic decisions...at least the right ones, are at the heart of survival in business. It is one I think we...that Victor will have to make...soon."

"What do you think Victor will say?"

"I think he will discount anything I say and insist we can survive around here forever. Only time and developments will impact what he decides...not what I say."

"You are confused about the Frangelettis?"

"Right now I have not figured everything out. What else is going on with them? Why is it nagging at me?"

"You are probably trying to make more of it than there is to it. Most likely it is as you see it...no more, no less. And we are in their way, big time."

Cuzo and Luis bantered back and forth for another hour enjoying the afternoon as best they could, considering the seriousness of their meeting. They finished the beers and walked to the park Lodge to use the men's restroom. Luis had dumped the remaining ice from the case and put the empty cans inside without zipping it closed. As they walked by a trash container on the way to the Lodge he turned the case over letting the cans fall into the plastic bag.

"We drop the man with the ice pick," he said to Cuzo.

"We will talk to Victor," Cuzo replied.

3.

While Cuzo was heading to meet Luis, the two men from the plaza drove Jerry's car and their van eastbound on the Turnpike for an hour. The tall fellow, who drove the car with Jerry in it, pulled off the Turnpike and parked against the abutment of an overpass. He got out and stood by the sedan as the van pulled alongside to shield the car from anyone going by who might pay attention to them.

"This okay?" he asked the stocky one in the van.

"Good as any. Lock that thing and get in here."

The tall fellow did as he was told. The two men drove on to the next exit where they got off and headed west towards Toledo on little-used country roads. Getting rid of the car had not been difficult, it was merely a matter of leaving it someplace along the Turnpike. The tricky part was to not be seen. They were careful, the tall one moved deliberately and without haste in such a way as to draw as little attention to them as possible from passing motorists, hoping no good Samaritans happened to see them and stop to offer help.

The Ohio Highway Patrol conduct patrols of the Turnpike on a regular basis. Back and forth from each station along the I-80 corridor across the state. They monitored the speeds and they looked for the unusual, the problematical. The sedan with Jerry in it would get noticed in a routine way, another abandoned vehicle that needed to be checked and reported. Nearly forty minutes after the men left the car, it was spotted by a Trooper making his usual pass of this section.

The Trooper parked his cruiser a few yards behind the car and got out to assess the situation. As he neared, he was a bit surprised to see that there was someone inside, slumped against the dash. The sedan was parked so closely to the concrete wall of the overpass that he could not use the right-hand door to reach the man. He pulled at the locked door on the driver's side, yanking at the latch in frustration. He thought the man might still be alive and need help. The Trooper went quickly to the trunk of his patrol car, retrieved the jack handle, and brought it back to the sedan. This was a case where a slip stick wouldn't work, so he had to break the window. With one sharp blow, he disintegrated the tempered glass. He reached inside and pulled at the door handle to unlock the car. Even before he could get close, before he scooted on his knees across the front seat, the sickening smell let him know that Jerry was dead. The heat had turned the car into a broiler, affecting the condition of Jerry's body, intensifying what would have been unpleasant under normal circumstances of death. He had not seen the blood before, but now, holding his nose, as he reached for the slumped body, he could see the dark stains. His excitement at discovery abated, the overwhelming smell made him back out of the car to catch his breath. He choked for air as he emerged and stumbled back to his patrol car, swallowing, swallowing, fighting the urge to vomit. He leaned against his car sucked in and swallowed until he had control.

The Trooper had not stayed in the car long enough to check the man for identification and went back to the sedan to determine what the man carried. The smell had lessened somewhat since the window had been broken and the door opened, but still the stench was powerful. Powerful enough to make the Trooper fight the urge to gag.

He gave up quickly on that course of action and went back to his Patrol car again, feeding the license plate number into his computer link. It didn't take long for a reply to come back to him with a message he didn't understand and he got on the radio to the dispatcher. He waited silently as she worked on an answer for him.

"That's one of ours," she informed him solemnly.

"Notify command," he replied, and gave her his position.

The Trooper remained in his car for a few minutes wondering what he should do while he waited. Finally, he got out and approached the car once more. This was a State car. He wondered to himself, what had happened here? Was this guy one of us? He felt helpless as if he were suspended in some time warp while he waited for someone from command to arrive. It seemed to take forever for this Trooper.

His post commander got to him in about fifteen minutes and together waited for Highway Patrol brass to arrive. They spoke little as the time crawled and the heat sought them even as they sat in the Trooper's air conditioned car. The senior officers finally came to the scene by helicopter about thirty minutes later.

One of their own. The Highway Patrol officers who came to the car shook their heads and talked among themselves about the man, the tragedy, and what they thought their plight was trying to enforce the law. Theirs was conversation of self-involvement, rather than real concern about Jerry; a mutual assessment of how lucky they were to have escaped such fate in their careers. They talked nervously, trying to maintain their composure, not wanting to show the way they each felt, nor reveal the horror they had upon seeing Jerry's body. They all had been witness to car crash scenes where bloody death came to nameless strangers. Those times were bad enough, but this was different and it was worse.

Jerry was to have been a new face in plain clothes for them, a new chance to find out what was going on with drug traffic on and off the Turnpike. He had been given special training in Columbus for about four months, but the real world that he was trained for could be brutal, unexpected, and deadly.

The command of the Highway Patrol had received a tip from an anonymous source that something was going on with the Nicky's restaurants on the Turnpike plazas, so someone had to find out what the action was. The source said it was drugs, but no indication of that in connection to Nicky's had ever come up before.

Jerry was picked because he was sharp, smart, had seemed to have a sense of what was going on in the drug world, and they felt he knew how to blend in with the outside, the general run of society as they termed it. In reality, Jerry stuck out like a bad scarecrow. With all of his training of only four months, he didn't have the years of street experience to do the job. He was a babe in the woods, spotted right away, targeted because he got too close, too fast. Jerry was smart, but he hadn't figured out what was going on with the Frangeletti way of doing things for the drug market. His reports up until then described their shipments, which were regular and routine, their timing, and not much else. If Jerry had any speculations about what was going on with the Frangeletti restaurants along the Turnpike, those ideas had never been committed to paper.

Captain Carter Walker had picked Jerry himself, convinced that this young man had the stuff to help put the squeeze on the drug trade that paraded up and down I-75 and across the Turnpike. The Highway Patrol knew it moved and once in awhile they would, by accident, catch some small time courier who got stopped for a traffic violation. They were aware there were big scale operations going on, but they didn't know who it was or how they worked their shipments. The tip that was phoned in merely confirmed what they believed all along: there was an organized effort controlling the drug trade across highways where they were responsible.

The tip prompted the command to take action. It was the opportunity they had been looking for to set a specific detail in motion with a specific assignment. It was a chance to put the department in a positive light for the public and the legislature, a chance to enhance careers. Jerry was the choice for that detail. Walker had submitted only his name and when command came back with a request for other candidates, he declined to make any other names available. He believed Jerry was their man and convinced command to go along with his recommendation. Command wanted to find out if the tip meant anything and see if there was a chance for arrests. Or at least a chance to provide the DEA with some hard information to go on so they could move on some operation.

Walker rocked on his heels, his body racked with agony. He was responsible for putting Jerry Bowen in jeopardy probably without as much training and background as he needed to survive. Command had felt something should be done quickly to take advantage of the tip or at least that is what they had convinced themselves. It really should not have been the job of the Highway Patrol to go after this tip, he thought, it should have gone to the DEA. The Drug boys should have handled this, but command wanted to be responsible for the Turnpike, for their turf.

The Trooper who discovered the car was ordered to call for a local tow truck to get the car away from the abutment. The keys were still in the car, but Captain Walker did not want anything touched before the crime lab had a chance to go over everything. The Officer also got backup help from two other patrol cars to block off the right hand lane so that onrushing traffic was not so close. State Police crime lab investigators got to the scene soon after the tow truck had done its job.

As they moved Jerry's body to an ambulance, Captain Walker clenched his teeth to keep from weeping out loud, while inside he was screaming and crying at his own image, knowing the waste of this death. It was of no consequence to him that he had talked with Jerry several times and at length about the potential dangers that lurked for anyone working drugs. Even the free-lancers in the drug business were ready and quick to kill anyone they could who would disturb their chance for a score. He would tell Jerry's wife himself he decided, but right now he was struggling to keep from getting sick, blinking incessantly to keep back the tears.

4.

Carter Walker approached the Bowen house gripped with as much anxiety as had ever possessed him. He was racked with frustration, filled with doubt about what he would say. He had been practicing those first words he would use when confronted by Jerry's wife, revising and changing, testing phrases, trying to feel secure that the sound of them would be appropriate. He had met with next of kin many times to inform them of a loss. Those had been professional duties handled dispassionately in the detached way one does when death is a factor of the job. Most of those had been auto accidents, a couple of shootings, a suicide, but without the jagged emotion that was now a part of what he had to do. I am like next of kin, he figured, I would have liked to have been carefully told and comforted, not shocked with it out on the Turnpike. I could have used the explanations for meaning that survivors always struggle for and that pale with most attempts to give meaning to death. Words hollow, words falling away without being heard, words spoken, making no sense whatsoever. What would those words be for this woman?

He had met Pam numerous times over the years, in limited social contact, with a limited sense of who she was. He knew of her from what Jerry had said and from the comments of others, gossip that he factored somewhat in his opinion of her while discounting their biased, subjective sources. Gossip was still gossip, not fact. An indicator, maybe, but not fact. He thought of her as tall and pretty, maybe a bit of a flirt, bright, and in control of herself. She had taken exception to something he had said once, although he couldn't recall exactly what the subject was. He did remember what she had said was clever, disagreeing with him without being disagreeable. He wondered how Pam would handle this disagreeable circumstance.

When he assigned Jerry to follow-up on the tip about drugs and Nicky's, he believed Jerry was ready. His misgivings only came to him in full force on the long drive to let Pam know that Jerry was gone. Walker had recognized Jerry's potential way before the time came to move him from patrol duty to plain clothes work. Jerry had it all, the diligence, the ability to work within the framework of Patrol rules, willingness for any assignment, the general desire to get ahead. Jerry was, in many ways, Walker's project as a mentor and he made decisions for Jerry that imposed a positive impact on the younger man's career.

Jerry had been just another average type of young guy that came into the Patrol to get away from the boredom of some other kind of job. A chance to take responsibility, a way to distinguish himself, a line of work where the activity was never the same from day to day. He could be somebody. He had confided in Walker over the years how much it meant to him to be a part of the Patrol. Jerry was excited each time he got promoted and especially so when he was named to be a plain clothes investigator. He had called Walker to thank him for all his help. Jerry knew who had blessed his career; he knew it never would have happened without Captain Walker.

Walker pushed the doorbell as he surveyed the small yard, pleasant enough, yet without distinction in the short block of companion houses. The neighbors actually did a better job with their yards: more flowers, better tended. The place was not shabby, just okay in its appearance. Not a lot of effort placed on the yard here at the Bowen's, Walker surmised, it probably was not that important to them.

Pam pulled open the inside door and stared at him through the screen. She had only recently gotten home from work, still in her finely tailored suit, a beer in her left hand that hung by her side. She gave no sign of emotion, nor did she speak. Always calm and cool, he remembered, always seeming to be in control. She stared at her husband's commander, his uniform registering the official nature of showing up on her porch, the grim look on his face, each a symbol of the news she knew was to come. The realization instantly chilled her heart, stopped her breathing.

"Pam..."

"He's dead, isn't he?"

She already knew it was so before he spoke, her body steeled to the bitter words he would utter, her mind compressed and compartmentalized to contain all feeling, to firmly maintain her composure. She would not outwardly react, only the agony within her made any difference and inside she could deal with her feelings.

The impact of her own words, uttered as a way of determining events, stated so directly, these words triggered a sensation for her of stiffly falling backwards like a board as if she were fainting. The sensation transported her beyond where she was, away and outside, a strange easiness of floating, drifting apart from her body. She had not fainted, however, she still stood rigidly, waiting for his answer, knowing full well what it would be, yet feeling separated from her anticipation of and her reaction to what it would be.

Pam watched Captain Walker talk to her and she watched herself stare back at him, and realized she was now outside of herself. It was such a powerful sensation to be able to view herself from a position floating just above, looking down with an apparent omniscience for what she surveyed. Suspended as in a dream, watching herself while still being herself. Only in a dream does it happen this way, only in a dream can one be outside of, yet coexist with oneself. It seems so real. How can any of this be real, she thought, how can this be happening to me?

"Come in," she said without moving.

She listened to herself speak, evaluated her voice, considered how it sounded. There was a lifeless quality to it, she thought, and why not, life has been taken away from me. Jerry's life has been pulled from me without warning, with no way to be prepared. She had not understood the gravity of his new assignment nor realized the risk he was taking. In truth, neither did the Highway Patrol, although in a perfunctory way the warnings were presented to Jerry. Command never thought that he would get killed. As Jerry had told Pam: any law enforcement officer faces potential danger all the time, but with the new job it would be less, he would be an investigator, checking records, working on the phone, observing people. When she reminded him that when drugs were involved you had danger, he brushed off that notion and told her not to worry.

She took note of how calm she looked, how serene she felt. He was dead; it was a matter of being told the circumstances. She would try to make it easy for Captain Walker.

He pulled open the screen door and stepped inside. At first, for a moment, a matter of seconds, he could not look her in the face.

"I'm sorry to come here with the news about Jerry. Jerry's...ah...um..."

"Jerry's dead," she finished.

"Yes, ma'am. I'm sorry to be here like this...I wanted to come talk to you personally so you could hear it from me...not a phone call or something...but personally. I put him on the assignment...I'm responsible. He was well trained, Pam, worked hard at everything during training and did well."

"Did well," she intoned flatly. "What was 'did well'...what did it mean for him?"

"Scored very high on all the test work, Pam, very high..."

Walker knew he was in trouble with this subject by the way she asked the question, knew he should not have even brought up the training.

"Of course, the physical stuff...hand-to-hand, firing range...the practical stuff, how to interview, recognize certain conduct profiles, matching up..."

She admired her own calmness and self control, pleased with the smooth way she was functioning. At the same time, she was fascinated with her role as independent observer of herself. What a wonderful thing to have this dual role, she thought.

"How did he die?" Pam asked.

"He...he was stabbed. It was..."

"Stabbed?"

Pam watched herself react to that news. To be stabbed meant that the killer had to be very close to Jerry. How could the killer get that close? Why wasn't he prepared? Why couldn't he defend himself? She saw the look on Walker's face and knew those same questions were with him. How could it happen? Walker was also asking himself. She watched herself respond in a numb, uncomprehending manner.

"Stabbed?" She repeated the word in the same flat tone, again as a question.

"Yes, ah, he was stabbed in the chest. We're sure by the wound placement that he did not suffer...he probably died almost instantly...he was...ah...we think maybe..."

"Captain Walker, please just tell me what happened."

He sighed.

"We're not sure what happened, but..."

"Please tell me what you do know."

Pam was proud of the positive way she now saw in herself, her strength returning, the shock of the news insulated by her sheer will to maintain control of her emotions and by being able to look at herself in action from a distance. It was working well. Yes, she was in control.

"He was stabbed with something thin and sharp like an ice pick. He died right away, and his car was taken east on the Turnpike for sixty miles or so and left by an overpass. He was found by one of our troopers maybe two hours after it happened."

"Who did it?"

She enjoyed watching herself exhibit real intensity in her demand for such information. Anger must be creeping in already, she surmised.

"We don't know that yet, Pam, we've just started to investigate. There are some leads and we'll pursue all of them."

"I want to know who did it," she insisted.

"I'm sure you do...and so do we. We're working on it."

"If you don't find out, I will. Some way, somehow, I will find out who killed my husband."

"Now, Pam, I know how you feel, but..."

"You couldn't possibly know how I feel."

"Let us handle the investigation. A very strong effort will be made...let me emphasize strong...you can count on that. A most diligent effort."

"I want to know."

"I know you do and we'll keep you posted to our progress."

"Thank you, Captain Walker for your kindness...I know this was not easy for you."

"No...it wasn't. I'm sorry.

She watched as Captain Walker left the house and walked to his car, his image becoming a blur, a surreal portrait of how she thought it should be. As his image faded from view, she slowly was one within herself again. Still silent and stoic, still waiting for meaning, not understanding death any more than anyone does, rigid and stationary, hoping that this were indeed all a dream. The essence of a dream was about her in memory, but she knew it was not a dream. There was the pall of sadness that now overwhelmed her, an emerging mark of grief becoming part of her senses. The sadness was a hammer upon her chest, but right now she would not let herself cry from this pain.

5.

Cuzo knew what the answer would be even as they began talking with Victor. He deferred to Victor because Victor had an intensity that he could not muster within himself. Long ago, he had realized Victor's limitations intellectually, but the drive to succeed was there, and so was a profound charisma that unified the Mexicans needed to fulfill their venture in selling drugs. Victor knew what it took to compete against the black shooters from Toledo's inner city and the smooth, well oiled machine of the Frangeletti group. Victor could make his organization successful with the sheer force of will that was his spirit and with brains that Cuzo provided. Cuzo knew his place. He didn't like it much, but he knew how he fit in, how he could help make things happen. He was well rewarded and well regarded for his part in their system. He understood how fragile, how temporary everything was in the drug business, how easy it would be for their system to collapse in just a few hours. He trusted no one to any extent, except Luis, and Victor, slightly. As a result, he kept his share of the organization's profits close at hand at all times in real cash money, not relying on a bank or any other financial contrivance that the establishment used. His money was in a small satchel locked in a two-drawer file cabinet, ready to pull out and leave at a moments notice. He believed you never knew when it might come to that. Drugs attracted big time trouble from the competition and the law. He was prepared for trouble.

Victor had grown up in violence in Mexico City and came to the United States to escape that life. But there was a thirst for violence within him that he could not escape, so it was with him wherever he was. He had a quick smile that made him seem easy going and friendly, but just beneath the surface of his personality lurked an animal-like craving for violence. He had learned over the years to control the burning sense for striking out, to keep it in check, and now, at age fifty he was more at ease with himself.

Prison had helped do that for him, he had explained. Once in Texas and again in Florida for a total of fourteen years behind bars. The poison of prison was in his body still, not fully expelled, and the ravages of those caged ordeals still showed in the scars on his body that would never completely disappear. Prison, he had said, made the rage worse for a man or calmed it down. He explained that he was calmer now.

Victor had first come to northwestern Ohio as a drug courier for a Houston syndicate, traveling the I-75 corridor several times a year, each time in a different vehicle. When he decided to form his own group to do drug business it was a simple matter for him to settle near Toledo. He had avoided conflict with the Houston syndicate by keeping a low profile for several years in Florida before beginning his venture in the North. His temper, not drugs, had gotten him into prison both times, so he had not come to the attention of the DEA.

Getting into drugs for a Mexico City gang kid looking for thrills and pleasure is a certain destiny just as it is for many urban Chicanos or blacks in the U.S. As a result, these kids look at drugs with an eye toward enterprise. Drugs were a business, a preordained right for them to make money, lots of it, a great deal easier than any other way they knew. Courting trouble with drugs was still much easier and much quicker than the ways respectable people they knew worked for a lot less money.

It was there on the streets of Mexico City that Victor learned how violence paid off, how the intimidation from the fear of his violence made things go his way. It was there he made the connections for moving drugs that would later feed his system. It was in his school on the streets that he learned what the drug business might one day do for him. He knew that if somehow he could get north of the border he could make himself a rich man. It was to be, but not without considerable struggle, falling victim to his temper, and a rage that always simmered.

Cuzo, on the other hand, came to the drug world with the gentility of a pampered rich man's son, drawn to their potency for attracting and having women. He was forever fascinated by that aspect of drugs, but soon realized they could make him as rich as or richer than his father and with substantially less work. Every business had risks, he concluded, the illegality of drugs was just another downside of a business operation.

For Cuzo, from Guadalajara wealth, to cross paths with Victor, from Mexico City street poverty, the irony was immense. They each recognized and respected the fate that made it so. Some demon God of the universe in charge of their lives in willful ways was, directing, moving, channeling these two men to the circumstance of their meeting. They each knew that a master hand was at work with them and it overcame them with awe, almost frightened them, whenever it was that they spoke of it.

Victor had just gotten out of Florida State Prison and headed for Tampa. Someone he knew from the Houston syndicate was living in Tampa. He never got to them. When he got off the bus in Tampa, he went down the street looking for someplace to get a cup of coffee. Cuzo spoke to him outside of a coffee shop two blocks from the bus terminal. It was a direct comment that struck home with him.

"You look like you just got out of trouble or are headed for trouble."

Cuzo said it in English and with a smile.

"Both." Victor had replied.

This chance meeting could not be explained even as they compared their lives over coffee, and Cuzo could not understand why he had even spoken to Victor. The eerie effect clung to them creating a bond between two unlikely comrades. They were simpatico even though they came from such different backgrounds.

It did not take long to establish their mutuality of desire to make big money in drugs. Victor knew how it could be done from working with the Houston syndicate, but he needed help. It takes an organization, he told Cuzo, people in a system that has been structured and has some planning behind it.

Cuzo was his man, but they each did not know it yet at that point. It would, however, be determined by Victor quite quickly. Cuzo had gotten to this coffee shop, this place of business beginning, by a far easier path than had Victor. His parents had sent him to school in the U.S. to study business at the University of Miami. Although he had done fairly well with his studies, his specialty was drugs: the ready supply, the quick delivery, the reasonable prices. He used friends in Guadalajara to fulfill his orders and they did so readily, fully prepared to stay rich and flaunt the laws and legal efforts to thwart them.

Such activity gains attention from a variety of officials wanting to put a stop to the business. University administration, city police, the DEA, all wanted to get at Cuzo. He realized he had drawn too much attention to himself by having public fun with several young coeds and flashing lots of cash as he went about his business. He stopped selling abruptly, cut off all ties to his buyers, and concentrated on being a student. He stuck with his classes for the term, finished with good grades, and dropped out and away from the University at the end of his second year, although he didn't let anyone know that was his plan. He felt he already knew how to run a business, at least the kind of business he wanted to run.

He was aware that someone was watching him. He didn't know who, maybe the DEA, or the FBI, but somebody shadowed his movements. He got a job with a company that made calls to sell a variety of products over the phone. He stayed in the same apartment he used as a student and even filled out the forms for the next term. Quietly, carefully, he left the apartment early one morning before daylight. He had parked his car some distance from the building the night before and so now walked through the dark to its location several blocks away. He made sure he stayed out of sight, made sure he was not seen or followed as he walked the distance. He started the car without turning on the lights and slowly eased down the street and drove away from Miami. He was quite sure, as he headed for Tampa, that he was not followed. Within the year he met Victor.

Cuzo and Victor put together a group of men they could trust and who would work well together to make an organization successful in the drug business. They established the organization in Tampa, readying themselves for the business ahead. They moved to Ohio as one, in one day, and no one ever went back to Tampa. Once they were located in Toledo, they added several others to the group, but in all, they were committed, dedicated to making money. None of them had a sense they were doing anything wrong from a philosophical point of view, although they all knew that what they were doing was illegal. They were engaging in an enterprise that many others thrived in, feeding the channels of drugs that relentlessly, constantly flowed into the U.S. on a daily basis, a multitude of systems that fed an insatiable, ever-increasing appetite for drugs that Americans craved as a kind of national cotton candy for the hip, the disenfranchised, and the forgotten. Drugs were as American and in use and wanted and as accepted as coffee, cigarettes, or booze. Cuzo knew the market was already there for them to exploit and to get rich.

Their first year in Ohio, they kept a low profile, sorting out where they would sell. It was easier than they had believed it would be. A contact here, a word there, and the business began to roll. In large measure, Cuzo financed the start of the organization from his take on the Miami campus. It wasn't a big number - $15,000.00 - but it was the start they needed.

Cuzo came up with the car wash idea as a cover for their operation. Lots of cash, coming and going of those needed to service the car wash, and plenty of ways to exchange merchandise. Victor accepted this idea as his own and soon had two units under construction. Once established, they built five car washes in and around Toledo. Year two they started ten and year three they opened twenty.

The Padillo organization supplied a group of dealers - they never sold directly to users - although most of the dealers were users. Cuzo thought of the business as that of a wholesaler providing a secondary market with the product which was in demand. It was illegal, it was dangerous, but it brought in tremendous amounts of money. The car washes were the place where orders for drugs could be received. Deliveries were made along back country roads, at night, under cover from the Organization. For the most part it worked smoothly.

The Frangeletti guys soon learned that somebody beside the black boys and other free-lancers were trying to move in on their market. It didn't take long for Nick to find out about the Padillo organization. The Frangelettis watched the Padillo operation very carefully, but left it alone. Nick didn't want a war over drugs that would bring the Feds into play. Besides, they had not noticed a decline in their volume. Whatever the Mexican boys were doing it was not affecting the Frangeletti business in drugs. At least in the beginning this was true. Eventually, however, the encroachment on the territory would have its effects. Bottom line losses in the drug business. The Mexican boys began to cause a problem.

Cuzo and Luis sat facing Victor in the large family room of a sprawling ranch style house located on one hundred fifty acres of former cornfield southwest of Toledo. The house was almost half a mile from the county road, surrounded by stands of maples and pines. A brick courtyard connected the house to a swimming pool and adjacent bath house. Another hundred feet or so away was a large pond stocked with fish. The house contained a master bedroom, four guest bedrooms, an office, formal dining room, kitchen and pantry, and the common room where the men sat talking. Behind the three-car garage were separate quarters for the maid and handy man. Close by were the dog kennels. Unlike other houses in the area that were built on slabs, Victor's house had a basement. He felt safer with a basement in case of an attack. A cyclone fence surrounded the trees, house, buildings, and pond, and four Doberman dogs ran free throughout the fenced area.

When the organization first got started, Cuzo and Victor felt safe in what they were doing, knowing that no one from the Frangelettis or the black boys would be able to spot them. But that changed and Padillo Development employees took turns living in the house for a few days at a time with at least two of the men there twenty-four hours a day. It was seldom that Victor ventured outside of this compound. This was a precaution that Victor wanted. He knew there could be war about the drugs, he knew that eventually the Feds could come.

Victor had never married, but had fathered children in Texas and Florida with three different women whom he sent money when he thought about it, which wasn't often. He had never let these women know where he was. The children were Carlos in Houston, Ernesto in Tampa, and Maria in Dallas. They did not know much about their father and had little contact with him over the years. Victor did not care.

Gloria Smith lived with Victor and had been around about five years. That's the name for her Victor used when he first introduced her to the organization. Cuzo had wondered if that were her real name. She had appeared one day with little fanfare and no advance notice to his men. One day no Gloria, the next day there she was. A girl in her mid twenties, she stayed in the master bedroom all of the time that Cuzo and

Luis were in the house. In fact, neither of them had seen her much over the years that she had lived with Victor. She was not involved in any way with Padillo Development and apparently had only one function in Victor's life. Since he did not socialize outside the group, Gloria was not needed as a companion for parties or other engagements. Victor never really explained who she was or where she came from. He didn't have to and none of the men asked. Over time, he had told Cuzo that the girl was sent to him by a friend in Florida. On another occasion he told Luis that the girl was a runaway who was sent to him for protection. Still another time, Victor spoke of her as a child of a friend, pledged to him in payment for an old debt. In any case, it was Gloria's appearance that made Cuzo realize he did not know his partner as well as he had thought he did.

Cuzo believed the truth about Gloria was somewhere within the stories Victor told you something, but didn't care much what the truth was. Cuzo knew he would never know much about Gloria and that was okay. She rarely spoke to him directly even on those few times she was in the same room. A quiet hello from her was about all he had ever heard. She was damned pretty, though.

Victor listened intently as Cuzo talked about what he had seen, what he thought it meant. Victor watched Cuzo speak calmly and rationally about what the Frangeletti guys were up to and what he thought was going on. This was the first full report since Victor had given the assignment. He looked at Luis watching and listening to Cuzo and knew that Luis was angry. He related to that, but reminded himself to keep control. When Cuzo had finished, Victor asked him what he thought was missing, what was bothering him.

"You theenk something is missing. Does it matter?"

"It may," Cuzo answered, "it may in the way we handle them. I just don't like not knowing what else there is and how it fits. But what I do believe is that there's not much we can do about the Frangelettis."

The older man smiled because he knew how smart Cuzo was, how precise, how thorough.

"Jewno, Cuzo, you can theenk about it, but meantime we gon take care meester ice pick."

After all these years, Victor's accent still came through, unlike the two younger men who spoke with no discernible trace of the Spanish. He could not hear it in himself, so it didn't bother him, but somehow it did bother Cuzo.

The three men talked for another half hour or so with Victor doing most of the talking. He wanted the ice pick man to be handled in a certain way that would send a message back to the Frangeletti guys. It was a method he believed would be understood: Don't fuck with us because we can hit back and keep in mind that we are going to operate around here just like you guys. He had a sense for what would get their attention and the controlled rage that had always been a part of him brought answers to situations such as these that were brutal and ugly. His solutions were simple and usually bloody.

6.

Buddy Cappeletti did not carry a gun, but he usually had an ice pick at hand that he could use if necessary. He preferred the plain, standard ones with the simple, natural finish handles. He kept one in the glove box of his car and another on a shelf by the door of his apartment. He had acquired ten of them from a variety of places over the last few years and was always on the lookout for a new one as he traveled about the state. For Buddy, using an ice pick was merely a symbol of how he liked to strike out at the world, a slick element of the brutality that overrode anything about him that one would describe. Bludgeoning someone with a baseball bat would be good, he had once considered, but a bat was awkward, too difficult to conceal, the result of attack not as sure and swift as the pick.

He could not remember exactly how the idea to use a pick to kill someone had come to him, but he remembered clearly that first incident when he relished driving the sharp point into an adversary. They had argued over a minor wager on a pro football game: Cleveland Browns against the Pittsburgh Steelers. Buddy's team was the Browns and they had squeaked out a victory. Buddy wanted the hundred dollars he felt he had won. When the money was not readily forthcoming, he went to collect. He accosted the man in the Westfield Mall parking lot in the middle of a Saturday afternoon. No one paid any attention as Buddy drove the ice pick into the man's chest. He struck with the pick several times, holding the man's body against a car, slowly letting the body slide to the ground. It had been so easy, so quiet, so quick. He felt quite satisfied that the pick was meant to be his weapon. Not a new weapon to be sure, but one that Buddy took as his own creation, his own way of striking out when he wanted to settle a score or record a cap of someone. The pick was beautiful, he thought, satisfied that he had adopted an untraceable mode for killing.

Short, powerfully built, Buddy had tremendous upper body strength that he could leverage very effectively in a fight, even with his shorter stature. He liked to fight, he eagerly looked for a fight, provoking one at any opportunity. In his current assignment, Mr. Frangeletti had cautioned him that such an instinct could get him in serious trouble. Containing the urge to fight festered within Buddy, a wild rage running loose inside him, calling to him constantly for release, tantalizing and teasing the control of his behavior so that it jeopardized his work for the Frangelettis. Working for the family probably kept Buddy from being a serial killer, where he would have exercised a steady compulsion for satisfying the urges he had, regularly finding, systematically tracking down, and routinely killing chosen targets of his rage.

With his own physical system working on overload much of the time, Buddy had started to drink too much and at the wrong times. He couldn't get enough of killing, involving himself eagerly in the power over someone, taking away their life. He was thrilled with killing, something that he discovered when he was about nine years old. He had the typical childhood profile for this type of condition: smothered a pet rabbit of his cousin's, killed his grandmother's pet canary. After that, came a succession of pet deaths for other family members and those of neighbors. People who lived in the north Toledo neighborhood where he grew up knew full well that Buddy was the one who did it each time, but they couldn't catch him.

Finally, at seventeen, he took another person's life. He used a jack handle which happened to be the nearest weapon, ending an argument with Rod Boyer who did not realize such danger from Buddy. No one saw it happen, but he was suspected, taken down to Child Study Institute for questioning. He was quite familiar with CSI, having been hauled in several times accused of a variety of offenses from shop lifting to burglary. Nothing would stick and to the CSI counselors he seemed absolutely fearless. Nothing ever came of Rod's death. He claimed that Boyer had fallen on his head while they were working on Rod's car. There was no evidence to refute his claim and he was released. His times in prison over the years were for other antisocial aggravations, but not for murder. He just didn't get caught. He had killed another eight times up to this point, mainly with an ice pick, striking without warning, using his strength close in and the surprise to overwhelm or preempt any resistance.

Buddy sat staring at his office wall, eyes somewhat glazed, shuffling some papers without looking at them, desperately wanting a drink, wishing he could kill someone right now. As the Frangeletti enforcer, Buddy had made a mistake. He had gone in for the kill when he should have waited to find out what was going on with the guy who had been spotted. Now Nicky was pissed and Nick did not want to talk to him.

Nick had warned him: 'Don't let your fun and excitement of killing rule. It is your thing and it doesn't make sense most of the time. Your head must rule or you will put us in jeopardy.'

When Buddy had been told that Jerry was watching Nicky's on the plaza, his first reaction was to eliminate the snoop. He thought about this information for a couple of days, but did not consider what the consequences would be. Unfortunately for Buddy, his brain was not blessed with analytical capability. He was on Nick's shit list and he knew it and it bothered him a lot. He wasn't bothered, however, because he made a mistake in the Frangeletti's eyes, because he didn't think he had done wrong, he was only bothered because a big deal had been made of it and that now it was a problem for the boss.

The Frangeletti offices were on the second floor of a modern, highly efficient warehouse building in a commercial district of north Toledo. The warehouse was equipped with the most modern material handling systems and inventory control database that resulted in its ability to move tons of supplier foods and sundries in and regularly ship them out on delivery trucks to the various Frangeletti food service operations. The offices were modest, very professional looking, with pleasant decor. It had been kept modest on purpose so that IRS auditors would not be overly impressed. The plush offices for the Frangelettis were in a condo on Lake Erie in the little boating and fishing town of Port Clinton.

Buddy rose to his feet. He did know better than to have a bottle in his office, so he needed to get to some booze as soon as he could. He looked at the wall clock reading 11:30, almost lunch. Lunch with little Allie his assistant. Little Allie the jerk. Little Allie the moron. Little Allie the twerp. Little Allie the asshole. For a man with no sense of humor, Buddy was somewhat amused at the term, assistant.

Allie had been assigned to Buddy by Nick to help keep Buddy out of trouble. Buddy had refused to listen to Allie about getting rid of the snoop. Allie had told Buddy that it would get him in trouble with Nick. Mr. Frangeletti does not want to draw attention to us if it's possible to avoid, Allie had warned.

He went out to the main office area where Lisa was opening mail and answering the phone. She had been hired as a receptionist, but he thought she could be more than that for him. He sat on the edge of her desk as she handed him several messages.

"You been fucked really good lately," he asked her casually.

She did not respond, ignoring him in an offhand, yet officious way.

He persisted with, "Hey, Lisa, yeah Lisa. How do you like it...do you like...?"

She cut him off at that point, but never turned to look at him.

"Mr. Frangeletti," she snapped, "says to tell you that he expects you at the condo office at the marina tomorrow at nine o'clock sharp."

She headed for the copier with Buddy in close pursuit.

"Ya know Lisa," Buddy insisted, "between now and then you and I could get a lota fuckin' in."

She turned on him in a rage, pointing at him with the papers she held in her hand.

"Listen, shit head," she screamed through clenched teeth, "if you ever say anything like that to me again or try to get close to me, I'll tell Nicky. He'd cut your balls off if I asked him to, so back off."

It wasn't what she had said, but the way she had directed it at him that bothered Buddy. She was confidant in her defiance, almost with some knowledge of something he didn't know, but could only suspect. He believed it meant that he was in deep trouble with the Frangelettis. He needed a drink.

"Sure, sure," he responded with false bravado, "you do that, you tell Nicky, and while you're at it tell Nick I'll be at the meeting tomorrow, don't anybody worry."

He walked out of the air conditioned office into the scorching midday July glare. He stood there for a few moments, gripped with anxiety, wondering what had really just happened with Lisa, hoping she would not say something to Nicky. The heat made beads of perspiration pop out on his brow, made sweat run down his chest and back, and intensified his desire for a drink. He pushed his large sunglasses onto his face.

It took only a matter of a few minutes to make the short drive over to Francesca's where he would meet Allie for lunch. Francesca's was one of the best of the Frangeletti restaurants with quiet, expensive furnishings, and an excellent Italian menu. There was superior service from the corps of waitresses, specially selected by Nicky. The restaurant was packed seven days a week for dinner and also for lunch Monday through Friday. Since it was Friday, there was a jam of people almost elbow to elbow in the waiting area by the bar, buzzing with conversation as they tolerated the thirty to forty minute wait.

Buddy pushed his way through the waiting crowd and was shown to his booth in a back corner off the main dining area. The place catered to lawyers, executives, and others who wanted to conduct business or otherwise wheel and deal. The floor plan was set to accommodate semi private sections where confidences could be shared with little chance of being overheard from another table. Allie was already sitting in his booth.

"You're in deep shit, man," he said to Buddy, "you had to know that was law. If you were going to get rid of him, it should have been different. Away from the pike, out in the country someplace."

"Who the fuck do you think you're talking to, you scumbag asshole?" Buddy responded. "You work for me, get it."

"All I know," Allie went on, "is that big Nick is pissed. I tried to tell you not to do that guy like that. You should have cleared it. You should have..."

"Shut up, just shut," Buddy commanded. "Where the hell is that bitch? I need a drink."

Buddy spotted the girl assigned to his section, a tough little girl of nineteen who knew Buddy would be there every day at lunch. She dreaded waiting on him, but he was usually gone in an hour. He pointed his finger at her in a jabbing motion without saying a word and she knew he wanted his martini right away. She got his drink from the bar and took it to the table. She spoke first to defuse his anger.

"Sorry Buddy," she said, feigning being out of breath, "that jerk over there took too long to make up his mind and he wanted to chit-chat."

"Don't give me that bullshit, just get us a coupla plates of spaghetti," Buddy demanded without looking up.

She turned and headed for the kitchen without saying another word. Naturally, since Buddy ate here every day he knew the menu by heart. It was a Frangeletti place so all he had to do was sign the tab, one of the benefits of working for big Nick. He liked to start with a side of spaghetti before he even decided what else he would order. Allie had no choice in the matter as to whether or not he wanted spaghetti to start because that's the way it was when he had lunch with Buddy. Buddy did let him order the rest of his lunch without interference, but he did not want to eat the spaghetti by himself, besides its good for you he would say.

He had already sucked down most of the martini and was shaking up the ice so that he could get the rest. Karen was back with the spaghetti and Buddy was pleased.

"That's better," he told her, "and you can get me another drink."

"Hey, wait a minute," Allie protested, "you're supposed to be waiting on me too and I want an ice tea."

"I'm sorry, Allie," she moaned in her little girl way of dealing with the two men, "I didn't mean to overlook you, but we're so busy and I just don't have the hang of this yet."

She had the hang of it all right, but Buddy was unreasonable and Allie was an idiot. She never wanted them to know just how much she had the hang of it.

When she returned with the ice tea and second martini they were ready to order, but Buddy had something else on his mind. He looked right at her now to get her reaction to his question.

"You going boating with us tomorrow?" he asked.

She did not respond for an instant, her hesitation brought on by the flicker of fear that she might have to deal with him in a situation that was way out of her control. She knew about the importance of control, she knew to struggle for it whenever she could, and at nineteen with no money, no resources, she knew she had little chance of getting control of her life. She knew her fate for the time being was in the hands of the Frangeletti organization. She accepted that, knowing, too, there was no liking or disliking to it, it just was.

"Yes," she answered quietly, "it should be a beautiful, sunny day. I hope to work on my tan. It's hard working in here all the time to get a good tan going."

"Well, good," Buddy said, "maybe you and me can get better acquainted."

She did not respond, but merely smiled.

"Better get me another drink and we'll order," Buddy grinned at her in return.

As they ate their lunch, Buddy and Allie discussed the screwup and what Nick might put down as punishment. They could not come up with anything that made sense, but to Buddy who by now had five martinis, little made sense. He just knew he had to get back to his office and hide for the rest of the afternoon and get ready for tomorrow's meeting.

As they walked out of Francesca's into the bright heat Buddy handed a five to the young Hispanic who had parked his car.

"Yessir, thank you," the kid said, "car's ready for you, sir."

The young man had the big car running with the air conditioner full blast and parked close to the front door.

"Cooled down, sir. Have a nice day."

He opened the door for Buddy and closed it once he was inside.

With the amount of alcohol that Buddy had consumed, he was very drunk, but he didn't realize it yet at this stage because of the tolerance he had built up over the past year or so. He pulled out of the restaurant parking lot and headed back to the office, driving through a modest residential neighborhood of narrow lots and small, cookie-cutter frame houses, one after another, block after block. Because of the dimmed mental state he was in, his guard was down and he was unaware of the Chevrolet Suburban that was now following him quite closely. He was in the heart of this neighborhood where he usually ignored the speed limit and the occasional stop signs that monitored the intersections.

His condition began to be apparent to him and, as is usually the case for those who realize they have had too much to drink, it reveals that they don't have as much control as they should. He became cautious about his driving. His first precautionary measure was to come full stop at the next corner where he saw the red sign.

As Buddy halted his car, the Suburban rear-ended him with a loud bang. The impact, although not severe, snapped Buddy's head backward and, because he wasn't wearing a seat belt, threw him against the steering wheel. He wasn't seriously hurt and very quickly was over the shock, although the snap and contact made his upper body sting from the jolt. Anger raced through him with an adrenaline-kicked surge, his readiness for violence took over and he pushed himself out of the car primed for a fight, not prepared for what greeted him. Four Mexicans surrounded him, having counted on such a reaction from Buddy, each with an automatic pistol against his head. His arms were pulled behind his back and tied with a nylon cord before he could even resist. He was shoved into the back seat of his own car.

"What the fuck is goin' on?" he yelled.

"Jewcoin for a ride, sénor," one of the men said. "Jew not likit, no way."

The Suburban was already gone from the scene when two of the remaining men got in on either side of Buddy, while the third drove the car quickly away. The entire incident took less than two minutes. This was a very working class section where everyone in the household who was able to work was at work or asleep from the night shift. No pedestrians were around, no kids were in nearby yards, and no one came out of their house to see what happened. It had been a perfect snatch.

Of course it was the Padillo shits, Buddy reckoned. Would they kill him, he wondered? Why not? He figured they had him pegged for getting their guy at the car wash. No, he shouldn't have capped the guy, but what the hell, he thought it would send the right message. Besides, it was another excuse for what he liked best. He had been stupid to drink so much. He knew he needed to quit drinking like he had been doing, to ease off, a beer now and again, maybe. His brain was in a fog and he had a hard time now even trying to think. There was no way out of this, his mushed thoughts told him.

Buddy started to feel the pain in his wrists where the cord held him tightly and he tried to move his hands against the restraint without success. His neck and back were hurting now from the whiplash, intensified by having his arms behind him. He could feel the automatic pushed against his side. No one would miss him at the office, since he often did not return after lunch, and Allie was headed for the condos at the lake. He figured he was going to die.

"Listen," he began dealing, his words slurred "what is it you guys want. Money, you want money? Waddaya want?" He was struggling for survival.

The man driving responded. "No, sénor, what we want is to teach you a lesson."

Buddy decided right away not to give them any satisfaction by begging. He would be quiet and take whatever they dished out silently. He would teach them a lesson on how to be tough, how Buddy Cappeletti could be very tough.

Soon the car was on I-75, moving through Toledo, heading south. At Route 20, the car exited, heading east for awhile, and south again over a two-lane country road that ran between two large fields of soybeans. The car pulled to the side of the road and stopped on a grassy strip that ran between the road and field.

The two men in the back seat pulled Buddy from the car over to the edge of the field.

"Fuck you guys, you wetbacks don't scare me," Buddy yelled.

This was the bravado he wanted them to see, to see how tough he was, how unafraid to die, how easy it would be for him to endure pain, to withstand their threat without collapsing into a sniveling mess. He would show them.

The two men walked away from him, turned and took turns firing their automatics at Buddy. They systematically shot at Buddy's knees, ankles, and wrists, each man aiming at a side, starting at the knee, the ankle, and finally the wrist. Although the first shot fired hit Buddy just above the right knee, the men were not experts with the automatics and most of the following shots missed their target. A few did. Buddy had stumbled backward with the first hit, fallen writhing on the ground as other shots tore through him. As he moved, tossing and turning, they tried to pick their shots with limited skill, mainly missing. Still, they did considerable damage with the hits they made. He tried to crawl away, but collapsed face down after several feet. Before he passed out, his screaming pierced the quiet summer afternoon and could be heard across the fields for almost a mile.

About fifteen minutes after he was dumped and shot, a passing farmer stopped his pickup truck when he saw Buddy lying along the road. He cautiously went over to see what was wrong. Buddy's eyes were closed and he was blood soaked, but the farmer could tell that he was still breathing with life. He jumped back into his truck and sped on to the next farmhouse to call 911 before going back to where Buddy was to see if he were still alive and to wait with him for the Sheriff.

The Deputy Sheriff who got to Buddy first recognized the bullet wounds and knew there was not much time to get medical help or the man would be dead. He radioed for Life Flight and it wasn't long before the sound of the helicopter from St. Vincent's Medical Center in Toledo approached the field near where Buddy was continuing to have his life run out of him. The dark blue and white chopper landed in the center of the road under the direction of the Deputy. Buddy was quickly loaded onboard.

Buddy did not die, but for many years after he would wish secretly to himself that he should have. Unfortunately for him, his toughness intensified his suffering because he did not lose consciousness. He felt the agony of pain throughout the entire experience of being found and flown to the hospital. He was in the operating room for about five hours after they first brought him in, again for several hours the next day, closing the wounds, repairing the damage. He would be months healing, years recuperating and going through rehabilitation, always a cripple, and forever caught with the special rage trapped inside of him that he had nurtured and indulged.

Los Tigres taught Buddy a lesson and sent a message to the Frangelettis all right. But Victor figured, and Cuzo certainly knew, this was probably not the end of it. In fact, it probably was only the beginning. They would have to be prepared for an answer.

7.

The idea for holding business meetings at the lake was strictly Nick's. He loved being at the lake during the summer and wanted to spend as much time there as he could, especially since his wife died several years ago. From late May until the chill of autumn, he ran the operation from the office condo in Port Clinton rather than the office in Toledo. He usually called a nine o'clock Saturday meeting for key staff members that lasted about an hour. They discussed items that were on an agenda sheet that he had hand-written, run through the copier, and passed around to everyone attending.

Once a month, all of the managers from the various food operations came to the condo office to give their reports and listen to Nick talk about the business. On those Saturdays, the managers met with Nick at eleven o'clock, after he had conducted the staff meeting. Attendance was mandatory for those invited to these meetings and no one wanted to miss being there. Not making the meeting meant incurring Nick's wrath. When someone did not show up, which was seldom, Nick would give them a phone call and proceed to explain about their responsibilities. Anyone who had ever received one of those talks from Nick never wanted to get the lecture again. Missing twice did not happen.

The Saturday meetings took place in a condo at the North Coast Marina Club which was used exclusively for business and entertaining. It was set up that way when it was originally built, with the rooms never having been designed or decorated for bedrooms or living accommodations. The kitchen and bathrooms were completed in the usual manner, but the rest of the condo held desks, tables, computers, and other office equipment.

The North Coast Marina Club is situated on a prime piece of lakefront property in Port Clinton about an hour drive east of Toledo. The Club offers a series of luxury condominiums facing northward to the lake with a boat basin and dock space behind them. The boat basin is reached by a channel that runs from the Port Clinton harbor where the city docks are located. The harbor is at the southern most spot of the bay that is formed from Point Catawba to the east and Locust Point on the west, and protected from northeasters by the Catawba Peninsula extending several miles into Lake Erie.

Commercial fishermen found out years ago that Port Clinton was strategically located between the Toledo and Cleveland markets. Plus, it was a safe haven from storms that blew up quickly on Lake Erie, roiling the water in dangerous fury. Shallowest of the Great Lakes, Erie, at an average depth of sixty feet, could be churned and whipped to a frenzy in short order by summer storms that blew in from the southeast or northeast. Charter boats after walleye or perch were based here, close to the action for sport fishermen. Hundreds of boaters took advantage of the numerous marinas in the area. During the summer, Port Clinton swelled with out-of-towners who wanted to be on or near the water in the sun and have fun in the bars at night.

When Nick Frangeletti was a boy, his father brought him to swim at East Harbor State Park on the other side of the Catawba Peninsula near Port Clinton. Nick never forgot those wonderful warm days in the water and on the beach. Wading in the surf, swimming, playing games in the sand with his sisters and brother were fond memories that stuck with him. He realized over the years that he wanted to spend more time around here in the good weather, in summer time, to enjoy the pulse of the water, and feel the warm wind move across the shore.

The idea for developing property in Port Clinton was not original with Nick, but rather came to him as a suggested plan from a friend of son Nicky. It was during the early eighties when Savings and Loan money was available for construction. All kinds of projects were built that went way beyond the home building financing which S and Ls were meant to handle. The plan incorporated a private, sixty boat marina with a first class restaurant and luxury condos on what was very valuable land overlooking Lake Erie. The grounds would be exquisitely designed and landscaped to create a feeling of seclusion and exclusion.

Buying the land had challenged Nick. There was a certain degree of difficulty about it and somewhat of a complicated transaction. A Columbus lawyer representing a Frangeletti subsidiary company negotiated the deal. The movers and shakers in Port Clinton who were jockeying for investment opportunities assumed that big money from Columbus was making its move. Little did they know at the time that Grossman Real Estate Development operated primarily to locate and secure land or establish facilities for the Frangeletti restaurant operation. Only much later, after the deal was signed, sealed, and underway, did they learn it was really Nick. There was nothing they could do about it, but they didn't like it. They knew who Nick's father was and that was enough to cause concern about what might go on at the new marina. Dominic Frangeletti had been one of Toledo's rum runners and booze brokers during prohibition. He fought both the Licavoli gang and the police for position in that lucrative business. Even behind the Grossman cover it took considerable time, effort, and money to convince the town's power brokers to allow outsiders to pull off the development.

The Frangeletti Corporation, as owners of the Club, took four of the condos for their own use. One was strictly for business, Nick and Nicky each had one, and the fourth unit was for guests, usually members of the organization and their families.

The Saturday meetings were held in a large open area of the business condo in what otherwise would have been called a family room. A large round, solid wooden table dominated the space, surrounded by a dozen executive style office chairs. Against each of the two available walls was placed a large black leather sofa. Above one of the sofas was a mounted map of Ohio with designations for each of the Frangeletti establishments. Numerous floor lamps were strategically placed to provide light when necessary. There was a view of the lake through large sliding glass doors.

Ten of the chairs around the table were occupied and the men in them were talking incessantly to each other, causing a din that bounced off the bare walls and flooded the room with noise. It was 8:55 A.M. Nick was sitting back in his chair savoring his first cigar of the day, his watch on the table in front of him. Promptly at nine he leaned forward, tapped the ash from his cigar in the glass tray, and looked at his son across the table who was intently gesturing to make a point. Nicky saw his father's movement out of the corner of his eye and turned to verify the signal. He stopped talking immediately and focused his full attention to his father. The room became very quiet.

"I think the Mexican boys have spoken to us," Nick began. "I think they have told us they don't like it when one of their boys gets nailed. It's clear what they did to our boy Buddy. They didn't want him to die, that would be too easy. They wanted him to suffer and he is suffering, let me tell you that. And he will suffer more. They want us to leave them alone. It would appear they don't scare very easy."

Nick paused, puffing on his cigar, now putting his forearms on the table, his hands folded with the cigar sticking through the interlaced fingers. No one else said a word, almost as if holding their breath in unison.

"You know," Nick continued. "It is very interesting that the Mexican boys knew who to go after. Do you think they figured out about Mister Ice Pick? How would they do that? Or did they know because we have a leak somewhere?" He did not expect a response and there was none. "I think the Mexican boys are smart enough to find out about Buddy on their own, but my guess is a leak and we should check that out very thoroughly." He pointed at Nicky with his cigar and nodded. It was a gesture that indicated an assignment had just been made to Nicky. "Poor Buddy...we would have had to deal with him today if he were here. In fact, Buddy would have been the number one topic for us. But instead, the Mexican boys punished Buddy. By the way, Tony, what's the story at the hospital?" He turned to his right when he asked the question and directed it to a thin, dark haired young man.

"Jack's there with him now," Tony replied, "I was there most of the night and we'll have someone with him round the clock."

"Yeah," Nick emphasized, "we don't want our beloved Buddy to say something he shouldn't when he's in some kind of fog from all the dope and shit they give him. You guys make sure that doesn't happen. Okay?"

He got a nod from Tony as he turned to Nicky who also nodded in agreement. Everyone else still seemed to be holding their breath. They knew Nick was angry, but he was so calm, very quiet with his voice, his face relaxed. Would there be a tirade from him and when would it hit? Nick continued to suck on his cigar, blowing the smoke at the ceiling.

"Yes, indeed, my friends and associates, Buddy would have been point one on our agenda." Nick paused, looked right at Allie. "Did that sonofabitch know he was sticking a law officer?"

Allie was prepared for the question he was sure would come from Nick. He remembered asking Buddy about the hit on the guy in the car, but Buddy would not listen. Buddy knew someone had staked out some of the plaza restaurants and didn't care who it was, they had no business getting nosy. "No, no," Allie lied, "Buddy thought it was one of the Mexican boys."

"You're full of shit. You know as well as I do that Buddy liked to stick people and he saw his chance with that guy. It was stupid and so was sticking one of those Mexican boys." Nick blew more smoke at the ceiling.

"Now we've got a goddamn mess to clean up, first of all, and second, we have to make some adjustments to the operation." Nick's voice rose in pitch just slightly when he said that.

Nick looked at the ceiling and blew a perfect smoke ring. "I thought about playing doctor Kevorkian for Buddy to take him out of his misery, but I decided to let him be. He got us in this mess, let him deal with his mess. Anybody got any ideas?"

He looked first at his son before scanning the table, checking each of his lieutenants. No one said a word at first. After a short pause, Eddie Majeski said there should be retaliation with several others chiming in with agreement.

"Come on, wadda we gonna do, get in a goddamn war with these Mexicans? Whose got more to lose with a war, them or us? A war blows the lid off everything. If there's a war we win. If there's a war we lose. That simple."

He looked around for reaction from the others, but did not get any. He tapped his cigar on the glass tray several times to examine how it was progressing. He must have been pleased with what he saw because he nodded his head up and down slightly, closed his eyes, and drew on the Cuban master another time. He kept his eyes closed while he continued.

"Besides, the truth is that Buddy Cappelletti is not worth a war, not worth losing control of our system, not worth the effort. That's the sad truth. But for our honor and self respect we need to answer their message. They sent us a message, now we gotta answer. Nicky, I want a plan by Monday. A plan that does not involve somebody killing somebody."

Nicky looked down at the table top briefly, then looked at his father. "Like what," he asked, with just a tinge of sarcasm.

"You think about it, Nicky, talk to me on Monday. Think about it while you're enjoying the boat ride today. Think about it tomorrow while you're at Mass. Talk to me on Monday. Right here. We'll talk right here."

The meeting moved on for about twenty more minutes, covering a variety of business items that Nick wanted settled. No one else spoke and they all listened intently as Nick spelled out what he wanted to happen, punctuating his remarks with jabs of the still smoldering cigar, now down to a mere nub of gray brown.

"That's it," he stated emphatically. "We will have an action plan for the Mexicans on Monday and we go from there. This was a good meeting, thank you. Always a good meeting with you guys. Business is good, we just have to stay out of the way of people who want to do us harm, want to take away our business. Remember, be on your guard. More people than the Mexicans want us to fuck up. Got that?"

Everyone remained seated at the table waiting to be excused. Nick never, ever excused them in so many words, but rather gave a sign, a gesture of unspoken release from his meeting. Today, he would lay the still burning cigar butt in the tray and nod his head in approval, and silently stood. When he did, everyone stood with him.

"Let's have a boat ride," he said in finality. He turned on his heels and left the condo, heading back to his own unit. It was understood that Nicky was now in charge of the day's events.

"Hey, Eddie, Frank, Willie. Get the bags on board. Tony make sure all the food and beer is on and tell George we want to leave at eleven. Listen, hey, wait a minute. Let's see. Two, four....eight of ya. There's only six girls, so you guys will have to take turns. There's seven, but one of 'em is mine, I already know that, so you guys got six."

The four men Nicky gave work assignments for the boat ride headed to the dock while the others moved on to the guest condo. Nicky went back to his own unit. When he walked in, three of the girls were in various states of undress, but they didn't seem startled by his sudden appearance. One girl, totally naked, stood in the family room facing him as he came through the front door. She merely smiled, said hi, and started to pull on her bikini panties.

Lining up the girls for the outings on the boat was Nicky's responsibility; one that he took very seriously and worked at quite diligently. He also had a hand in the hiring of waitresses for Francesca's and their other restaurants, using that situation as a way of recruiting the young sexy ones he wanted, keeping them available by keeping them on the restaurant payroll. Meeting the young girls was easy. Nicky hung out at several bars where the music and atmosphere catered to a younger crowd. There were always young girls on the move looking to hustle or be hustled. They all needed money and would do most anything to get it.

He also had an efficient referral system. New faces were brought to his attention from enterprising girls already in the fold and from other members of the Frangeletti organization. It was well known by those close to the action that Nicky was extremely generous in rewarding you for a triple A prospect. Girls were rated by Nicky from AAA to A and what he gave you matched how your referral ranked on his scale. Every girl selected went on the Frangeletti payroll working somewhere in the organization, usually as a waitress or, sometimes, as a hostess.

Nicky's way of rating a prospect was purely subjective, based on some set of criteria no one understood and which he did not share with anyone. Curiously, he did not appear to have any preferences in type. Blondes, brunettes, redheads, it didn't matter. Personality didn't matter, but if they talked too much they were gone. Smarts didn't matter either, but if they were too stupid they were phased out. What really mattered to Nicky was their willingness to be involved in the sex parties he wanted and their proficiency in making those outings exciting for him. New girls were on trial to see how well they reacted and performed. The keepers usually knew what was required and enjoyed the benefits Nicky provided.

Once in a while an AAA girl who was sex shy or inexperienced caught Nicky's fancy and he would train her himself, relishing the chance to show her some things, savoring the sex with insatiable desire. Girls who didn't cut it in the sex department kept their jobs, but were not invited to the parties any more. Eventually, they were gone.

Nicky ignored the young girl's greeting, not even looking at her. "Hey," he yelled at no one in particular, "you gals ready for a party?" There was some laughing, a little giggling, with a generally voiced consensus of yes. Sounds of assent came from various corners of the condo.

"Get yer stuff and line up right here," he demanded, pointing at the living room floor. "Come on, let's get going, we gotta get ready for fun in the sun."

The girls dutifully moved to the room where Nicky held court, their variety of carry bags and overnight cases swinging with them as they shuffled into review. In an unspoken, yet predicable way, they formed a single file in front of him; a ragged lineup, ready for the trip, wanting only to be told their next move.

He looked at them from left to right and back again. He didn't say a word. His examination took several seconds, but it seemed a lot longer to the girls standing there being evaluated, being reviewed for their sexiness, their willingness to perform.

He unzipped his fly slowly. He looked at the ceiling. "We're gonna have a lotta fun today. You better be ready to get hot, 'cause we want it hot."

"Don't worry, we're hotter than hell," responded a tall redhead in the middle of the line. "You guys will scream for mercy." All of the girls laughed at this and evoked a posture of sureness and self possession.

Nicky could not help himself and laughed at their presence of arrogance. "Hey, shit, that's great. We're gonna have fuckin' fun that's for sure."

He looked them over quite closely now, inspecting this crop of sexy young girls in a way that a horse breeder considers his thoroughbred for the next race. He smiled in a disarming way for the girls to try to understand, keeping his gaze fixed on one of the seven.

"You," he pointed at Karen, "move out." He wagged his finger indicating that she move towards him. "The rest of you get on the boat, now. Take yer stuff, get on board."

He pointed at Karen again. "You go upstairs. We need to qualify you before the trip so you can help everybody have fun."

She started up the stairs quickly ahead of Nicky, but before she reached the top he had caught up and slid his hand between her legs from behind. She was prepared for it, having heard him take the steps two at a time, knowing something like that might happen. She stopped dead on the top step, spread her legs, and bent over to lay the palms of her hands flat on the upstairs floor. He rubbed between her legs for several seconds, stood on the same step where she was standing, and pressed his body against hers as he leaned over her to grip her shoulders from behind. He pulled her slowly upright in a delicate balancing act to keep from falling backwards down the stairs. He had broken into a sweat, partly from the quick strides up the stairs, but mainly from the excitement of the prospect of having this girl. Now, standing pressed against her, he could sense her excitement also. She hardly dared to breathe, feeling that at any second they would both pitch down the steps. He kissed her neck, slightly pushed her forward so that she regained her bent over position, and stepped over her.

"Come on," he directed, as he walked into his spacious bedroom.

"Should I take my clothes off?" she asked, as she walked to the center of the room.

"No. Stand right there. I'll take 'em off." He proceeded to pull off his own clothes, tossing each article onto a nearby chair. When he was completely undressed he stood facing her with his hands on his hips.

She was impressed with what she saw, both in his well formed body and in his semi erectness that was on display. Nicky was not a body builder, he just naturally had a very good physique, and nature also made him well endowed.

"Do we have time?" she quizzed. "I thought we had to get on the boat soon."

There was a casual, teasing aspect to the way she asked the question that Nicky read as coyness. "We've got time. The boat doesn't leave without me. Or you." He paused, told her to turn around. When her back was to him he approached her, reached around to undo her shorts, and let them fall to the floor. He got on his knees and slowly pulled her panties down her thighs, over her knees, and to her ankles. She stepped out of them without being told and without looking down. He put his hands on her hips, moved his mouth to her left butt, and nipped the soft under part of the cheek with his front teeth like a playful puppy.

She made a sound inhaling with the effect of the bite and reached around for his head, caressing his face slightly. She gave his face a firm slap. When she did that he laughed, pushed his right arm between her legs to spread them, and began to massage her again, this time running his tongue lightly on the cheeks of her butt. She was excited with his attentions, pulling off her top and bra, leaning back her head, hands on hips, voicing quiet approval of the contact.

Nicky stood, still at her back, and wrapped his arms around her to hold her breasts cupped in each hand. "Nice nipples," he whispered to her as he fingered them gently. She remained silent, but pushed her head back against him in a way that offered encouragement as well as responded to the pleasure she was feeling. She liked this sensuality, disarmed by his soft manner, when she had expected it to be rough stuff from a tough guy.

He pushed against her to move her to the bed where he turned her around and, taking hold of her upper arms, sat her down on the soft mattress. He reached down, grabbed her ankles, and tipped her back on her shoulders. He mounted her with an agility that took her by surprise.

Her legs were over his shoulders in a coupling that aroused her passion and heightened the excitement. So far, on her day off, she was having a good time.

8.

The boat was fueled and loaded when Nicky and Karen walked down onto the dock. It was five minutes to eleven and everyone else was on board. They jumped on the boat and Nicky headed for the flying bridge, throwing his duffel at Karen as he went.

"Put that below," he ordered, "someone will show you where."

Nick had taken his usual spot for the start of the boating excursions in the rear deck salon where he could be out of the sun, yet see all that was happening. He watched intently his son's arrival with the girl, but said nothing. When Karen went by him with the bags, she did not speak to him. She did not know who he was. Nick looked her over carefully as she went through the salon, but turned his attention to the process of getting underway. He enjoyed being by the water, but not always sure that he wanted to be out on it, confined in a boat. There was a sense of vulnerability he had about being on the boat, even though they were always out in the open, usually in view of other boats. You never knew what might happen, when someone might take advantage of the situation. However, he made the best of being on the boat, coping with concern for his safety, because he wanted the fresh air and the view of the lake along this shore.

Nicky bounded up the steps to the flying bridge to speak to the captain who was overseeing the release of the dock lines.

"George, no matter what, we gotta be back here by five. My wife expects me to take her out tonight. Understand?"

The captain turned his head to Nicky and nodded affirmation with an added 'yessir.'

"It will take us about an hour to get to the rendezvous point," George stated, "so it should be no problem even with a couple of stops. Anyway, the marine forecast says we'll probably want to be off the lake by late afternoon."

"Good," Nicky shot back, "because we want to make at least one stop in open water. Everybody wants a swim."

They both laughed at his remark and Nicky headed for the rear deck.

The large cabin cruiser eased away from the dock, its powerful engines held in check, and pulsed a throbbing reverberation from the exhaust ports beneath the fantail. The *Francesca* glided slowly out of the marina and into the boat channel that led to the open water of the bay. Moving along through the channel at a no-wake speed of about three knots, the boat passed under the tilted spans of the Water Street liftbridge, raised to allow her passage. Weekend traffic was stacked up on both sides, waiting and watching as the big boat came by in review.

The *Francesca* proceeded by the city docks loaded with tourists waiting for the charter boats to shove off or who were just simply milling about watching the boats and boaters. There was an air of excitement from all of the activity taking place here by the water. The Port Clinton city docks form the demarcation of where the boat channel widens and stops being a channel and where the lake begins. The docks are a focal point for action and attract people and cars until there is hardly room to move about.

Nicky stood on the flying bridge, surveying the crowded dock from behind his mirrored sunglasses, wondering who or what was out there to screw up the operation. Cops, narcs, Feds, the Mexicans? He saw nothing suspicious, but somehow felt uneasy. He shrugged off the uneasiness and turned his attention to today's operation, telling George to head for the spot on the lake where they would be meeting another boat.

"Let's get up there and anchor before our friends arrive, so we can be set and waiting. I like that advantage, George."

Among the press of sightseers and fishermen on the dock, Cuzo stood with binoculars held to his eyes, carefully watching the *Francesca* gathering speed as it moved out into the lake. He saw Nicky on the flying bridge talking to the captain, wishing he could hear what was being said. He could see four or five very attractive young girls in bikinis moving about so he knew more than just business would be going on this afternoon. In fact, as the boat got steadily smaller in his view, he could see that one of the girls had already removed her top. Cuzo smiled. Mr. Nicky, he mused, likes to mix pleasure with business and that makes him very vulnerable. Yes, very vulnerable. I like that a lot, he thought.

Cuzo walked quickly off the dock and up the street about a half a block away where there was less crowd, less noise. He flipped open his cellular phone and hurriedly punched in a number. After a short pause he spoke into the phone.

"Luis, they're headed out. Yeah, just a couple of minutes ago. Right."

He closed the phone, put it in his pocket, and walked to the restaurant across the street.

Nick saw the bare breasted girl and yelled.

"Hey, Judy, keep your goddamn clothes on till we get out in the lake. Too many boats around here. Draws too much attention."

He watched as the bikini top went back on, the girl playing with her breasts and the skimpy cloth in a sensuous way that was almost a reverse striptease.

"Let me know when," she laughingly responded, "I've gotta get these fabulous rays."

Nick did not have a chance to answer, because Nicky came down the ladder from the flying bridge at that moment, shouting at her before he hit the deck.

"I'll tell you when, goddamnit. Get below."

She didn't move, wide eyed at his anger.

"Get below, I said. Now."

She quickly moved through the salon and down the passageway to the lower deck.

"Let's keep a lid on things for awhile," Nicky said, looking around at the other girls. "I'll tell you when the party begins. In the meantime, have something to drink, get something to eat. There's plenty of time to have fun. Work on your tan, but keep your clothes on, stay cool till I say so. Mitzi's getting the food ready now."

With that, he whirled around and jumped down the steps leading below. He found the girl he had chastised in one of the cabins strewn with tote bags, shoes, women's underwear, and various articles of women's clothing. She was lying on her side on the bunk, propped on her elbow, facing the doorway when Nicky entered. Without saying a word he rolled her over on her belly and slapped her butt with the flat of his hand all in one continuous movement. He struck her with a force that left a red print of his fingers on her white flesh. She cried out, but did not move. He slapped her again, this time on the other cheek of her butt. Again she did not move, but the slap brought another sharp cry. She trembled after each blow and the skin on her legs and arms were pebbled with goose bumps.

Nicky leaned over close to the back of her head and asked quietly, "Does that hurt?"

She did not answer. He stood up straight and slapped her on the upper left thigh with a snap of hand against skin that produced another bright red mark. She cried out, but did not answer his question. He slapped her right thigh even harder.

"Oh," she cried in a high pitched voice, "yes, yes, yes. That hurts. It hurts."

"You like it to hurt, don't you?" he laughed, slapping her again on the butt, but this time not so hard. "You like it, you like it a lot."

She rolled over on her back and slipped off the bikini panties. Her face was flushed with excitement, her lips formed a slight smile. "Yeah, I do," she said as she reached out for his crotch.

He moved slightly so she could not reach him.

"Later," he said, "we'll finish this later."

She was now on her knees on the bunk facing him.

"Promise?" she queried.

"Yeah, promise."

He turned and went topside.

Mitzi was busy getting lunch set up on the big table in the main salon. She padded around the table in cloth slippers, shoulders hunched, arms extended, making sure the food was arranged just as she wanted it to be. Muttering to herself, she pushed a plate one way, pulled a platter over a few inches. Satisfied with what she saw, she turned to Nick and bowed.

"Leady, for you, yes," she pronounced, a tinge of her accent coming through. She had the placid, ageless face of the Japanese, unruffled by circumstance, revealing neither pain nor pleasure.

Nicky moved past the table, nodding his approval of what Mitzi had laid out, and went to the rear deck where the girls were engaged in banter with the men. It was a verbal jousting edged with sexual tension which came from their understanding that later in the afternoon more than words would be part of the interaction among them. He sat down next to Lisa, the office receptionist, to wait for Nick to announce that lunch was ready. He was hungry - they all were - but it was up to Nick to pronounce the meal.

Lisa turned to Nicky, leaned towards him to speak quietly into his ear so no one else would hear, and told him what Buddy had said to her in the office.

"Can you believe it?" she whispered, "that bastard actually thought he was going to fuck me today. I hope he enjoys himself in the hospital."

"Lisa," Nicky said calmly without looking at her, "if Buddy had been here today, he would have."

She sat back against the boat cushions and looked at him, not knowing quite what to say. "Is that right?" she said finally, her face tight with anger.

"Yeah, Lisa, that's right. Keep that in mind the next time you want to shoot your mouth off about one of our guys. Keep in mind that your ass is mine and you will do as I say when I say. And I say you would have fucked him if he'd been here. In fact, maybe you should visit Buddy in the hospital and make him feel good. That would pick up his spirits. He's real down right now. He could use some cheerin' up. You have the mouth for it. I'll think about that. I'll think about that as an assignment for you. I'll let you know."

The boat was moving northeast across the lake at a steady fifteen knots. With no wind, the lake was a flat sheet of blue, oddly quiet for a body of water so large. Every so often, the *Francesca* would cross the wake of another boat and there would be a slight roll, but otherwise it was a smooth ride. Nick had announced lunch with some fanfare about the menu and praised Mitzi, whom he directed to take a bow. She bowed several times in all directions and scurried below.

Two bottles of white wine from Veneto were on the table and a large pan of ice was chilling German beer. They all gathered around the table filling their plates with Mitzi's lunch. Nicky worked on two plates at once, picking out white meat of the fried chicken, loading on potato salad and baked beans. He took both plates up to the flying bridge and handed one to George who was guiding the cruiser across the open water.

Nicky went back over to the ladder leading down to the salon and bellowed for someone to bring up some beer. Karen responded, negotiating the tricky climb up the stairs carrying her plate in one hand, holding three bottles of beer between the fingers of her other hand.

After handing a beer to George, she went over to where Nicky was sitting and handed him a beer as she sat down next to him. The flying bridge had two large built-in upholstered bench seats that provided a comfortable spot to view the lake as the boat cut across the green water, sending a white trail of foamy wake at its stern. Nicky held his beer up and clicked the bottle against hers.

"Here's to this morning," he toasted.

She looked at him, smiled, and clicked her bottle back against his. "Here's to Mitzi's food."

Nicky started to respond, but George turned around to report the boat's progress. "We're less than thirty minutes from the spot, Nicky," he announced, "I'll drop anchor as soon as the position comes up on the GPS."

"Okay, good," Nicky answered. He turned his attention back to Karen who was licking her fingers. "Yeah, right, Mitzi puts out a nice spread. You put out a nice spread, too, and we're gonna look into that this afternoon, later. Come on, let's get below."

Once back down in the salon, Nicky began giving orders. "You girls take your stuff below, yeah take your plates, beer, whatever you're drinking, take it below. Eddie, Phil, you guys get up there with George. Frank, Willie, you guys help get them tied on to us when they get here. Tony, you're in charge of protection. Allie, you handle the stuff, have two guys to help you. Remember now, keep guns outta sight. We don't want to spook these guys. And you broads keep still down there when these guys are on board. Yeah, okay, we're gonna have visitors. You just stay down there with your mouths shut and mind your own business. Once we take care of our visitors we'll have some fun. Okay, move it."

The girls started filing down the passageway to the cabins below where they had changed their clothes and left their belongings. Allie and the two other men followed the girls down the steps, but went to the storage locker just off the galley. There, neatly stacked, were ten large athletic duffel bags much like those that pro tennis players use to carry all their gear. Each man took two bags, one in each hand, and went back up to the salon where the bags were placed under the table that was still covered with a large quantity of food. Allie directed the two men to get the remaining four bags which were also placed under the table with the others.

It wasn't long before George told Eddie that they were almost in position and that it looked like the boat they were to meet was bearing down on the spot. Eddie yelled down from the flying bridge to notify the others that the boat was coming.

No more than ten minutes or so had gone by before the other boat was alongside, churning the water as its skipper maneuvered for position, hitting reverse, pushing the lever forward, and back to reverse again, controlling the dual engines so the boats got closer and closer. Frank and Willie who had thrown bumpers over to protect the hulls of both boats, were at the rail to catch lines tossed at them, and began to pull the boats together. George had throttled down to idle and dropped anchor, so that when the two boats were secured to each other they stayed together at that position. Once the other boat throttled down to idle, the water began to get calm again and the rocking and bouncing that occurred from the maneuvering slowed to a gentle roll as the two boats bobbed slightly on the lake.

They were over fifteen miles from the nearest land. It was a beautiful and peaceful spot to have a meeting when you didn't want to be disturbed. The sky was cloudless, deep blue, and the relentless sun brutally heated anything not in shade.

Two men climbed over from the other boat and came right into the salon. The older man looked at his watch and moved towards Nick, his right hand outstretched.

"Nick, hey, great to see you. I know, I know, we're three minutes late, but we got slowed down a little...sight seeing."

He laughed at his own attempt for humor and Nick indulged him, laughing and pointing to his own watch.

"This watch," Nick replied, "says you're right on time. Anyway, what is important is that you're here. Have a beer, maybe a glass of wine...real good Italian wine. It's lunch time, there's an excellent selection of food prepared...eat, drink, enjoy. Go on, go on, grab a beer, get something to eat. Jackie, come on, get a beer, sit down here tell me what's goin' on with you."

The older man took the beer that Nicky held out to him and sat down next to Nick.

"Thanks, Nicky," Jackie said, "we really appreciate the hospitality, but we'll only stay a little while. Business is business, and we gotta get goin' to do some more sight seeing." At that point he saw the duffel bags under the table and pointed at them using the beer bottle as an indicator. "You must have a bunch of tennis players on board to have all those bags," he laughed. "You know what, we've got some bags just like that. Wanna trade?"

Nick looked at him with raised eyebrows and answered in mock astonishment, "Same colors? Same size?"

Jackie nodded emphatically. "You bet," he confirmed.

"Okay," Nick agreed, "let's trade. I might like yours better."

Jackie turned to the young man who had come aboard with him and motioned to him with his thumb, pointing back to their boat. The young man who had stood motionless and silent through the previous interchange knew what he was supposed to do. He went to the rear deck and whistled at the other boat. Soon, athletic bags like the ones under the table were pitched across to the *Francesca*. Ten in all. He brought them into the salon with the help of Frank, Willie, and the others. They were placed side by side in a row near the table.

Jackie unzipped one of the bags to reveal wrapped bundles of twenty, fifty, and hundred dollar bills. "Do you want to count it?" Jackie asked.

"No," Nick said, "but let's unzip the others and take a look. I'll let Allie count it when we get back to Toledo. That's soon enough. Willie, pull one of our bags out for Mr. Zimmerman so he can see if he still wants to trade."

The bag was placed in front of Jackie, who eagerly pulled the zipper open. The bag was completely full of oblong plastic bundles, white in color like corn starch.

No one said a word. Jackie pulled one of the plastic bundles out of the bag and turned it over several times in both hands. Sweat oozed from his temples, his colored shirt dark with wet in the armpits. Even in the shade, even out here on the water, the ninety degree heat affected everyone. Beads of sweat had popped out on each face, especially the men who had handled the bags, and the tension everyone felt intensified the effects of the heat.

Jackie broke the long silence with a grunt, a low pitched animal-like sound that came up from inside his mammoth gut and out his closed mouth. It was a sound of satisfaction, much as when a brood sow moans contentedly as she wallows in cool mud. He smiled slightly, as he declared, "We've made a good trade. I like my new bags. Do you like yours Nick?"

"Sure I do, Jackie," Nick confirmed. "Now," Nick continued, "why don't you have a bite to eat? Relax."

"Naw, we gotta get goin'. Thanks anyway. You're always very hospitable Nick, I appreciate that. By the way...I may have another kind of request from you soon. I'll let you know."

"You just ask," Nick said, "and we'll take care of it. We appreciate our valued customers."

Both men laughed and Jackie waved his hand at Nick as if to say 'aw go on, don't flatter me,' as he moved to leave.

The deal was done and Allie and the boys helped get the bags with the white powder over on the other boat. Lines untied, Jackie Zimmerman was on his way, his big boat gaining full speed, quickly getting smaller as it moved out over the lake headed north.

The bags from Jackie were being taken below when Nicky went into action.

"Okay, get that anchor up, let's get moving. Time to party."

He directed George to head for North Bass Island, and shot down the passageway to get below. In the main cabin, hidden beneath a built-in desk, was a safe large enough to hold a briefcase. Nicky twirled the lock dial back and forth through the combination and jerked the handle to get it open. He pulled out a thin, brown leather case, closed the safe, and spun the dial. He bolted back up to the salon, case in hand, yelling at the girls as he went.

"Party time," he bellowed, "get topside."

He went right to the table, moving plates and dishes at one end to make room for the case which he placed in the cleared area. The girls came up and into the salon, gathering around the table as close to Nicky as they could. All except Karen, who was new and had never been on one of the boat trips before. She stayed at the other end of the table checking out what was happening, wondering what was next in this surprising day for her. Nicky motioned to her to come closer. He opened the case slowly.

Inside, the case was filled with dozens of what looked like cigarettes and four small clear plastic containers with white powder in them. Several of the girls gasped when the contents were revealed, but none of them said a word, they just stared.

"Ladies, this is worth a lot of money," Nicky said, "and it's all for you. Think of this stuff as your reward for helping make this a great cruise on a beautiful, hot, sunny day. We always appreciate a fabulous party. Enjoy."

With that, he backed away from the table. He saw Nick moving up the steps to the flying bridge and followed right behind.

Nick had put on a wide-brimmed hat for protection now that he was out of the shade. And when George set up a folding deck chair for Nick, he stationed himself near the captain. Nicky came up beside the chair, turned, and leaned back against the instrument console so he could talk to Nick face-to-face.

"No, no, it's okay," Nick said, "you have your party. I'm gonna enjoy a cigar."

Nicky looked him not knowing quite what to say, stumbling to get started, not really able to find the right words.

"Listen, I know...I mean, you can't..."

"Nicky," Nick interrupted, looking directly at him, "I don't like the drugs. I think fooling with that stuff is crazy. That will never change. I know you aren't personally, but...but even with the girls and some of our guys...I think it's askin' for trouble. I don't want the trouble that could come from it, that's all. Make money, that's another story. That's okay. It's a money thing. Its part of the times. But I don't like 'em used around me. You do. You don't mind. Okay, so that's the way it is. I know you like these parties on the boat. Okay. But let's not screw up the operation with dope. As long as we don't get screwed up by it, okay. I just don't like it. Just be careful...just be careful."

"Look," Nicky explained, "this stuff makes the girls loosen up. They like it. They're used to it. They want it."

Nick did not reply. He had lighted his cigar and drew on it very carefully, savoring the aroma. He blew the smoke up into the breeze created by the boat's movement and closed his eyes. He was done talking.

Nicky went back down to the salon where the party was on its way to being a big success. All of the girls were already well into their high. The addiction was worse for two of them than for the others, but they all depended on Nicky for drugs and to keep them insulated from the world of buying and dealing. Nicky took care of all of that. He doled the drugs out to them as he saw fit as a way of controlling them, controlling the sex, gaining their attention, and as a means of keeping them around so they didn't run away. Nowhere could they go and have a life as good as he managed for them. Four of the girls were already hooked when they were recruited. Nicky knew they were, but they met his requirements and that was all that mattered.

He sat down at the big table in the salon that Mitzi had cleared of all the food. The wine bottles were at the center of the table and there still was some beer that hadn't been opened. He called out the names of three of the girls as a drill sergeant would: 'Judy, Karen, Lisa'. The three stopped what they were doing on the rear deck and walked into the salon. They were each smoking one of the cigarettes from the case. Karen carried a beer with her. He motioned for them to sit and they silently, obediently complied.

"Lisa, I been thinking about you." She put her arms on the table at this point and hung her head. "I told you I would consider sending you over to console Buddy..."

"Shit, don't make me do that," she interrupted. "Please, please."

"Well, I've thought about it," he went on, "and I'm not going to make you do that, but..."

"God, thank you, Nicky," she sobbed, tears welling from her eyes, running down her cheeks.

"But, you will take care of Allie this afternoon. Make him feel like a man, make him feel good. Okay?"

"Yeah, okay," she answered, throwing her head back as if to shake off her feelings. She got up and headed aft to get Allie.

At that point, George throttled down the engines to idle and the boat rapidly lost headway in the water. Once the forward movement slowed to his satisfaction, he dropped anchor again. The gang on board knew that it was swim time. There wasn't another boat within a mile of the *Francesca* and she was about two miles from the North Bass Island shore. Going in the water without benefit of a swim suit was understood. In fact, after several moments at anchor, George, Nick, and Mitzi were the only ones on board still dressed. Mitzi hid below, George and Nick looked out over the water, ignoring the others.

Nicky had taken Judy and Karen below to his cabin where the three of them began to explore each other's bodies and enjoying getting better acquainted. Lisa was in the embrace of Eddie, passionately kissing. She had already taken care of Allie, who had passed out on one of the couches in the salon. Two other couples were having sex on the aft deck, while the rest had moved to spots below. There was almost no talking, but there were the quiet snorts of cocaine, the puffs of the mj cigarettes, and the moan and groan of continual sex. This was the kind of party Nicky and guys liked best.

George and Nick stayed up on the flying bridge, out of everyone's way, silently looking at the lake, keeping an eye for boats closing in, and only occasionally making a short comment about the heat or the fishing or something else innocuous. Mitzi had cleaned up the galley and closed herself into the small cabin in the bow. She packed cotton into her ears trying to ignore the proceedings and take a nap.

More than an hour had gone by when, suddenly, a quick draft of air swept over the boat causing it to rock somewhat. Less than a minute later another gust of wind snapped their pennant around on its lanyard and pushed the boat against the anchor line.

"That's the signal, Nick," George offered, "storm's on its way. That's how quickly they blow up on this lake. Marine forecast was right, so we need to head back."

With that, he made sure everyone was on board, powered up the anchor, and throttled the boat forward, easing the speed to more than three quarters full. They were pushing twenty knots.

As they headed south across the lake towards Port Clinton, random blasts of wind jabbed at the boat and pushed the water up in sprays that splattered against the flying bridge windshield almost as if it were rain. The sky had quickly gone from bright blue to muddy gray to blue-black gray as clouds piled upon clouds to wipe away the sun and drop the temperature twenty degrees. What had been a searing hot day now felt chilly from the quick change.

The boat plowed across the water towards the safety of the harbor channel in its attempt to reach port before the full brunt of the storm could sweep over them. George wanted to get the boat into the channel before the waves that were building got higher and made the entry dangerous. Even now, the water was beginning to pound the city dock and as he looked across the lake, the puffs of white foam could be seen as the water churned. It was a challenge, but they made it into the channel and ahead of numerous other craft that were scurrying for shelter. Even the channel was starting to get rough and the *Francesca* bounced her way along, under the raised bridge, finally reaching the dock. Help was on the dock to grab lines and secure *Francesca* with some difficulty as she rocked from bow to stern. Safe in the Marina, George shook his head and blew a discordant whistle as his notification of relief that they were tied down. The time was not yet four thirty.

The steady buffeting of the wind pulled at the boat and rocked it against the bumpers. At first, large drops of rain began to hit in a random pattern as the storm rolled through with persistent force, followed by sheets of smaller rain drops that slashed across the marina. Lightening laced the sky with jagged darts, sending flashes of light in all directions as it reflected from all the water, casting eerie shadows onto the boat.

Cuzo sat in the dry quiet of the Marina lounge. Mid afternoon he had taken a table next to the large windows that looked out over the boat basin where he had a direct view of the Frangeletti dock. He had opened the brief case he carried and passed the time pretending to work on some business papers while he slowly drank several beers. He watched as the *Francesca* was attended to, noting the absence of anyone on deck or in the salon. He was amused seeing Nick and George scurry down from the flying bridge when the rain hit. He was most interested when, after ten or fifteen minutes, several of the men carried sports bags off the boat, even in the driving rain. These were the same bags Luis reported had been exchanged with the other boat out on the lake, he realized. Amazing, he thought, that Nick himself would be involved in a transaction. Nicky, maybe, might do something like that, not the old man. But he did. Probably for a long time friend; that way a personal contact might be needed. Damn, those bags gotta be full of money and right out here in the open. Pretty slick, he judged to himself, pretty slick.

9.

Butch Greiner was alone, nearly finished with his usual morning run. He moved steadily along the city streets, content with the solitude, comfortable with the easy pace, enjoying the moist morning air. As he ran, he thought about Pam, how she might be handling Jerry's death. Probably not very well, he figured. Who would, what with the suddenness, the terrible shock of how he died?

He had been out of town when Jerry was murdered and now had to play emotional catch up with Pam, a responsibility he felt strongly, but didn't relish fulfilling. Butch had looked upon the potential task of comforting Pam with considerable concern because of his own perceived deficiencies. He believed that his ability to bolster her spirit did not measure up to what might be required. He didn't think he had the emotional skill or the emotional fortitude to comfort her. He was still wrapped in the confusion and pain of his own loss. Dealing with a loss for someone else seemed to be a burden beyond his current ability to cope with her effectively.

The morning after Jerry's killing, Butch had been in his room at the downtown San Diego Marriott getting dressed and readying himself for the upcoming morning meeting. The television was on in the background, but he paid little attention until some of the words struck home with him. 'Bowen,' 'Ohio Highway Patrol,' and 'Perrysburg' grabbed his attention. At breakfast, he read the details in the morning newspaper. There's not enough time right now, he thought, I'll give her a call later. Later in the day when he had the time, he decided to wait until he got back to Ohio. He chided himself for the procrastination, but it was a call he did not want to make.

Butch tried to define his friendship with Jerry. It was loose, but had a certain kind of value. They lived in the same neighborhood, but not close. Their wives had not been buddies, but they were congenial. They didn't socialize that often, but the times together were fun and worthwhile. The connection with Jerry, he decided, had been sports and law enforcement. They had met playing for the same softball team, Butch the brunt of teasing because of his age, while Jerry felt the barbs for limited athletic ability. Neither man faltered under the barrage of words from their teammates. The good-natured chiding came as the team suffered another loss in the closest tavern to the ball park.

Law enforcement was an issue that gave some meaning to their relationship. He knew that Jerry believed strongly in maintaining a stable society that resulted from the able and conscientious actions of those working against criminals. Jerry had taken an approach to the whole criminal world with a defensive attitude.

"I know, I know," he had stated, "lots of people are critical of the police effort, but I believe it's important and I'm going to be part of it. There's no way we can give up to the drug dealers and pimps and the rest who want to take advantage of us. Shit, I don't care...call me an idealist, but I believe its right."

You had to admire him for his convictions, Butch thought, he sure wanted things to be right. Not sure he fully knew what a tough battle it would be dealing with organized criminal activity, the multitude of antisocial and sociopathic bozos who roamed the streets looking for ways to get into trouble, and how difficult it was to get the upper hand with the bad guys. There were lots of bad guys...they just keep coming with new ideas, new scams, new ways to work what they want, sell what they want, overcome the efforts to slow them down...let alone put them out of business. He liked Jerry's idealism and had hoped it would not blind him to how difficult his job could be.

He respected Jerry, even though he believed the idealism that Jerry had clung to was a forgotten dream of law enforcement. He knew that Jerry would give it his best shot. For that idealism, Jerry paid with his life, Butch reckoned, and hoped that others would appreciate the effort. Probably not, he conjectured, he will be forgotten quickly and all will remain the same in the legal and illegal systems. Business as usual on both sides, good and bad.

Butch remembered a night after one of the ball games where Jerry had gotten a couple of key hits that helped bring the team one of its few victories. Jerry had been pleased with himself, ready to celebrate. After a few beers, Jerry had lapsed into griping about his new job as an investigator, how boring it really was, how much he longed for something exciting to be part of his work.

"Don't misunderstand me," Jerry had said, "I'm proud of the promotion, but it doesn't seem to amount to anything. I mean, it's checking records and interviewing people, doing surveillance...it's not like being on the firing line."

"You are on the firing line, partner, and don't forget it," Butch cautioned, "whether you know it or not. Keep your eyes open...be alert for the unexpected. It's easy to get nailed by somebody, so watch your step."

"Come on, what I'm doing isn't like that."

"Just be careful. You have to always be ready for it."

The words of that conversation were with Butch as he ran down Louisiana Avenue at an even stride, dodging puddles, ignoring STOP signs and traffic lights, intent on maintaining the speed he wanted. At Indiana, he headed directly across the intersection towards the group of buildings on the other side where his office was located.

It was Sunday morning about nine thirty and there wasn't a car within three blocks. Once across, he cut through the office complex parking lot to reach his building. He ran right up to the door, and slapped the wall. He sat down on the stoop, panting heavily in the hot sun and the brutal humidity that was intensified by the overnight rain. Water was still dripping in down spouts and drops fell from the overhanging eave. The water-laden tree leaves in the green space shimmered and glistened from the sunlight.

Butch loosened the laces of his running shoes, eased off the saturated sweatband. He leaned back, bracing himself with stiffened arms, palms flat on the still cool concrete. Staring up at the blue sky dotted with giant puffs of white clouds, he figured this was going to be a great day.

He had already run five miles, an easy distance for him, and was ready for breakfast. But, he thought, better check the office for messages and mail, sort through the faxes and e-mail before I eat. He had been away from his office for more than two weeks and felt the need to catch up. He didn't have a secretary or anyone else working for him, so the task of culling the messages, going through everything was his chore.

Butch had his own private investigation business handling special cases for a number of large clients, mainly corporate, business he got from friends that he had made over the years. It was work he enjoyed for the most part because it was somewhat interesting and easy, and it gave him a lot of latitude to pursue his own interests. He used much of his spare time training for and participating in several triathlons a year. Running, lifting weights, and staying in shape were all part of his life, made him feel good, feel complete. Being in the gym and swimming laps several times a week were part of his routine. Naturally, watching his diet and eating healthy were also part of the regimen. He knew he was in good shape and liked the feeling, and liked being an athlete in training. Training compensated for a lot in his life that was missing. And he knew very well what was missing: he lacked a partner, a soul mate. He had one once and she was gone and he felt the void, sometimes desperately so.

After he rested for awhile, he rose, shoved the sweatband in his pocket, and walked up the steps, the untied laces flopping and jumping around his shoes. He disdained the elevator, believing that only the handicapped, old people, and certain losers would use it to go up one level. He went down the hall, the laces clicking and clacking on the tile floor. He unlocked the door and went into the very warm, stuffy two-room office. The phone had been ringing as he came down the hall, but he did not change his pace. Screw it, he thought, the answering gizmo will take care of the call. Which it did.

The door brushed aside the small pile of envelopes that had gathered after the days of being dropped through the mail slot. Not much worth his time, a few bills, several notes of inquiry. Nowadays, most of the important assignments came on the fax or directly to his computer through e-mail.

He threw the mail on his desk, walked over to one of the few windows that could be budged and pulled it up and open. The air that rushed in was even hotter than inside, but at least it smelled better. He picked up several sheets from the fax machine and sat down at his desk to plod through the phone messages.

His business, this business, any business like this one, wasn't really that much fun anymore, but what the hell, it was all he knew. A lot of digging for information to protect some large corporations, without much action, and little sense of danger. Kind of like Jerry felt, I guess. It was the danger he missed, he admitted to himself, the conditions that tested the acuteness of your ability, that presented the thrill of death potential. Death potential: the statistics of risk that overrode an assignment and gave him such exhilaration. The elements of risk were considered, balanced against the assignment goal. It had been great excitement and this business was no match for the fun he once had taking those risks.

Butch glanced at one of the fax sheets as he punched the answering machine buttons. It was headed: *TO-RA*

GREINER. Someone who doesn't know me, he said out loud.

Richard Alfred Greiner was the name that brought him into this world as the second child of parents of German heritage. He was now the third generation removed from the immigrants who had started in the region of the Junkers, who had forged a new life in America. He could still remember that call of his mother's on late summer afternoons, calling him home for dinner with a plaintive, yet distinct cry of *Rich-ard, Rich-ard.* She retrieved him with that call of his name so clear, so sure a beckon for the meal at hand. She would ever call him Richard, although no one else would. His older sister saw to that.

Sister Kate started calling him Butch before he was two and no one ever figured out where she got that name. She didn't know and wouldn't tell if she did. She liked calling baby brother Butch, because for her the name was a signal of the derision she felt. How dare this little wad of flesh, this brat, come into our lives and spoil everything? He got the attention I should get, Kate figured, at least I can stamp him with a label of contempt. For everyone but Momma, and eventually Kate herself, the label stuck and he would carry it into adulthood. On his part, when Butch reached an age when he realized what she had done, he didn't care. He adored his sister so the name never was an issue between them and he allowed it to stick. In time, she could not refer to him or address him as anything but Richard and regretted she ever placed the name Butch on him. But Butch the name and the person endured.

Although his nickname was not an issue for him, his size surely was a bother and an irritation. At every age, in every class at school, he was one of the smallest, if not *the* smallest kid. This was a burden for Butch and he worked diligently to overcome stature as a stigma. The usual doses of over compensation came about as he lifted weights and ran mile after mile to prove his worth in physical terms. These activities made him sinewy and tough, but, to his credit, without the swagger and puffed chest that might otherwise accompany such compensation. Instead, it brought him to a sense of what he could do. It did not take away the desire to run after risks, to take many a dare. Putting a sense, a feeling of risk into his life became very important. Sky diving, race cars, steep and dangerous ski runs, these became the companions of his life even as a young man. It helped that his father indulged him so that he could explore these options. They would prepare him for challenges in the future.

The direction he got from his father was constant, although it seemed quite domineering to some. For sister Kate, their father's control was too much and she fought it constantly, harboring resentment against it's confines. The friction with her father simmered within Kate for years, well into adulthood and the development of her own marriage and family. On his part, Butch didn't seem to mind his father's direction, or at least he didn't react to it. He had a feeling that the direction came from some unspoken well of love that his father had for him. So it was okay and he responded positively. It was okay and he blossomed under the guidance.

Butch graduated from Ohio State University, majored in political science, minored in European History, pushed to excel and succeed in a field he did not care about nor want. Good prep for law school, his father had expounded, you get your law degree you'll have it made. Truth was, Butch wanted to be a geologist, work out in the open, prospect for minerals, explore for oil, and be released from the workings and trappings of offices and bureaucracy, of people constantly colliding with each other in the confines of an office. Outside where he belonged, that was his desire. No, no, his father insisted, lawyers control the world. You must be one of them, you must be one of the controllers, the directors of action. His father felt that being a director of action was very important, and, of course, worthwhile in the sense of making a lot of money.

The idea of being a geologist faded as Butch pushed his way through law school. He had done well as an undergraduate in political science, even though it was not his choice. Once he made the move that pleased his father, he gave it a decent effort, graduating with honors. He was accepted into the Ohio State Law School quite easily and slugged it out for three years, graduating in the top third of his class. His father was excited and proud, his mother stood by smiling silently as her boy accepted his father's praise. She was proud of him for two things: he always did well and he did what his father wanted him to do. Both issues made her life so much easier. She loved him for that and she loved him because he was so bright and quick and funny. She had no idea what he would do as a lawyer.

Butch never took the bar exam. Two weeks after graduating from law school, he and a friend went to a careers conference on campus. Chuck Logan, his friend, got button-holed by a representative from IBM, and when this happened, Butch wandered off a bit to see what was going on at some of the other booths. The CIA display table caught his attention and he stopped to talk. He was surprised, a little taken aback when, after identifying himself, he realized they knew all along who he was. We think you'd like this work, they said, you would be perfect for it. One man in particular, Gary Crossman, impressed Butch with his pitch for the agency. He remembered the name as if it were yesterday and could recall his face clearly, still hear the excitement in the tone of his voice, the sense of urgency he gave Butch to get involved. It was imperative, Butch needed to be an agent for the CIA. His country wanted him to help protect itself against the Communist menace that was a plague upon our Democracy, a constant threat for our future. Butch could be a part of the service of secret defenders who protected all that we as Americans held near and dear. It was a call he heeded, it was a task he relished, and it would become the definition of his life.

Surprisingly, his father only shrugged when Butch told him about the CIA, a signal of resignation for accepting Butch's choice. However, his furrowed brow also signaled his displeasure. "So much for making good money," he had commented.

The numerous calls from Pam Bowen were all that interested Butch from the answering machine, the last one having come in while he was walking down the hall to the office just a few minutes earlier. She sounds pretty depressed, Butch thought. Jerry's death would surely do it to her. Better call, he said to himself, better call, better call. He looked through the faxed material, then turned to his filing cabinet to pull out folders to match up with each of the faxes. Better call, he kept repeating to himself. He got up and walked over to the window where he stood and stared out at the flowers in bloom in front of the building. Yeah, I gotta call her.

Pam answered the phone on the first ring. She was calm when she answered, but as soon as she realized it was Butch calling, she started to cry. Butch told her how sorry he was about Jerry and how badly he felt for her. She sobbed softly. "Butch, I need to talk to you. Will you come over?"

"Sure, I'll see you in a little bit. I'm at the office...just finished a run, so let me clean up and I'll be over. Okay."

"Okay," she sniffled.

He wondered what he would say to her, he knew it wouldn't be easy.

10.

When Butch got to Pam's house he didn't get out of his car right away. He let the engine continue to idle so the air conditioning would keep him cool through his hesitation to meet the situation at hand, although the beads of sweat on his forehead belied its effects. He sat looking at the little bungalow, his hands firmly griping the steering wheel. It was as if he could not let go, as if by squeezing tightly some inspiration would come to him. He drew a blank for what he might say, lost in an inspirational vacuum. Finally, he relaxed his fingers, put his hands together as if to pray, and cracked his knuckles with a quick reverse flex. That sound of his joints being stretched was his call to action.

He turned off the engine, jumped from the car and strode briskly to the porch, and rapped on the screen door with a sharp stab of his index and second fingers. He hadn't even considered using the bell. The door rattled in its frame from the intensity of Butch's knock and the sound bounced around the wooden porch with an unsettling reverberation. Pam did not answer the door right away and Butch involuntarily started to pace. After a few minutes he could hear her moving through the house towards him. He heard the metallic click of the deadbolt being drawn back. The inner door was pulled open. She pushed the screen door wide and moved to hug him in one continuous motion, the door flapping back against them as she clung to him.

"I'm sorry," she breathed into his neck, "I've been so upset."

"It's okay," he said as he gently released himself from her embrace and guided her back inside. "I'm sure it has been tough for you."

Oh, man, that was not one of the things he was going to say to her, so he had no idea where it came from when he said it. He realized it sounded all right, though, so what the hell. Now what? A big part of Butch's concern for what he would say to Pam came from his feeling that consoling her too much or in the wrong way might precipitate something with her that he did not want. What was the wrong way? Maybe too much touching? She had come on to him before, when he and she were alone together, and again in a couple of phone conversations. Each time, Jerry had been out of town. Each time, her suggestiveness made him uncomfortable. Now, he did not want that to be a part of the aftermath to Jerry's death, some kind of attempt by her for a romantic development. He had the uneasy sense that it could happen if he were not careful.

"I feel badly that I was away when it happened...pretty frustrated. I only wish I could have been here to be some support. I...I couldn't even call. After I heard on the news on the TV where I was staying...the way my schedule and commitments worked out...and the three hour time difference didn't help...I simply wasn't able to get a call in."

There was no way he would admit to putting off the call, that he couldn't bring himself to make the call to her. Butch felt this was a case when a little lie was best. At least for him it was and probably for her, too.

Her entire experience of the last several days spilled from her in a jumble of unconnected sentences and random thoughts, each separate idea related to the sorrow she was feeling, each memory a part of her sadness. Her voice sounded the frustration she felt as she lapsed into a description of the life she and Jerry had together. It was information Butch believed he shouldn't know and didn't want to hear.

At first the words came quickly, but as she pondered what she was saying, they slowed and her voice became a soft monotone. Her words were laced with sighs and little explanations that made it seem as if a kind of relief overrode her sadness. It was an aspect of her rambling that he found puzzling, but perhaps he just didn't understand what she said.

Butch sat silently trying to formulate how he might respond. Right now, no response was necessary. As she continued, his thoughts wandered to other times and places when Jerry was still alive. He would miss Jerry, miss the easy smile, the fun, the teasing.

"...it was," she said, "it was...it was that...I don't know, I don't know...strange in the last few months. Not that we'd drifted apart...we hadn't...I don't think. But things were different somehow."

He must have been more into his own thoughts than he realized, because he had not caught it when she switched her frame of reference from the events of learning about Jerry's killing to their relationship. That's the trouble with women, he thought, their damn thought process changes direction too fast, especially when you least expect it.

He looked at her carefully, trying to figure out what was really going on with her. Her teary eyes looked back at him without revealing more than the sadness they already showed. She had taken his hand, but it was not an act of flirtation, rather it was a matter of clutching something to maintain composure. She had, so far, given no signs of romantic notions. That was good, he thought, keeps this from being more unpleasant than it is.

Pam was a large angular woman who never looked comfortable when she sat down. Her thin body never quite settled in, but rather seemed to protrude from whatever chair or sofa she was seated. At a tad over six feet tall, she looked better standing, Butch decided, and being very strong willed, had given Jerry a lot to contend with in their relationship. She was attractive, not beautiful, he assessed, but striking in a way that made men want to look again. Plus, she could be provocative with a certain pose of her eyes and lips that had, on occasion, made him uncomfortable. A flirt, she had made Jerry jealous numerous times. He wanted to avoid saying anything about her 'drifting apart' comment, but she wasn't ready to leave it alone.

"Had you noticed?" she asked. She pulled at her hair and twirled it into a bun that she held at the back of her head with her hands.

"No, I really can't say I had."

"You must have seen something." She let the hair drop back to her shoulders and raked her fingers through the thick strands.

"No, not at all. Nothing comes to mind. You guys seemed to be doing fine."

"Well, something had happened between us."

"Truthfully, Pam, I hadn't seen you two all that much lately, so I'm not one to be able to judge..."

"I guess that's right," she said. "How did you feel when Cindy died?"

Damn, he thought, the quick change again. Her question stunned him and he struggled for a response. He had not thought about his wife's death for awhile, maybe a couple of weeks. She had been dead almost five years. As those first years went by he thought about Cindy every day. In the last year or so he thought about her frequently, but not every day. It had been days since he had been conscious of her memory and this bothered him, now that Pam had drawn his attention to the fact.

"It took so long," he said quietly. "longer than I could have imagined. When we first talked to the doctor...I...I was so rocked by what he said that I thought immediately that I had started to lose her. The feeling never let up, in fact it got worse and worse as she was in treatment...she suffered so...the treatments were brutal to her..."

"The loss," Pam interrupted, "that's what is so hard...the loss...your connection with another person is gone and there's no picking up the cell phone to get it back. They are gone...like forever...there is no reconnect."

"I don't know how you must feel Pam; I only know the sadness I felt back then. It happened so quickly for you it must have been a shock. Takes time. In time the shock will wear off, the sadness will lessen, life will move on."

"I feel nothing Butch, no shock, no sadness...but I feel everything." She started to cry.

His instinct was to reach for her, to offer comfort, to help rally her from the anguish he thought must possess her, but he did not. The vague suspicion that she might misinterpret his actions was still with him. He did not want her to think there could be more to his comforting than a friend's support.

She had regained her composure, ready to move on to other subjects.

"When I first heard about Jerry I was calm. I saw who was standing on the porch and I just knew. I knew he was dead before Walker said anything. I just separated. I went out of my body and watched myself stay calm. I was very satisfied about that. It was so unreal, yet so believable, so right. Weird, but right. I guess I just accepted what was happening to me without fear. I could watch myself and see that I was okay. It's a little weird when I think about it, but it sure got me through the experience of dealing with the news. The funeral was tough, but I got through it. Friends helped, of course, but the finality...the finality was not there. The finality is missing and I want it. I want that finality, so I can go on. If I don't get that finality, I think it's going to be a struggle to move on with my life."

She saw Butch's expression which she could not read and she stood up.

"I want to know who did it and why."

"Is that going to bring you the finality you want?" he asked.

"I want the person punished," she said, ignoring his question.

"Pam, more than likely..."

"I want to know. Yes, that's how I can finalize it. If I know. Because right now it's just nuts, and nuts I can't deal with. I need to know."

"The Highway Patrol..."

"Them? Spare me. They won't find out."

"Jerry was one of their men. Believe me, they'll work very hard on this. Very hard. The investigation won't be tossed aside. Let them do their work. I'm sure he was part of something very important so they won't give up very readily on trying to get his killer."

"Please find out for me, will you Butch? Please."

He knew the meeting with Pam would be touchy, but he hadn't expected this request. With the cases he was currently working on, he didn't need this. It wasn't reasonable for her to ask, he thought, but what could he do? Jerry had been his friend. Pam was his friend. What could he do? Even though it was a task he didn't want, didn't have time for, Butch knew he could not refuse.

"Okay, I'll look into it," he said as he rose, "but don't expect..."

"Thank you," she said, as she put her arms around him.

"Don't expect too much. I'll do what I can, but don't expect any answers. It smells like the touch of a pro. Maybe the mob or drug dealer. Those kinds of murders don't get resolved very easily."

She kissed him softly on the cheek as she held him tightly to her. He patted her back and hoped that small sign of comforting would not encourage her. It didn't seem to and he was relieved.

Once back in his car he looked to see Pam at the door. She waved and he returned the gesture. "Damn!" he said out loud. The meeting with Pam had been brief and it had been unsatisfactory for him. He hadn't said any of the things he had thought about saying and he was left unsettled. It had been a maddeningly irrational experience with Pam, one that poked at his subconscious, that could not be defined. "It makes my head hurt," he said to himself. Lack of a rational exchange with someone was always troublesome for Butch.

Being reminded of Cindy by Pam left Butch edgy and he drove around for several hours trying to decide what to do next. Slowly the edginess turned to resolve for never forgetting to honor the memory of his wife, resolve that he would find out something for Pam, and move on with his other cases.

Butch figured he would try to reach Tom Wachowiak even though it was Sunday, so he drove back to his office to make the attempt. That man would be the best place to start. Tom had been with the Toledo police for about 25 years, the last ten as a detective. As Butch had developed his investigation business, he and Tom had become friendly. Theirs was a friendship based on mutual cooperation and the passing of information to each other. Tom could always be depended upon for a straight answer. Besides, Butch had always made it worthwhile for Tom with a gift of some kind or an envelope with money. Tom was especially fond of Detroit Lions football tickets.

"Julie, Tommy there?" he asked. He tapped his felt tip pen on the desk as he talked.

"Butch?"

"Yeah. Sorry to interrupt your Sunday...it's important."

"Hang on."

Butch could hear her calling and after a few seconds Tom was on the phone.

"Tommy, how you been?

"Good," Tom answered, "Butch?"

"Yeah. Can you talk?"

"Naw, too much goin' on here. Waddaya need?"

"A friend has been capped and I need some answers."

"Official?"

"No, as a favor to the widow."

"I'll meet you for lunch. Tomorrow. At Murray's. 11:30."

"You got it."

11.

Butch eased his way into Murray's, pushed through the crowd at the door, and nodded to the bartender as he moved to the far end of the bar. He had called Murray's that morning and reserved a table in the back where it was quiet. He didn't want to sit right away, although the table was ready. He wanted to check out the room. It was always a surprise to him the mixture of law enforcement, lawyers, and bad guys who frequented this place at the same time. Lunch drew the biggest crowd. It was supposed to be non-smoking, but that didn't stop anyone who wanted to indulge. Murray's was where the big shots came for lunch: you don't tell big shots what to do. At least Murray wasn't so inclined.

A typical cast of characters, Butch thought, as he surveyed the crowd. No one here to worry about in the faces he recognized, but he was more concerned with those he didn't know. A couple of them looked like Frangeletti guys. He would watch closely to see if he were followed later. Right now, it was hard to tell. The Frangelettis had kept track of him ever since an insurance scam he investigated got a little too close to them. Butch never could find proof of the connection, but he knew through his sources that they were behind the fraud. A no-name stooge took the heat for them, doing several years in prison as a result. They were wary of Butch because he had pushed into their domain and he made them nervous. Butch figured the front man who did time would have been nicely rewarded for keeping his mouth shut, although the alternative if he wouldn't take the fall probably would have been for the guy to disappear.

Murray's was the kind of place men liked. There was a rough and tumble atmosphere about it and the food was basic cooking, well prepared. You could slug down whiskey or sip ice tea, no one cared. And there were no women. No rule against them, but most of the women who worked in downtown Toledo knew better than to come into Murray's. Those who did seemed to be tough enough to handle the situation, but they were rare. For most women, Murray's was not worth the hassle. So, by default, Murray's was a men's club. It got rowdy and the language was crude sometimes, but men liked that, that locker room macho that even piss-ant wimps reveled in and took for some kind of male reality in a world without women, in a world that was really devoid of gender and tantalizingly deceptive in its sense of well being and self content.

Butch waited for Tom to come in before heading to the small table in the corner. He caught Tom's notice with a raised hand and moved away from the bar. Tom got to him quickly, trailing behind to the table, and they pushed themselves into their chairs almost in unison.

"Late. Sorry. Got tied up. Case I'm working on."

"It's okay," Butch responded, "gave me time to check out the place."

Tom gave him a look, but said nothing.

"I always do that. It's defensive. Habit I picked up. Saves surprises you don't want."

"What's going on?"

"A friend of mine got capped out on one of the Turnpike rest stops. A Highway Patrol officer in plain clothes. He must have been on surveillance - I haven't talked to his command yet - when someone got him."

"Bowen?"

"Right. Jerry Bowen. I know...knew him, and his wife, Pam."

"Bad. Real bad. Ice pick in the heart."

"Tell me about it," Butch asked casually.

"Well, we think we know a lot, but there's not much we can do. Or should do. All out of our jurisdiction. And nothing that could be proved."

Butch looked at Tom intently, a look that meant keep talking.

"That's the way it is with a lot of the crap we deal with. It's rare when we don't know who did something, or how and why it went down. But proving it is another matter. Like this thing with Bowen. He's sitting there in his unmarked car. Someone gets in and puts a pick in him. Now, we know that Buddy Cappeletti..." He paused. "You know our friend Buddy?"

Butch gave a slight, almost imperceptible negative shake of his head.

"Buddy is a Frangeletti tough guy...an enforcer, the muscle. You know how it works: he puts his thumb on anyone that needs the pressure. Buddy is kind of a free-wheeler with the pressure. He applies it whether it's needed or not. Guys sometimes die from his pressure. Nick gets pissed off, but Buddy is hard to control. He's been reprimanded in the past for stuff he did, so I hear, but this time old Nick didn't have a chance."

"How so?"

"Well, the word we get..." Tom paused and looked around to see who might be listening. "El Tigres took care of Buddy. El Tigres are a bunch of Mexicans who run drugs. Now *they* are some guys we would like to nail. DEA knows about them. We're working to get evidence, working to nail 'em. We're working pretty closely with DEA. Nothin' solid yet. We're covering all the bases here in the city, DEA is doing their thing, closing in slowly, but surely. You'll see a hit on them soon, I think, a solid bust."

"How did they take care of Buddy?"

"We think they picked him up here and took him out in the country and shot him up. Not enough to kill him, just enough to make him suffer. Probably end up a cripple. Shot him bad in the legs. He'll be a long time in rehab. Saved Nick the punishment."

"Could be your deal if they picked him up in the city."

"There has to be proof and there has to be a complaint. So far, no one has come forward to ask us to investigate. Besides, we like what happened to Buddy, we're not going to get into it."

By now the waitress had gotten around to them and they ordered. Butch kept it light with soup and salad, but Tom went the burger and fries route.

Butch surveyed the room again and realized he recognized a man seated at a table about twenty feet away.

"Who is the guy with the gray shirt? Over my right shoulder, by the wall. A funny blue tie. I know him from somewhere, but I can't place him."

"That's a Frangeletti guy. Can't come up with his name right now, but he's one of Nick's army."

"Who's he checking out...you or me?"

"Me. They keep tabs on me. I watch them, they watch me. It's a funny game. I guess they just want to know where I am all the time. They stay away from my house, but they dog me a lot of the time."

"How do I make contact with the Mexicans? I want to know some of the details. My client will want to know, I can anticipate that. She's going to want to know what happened."

"There's a point man for those guys. His name is Mosca. Cuzo Mosca. He makes things happen for Victor Padillo, who runs the Mexican show. Victor has a lot of connections back home or somewhere here in the States, is what I hear. They get the stuff into the country and Victor makes it happen around this area and even over toward Cleveland. Real problem for them is that Victor's El Tigres and the Frangelettis are jockeying for position on the same playing field. Lots of competition. There's just so much money to be made that neither of them is afraid of the other. It's rough. Guys are dying over struggle for control. We think that Buddy was a payback for one of Victor's guys getting nailed. It's almost a coincidence he was the guy that stuck your friend."

"How so? I mean why?"

"Well, there was a guy on the Padillo carwash payroll..."

"Carwash?"

"Yeah, that's Victor's front. Cash business. Easy to launder money. No pun intended. Legit front operation. Someone has to go around to the different carwash operations on a regular basis to empty the coin machines. Fill the bill changer and make sure the place is okay. Get the set up?"

"That's one way to do it."

"A while back, a young Hispanic kid was found dead at one of the washes. There was an ice pick stuck in his chest. He died fast, just like your friend Bowen did."

"A warning from Frangeletti."

"Yeah, that's what we figure. Buddy nailed this kid as a signal to Victor to lay off...stay out of their territory. Word was Buddy loved to stick guys with an ice pick. More than likely, Buddy stuck the Mexican kid and Bowen. But it was his own overreaction to Bowen snooping around - Nick never would have ordered that - and probably, he wasn't supposed to kill the Mexican kid either, just rough him up. But Buddy likes to play for keeps. We figure somehow Cuzo or one of the Mexicans saw what went down in the plaza or heard about it and put two and two together, but they acted on Buddy. Maybe they already knew and were watching

Buddy, I don't know. But we're pretty sure that's about what happened."

"Where can I find this guy Cuzo?"

"I dunno. We don't see him and he's never been picked up. Once in awhile we hear about him. His name gets kicked around from informants. Nothing we could ever use, however. Let me check on him. Lot of the Mexicans hang out at a bar out on Broadway. Just remember, they don't blend in well unless their skin is very light. The dark skinned stand out. And most whites aren't comfortable having a bunch of dark skinned Hispanics sitting around in their places. Almost like with the Blacks. Nobody is prejudiced until it comes to their joint. They want that pure white. I don't know what he looks like 'cause he's stayed out of trouble, so maybe he blends. I'll see what I can find out. I know he hasn't been in trouble with us."

"Thanks."

"Have you checked with the Highway Patrol guys to see what they're doin' to get their boy's killer?"

"Not yet. I've got a meeting with them this afternoon."

"They won't find out much."

"Why do you say that?"

"Don't have the manpower, don't have real experienced investigators...I just don't think they'll get far...maybe so, but I doubt it."

Butch made no comment to Tom's remark.

"Be alert, Butch. There's a lot of stuff gonna go down. At least that's what we hear. Wouldn't want you to get caught in the crossfire."

"Like what?"

"Not with us. But there's the FBI and DEA chasing after drugs. The ATF is scrambling to get a lead on some guns and plastic. They don't all talk to each other. Like to protect their own world. Keep their own secrets, so that they can be heroes when they make a bust. What I hear is that the Frangelettis and the Mexicans are both mixed up somehow. In all of it, guns, drugs, plastics, pornography, you name it, they're connected somehow. That's the theory of the Feds, anyway."

"Drugs, I understand, but what's this guns and plastic stuff?"

"It seems there has been a systematic disappearance from a couple of Army bases of several kinds of rifles and plastic explosives. Somebody finally got wind of it."

"Explosives, I can understand, maybe, but not rifles. There's too close a check on weapons."

"I'm told it's been happening. That's all I know. The stuff is missing. They figure it's in the pipeline to the mob. Not to use, but to resell or to trade for big drug shipments."

"Where did...?"

"My buddy, Tim Connelly, with the FBI. He's been a big help to me. Seems to have a bead on what's going on around here."

"I know his name, but I don't know him. Would he know about this guy Mosca?"

"Hey, he might. Worth a try. Give him a call. Mention my name."

"Thanks, Tom."

The cop reached for the check the waitress had left, but Butch got it first with a quick swipe of his hand.

"On me," he said with a smile, "you've been a big help."

Outside, the two men shook hands and walked in opposite directions. Butch went about twenty yards and stepped between two delivery trucks parked at the curb. From that vantage he could see Tom headed toward his unmarked police car waiting in the next block and could also see the front of Murray's. It didn't take long for the man in the gray shirt and weird blue tie to emerge. He lit a small cigar and watched intently as Tom walked up the street. He pulled a cell phone from his pocket and called in his report as he walked to the corner and disappeared around the building. He had not seen Butch watching him.

Butch retrieved his car and headed for his meeting with the State Highway Patrol.

Butch figured that Tom probably had it right. With one foot on each side of the law, the cop guys often knew a lot more than they were able to use or pass on to the Prosecutor's office. Poor Jerry never knew what happened. What a waste. Jerry had been caught in the middle and Butch didn't want to be in that position. He would have to be careful. Get some information for Pam and get away from it. Keep a low profile, don't get involved. It seemed that both factions kept close tabs on what was going on. It wouldn't take long for the Frangelettis and Los Tigres to know he was in the picture. Stay sharp, stay sharp. He made a mental note to himself to be alert. He knew how necessary that was for survival.

Let's see, Butch said to himself, if the Frangelettis and Mexicans seem to know so damn much, they must have informants, moles in the police department or in one or more of the Fed agencies. No other way. Money buys a lot of information on the street, but an insider gets it faster and more accurately. There have to be lots of leaks.

Butch sat down in the chair indicated by Carter Walker. There was no cordiality about the way the man had received Butch. Their meeting could not be avoided, but it was certainly unwanted. Walker was wary of the entire situation: a man he didn't know anything about, now working on behalf of the widow of his dead officer. Was this a setup for an impending lawsuit? The possibility of legal action by Pam was a consideration that concerned Walker since he got the call from Butch wanting to meet.

"Thanks. I appreciate your time. I know that this is difficult, but the wife wants to know some things. She's pretty distressed. Insisting to find out who killed her husband. She says when you came and talked to her it wasn't very satisfactory. To her. Too many questions unanswered, too much up in the air. She is looking for some answers. She asked me to help. I tried to talk her out of it...told her you guys would make a supreme effort to get Jerry's killer, but she's strong willed...and determined to find out. She wouldn't be dissuaded."

"I see. What's your connection...and...and...?"

"Credentials? If that's the word you're looking for...I'm a private investigator...and a friend. Handle insurance business mostly. But it's because I'm a friend that Pam asked me to find out something. And I have a vested personal interest. I also want some answers. And I want to cut through any smoke and mirror attempts by you guys. So please don't fool around with me or I'll make your life miserable. Up to now, the press is not really hot on this. I could change that real fast. Now, what do you know?"

Walker didn't respond at first. He sized up this diminutive, balding man sitting there in front of him and sat down. He was not a veteran of field experience, rather a practiced administrator and canny manipulator of the system, skilled at the paper work, keenly knowledgeable of what it took to progress through the ranks. Every bureaucracy, every business has these types. They do well by being good at managing paperwork and by fostering the correct relationships. Their efforts often transcend reason and the results are strictly their own personal reward. They know no other way to exist. He wanted Butch to feel he was being cooperative. Besides, Walker dreaded bad publicity or a lawsuit that would be messy for him and the Department.

"We don't know a whole lot about what happened, but we do have some speculations. I can fill you in on what we do know. That's no problem. We want Mrs. Bowen...Pam...to be satisfied that we are doing all that we can to learn the truth about her husband's death. It's an ongoing process as you probably know and takes a great deal of man hours and effort on our part to uncover the whos and whys."

Butch settled back in his chair and listened carefully as the officer gave him much of the same speculation he had just heard from Tom. These guys had not discovered much, Butch decided, just wired to the same sources of law enforcement knowledge that gave Tom his awareness and insight. However, Walker had hard information Tom could not have known, and it was contained in Jerry's surveillance reports of the previous weeks: something was going on with the Frangelettis. It was a slip for him to make reference to the reports and he stumbled over his words to cover the mistake. Butch pounced on his revelation quickly, but Walker was reluctant to share that information.

"I...I can't really fill you in on that...I...shouldn't have even said anything about them...but...they are something we are working on."

"All I want to know is if there is something I can share with Pam, something that explains, or..."

"No, there isn't. It helps our investigation, but doesn't do anything to give her piece of mind."

"Buddy Cappeletti is the man?"

"Probably," Walker answered, looking away from Butch, doing so to avert the intensity on Butch's face.

"Thanks."

Butch left without saying another word and headed for his car. He wanted to talk to Cuzo Mosca, he wanted away from this mess.

12.

Chick Frangeletti wasn't uncomfortable in prison, since it was not that much of a change for him from the outside. He preferred the company of men, although they were not his sexual preference. He had, in fact, no sexual preference. He was neutral, simply not interested. Oh, he had had sex with women because it had been arranged for him and that was what men did. He was used to having his life arranged for him as his father and his cousin Nick had always done for him.

He was not retarded, but not quite normal. He had been different from other children and the family knew something was wrong with him when he was very young. Papa Al watched over little baby Francis very diligently, waiting for more response, hoping that what he suspected was not true: the boy was not right. The prospect that his son was less than perfect bothered Al considerably, so he prayed time and again for him to be all right.

He's not right God, I don't know what is the matter with him, he's not right, make him grow up to be okay. He accepted the outcome of birth as God's will be done. So it was like a miracle when Francis grew older and was healthy and could function in a fairly good way. Yes, he was a little slower witted that the other boys, but he was going to be all right.

Nick started calling him Chick after a pro football player his father and his uncle had talked about, so he could not be teased about his name. To have his cousin named Francis and be teased about it was more than Nick could bear. He assumed that certainly the sissy name would be a reflection on him.

Papa Al doted on little Francis, knowing he needed special attention, needed to be cared for if he were to survive. He requested from Dominic that older cousin Nick help with the protection. Dominic believed that such help should be given to his brother's son and directed Nick to watch out for him. 'That unfortunate boy,' as Dominic described him. Nick heeded well the command from his father, making sure that even as an adult his younger cousin would be watched out for and insulated as best he could from difficulty. Nick and Chick were almost inseparable in the early years as Chick got used to being protected, directed, and nurtured by his uncle.

But Chick had not been able to avoid getting into trouble. He broke the law, got caught, and caught up in the legal system for something he didn't think was wrong. To have his life directed, programmed the way it was in prison was merely a continuation of what he knew. To have power accorded to him by deference was also something that he knew. Being in prison was not much different than outside, except that he couldn't drive a car. He loved to drive, to drive fast. Causing an automobile accident was bad enough, but he fled the scene. There had been witnesses who got his license number and the woman he left lying by the side of the road died later in the hospital. He hid at Nick's, but it was only a matter of time before the police came for him. He did not realize that Nick had called the police to tell them where he was. Nick's attorney thought it would be better that way and might go easier on Chick at trial. But he was summarily convicted and given a stiff prison sentence. And that is what put him in Mansfield Correctional.

Mansfield Correctional Institution is situated in rolling rural landscape just north of the town of Mansfield, Ohio, a facility of the Ohio Department of Rehabilitation and Correction. It is an interesting name for an agency that, on the whole, produces neither. Just simply Incarceration Department would be more accurate. Not that the attempt isn't made, it certainly is. There was school, with high school equivalency mandated and college available; various work assignments; trade training; jobs in contracted manufacturing; and recreation of all kinds. But the system, with all its worthy intentions, did not rehabilitate to any extent, nor correct effectively. It did, however, bring together like minds who discussed their exploits and collaborated on how they would be successful with future crimes. The less proficient learned how to better their skills at stealing, scamming, or robbing so they believed they would not get caught the next time. Most of them would churn through the system again, as surely as nightfall passed over the prison.

The Mansfield facility was designed to resemble a college campus, with a large open quad, the neatly arranged cellblock buildings, the strategically placed school rooms, mess halls, and training locations, all unified in one integrated architectural message of confinement with compassion, imprisonment with meaning. For many inmates, it was the best social and living environment they had ever experienced. And it was all under the specter of the Reformatory, the aging former prison that stood on the hill in the background, a constant reminder that prison was once brutal, that doing time meant suffering the indignation that society had wanted criminals to endure. Mansfield was today a new world, the reflection of a new society where civil rights and personal esteem and racial diversity were critical elements in the process of being penalized for deviating from accepted norms, for breaking laws. But it was not bad time served, it was merely an inconvenience for the professionals and case hardened.

In large measure, drugs were the reason most inmates got to Mansfield, not killing someone with a car. Buying, selling, or using drugs. And just because they were inside didn't mean the drug commerce stopped. Inside, drugs were bought, sold, and used on a regular basis. Not in volume, but with steady continuation.

Chick Frangeletti controlled much of the drug commerce in Mansfield, along with cigarettes, pornography, and other specialties that might be ordered from him by mainly white inmates. The blacks had their own source, as did the Hispanics. This control gave him a special position among the inmates, although his name alone would give him certain rights. The insidious web of Frangeletti influence reached well inside the State's prisons.

On Mondays, Wednesdays, and Fridays, an unmarked Frangeletti semi brought provisions to the Mansfield commissary. The Frangeletti operation held the food service supply contract and these were the fulfillment days. Routine and consistent in time of arrival, with the same driver, and the same tractor and trailer with the same license number, these deliveries lulled the guards into a false sense of acceptance and a weakened posture of security.

The truck entrance pen was wrapped with razor wire, the driver was patted down, and the rear doors of the trailer were opened for a cursory inspection. Mirrors were used to check underneath the tractor and the trailer. After dozens and dozens of these deliveries, the guards did not put the same effort into the inspections as they had at first. The commonalty bred laxness, carelessness on their part. It had become too routine to bring about much interest or concentration by the guards.

Today was a very special day for the Frangeletti delivery, and it happened that it was also the same day that Cuzo Mosca observed the truck's passage into Mansfield.

Cuzo had patiently followed the truck from the Frangeletti restaurant at the Commodore Perry service plaza, a boring ride of little more than an hour and a half. While at the plaza restaurant, it had off-loaded a batch of boxes and cartons and on-loaded what looked like the same boxes and cartons. Besides the nondescript tan cardboard containers, there also were bags of bulk staples such as beans or flour, and cans of olive oil. He had, as Jerry had, watched this action numerous times and had finally decided to see where the truck went. At first, he had no idea where the truck was headed, but after awhile suspected the destination. He wanted to make sure. Mansfield, he said to himself, this guy is headed for Mansfield. It must be part of their usual business. Diós mío, what a thing they've got going!

Cuzo slowed as he saw the truck turn into the delivery driveway, just south of the prison. He drove on past the truck entry a short way and parked his car well off the road. It was the road that ran by the front of the prison. He got out of his car and walked up a slight rise to check the truck's progress. He stood with binoculars pressed to his eyes as the truck sat within the cocoon of razor wire at the check-in pen. The casual way the guards inspected the truck and trailer did not go unnoticed by Cuzo. Pretty loose, he thought.

Soon the truck moved through the check-in pen onto the grounds of the prison. This is it, he reasoned, this is how they get stuff inside, big time. All boxed as food items. What a set up. It would be, he thought, an operation very easy to screw up. The disruption would cause serious problems. He held the binoculars at his chest and watched as the truck slowly moved away from the check point and disappeared behind one of the buildings. He walked slowly back to his car, all the while factoring what he had witnessed. Clever, very clever, he said to himself, I admire such a method, it is so sweet. But, he concluded, here also was a vulnerability that could hurt them. He got back in his car and headed for Toledo.

The Frangeletti truck moved across the prison grounds on the approved road to the primary commissary, where it cut a wide circle to its left. It carefully backed up to the loading dock. It was the right day and the right time, so several inmates and their guard were waiting for the delivery. As soon as the trailer touched the dock bumpers, the loading door was jerked open and the trailer door was released. The driver got out and walked to the rear of the trailer. There in the loading dock opening stood Chick Frangeletti, hands on hips, a broad smile on his face. The guard who had watched the truck move into position, walked back into the storage area. He would neither observe nor interfere with the unloading.

"I hope you have everything we ordered," Chick asked the driver.

"Yessir, Mr. Frangeletti, its all here."

"Go inside...get a cup of coffee. Relax. We'll take care of everything."

Chick was excited about pulling this off, but he didn't want anything to do with the girls himself. He did not want to see them or talk to them. They were, for him, merely part of the goods he got inside Mansfield. He tried not to even think about them being there behind the boxes. He went on about his business of checking out the other items that had been ordered, making sure the shipment was right.

All of the special order merchandise was prepaid by someone on the outside. It didn't matter: if you wanted drugs or anything else from Chick, you had someone deposit the required amount with a Frangeletti Corporation contact in Toledo. The transaction was cash only and off the books. It didn't matter what was purchased, the money was with the Frangelettis before delivery. But it was possible to get almost anything.

There had been a special request to Nick which came about as the result of a tease by Chick to some of the inmates. The tease bloomed as a potential offering and subsequently took on a life of its own. More than two dozen inmates responded, the price put down for them with the Frangelettis. Today was the day that request was honored, was delivered. The price for this merchandise was actually less than for most of the drug orders. It was the delivery of sex. Available, real sex for those who had the money and got it paid. A thousand dollars a dip, Chick had promised, and that was cheap considering the quality of the girls that would be delivered.

It had taken considerable planning and coordination to get it done, but Chick's request was not to be denied. When Nick heard about the message from his cousin he was angry at first. It seemed like another chance for this less-than-swift problematical relative to get into trouble and compromise their operation. But he thought the proposition through and understood that it wasn't the sex Chick wanted, it was the chance to make money. Chick was not interested in the girls for himself, he reasoned, of course not.

Such an arrangement would be difficult, but not impossible. And, with further consideration, he figured it was no worse, no more dangerous than drugs. He had never been comfortable with the sex part of the business, so his first reaction to any enterprise that involved sex was always negative. He assigned Nicky and Allie directly to make it happen.

Nicky laughed when he heard about the request that Chick made for the girls and took great delight in arranging such an operation. Anything at all that involved sex got his full attention. He insisted that it was his devotion to duty for the Corporation and for family that prompted his diligence in these matters. He swung into action as soon as he finished getting the order from his father by reviewing his files of special females that worked for the organization. These were the young women he had personally selected. It was a group of about fifty, graded and categorized by him to fit his criteria of looks and ability to deliver sex.

He evaluated the pool of potential candidates for several days before finally choosing two young waitresses from Francesca's and another girl from the Nicky's restaurant in Norwalk. Of course, the women had no idea they were being considered by Nicky for the assignment. Once he made the decision, they were summoned to the Frangeletti offices in Toledo. He called them into his office, one at a time. To each he made the same short speech about doing what was important for the organization to insure the success of their careers. He told what was in store for them. Each of them knew there was no choice in the matter short of suicide or running away, and running away probably would be suicide.

Nicky's selection of the young women was based on his assessment of their physical stature. Each was fairly tall, large breasted, and ample of size through the hips, thighs, and buttocks. He felt they could withstand the rigors of the assignment more than some of the petite girls, although petite was not a word in his vocabulary. The smaller ones he called pixies, a word he had learned from his mother years before. Pixies will never do for this, he told Allie, we need broads that can take on the world, that have stamina, staying power.

The three young women were brought to Toledo the night before the delivery and met with Nicky. He explained the arrangement, but did not tell them they were headed to Mansfield, he merely said they would be the stars of a party in a truck and there would be a few guys to satisfy. They would each get a week of vacation and a thousand bucks. Somehow, somewhere deep within him he knew that this whole deal was crazy as hell, but he could not put his finger on what it was that made him feel it was so nuts. The excitement within him, knowing that the three girls would be screwed by those guys, gave him a sense of purpose. He could relate to the inmates desire, he could relate to their longing for a woman and the sensual pleasure with them that would ensue.

Allie took care of the trailer for that night. It was setup in the main Toledo warehouse where it was outfitted. He had carpeting put down at the head of the trailer covering the first ten feet. Three mattresses were brought in and positioned on the carpet. A row of cardboard boxes full of pasta were lashed in place to form a wall between the girls and the rest of the cargo on the trailer, but with a spot through which you could pass by carefully removing several boxes. There the girls would spend the night. Once he had the special section ready, Allie brought the girls on board.

"Here you are girls," he intoned, "ya got yer mattresses and brand new blankets, ya got yer bottled water, ya got yer snacks, ya got yer paper towels, ya got yer battery powered lanterns, ya got yer boxes of condoms, and ya got yer portable toilet. Yer all set. A little crude maybe, but it'll work."

The girls plopped down on the mattresses almost in unison and checked out their surroundings. "This is it?" the girl from Norwalk asked.

"You got it," Allie replied, "and don't bitch or I'll tell Nicky yer ungrateful."

"Ungrateful for what?" the Norwalk girl shot back, "for being fucked to death in the back of a truck, like some pig."

"Just do yer job and I'll see you back here tomorrow."

The girls listened as the trailer was loaded and it became pitch black. Now, nearly midnight, they didn't bother turning on a lantern. What was the point?

They were sound asleep at six in the morning when the trailer was dropped onto the semi tractor and moved out of the warehouse, headed for the Commodore Perry service plaza. They barely roused from sleep at the sounds and movement of that action and did not fully wake until the truck stopped at the plaza.

The girls listened with a sense of curiosity and anticipation as cartons and supplies were taken off the trailer and others replaced them. The voices of the men unloading and loading were muffled, whispering to each other as they worked. In short order, the truck was again on the move.

The three did not know they would be in the trailer for so long, so that their sense of anticipation intensified with the changes of speed, periodic stopping for traffic lights, various sounds, and the sway and bounce from different road conditions.

"Shit," Norwalk complained, "where the hell are we going and when are we gonna get there?"

When the semi pulled into the Mansfield check-in pen and stopped, they heard voices, saw a crack of light from the rear doors being opened. Their alertness at this became anxiety, especially when the truck began to move again. They felt the truck back up and settle against the loading dock. Finally, the sound of the engine stopped. They figured they had finally arrived.

The three young girls were each in position on her own mattress. No one would suspect, no one would check. Now, the portable whorehouse was in business.

Word was passed to the participating inmates about the girls in the careful way that any information is passed in prison. The knowledgeable speak to the uninformed. In time, everyone knew they were there, but only the legitimate buyers could respond. This was a time of reckoning for Mansfield: most of the inmates knew what was happening, few were participants. Those inmates excluded from the sale knew it was because they had not responded. Now that it was for real, they certainly knew what they were missing. This was an invitation for another circumstance of relief for those who wanted to and failed to participate in this excursion into passion.

The men who knew they had paid and were entitled to get in on the action with the girls carefully moved to the main commissary, sure that they were not being watched, hopeful their actions would not be reported. It was a subdued bunch that descended on the commissary, sure of their entitlement for sex, unsure that they would be discovered. This was, after all, a controlled environment, where men were watched for deviancy rather than action. Where fulfillment of desire was deemed impossible and circumstances guided all actions.

Enough boxes were removed to form a path to the front where the three young women waited. Those inmates who had paid moved to the commissary, into the kitchen, through the loading dock, and into the truck. There was controlled movement orchestrated by Chick so there weren't bunches of men, and each man had a story for why he went to the commissary. It was still awhile until lunch, so guards might ask what they were doing.

It didn't matter which girl, which ever one was free would do. Although robust of size and shape, in truth, each was a luscious specimen. Nicky had seen to that, so there was no quarrel over which girl was had. Twenty seven men paid and showed up to collect, so the girls were busy. The truck usually stayed for an hour and a half, so the sex was rapid fire, non stop.

It was the sex of extreme convenience, ordered, paid for, and delivered. It was the sex of extreme excitement for men isolated from its pleasure for a time longer than their souls could bear. It was the sex of extreme emotion as these buyers of pleasure exalted with the moment. It was the sex of expediency as the men struggled with the precious moments of ecstasy, the enchantment of the day that would carry them for a long time. It was the sex of debilitation as some clutched to an unknown meaning for the sense they had lived through, the transcendent, overriding characterization of them they might not want to face. It was the sex of baseness that locked each participant into a channel of degradation. It was the sex of wild fun and exhilaration. It was the sex that symbolized freedom and the reason for having it. It was a day that would be talked about at Mansfield for years to come, and in the future, every con, every single con there, was a part of the moment, everyone was a part of the glorious sex of the day. There was shared mutuality of pleasure and excitement.

The unloading was paced with precise control until the last of the twenty seven men was finished and the final boxes were taken off the trailer. The naked girls lay there exhausted and spent as the trailer doors were closed. The men who unloaded the trailer neither looked closely nor remarked on the scene they had witnessed of the young girls. It was a delivery that was ordered and that was that - complete.

For Chick Frangeletti, this delivery was, as any of the others, important to insure his presence and power within Mansfield. He neither understood nor cared about the exchange that had taken place. He was only concerned with his own position in the prison. This confined universe contained several men who competed and jockeyed for power and prestige. The black gangs, the Latino gangs, each had someone who wanted kingpin status. Chick held that position with most of the whites and a few blacks. The Latinos held out for their own man. Few, if any, of the very oldest inmates -regardless of race - got involved with such maneuvering. They knew better. However, any one of them who wanted anything bought it from Chick. He controlled the supply.

The idea for bringing the girls in had come from Skippy Decho, a runt of a man who was Chick's shadow. Wherever Chick went, Skippy was close at hand. They shared the same cell and Skippy acted as valet, right hand man, and general all around flunky. Skippy liked the arrangement because it made him feel safe. He had been in and out of prison most of his adult life and he knew the dangers that awaited anyone as physically weak and powerless as he. Being connected to Chick gave him a feeling of safety.

As the truck pulled away from the loading dock, Chick turned to Skippy and poked him in the shoulder. "You did good, Skip, real good. I'll tell Nick to put some extra in your account."

This was high praise for the skinny little man and he grinned broadly in response to the reward.

The process of distributing all of the other purchases was now underway. Slowly, but surely, each item moved from the storage area of the commissary to the buyers throughout the complex of two story cell buildings. It was well organized by Chick with men he could trust, accomplished with simple efficiency. Transfers were made in the open quad, near the recreation field, and in the dinning halls. With the movement of inmates relatively unrestricted during the day, it was done without arousing suspicion from the guards not in on the action. The few guards key to insuring the success of Chick's commerce were taken care of by Nick. Cash found its way into their hands on a regular basis.

"We gotta make sure this business don't get messed up, Skip...gotta be careful. Can't get cocky just because we pulled this off. I'm outta here in less than two years. I don't want that screwed around with. Right?"

"Right...that's right Chick. Gotta be careful."

Skippy was always careful. He knew the operation could fall apart at any time. Somebody talks, there's some kind of slip up...it could end in a blink. The results would not be pretty.

Cuzo also knew how delicate it was to be bringing merchandise into Mansfield. The random patterns of well tended farmlands raced by as he drove back to report to Victor, deep in thought with no inkling of what had transpired with the girls. If he had known, he would have been filled with awe and admiration. He appreciated a good operation no matter who pulled it off. He wondered how the Padillo organization could use the knowledge of what he had seen. It just might be leveraged in dealing with the Frangelettis. Certainly, the Frangelettis, especially Nick, did not want Chick to do more hard time. There could be valuable consideration with this knowledge.

13.

Butch understood very well that trying to find someone like Cuzo in a large metropolitan area was not particularly easy, certainly not as easy as the cops on television and in the movies would have one believe. That kind of action had all been glamorized. It didn't reflect all of the hard work that was done day in and day out to find the bad guys. It wasn't easy, the real chances of solving a crime were limited, the results of pure detail and investigation tempered by the fact that most criminals get away with their crime. The bad guys slide through each day knowing they can steal or rob or do whatever they want to do without ever being touched by the law. More often than not, dumb luck played a large part in finding someone, quite as it was in solving most crime. Luck, hard work, circumstance, and informants were the ingredients for investigative success. Flat out being smart, with the ability for associative thinking could shortstop some of the work, but sitting around thinking didn't cut it. The smarts and the fitting together of random pieces of information had to be a factor while you were full speed on an investigation, when the tedious work was being pounded out and the leads pursued. Butch didn't much believe in coincidences or luck when it came to investigative work.

Butch had what it took - smarts and so forth - but he was older now...and tired. With Tom putting the word out, he wondered, maybe I should just stand still and let this Mosca find me.

He punched Pam's number into the phone and leaned back as he began to open a large envelope that had come in the mail. He had the receiver tucked between his cheek and shoulder.

"Pam," he said softly, soothingly, "reporting in. How's it going?"

"Okay...I'm okay. What have you learned?"

"There's this guy named Cuzo who might know something. My friend Tom with the TPD says this Cuzo would be the start of finding out anything. I'm trying to run him down. Nothing at this point. Tom was going to tell some of his contacts to let him know I was looking for him, but he hasn't touched base with me yet. I really doubt if he will."

"Why?"

"Hunch, I guess...I just don't think so. This guy doesn't want to be bothered with me. Hey, listen, I'll stay in touch. Talk to you later."

He dropped the receiver back onto the phone base and stared at the photo he pulled from the envelope. He pushed the envelope open wide: no letter, no note. Just the photo. On the back was written - *Mosca. Tim.*

Well, isn't this interesting, Butch said to himself, the FBI wants to help me. Wonder why? Something's going on. They want something, or they want me to stir up the Mexicans. There's an angle here for them, most likely. Get Cuzo out in the open would be one thing, get him isolated, get him separate from the rest of his organization. No matter, we've got to run him down. Butch felt he was being squeezed to some point where he probably did not want to be. He would be glad when this was over.

He punched in the FBI number, finally reaching Tim Connelly after a long wait.

"Connelly."

"Thanks for the photo. It'll help."

"Greiner?"

"Yeah."

"Heard you were looking for the guy. Well, I thought it might be easier if you knew what he looked like."

"Any chance we can get together and chat awhile?"

"What do you need?"

"I'd like some background on Mosca. I figure if you have a photo, you must know something about him."

"What you have is a blow up from part of a surveillance photo. He's elusive...we don't know much. The DEA guys probably know more, but they won't give you anything. He seems to be a character worth watching. What's your interest, a client?"

"No. Personal. A Highway Patrol officer named Bowen was a friend of mine...had an ice pick pushed into his chest while he was on surveillance at one of the Turnpike plazas...wife wants me to find out what happened. I would have thought Tom told you that..."

"No, just said you were looking."

"Where do I find him?"

"He lives in Maumee, but he's rarely home. Hangs out at Judd's once in awhile..."

"Yeah, I know the joint, it's also in Maumee."

"...but mainly he's at Padillo's house when he's not on the move. He's on the move a lot."

"He's being watched?"

"I can't answer that. Let's just say he has come to our attention."

"Enough said. Thanks a lot, Tim. Take care."

Butch looked at the photo for a long time, implanting the image in his brain. He knew he needed to do that so he could spot Cuzo when the time came. He would not be carrying the photo with him, again a habit from the past. Who is this elusive Mr. Mosca and what was he all about? Butch wondered what kind of man he was after, wondered how Cuzo would respond to him once they met. He assured himself they would meet.

As the afternoon pushed on into evening that retained much of the day's heat and humidity, Butch settled onto one of the bar stools at Judd's and relished the coolness the air conditioning offered. He ordered a beer. The place had a smell about it that Butch disliked, mainly the odor of smoke, but helped along by a generous amount of booze spilled onto an endless carpet of peanut shells. Not quite a dump, but almost so. Non-stop sports talk, blue collar drinkers, and cheap draft beer. Judd's was a kind of clubhouse to a weird cross section of regulars. No blacks. Hispanics, but no blacks, and the Hispanics had very light skin.

Butch surveyed the bar, sipped on his beer, and lapsed into thoughts about his work. What he did to help his clients didn't seem all that important, but he knew that, in the scheme of things, the results were worthwhile for the companies involved. Pam was something else. It was one thing to help a friend, but it was another matter altogether to turn your life over to an investigation like this. He already knew more than he wanted to know. It was time to talk to Cuzo, report back to Pam, and move on. Working for friends can get complicated and messy, and besides there's no money in it. He still was uneasy about helping Pam because of the potential for her to make more of the help than he wanted - the romance stuff - so getting the thing resolved and out of his hair was important for him.

These government agencies guarded their information jealously, he said to himself, reflecting on his brief conversation with FBI Special Agent Connelly. Secrecy was everything for them. The little bits of information, the knowledge of something happening, the low down on what was going down...they were elements of being more alert, of being on top in your job. There was little inclination to pass these details to another agency whose agenda and actions might show you up. No, these secrets, these tidbits of information, all were retained for an agency's benefit, for their protection and containment. There was power and control to be derived from such secrecy. He had experienced this from his time spent at the CIA: have the information someone else didn't have, have it ready in case it was needed, use the information for advantage. This was the power of information control used over and over to establish personal credit. It was inconsequential that the information might help someone else.

His former work with the Agency was an aspect of his past that he rarely thought about these days, a part of his life he hardly talked of or even mentioned to anyone else. Only his closest friends knew about his time with the Agency and it was an avoided topic by them based on Butch's lack of desire to reveal any details. Having been sworn to secrecy, much of what he had been involved in couldn't be discussed anyway.

Cat, mouse, cat. Cuzo sat in a far corner of Judd's watching Butch with quiet fascination, feeling in control, satisfied with his position, knowing he was master of his universe. It was he who dictated what happened in his world, for the most part, and he edged around adversity, stayed clear of danger, and simply looked down on the world around him. He had an arrogance forged from his privileged background, reinforced by his ability to skirt the law and survive the drug business. He believed he was master; he was the fox who outfoxed. He saw Butch as a stranger who would not know who he was. He didn't realize that Butch recognized him, spotted him when he came in, and knew right where he was sitting. It was a shock of some magnitude when suddenly Butch was standing at his table staring down at him.

"Mosca?"

Cuzo refused to fully look up, to truly acknowledge Butch. He did not respond. He sensed Butch's intensity and knew instinctively that he was confronted with someone worthy of his attention. But he was not about to grant that attention without some degree of resistance, while retaining full measure of his Hispanic bravado, charm, and wish for maintaining complete control of the situation.

Butch kicked through the two chairs by the table, his foot landing full on the table pedestal, bouncing it back into Cuzo's belly. There was a clattering noise as the chairs bounced aside and the table base shimmied on the tile floor. A large glass of ice tea bounced and tipped as it struggled for stability on the table top, but oddly enough did not fall over. This got Cuzo's attention. He looked up, but his face was turned towards the bar.

"That's not very polite," Cuzo said, still not looking at Butch.

Butch was not normally pugnacious, but he had a toughness about him that was visible, much as a tightly coiled spring - it wasn't doing anything, but you knew it could. He had a sense of confidence that projected his physical strength and his lack of fear. At five six and 147 pounds, he picked his spots carefully. This was one of them because he was tired, running out of patience, and didn't want time wasted playing games with the Mexican.

"I need a few minutes of your time and I'm not interested in your posturing," Butch said calmly.

Butch sat down across from Cuzo and propped his elbows on the table.

"I suggest you be nice and talk to me or I'll make this a very ugly day for you."

Luis started to approach the table, but Cuzo waved him off. It was a gesture that Butch ignored. He had seen the other Mexican - probably Cuzo's lieutenant - standing at the bar and was fully prepared to deal with him if necessary.

Cuzo now looked at Butch squarely, a smile slowly forming on his face.

"Of course. What ever."

He pulled the runaway glass of ice tea towards him, took a sip, and set it down. His outer calmness with pleasant countenance and easy gestures belied the anger that simmered within him.

"I need some information," Butch said, "you can help. Probably more than you know."

"Who you with?" Cuzo asked carefully. He assumed Butch was some kind of law.

"No one...I'm a PI...I represent a lady who wants me to find out about her husband's death. I'm told you might know something."

"Who was this guy?"

"Bowen. Jerry Bowen. You probably didn't know his name. He was Highway Patrol in plain clothes who got an ice pick shoved into his chest out on one of the Turnpike plazas. He was..."

"I know the situation," Cuzo answered matter-of-factly. "I did not know his name, you are right."

"What do you know?"

"I believe that the man who committed that crime was punished. I think that's the case. I think you can tell the wife it has been taken care of."

"You know for sure?"

"Nothing is for sure. Let's just say I have very good reason to believe that her husband's death has been avenged."

"And your guy's death has been avenged?"

"We had a certain interest in the situation...we were paying attention to certain things and we became aware of a person who was probably the guilty party...we..."

"Probably?"

"Nothing is one hundred percent...that is, nothing is one hundred percent without an eye witness. The probability is very high that the man who took out your client's husband has been dealt with. It's that simple...I can't tell it to you any different than that."

"What kind of nonsense is that?" Butch prodded. "Someone saw something...something gave you guys the idea it was that Buddy what's-his-name who used the ice pick. Let me repeat...someone saw something. Someone like you, maybe?"

"Yes," Cuzo said after hesitating, "I can say that I saw something, but part of my vision was blocked for a few seconds. I know I saw this Cappeletti get in your friend's car, I saw some quick movement by him. We had heard about him."

"Like what?"

"We had heard he used an ice pick...many times. He enjoyed stabbing people with the ice pick, we were told. A young man of ours, harming no one, merely going about his business, was killed with an ice pick. It was left in his chest still sticking in his heart when we got to him. It became a police matter, but they could find out nothing. We didn't expect them to and we knew we must deliver the justice that was needed. So you see, by accident, your lady got her revenge...and we, of course, got ours. That is all I know."

"Thanks," Butch said slowly.

Cuzo did not respond.

"You're not listed...give me your number. I may want to contact you again."

"I don't give out my number."

"Make an exception for me. Otherwise I'll throw your ass out the side window. You won't like it much."

Cuzo looked at him coolly. "You wouldn't do that."

Butch pulled a pen and small notebook from his inside jacket pocket. "You have till the count of three to give me your number."

Cuzo recited the number casually, as if he were telling Butch the temperature or giving a baseball score. He was not interested in a scene and Butch counted on that, counted on the fact that Cuzo liked to operate with a low profile.

Butch wrote the number in his notebook, realized from the three numerals of the exchange that it was for a cell phone. He sat back in his chair looking intently at the Mexican who would hardly look at him. There was no way to fathom what this man was thinking or feeling. I hope this is the one and only time I have to deal with this guy, Butch thought, as he got up and walked out into the oppressive night air.

14.

Victor Padillo rarely ventured from the compound he had built on former farmland. He didn't need to leave, because here were provided the amenities that he desired. The house had been setup to be well stocked with food, to be self-sufficient in order to hold out against siege, if necessary. A man of simple wants and needs, his was a minimalist lifestyle where many basic items most people took for granted were savored by him. A childhood in poverty and countless hours locked in a prison cell had given him that perspective. He had promised himself while he was confined the last time that when he got out, when he made some money, even big money, he would not be lavish in the way he lived. He could appreciate simple things, he reasoned, let the money build up for the future.

Cuzo had found the acreage while driving around looking for a place to establish their headquarters. He had been on his way to check out a farm that he had seen listed for sale in the newspaper, but figured building everything from scratch on raw land might be the better way to go. He sold the idea to Victor after a great deal of discussion to convince him of the advantages. It wasn't long before construction was completed and they moved the operation from the large apartment Victor used in Toledo on the east side of the Maumee River.

Victor ran the carwash and a vending business, and drug distribution from the compound. There was no need to have an office away from the house. Meetings with the men in his organization were conducted here. He didn't care much for restaurants, didn't care much for other people in general, so there was little reason to leave. He had Gloria, the fish pond that he used frequently, his dogs, and a pistol range in the basement. A man with uncomplicated tastes, he lived in a way that suited him.

He could fish the pond for several hours at a time, cell phone beside him, alternating between phone conversations and fussing with the tackle and bait. Catching a fish was immaterial to him. The fresh air, the sun, the sense of freedom he felt by the pond were satisfactory. When, as it happened infrequently, he caught a fish, he gently removed the hook and tossed it back into the green water. He found that its shiver and slide away into deeper water a comfort to him. He had been caught, he had been confined to the mind-numbing dullness of prison boredom, so he was sensitive to their freedom and it was important to him to put them back in the pond.

Sometimes Gloria would loll about on the grass nearby. She would sit, lie spread-eagled, eventually roll slowly, turning her body over and over as if to squeeze away the boredom that oppressed her. Cuzo gave her books to read once in awhile, but they were of subjects in which she had no interest. Besides, they were too difficult for her, so that the challenge to stick with them could not be faced without merciless, tedious effort. She gave up on them quite easily. She was entranced, however, by what she saw on television. There on TV, was a world that she understood, where she could relate, and where she could learn. She was not, as they say, intellectually stimulated. However, had her level of comprehension and intelligence been equal to her reach of physical beauty, she would have been a genius. Victor was not interested in her mind, so she matched the level of the rest of his simple desires and gratified his requirements for *love*. Love as understood by men with Victor's limited dimension of personal interaction. She was great to look at and fabulous in bed. So be it for him.

Once when they were out by the pond, he fishing and phoning, she lolling bored, she presented a concept to him that disturbed him.

"We're prisoners here," she said with her squeaky, pouty voice, "it's like we're in jail. We need to get away from here once in awhile."

He didn't answer at first. He was stunned by what she had said, but did not want to give her the satisfaction in knowing she had made a point with him. He did not want to give her comments validity, because that might mean that something was wrong with the setup here, and, worse, something was wrong with him.

"We can go anywhere any time. You can't when you're locked up." He controlled his anger at having to deal with this.

"But we don't go anywhere, so it's the same...isn't it? What good is all the money you make, anyway? We don't use it to have fun or buy much...what's the point?"

"Shut up! Damn! How can women figure out ways to do dees shit to us guys?"

He was confused and frustrated by this woman he held in so little regard. Does she make any sense? He hated to think that she did and he wanted to push the issue out of his mind.

"Am I wrong?" she asked, "tell me if I'm wrong."

"Sí, you are wrong. And don't theenk so much...it ees not good for you...geets you confused. We can buy anytheeng, we can go anywhere...de money ees...ees...ees like insurance. Now, shut up. You scare away de fish."

She had thought she might be right about her point, but didn't say anymore and Victor had gone on fishing and phoning.

On this particular day, however, they were headed out, leaving the compound, and Gloria was excited. She would be going with him and be allowed to shop at Westfield Mall. This was a special trip and it was necessary. She rose early to get prepared, slowly, deliberately doing her hair, her makeup, and finally her nails. She had worked diligently getting herself ready, fretted over the right outfit, and essentially ended up being over dressed and looking as if she were a well-coiffured and exquisitely tailored hooker. The stiletto heels were certainly a give away. She really had no sense of how she looked, she just knew the clothes and shoes were expensive and that she had carefully prepared herself. She sat waiting for Victor more than an hour after she had herself ready, patiently watching television. She had been too involved getting herself ready to even think of having breakfast.

Victor had been forced to plan the trip away from the compound because of his teeth. He needed a dentist. Years of abuse, lack of regular care, and disregard for normal oral hygiene, coupled with chewing tobacco and using pinch, had made his mouth a holy hell of constant pain. It had been pain he lived over for a long time, but now, he finally could not withstand the agony. Off to a dentist for relief.

When he came into the living room, still in his undershorts, Gloria sat prim and patient on the sofa waiting for him. It was less than an hour until the eleven o'clock appointment. He stared out the picture window at the pond and yawned.

"I'll bet you're afraid," she laughed.

"Shut up." He walked to the kitchen for coffee.

"We're getting out of prison and you're afraid," she mocked him, "This is a blessing for me. I'm not afraid. Sometimes I wonder if you have balls...I have felt something and seen something, but maybe you had a transplant...what I felt was not your balls, but something else in their place, some substitute for what you should be carrying there."

She knew he was out of earshot, so she kept going with the insults. "No manhood when they get cut off. Take away the sack of marbles and you are a miserable worm, crawling in darkness. When did you have them cut off? Or maybe the bag was opened and yours were substituted by a couple of olives. You have Italian balls, like two Martini olives..."

She knew she wasn't making any sense, but she liked the idea of talking back to Victor - as long as he did not hear what she was saying.

Victor stuck his head around the doorway and yelled. "What the hell are you talking about, I'm trying to get something to eat...some coffee..."

"Nada," she yelled back, "nothing. I was just talking to myself."

Fifteen minutes later, Victor was dressed and headed out the side door into the garage. "Come on, if you're going," he yelled.

Juan followed him into the garage, protesting to Victor that he should not be driving himself. "You should let me drive. You should not go alone."

"No one knows I'm out here, Juan. Eet will be okay. What...someone would shoot me? I theenk not."

He drove the nearly new Lincoln Town Car slowly out of the garage, headed down the drive, and pushed the control signaling the powered gate to open. He stopped at the edge of the road, poised for starting out, checked both ways for traffic, and, with no vehicles to be seen, turned left and headed north. Off the compound, he always had a sense of dread, of some ominous occurrence happening, though God knows what it would be, and he touched his shoulder holster slightly to reassure himself that it was there, his partner in time of danger. Feeling its substance against his chest made him feel a little better.

Within a mile or so from the compound, he suddenly caught an image in the rear view mirror that forced a surge of his adrenaline. A beat-up van was approaching, coming very fast, fast enough to overtake him, to run into him. He pushed hard on the accelerator, but the Town Car being the lumbering beast that it was, did not respond fast enough to get away from the van that came roaring at them. When the van hit their rear end, Gloria gave a yelp of fear as her head and Victor's were snapped backward by the impact.

Victor struggled with the Town Car to maintain control, but that effort kept him from pulling out the automatic pistol at his left armpit. It was all he could do to keep the car on the road as the van hit the Town Car three more sharp bangs, with solid smacks that snapped their heads each time. He did not want to lose control, to swerve into the ditch running alongside, a ditch that was six feet deep in some spots, a ditch that would more than likely cause the car to overturn and roll.

Suddenly the van was alongside, slamming broadside into the Town Car to force it off the road. Now going almost seventy miles per hour, it wouldn't take much for the van to brush them aside. From the open passenger side window of the van, a shotgun was fired at Victor's car. At close range, the shotgun blast was an explosion of sound from the barrel's discharge and the almost simultaneous noise of its shot hitting metal. The shotgun blasted two more times as the two vehicles careened down the country road.

Victor ducked instinctively with the first shot, believing they would soon be dead. He fought for control, trying to see the road without letting much of his head be a target. When the second and third shots were fired into their car, he knew they were not trying to hit him. The first one could have done that. He sat back up and kept the car on the road.

The van and the Town Car went through the crossroads nearest the compound without incident. Luckily, at this time of day there was little traffic in their rural countryside. Once through the intersection, the van pressed its superiority of power and speed and steadily pushed the Town Car off the road at a place where the ditch was a shallow dip. Victor steered as best he could, struggling to keep the car from overturning. They were soon into a soybean field, bouncing over the loose soil, scattering plants and dirt in all directions. He started to pump the brakes as they left the road, so the careening ride onto the field did not go very far, and abruptly stopped with dust and debris still hanging in the air. At least they had not overturned.

Through the scrim of dust, Victor could only vaguely see the van slide to a stop and two men get out of the rear doors. They walked toward the Town Car, one with a shotgun, the other with an automatic pistol in each hand. Victor knew, without clearly seeing, what would happen next. Instinct, experience, they kept a man from getting killed. He assumed this was just a job to scare him, but he wasn't taking any chances.

Buckling up may be the law, but it was just one more that Victor chose not to obey. Gloria, on the other hand, had dutifully snapped hers in place. He popped the release on her belt and pushed her towards the door as the belt slid away.

"Down. Stay down. Geet thee door open, geet out, geet out..."

She did not react fast enough, so he shoved her against the door as he pulled the latch. A shotgun blast tore into the front of the car and a second hit the windshield before he could force her out onto the ground.

The one with the shotgun had fired first and each of them kept firing until their weapons were empty. They quickly, deliberately reloaded and unleashed a new barrage until they were empty again. Tires exploded, glass burst and flew, metal and plastic fragments filled the air as the Town Car was made a shambles.

Victor and Gloria were sprawled on the ground, out of the line of fire. Dust was in their eyes and mouth, their faces bloodied from flying glass, and their sense of direction somewhat disoriented at first. Gloria rolled onto her back and closed her eyes. She figured they would soon be dead.

Victor yanked out his automatic pistol and crawled to the rear of the car. He worked his way on his belly through the dirt to where he might get off a shot. It was quiet now, save for the incessant buzzing of horse flies and the muted cawing of some crows in a distant batch of trees. The van had pulled away and through dust blurred eyes he could see it slowly getting smaller as it went on down the road. He stood up and squinted at their departure through the haze of stifling humid heat.

"Sheet, I guess dey dunlike our message to dat ice peek guy. Poor sports. Fuck dem!"

He looked over at Gloria, who was still cowering on the ground behind the car. "I know doze guys. Dey Frangeletti. Dey could keel us if dey wanted to. Jus scare, jus scare. Very funny." He walked to where she sat in the dirt. "Sorry, yer escape got spoiled. We do it another time. Maybe tomorrow. Come on...I call Juan."

Victor retrieved the cell phone from the car and punched in the compound number. "Esme...Victor...we had a little problem up de road."

The one named Juan said he would come get them right away.

Gloria carried the stilettos limply in her left hand as they walked slowly back to the road to wait for Juan. She had found one of them still in the car and the other was half buried in the dirt. They were precious to her and she had crawled around until she found the prized shoe.

"Do you think these will clean up?" she asked plaintively. "I hope so."

"Sí, dey weel," he answered without looking at her.

"I'm sorry about your car."

"Better thee car than us. But that is thee way dey wanted it. Eet was der answer to our little message to dem. Dey could have keeled us...dey deed not want to. Jus to scare us. Dey not know, we don scare so easy."

His anger and the wait in the blistering heat had Victor dripping with sweat by the time Juan got there to pick them up.

"Señor Padillo, you are okay?" Juan was very nervous about the mood his boss would be in when he got to him.

"We okay."

Victor seemed calm and Juan was relieved as he watched his boss help Gloria into the sedan. She was badly shaken and started to sob once seated in the car. She laid her head back on the seat, the tears streaming down her dust-covered face leaving little trails, her eyes tightly closed.

"Juan, dey shoot at us, run us off da road, shoot at us again, but we are okay. We deed not teep over so we got out of eet. Jew know, Juan, jew were right, jew should have been driving. Different story den. Nes time...jew drive."

Victor was exhilarated by the action that had just happened and smiled broadly as he spoke to Juan.

In a few minutes they were back in the house at the compound and Victor was barking orders to get the Town Car taken care of and to get Cuzo on the phone. Victor went to the kitchen and washed his hands and face thoroughly and carefully dried himself. Juan stood nearby, waiting with the portable phone that had Cuzo on the line. Victor took the phone and laughed before he spoke.

"Señor Mosca...they deed not like our message bout dat ice peek guy, dey give answer to me this morning. I theenk we give them message numero dos." There was a pause as he listened to Cuzo. "Sí, sí, dey shoot and kill a car. We are good...a little blood from the glass, but we are good. We can get another car...maybe that big BMW or a Mercedes. Why not? Let's cheet and chat Señor Mosca. I have idea for message dos."

No one in the house realized that Gloria was still sitting in the car in the garage. She had stopped crying, but her eyes were closed and she quietly sat clutching her purse.

15.

Duane Hargrove at the DEA and Ralph Simmons at ATF separately had learned that Butch was on the prowl, nosing around in what each of them assumed was their backyard. Butch might be able to help either of them in some way or, they figured, more than likely he could screw things up; it all depended on whose agenda it was and what point of view they had. Neither of these men liked anyone invading their jurisdiction. Neither man, however, was ever concerned if they moved in on someone else.

These two offices rarely spoke to each other, neither of them feeling the need to communicate with a companion government agency, since their focus was on their mission and did not necessarily include involving someone else's world. Never mind that information was gained that might help the other. Never mind that it made sense to give the other office an alert on special knowledge. It never would have occurred to either of these agents to confer with the other about Butch. Since they each saw him as having the potential for interfering with what they were working on, they didn't really consider whether he could help them.

For Hargrove especially, it was most disconcerting to have Butch make contact with Cuzo. The DEA had been keeping the Padillo organization under surveillance for more than a year. It had been a highly detailed operation and they were getting close to moving in for the kill. He was worried what Butch might know, what he might say to Cuzo that could alert the Padillo group of anything. After all the work they had done, all they needed was to have some outsider mess up the operation. He sat in his Lakeside Avenue office in downtown Cleveland and fretted, but he didn't talk to anyone about his concerns. He would talk to Butch himself, get his story, get him to back off. He didn't even contact the Toledo office of the DEA; he would wait until they were ready to move on Victor.

It took two days of phone calls and messages, but finally the diligent and hard working Hargrove talked to Butch.

"Greiner. You're one tough guy to get hold of. This is Duane Hargrove. DEA...Cleveland. Wanted to talk with you about a case you're working on..."

"Oh, really?" Butch cut him off, "What could I be doing to interest the DEA?"

Butch knew what he was doing all right and figured his talking to Cuzo might have made the DEA nervous if they had been keeping an eye on Cuzo. But he wanted to have some fun with the agent, so he toyed with Hargrove's beginning efforts to get information.

"We have a suspect that we're getting to know...someone we're quite interested in and you've made contact with our suspect. You're a PI...might be interesting for us to know what you talked about. We'd like to know what our suspect had to say. I also need to tell you that I don't want you to screw things up for us, if you know what I mean."

"Gee, is that a threat? Why would you sound like you're threatening when you haven't even told me who the suspect is."

"Hey, hey...don't play dumb with me, you know who I'm talking about - Mosca - so don't be cute just to pull my chain. You can tell me what you know now or you and I can have a little talk face to face. I can be over there and rattle your cage yet today if it's necessary.

Butch understood that no one wants to fool around with the DEA, not a licensed PI, not a former CIA agent, no one. They could make things miserable for anyone. He had tried to have fun with Hargrove; it was time to play it straight.

"Oh, yeah, Mosca..."

"Oh, yeah, Mosca...like you didn't know. Tell me what you two talked about."

"I was looking into the death of my friend Jerry Bowen at the request of Jerry's wife, who is also my friend. Jerry was an Ohio State Trooper, a plain clothes investigator who got murdered. She wanted me to get the details...that led me to Mosca. Mosca said he had information that one of the Frangeletti guys - you know the Frangelettis, I'm sure - was the one who x'd Jerry. Mosca told me that the Frangeletti guy had been taken care of...he knew somehow. That was it. All I know about Mosca. He could tell a lot more, I'm sure, but I got all I needed for Jerry's wife."

Talking to Butch was a waste of time, Hargrove figured. He listened as Butch talked and decided the man was not going to get in the way of their operation. Something in his voice, the note of being unsure, the deliberate minimizing of any circumstance about Mosca. This man was on the sidelines, he was not part of what they wanted to pursue, he was merely an annoyance, much as he had suspected from the beginning.

After talking to Butch, it was now a sure thing in Hargrove's mind what had to be done about the Padillo boys...and soon. He felt that the Padillo boys would not be ready for them yet and he wanted the surprise that this would afford them. They would move ahead on the Padillo organization, he committed to himself. Crushing the boss would be the first step.

Hargrove's DEA office had developed enough information to make him firmly convinced of the Padillo effort in moving drugs. They had carefully watched their carwash operation, noted the movement of their men. It was quite an operation. With Mosca as the front man and Victor Padillo behind the scenes, they were big time. Smart, very smart, Hargrove's men learned, smart enough to make setting up a sting a waste of time and effort. Better to systematically chart the operation, then raid Padillo's farmyard hideaway to get solid evidence. Hargrove was convinced they would have Los Tigres out of business soon.

For Ralph Simmons at ATF, Butch was not a potential problem, but rather a nuisance. He was just another in the cast of characters that had to be accounted for in his mission. Nosing about the Frangelettis or the Padillo group could raise suspicions, put either of the organizations more on guard, and bring attention where it wasn't wanted. But Ralph also thought that Butch might be able to help him with a dilemma that now faced his agency.

The ATF office for northern Ohio is located in a four-story, sand-colored brick building of a nondescript suburban office plaza just off I-71 in the Cleveland suburb of Middleburg Heights. This office, where Simmons operated, had been made aware, as all of ATF was made aware, of substantial theft of both armament and explosives from military bases. Regular, systematic theft had siphoned off hundreds of guns and hundreds of pounds of C-4 and Semtex. What the Cleveland ATF office knew from an informant was that a large order of both items had been placed by someone in northwest Ohio. Just who placed that order was not known, however, but Simmons figured it was either the Frangelettis or the Padillos. Who else could it be? It would take heavy duty money to get that kind of order paid for and fulfilled. Small timers and freelancers couldn't. Some of the black boys maybe, but not likely. It had to be the Frangelettis or the Padillos.

Simmons would have been very interested in just such a deadly cargo from Fort Bragg, had he known about it, one that soon was going to be on its way to Ohio. Bragg is a sprawling Army reservation of pine trees and sand, adjacent to the city of Fayetteville, North Carolina, and one of the country's largest military complexes. With Special Forces training and tactical deployment based there, it could be expected that Bragg would have strong security measures. Such expectation would be wrong. It was not a difficult matter for personnel in the right jobs, with the right connections, and the right help, to steal from the base. More materiel of all kinds moved off the base illegally than any authority wanted to acknowledge.

Besides the illegal removal of materiel by military personnel, vehicles with civilian personnel, almost anyone, can drive onto the base from the west side or what might be called the back end of the base. It was easy enough to drive onto the base with a car or truck, meet your contact, load your vehicle, and drive off. Such assignments were readily accomplished with uncanny regularity.

Certainly restricted materiel such as armament and explosives is registered and tallied. Stores are checked and rechecked. But for those grunts paid well to fudge check-in and to document what is not there, the job of getting guns and plastics is not difficult. The rewards are great for those who cooperate and, on Bragg, the group working on getting materiel out was making big money and not worrying one bit about the consequences. They didn't worry a whole lot because there didn't seem to be any consequences.

Command would be loathe to take action, even if it knew the extent of what was going on, because of the embarrassment, and no one wanted to account for the losses. It was simpler to pretend that nothing was happening.

There was one Daryl Hanlin. An uncomplicated, although far from simple minded, 30 year old Staff Sergeant from Arkansas, who had already spent twelve years in the Army. Daryl considered the idea of making the Army a career, but didn't look too far ahead in his life and signed on when each time came to re-enlist. He was married to shy, sweet Dorothy, a girl from back home, and they had Marshall, age 6 and Courtney, age 3. Marshall was the maiden name of Dorothy's mother and Courtney was just a name she liked a lot. Both of the children had been born in Germany during Daryl's four-year tour in that country. They had been back at Bragg for almost a year. Life was pretty good for them, the

Hanlins figured. Oh, they wanted some things, a bigger house, bigger yard for the kids to play in, maybe some better clothes, but all in all, they were satisfied with things. But Daryl wanted a new truck. The one he was driving was more than ten years old, a make-do piece of transportation he picked up used when they got back from overseas.

Daryl had been admiring an F-150 at the edge of the Alderman Ford new truck lot when he was approached by a well dressed man in a business suit. At first, he thought the man was a truck salesman, but quickly realized that no one at Alderman Ford wore a tie, including Mr. Alderman. His senses went on alert.

"Mornin'." The man spoke with a slight accent. It wasn't from the Carolinas, or like back home. It was Southern, not a drawl, not a slide of words, but smooth and silky. Maybe Georgia.

"Mornin'."

"Yer name Daryl?" the man asked quietly.

"Yeah, 'tis." Daryl's response was slow and just as quiet. He was now on guard.

"Good, good." The man reached out his hand offering to shake Daryl's. "Nice to meet you, Sergeant Hanlin. Name's Byron...Ned Byron. Mind if I buy you a cup of coffee?"

That was how it began at Ft. Bragg, a casual meeting with a Joe who wanted a new truck...and got it...right away. Daryl was the key ingredient because he had access and he had responsibility. Ned Byron - real name Alan Sidrow from Marietta, Georgia - provided Daryl with a kind of winning lottery ticket and Ned got what he wanted.

Even after he agreed, Daryl wasn't sure he had done the right thing. One day he believed he was nuts to go along, the next day the fantasies of what extra money could buy made him think he was right about it. He didn't tell Dorothy at first because the more he thought about the arrangement with Ned

Byron the more he thought it was wrong. Getting the Ford pickup finally convinced him that he had done right and forced him to share the news with her.

Dorothy was shocked at first and told him he shouldn't do it, but as Daryl regaled her with stories of what they could buy, how it would ease the strain of providing for Marshall and Courtney, she relented to his enthusiasm. Although she did acquiesce to his insistent pressure to approve what he was doing, she felt it was wrong and she did not like it. Her approval would be shown by not complaining or criticizing, but secretly she felt ashamed. He did not share with her the downside: he could get caught and go to Federal prison for a lot of years.

"Ned warned me to be careful about how I spent the money," Daryl explained, "he says if you git high and mighty with the money and show everybody you've got it...why...it would draw attention...people suspicious...someone might notice and start to investigate. So we've gotta be careful. We'll keep the extra cash here in the house...use it careful as we want...but careful. Okay?"

"I...I guess so," she replied. She still did not like the idea of doing wrong, but it seemed so easy, it seemed so all right the way Daryl had explained what would be happening.

They both went outside with the two kids and looked at daddy's new truck.

Nicky Frangeletti had met Sidrow through mutual acquaintances when Alan was working in Columbus, Ohio. Alan had bumped around the country as a con artist and general, all around small time hustler. He landed in Columbus and took a job for Nicky's friends running a car rental agency that was used as a front to launder money and move stolen cars. He and Nicky hit it off right away because they were so much alike. They each had an unquenchable lust for women and liked to cheat at whatever they did. During one all night drunk and numerous rounds with a handful of Frangeletti waitresses, he had talked to Nicky about stealing merchandise from Army bases. He was ex-Army and believed he knew how easy it would be.

"Hey, you girls go along now...git some sleep...git rested for tomorrow. If we have any more fun'n this somebody might have us arrested...go on now, me and Nicky gotta talk bidness...git...git some sleep...tomorrow's a new day and when that ol' sun comes up I'll be ready for another romp...you'll need your strenth."

They had been partying in a large suite at the downtown Hyatt, so the girls moved off to one of the two bedrooms connected to the large sitting area. Alan turned his full attention to Nicky for the proposition he wanted to make. A half bottle of booze and load of sex did not distract Alan from taking advantage of an opportunity to sell his idea.

"I been in the Army, Nicky, six years till they threw me out. I been on Bragg, Campbell, I know what can be done. Ya git help...I mean ya buy help on the inside...that's all it takes...the rest is sales and distribution."

Alan talked to Nicky about the idea for more than an hour and made it sound very good with his Southern charm and enticing drawl. Nothin', but nothin' could be bad about this plan, Alan had assured him, and they would make lots of money. So, Nicky asked him to put together his plan, not some hair-brained stunt that would get them arrested, but a real plan of action that he could take to the old man.

It took several days of scribbling on a yellow pad at the car rental agency before Alan had put together something that made sense. He scratched and erased endlessly, swearing under his breath as he worked. He finally had a handful of sheets of the yellow paper that he could give to the young girl in the office to type. She worked as his secretary and receptionist and also was one of the handful of girls with whom Alan regularly had sex. She didn't know about the others, but was the kind of girl who would not have cared had she known. Within a week of their conversation, Alan gave Nicky a plan, in writing, neatly typed.

When Nicky had come to his father about Alan Sidrow's idea and plan, Nick was not for it. There was in Nick a sense of patriotism. He loved America and stealing from the Army somehow was not patriotic. But Nicky prevailed, as he did about most things he wanted, and got the permission from his father to back Sidrow.

It was decided that Alan operate out of the Atlanta area because the bases they would use were in the South. Atlanta was a city that was satisfactory to the Frangelettis because they had lots of connections there. Alan Sidrow made good on his plan and the payback started relatively quickly. He used every misguided malcontent that he had known still working in the Army. He did, in fact, slick rascal that he was, convince several men to re-enlist so they would be able to take advantage of the operational scheme that he constructed for them.

Alan put together an admirable organization, one that could be the envy of any order taking and distribution system corporate America had to offer. Other than recruiting soldiers who could help, he never got involved directly in the mechanics of the scheme; he simply took a percentage of the selling price for all the merchandise that got moved. It was always by specific order only and restricted to small lots of whatever it was that someone wanted.

Although the Frangelettis set Alan up, they did not limit his ability to be an entrepreneur, so with their blessing he created a nationwide network that delivered to a series of contacts he made. The orders were primarily for guns and ammunition, but once in awhile someone wanted plastic. Such was the recent order from Nicky, and thanks to Daryl, the merchandise would head out from Fort Bragg.

With his job in the supply section, Daryl had access to the C-4 and Semtex that was used for general demolition training and for exercises by the Delta Force and other special CIA units that trained at Bragg. After agreeing to work for Alan - AKA Ned - he spent several months carefully removing C-4 and detonators from stores, two blocks and two detonators at a time using a coarse nylon briefcase that he always carried. Little notice was taken of his comings and goings at stores. He took the blocks home where he hid them in the crawl space under the closet floor in his and Dorothy's bedroom.

"Is it dangerous...I mean will it blow up?" she would ask.

"Naw," was his casual reply.

"Are you sure?"

"Look, I wouldn't put it there if it was dangerous." But he wasn't really sure; he just knew this was what had to be done.

When the order came for the plastic that Nicky wanted, Daryl removed ten of the blocks of C-4 from the crawl space and put them in a large drab olive athletic bag. The next day, he took the athletic bag as well as his briefcase to his office on base and set the bag under his desk. He was following instructions from a phone call he had the night before. He hadn't recognized the man who used the prearranged code; it was a voice he never heard before. He almost never heard from Alan.

"...no one will notice it there," the man had said, "make sure you're out of the office at five o'clock tomorrow afternoon...take a walk...go down the hall...just get out of the office for awhile at five."

At five minutes before five that afternoon, Daryl checked his watch and walked down the hall leaving his office unattended. At that moment, a late model, mud-spattered pickup pulled into a parking spot near the building where his office was located. The driver got out wearing Army issue clothing, although he was not Army. He casually walked into the building to Daryl's office, picked up the bag and walked out. Without hurrying, the man moved to the truck and placed the bag on the floor in front of the passenger seat. He got in and slowly drove away. No one paid any attention to his actions, but even if they had, they would not have been able to read the Georgia license plates that were obscured with caked on mud,

The pickup drove off the base down Yadkin Road and away north from Fayetteville to I-40 in Greensboro. Once on I-40, the pickup went west to Knoxville. At the Crider truck yard on the outskirts of Knoxville, the pickup was parked next to an unmarked semi that sat away from the administration building. The driver did not turn off the engine as he got out with the bag. He opened the passenger door of the huge Peterbilt rig, placed the bag on the floor and made sure both cab doors were locked. He pulled out of the yard and got onto I-40 headed for the I-75 interchange, south to Atlanta.

The plastics grab at Bragg was easy because the men involved knew to be patient and calm, the movement to Knoxville in step two was uneventful, and there now was only the simple task of getting the stuff up north to the buyer.

The operation for stealing from the military bases had been going on for some time, maybe a year or so, before the FBI was called in to the case. Security personnel at the affected bases had tried to find out what was going on, but their work went nowhere. The FBI didn't fair much better, so reluctantly, they passed off the investigation to the ATF. All anyone knew was that hardware was leaving bases, but no one realized at first that it was a single concerted effort controlled by one person. The FBI and ATF figured it was just some Joes who were stealing to make a few extra bucks. The ATF finally stumbled onto the fact the thefts were related when an informant tipped them to what was happening. The tip came in a phone call from a source that said he had just gotten out of the Army and had heard what was going on in service. He thought someone should know about it. The ATF still didn't have any idea Alan Sidrow existed, but they were working hard on it.

It was Ralph Simmons who stumbled onto another informant who began to give the ATF information that helped their investigation. The ATF learned through the informant that plastic explosives were on their way to Toledo. Simmons wanted to talk to Butch because he figured Butch might get a lead on who had placed the order.

Butch responded to Simmons' message on his answering machine and got right through to the agent.

"Ralph Simmons here. How can I help you."

"You can't," Butch said evenly, "but maybe you can tell me why you called. Butch Greiner here."

"Butch...thanks for returning my call. Hey, listen, I know about your background..."

"Oh..."

"Yeah. I know you can be trusted..."

There was a silence of several seconds and Butch did not respond.

"Anyway, I know you've had contact with this guy from the Padillos and you're looking around for information. I need information too."

"Like what?"

"Like who's waiting for plastic. I need to know that Butch."

"How would I know?"

"Well, just in case it came up or is something you run into...we'd like to know about it."

"What do you mean, 'waiting for plastic'?

Simmons sucked in a deep breath. He knew he was taking somewhat of a chance by telling this man about it, but he believed somehow an ex-CIA could be trusted.

"Either the Padillos or the Frangelettis have placed an order for plastic. We don't know which of them. Probably one or both of these groups have gotten guns and ammunition in the past...probably from the same source. Anyway, all our informant could tell us is that it is headed for your area over there. Someone in Toledo. He had heard about it, but wasn't sure where the order originated. If I had to guess who is behind this, I would say this is something Nicky Frangeletti is involved with...but I have nothing solid to go on. I would appreciate it if you find out anything about this you would let me know right away. That possible?"

"Yeah, that's possible. I have to tell you though, I know nothing about plastics...have heard nothing. If I do, I'll call you. I'm out of this thing that I was doing anyway. I've done what I can do for my client."

"Let me know if you hear anything."

16.

Butch walked with Pam toward Judd's from the parking lot across the street. She was eager to get to the bar and as a big woman with long strides, she closed the distance quickly. Butch hustled to keep pace with her. He could feel the sweat run down his back as they moved rapidly through the afternoon heat. He could feel himself anticipating the coolness of Judd's. Strange how it works, he thought, if I were lifting weights or in a 5K I wouldn't be uncomfortable. With a sport coat on, trying to keep up with Pam, I'm struggling with the heat. I love the heat. Go figure. Shorts and a tee shirt are just a whole lot easier to tolerate the conditions.

He had reported back to Pam about his conversation with Cuzo, explaining how it meshed with the story he had gotten from Tom. There was little question that Buddy Cappeletti had killed Jerry and for sure the Padillo guys had taken care of Buddy. It was that simple. There wasn't much to say after that. Jerry had been watching the Frangelettis. Buddy took him out. It was a mistake for sure. Nick Frangeletti would not have wanted that to happen. The Padillo boys made Buddy pay for what he did to their guy and, as a result, made him also pay for what he did to Jerry. He had tipped his hand to them because their guy had been killed the same way - with an ice pick. They knew about Buddy's reputation of acting without orders, that he liked to hurt people, that he liked to kill if the situation arose. There was no doubt in their mind that it was Buddy who needed to be shown a lesson. Death was too good for him, they figured, better he suffered for the rest of his life from the curse they imposed upon him.

Still, somehow that knowledge didn't satisfy Pam. The circle was not closed for her: she wanted to meet the man - Cuzo.

She wanted to complete what was still incomplete to her by saying thank you in person. She had gone on at some length as to how meeting this Cuzo would be the completeness she needed to put everything to rest.

To Butch this didn't make any sense at all and he tried to talk her out of meeting with Cuzo.

"Why would you want to meet this guy," he had asked, "he's a drug dealer and a...?"

"Because I need to...to help me get over this...this awful way I still feel. I think I'll feel better about things if I can talk to him. I can thank him for Jerry...I can thank him for me."

She kept repeating herself, first crying, and blazing with frustrated anger. She said she wanted to bring the finding out process full circle by meeting Cuzo and thanking him in person. To her, Cuzo was somehow a link to her dead husband. Cuzo was one step removed from Jerry. Such was her obsession with the prospect of thanking Cuzo that Butch could not relate to how it consumed her.

He eventually relented. There was no point in continuing to try to dissuade her, so he put in a call to Cuzo. But getting hold of him was difficult at best. Butch left messages several times a day, persisted for several days, and finally threatened.

"Listen up, Bud," Butch said, starting his message to Cuzo that he thought would get some action, "I'm tired of you not getting back to me. Here's what I'm going to do if I don't hear from you yet today..."

The hardball technique got Cuzo's attention. He responded quickly to Butch's suggestion that he might turn over the whole issue to the FBI - let the FBI talk to Cuzo and settle things for Pam. Or perhaps the State Highway Patrol could get involved. In any case, Cuzo called Butch and it was arranged for her to meet him at Judd's.

When Butch told Pam that he had a meeting set up for her to meet Cuzo, she insisted he go with her. Goddamn, would this not end, he thought. This thing is like having tar stick to your shoes - you can't get it off and it makes a mess with every step.

Butch wondered if there wasn't another motivation for Pam. Something about her insistence in meeting Cuzo didn't fit for him, didn't quite factor. Maybe it had been true that her marriage with Jerry had not been going well, maybe she now felt guilty about that and wanted to press for this meeting as a way of keeping her feelings for him alive, rather than putting an end to sadness. Maybe her feelings for Jerry had cooled in the last couple of years. There had been signs. Maybe she was refusing to let her feelings for Jerry die as he had died, even though for her they had lessened. Maybe she needed to talk to Cuzo to help resurrect the emotion for Jerry that was once within her. Who knows? Nothing she does brings Jerry back.

Cuzo came into Judd's from the back door, stopping first to get his eyes adjusted from the bright sun, looking around to see who was there, setting the scene in his mind, and assuring himself that the place was okay. He saw Butch with a woman and a certain sensation ran through him that he liked. His view of the woman brought the warm sensation to him, almost as if she had reached across the room to touch him. He felt as if he had been touched by a woman and he was surprised at his own reaction. He liked that feeling, whatever it was, that came to him when he saw a woman with *push*. That's what he called it: *push*. Push was what happened when the sex thing surged inside him in a special way, with a special feeling. For Cuzo, that was not often. He looked at most women dispassionately, with an off-hand casualness. His physical contact with most women was for release, with no more meaningful feeling than relief. This woman sitting with the little white guy was different because she had push. He turned to Luis, who was right behind him, and smiled, puckering his eyebrows as he did so.

"This could get interesting. What do you think?"

"She is quite attractive," Luis answered carefully, "but let's be careful."

"Always careful, Luis, always careful."

Luis walked past Cuzo to the bar and sat on one of the vacant stools, while Cuzo moved towards the table where Butch and Pam were seated. For these two men, it was a style, a choreography, a simple matter of positioning with ballet-like precision and timing. It was part of their constant need to be in control of any situation. Cuzo presented himself before the table in a posture of command, with the fingers of his right hand tucked into the top of his right front pants pocket, of demanding deference as a bull fighter would have done waiting for the charge.

"This is Cuzo," Butch said without laughing.

Cuzo looked directly at Pam and never once took his eyes from her as he sat down across the table from them. She reached for his left hand with both of hers and gripped it tightly. There were tears in her eyes.

"Thank you," she said softly.

"Nada," he said without thinking, but catching himself said, "you are very welcome. But for what?"

"For taking care of my husband's killer. Butch told me what you did..."

"I did nothing lady..."

"Yes, yes, I know...I know you don't want to admit anything, but I know and I appreciate what you did. You don't have to admit anything to me...its okay, its okay...but I...I wanted you to know how I felt. I was suffering so much wondering why someone killed Jerry...that's why I got Butch to find out something. I had to know. Now, I know. I think I know and I wanted to thank you...that's all."

She started to cry and laid her cheek down on his hands that she still firmly gripped.

Cuzo sat in stunned silence, not wanting to look at Butch, not wanting to acknowledge the woman in front of him, her face on his hands, her tears freely flowing over his fingers. He was embarrassed and looked around to see if anyone else in the bar was paying attention. No one was and he felt a little more at ease about what was happening, although still quite uncomfortable with the circumstances.

"I saw what happened. Not all of it, but most of it...enough to know what it was I didn't quite see."

"You saw the man kill my husband?"

"Yes...he and another guy, but it was the big one...Cappeletti...who did the work. I was there..."

Pam started to cry again.

"There was nothing I could do...it happened very quickly...it was over fast, but I knew what happened." He felt compelled for some reason to excuse himself for not saving Jerry somehow, to explain, to try to make her feel better.

Pam choked back several sobs, looked at Cuzo directly, again laid her face down on his hands, pressing her lips against them as she did so.

Although well recognized for its occurrence, little is known about the reasons for the instant, powerful attraction between a man and woman. When it happens it is electric, the supernatural supersedes the rational and the cosmos of uncertain gods and goddesses envelopes the two parties involved and possesses their hearts, minds, and loins. It is an extreme sexual stimulation.

It's mystical, Butch thought as he watched it happen right in front of him, crazy and mystical. Who would have guessed this lanky white gal and the handsome twerp Mexican could click. At least for Pam it was mystical, Butch was quite sure. For Cuzo he wasn't as certain, but Cuzo seemed locked in to her. There are a lot of perspectives as to how someone gets stars in their eyes about someone else at first meeting. A smell? Electro-chemical energy? Butch wondered about the reasons as he witnessed the process take place. Jesus, there's a lot of emotion in the air.

"Hey, bring us a pitcher of beer," he yelled at the girl behind the bar.

Butch marveled at what had transpired. Pam had wanted to meet this guy simply as a way of doing something for her - God knows what - and the next thing you know there's a big zing between the two of them. It didn't make sense, but why should it, nothing else about this business of helping her made sense.

Pam could not raise her face from his hands, so potent and captivating was the energy within her, a sense and reaction she could not quite understand. There could be no immediate expression for what surged through her. Cuzo slowly stroked her cheek and all of her feelings were expanded. She could barely breathe.

"We didn't know we were helping, but I'm glad we made it right for you," Cuzo said quietly. "It wasn't necessary...killing your husband...killing our guy...but he liked it...the big one...he likes to kill. We felt it was time for him to pay...for justice, our justice, to catch up with him. He had dodged the law for a long time. The law that is not justice. The law that is technicalities and trivialities and pretending to take care of things. Our justice is better and saves taxpayers a lot of money. Death would have been such a blessing for your husband's killer - the Italian gangster - death he would have wished for, death that was too good for him. No, lady..."

"Pam. I'm Pam." She looked directly into his eyes.

"Pam," he repeated slowly, mirroring her gaze. "Our Italian gangster will suffer as long as he lives. And especially so on cold rainy days."

She now knew for sure that Cuzo had watched Jerry, had seen him alive, and had been close to Jerry in death. She felt a closeness to Cuzo because of this, a closeness that now made the circle complete.

Butch had enough of the mystical stuff and wanted to get out of there. He also had enough of helping Pam. She was taking too much time away from other cases. This was a good chance to be done with it and he didn't even want to wait for the beer.

"I hope this isn't the last I'll see of you," Pam said to Cuzo, all but ignoring Butch.

"It doesn't have to be."

"Listen," Butch interrupted, "I need to exit stage left, but I want to know something first." He looked directly at Cuzo.

"Like what?"

"Like what do you know about plastic?"

"Plastic?"

It was a question from left field and it took Cuzo by surprise. Butch was surprised with himself at the abrupt way he had posed the question, but he had hoped to catch Cuzo off guard and this was his chance.

"Yeah, plastic...like C-4. Plastic...explosives. What have you heard, what do you know?"

"Nothing."

"The ATF thinks you do."

"They're wrong, we don't have anything to do with that kind of stuff."

"Just drugs?"

Cuzo ignored his question.

"Why do they think that we have something to do with...with that stuff?"

"Seems they have an informant who tells them some plastic has been stolen and is headed here. It's coming to you guys or the Frangelettis. No, it doesn't sound like something the Italians would order. But you wild Mexicans might order plastic for some reason."

"That's all bullshit. We don't blow things up. We have no need for explosives."

"Is that a straight answer or are you playing with me?"

"We didn't order any plastic."

"I'll tell the ATF that."

"You do that."

"Come on, I'll take you home," Butch said to Pam.

"Thanks Butch, but I wanted to ask Cuzo a couple more questions...you go on...maybe Cuzo could drop me off." She turned to him. "Could you?"

"Sure, why not."

"Oh thanks. And Butch, thank you so much for your help. I really appreciate your support."

She leaned over and gave him a kiss on the cheek.

"Well, as far as I'm concerned you've got your answers and the issues about Jerry's death can be put to rest."

Butch stood up, tossed some bills on the table to cover the pitcher, and was gone, without pausing, without turning around; he let the door close behind him. At least I don't have to worry about her hitting on me, he thought as he walked back to his car. Cuzo can deal with that, now.

Pam had been pleased that Butch brought her to meet Cuzo and now she was glad he was gone. It had been important for her to make the connection, to learn first hand that her husband's death had been vindicated. In her wildest imagination she could not have considered that Cuzo would have been so attractive to her. There was a quality, a sensuality that was magical to her, beyond what she had ever experienced. He had chiseled good looks and a confidence that shown from his face with an aura that gave her pleasure in looking at him. It was a look that Jerry never had. She felt badly about making the comparison, but it was true.

"Let's get out of here and go to my place," she said self-consciously.

Cuzo laughed when she gave that suggestion. It was a surprise to him the way things had turned out, but he decided to go with the flow.

He told her he needed to check with Luis before he left and walked over to the bar where the man was watching a baseball game on television.

"I'm going to take her to her house...she invited me. Seems like the right thing to do."

Luis raised his eyebrows, but said nothing. He nodded as he looked over at Pam and turned back to the game.

"I'll watch the house," he said without turning back towards Cuzo, "be careful."

They had driven most of the way to Pam's house, Pam giving the directions, before she really spoke to him.

"I...I...wanted to talk to you more...away from the bar...away from Butch and distractions. I wanted you alone to talk...I...I...wanted your impressions...I mean your feelings about...about what has happened."

She was not making any sense, but Cuzo did not seem to take notice and responded carefully in a way that would head him toward seduction of this woman. He was now intent on seduction. She had push and the push excited him to have desire for her. He wanted to make love to her and he knew that is what she wanted. It had happened quickly, he thought, strange the way things work. He checked out Luis' car in the rear view mirror, following a block behind.

Once inside Pam's house, she seemed confused and frightened, embarrassed maybe, terribly ill at ease, and unable at first to focus on interacting with Cuzo. He took her hand and pressed it to his cheek.

"Relax. Everything's going to be okay."

He pulled her to him and kissed her, softly at first, passionately, eagerly, pushing his tongue into her mouth, holding her tightly with his left arm, while he explored her breasts with his right hand.

It was an interesting sight of enflamed communion, their passion a connection in reverse of the usual: he, the short one, neck cocked back to engage her mouth, reaching upwards for her breasts; she nearly six feet tall, bending down to facilitate his physical address to her body.

With some sense of the reversal in size, she assured him, "It won't matter lying down. Why don't you take off your clothes?" She started to unbutton his shirt as she continued to run her tongue on his lips.

Cuzo was not used to the feeling he had for this woman and for the next several days, locked in passion, he put the Padillo boys out of his thoughts and concentrated on satisfying her...and himself.

17.

Cuzo leaned back against the towering weeping willow tree that stood close to the bank and watched the activity across the channel from the North Coast Marina Club. He could readily tell that the Frangeletti boat was being prepared to move out. Supplies had been brought aboard and there was extensive hustle and bustle from a variety of their personnel. With little wind to interfere, he could hear the laughter and periodic giggling of the girls. The boat's captain stood on the flying bridge, aloof and detached, merely waiting for the command to move out as the process moved ahead for getting the boat set.

Cuzo felt the day's heat upon him with an almost overwhelming effect that caused him to take a deep breath. He sucked in air for a few more moments the way a wolf or other predator tests the smells available in checking out their prey, a way to bring him closer to the movement and activity he was watching across the channel. He heard the complaints of how hot it was as the boat was made ready. He knew it would get much hotter.

As he viewed the action at the Frangeletti boat, he thought about the circumstances that directed him, the condition that made this condition. He had stood in the living room of Victor's house on the compound, resigned to the shit he would have to take, but resolute in his commitment to himself that he would not let Victor abuse him in any way. He knew he was wrong for not checking in, for not staying in touch. He knew that he had deliberately eliminated contact for several days and he knew that was exactly what he wanted to do. He knew that Victor would be pissed, but he was prepared for that response. He had never before put himself in jeopardy like this with Victor, but he had been overwhelmed from the sex with Pam, and yet he knew it was more than just the sex with her. There was a connection with her and he knew it. He was not sure what it meant, but he recognized the link, a binding to her and he consciously refused to speculate with himself what it meant. He had enjoyed flowing through space and time and he didn't give a shit what Victor thought. He knew, however, that Victor would yell, that he himself would respond carefully, and it would be over. They would go on to the business at hand. His confidence in such a scenario allowed him to stay calm and be patient with Victor's anger. It was justified, he assumed, but for the first time he just didn't care.

Now, as he slouched against the tree he tried to sort out whether it was because he generally did not like to be accountable or whether it was because he was a big fat sucker for Pam. When she wrapped her legs around him and they rocked and rolled, he could not distinguish any hard edges of his loyalty to the Padillo boys, to Victor. He reveled in the sensuality that Pam had provided for him and lost himself in her for a length of time he could not calculate.

"Where dey hell you been?" Victor yelled. "I been tryin' to git you, you shitass. We gotta talk. Comprende?"

Cuzo bristled at this, but he contained himself and made a very deliberate construct for his reply. He would not lie; he would not hedge because that would make the situation with Victor worse.

"I been shacked up with this white bitch fuckin' for a few days. Somethin' I needed, somethin' I wanted. I lost track of things...time...I lost track of everything. Sorry."

"You...you Cuzo, has been with a woman? That is amazin'...I did not theenk you wasted time with women. How interestin'. I hope it was good, my friend, I hope very good. Did you know I needed your counsel? No, course not."

Cuzo stood there impassively, waiting for the man's tirade to abate. He knew that Victor needed him, knew therefore that any anger Victor had would soon be gone and that Victor would be seeking his input about something. There was a thin veil between Victor and Cuzo in terms of his leadership role and Cuzo pushed at that veil on many occasions. Cuzo could just as easily be in charge, but it was the vicious, nasty dog that held the leadership role. Cuzo mostly accepted that, but he pushed and prodded so that Victor knew his role was somewhat tenuous and maintained only because Cuzo allowed it to be sustained. Cuzo accepted the other man's dominance, but sometimes wanted to pick at its vulnerability.

"Dey drive me off da road, I need to answer."

Victor described what had happened with the van driving him off the road. He knew that it could have been worse; he knew they could have killed him, but still he wanted to retaliate. He had been thinking about how that retaliation might be accomplished even as he rode back to the house from his wrecked car. He had rolled the idea around in his head for the several days that it took to finally make contact with Cuzo. For no matter how aggressive he was and how violent he might be with his ideas, he still wanted Cuzo's counsel. He had to talk to Cuzo with his idea.

"We fire bomb der goddamn boat, dat's what we do. We set dat sonabitch on fire out der on da lake. What do you thing of dat, sénor Cuzo?"

Cuzo stood there without looking at Victor, instead staring straight ahead out the huge picture window to the flower garden that lay in view, bright with color, silently shining back at him as blossoms bobbed and nodded in the morning breeze.

"It would take some planning. It would be dangerous. But it can be done. Carefully, it can be done. However, to do it will cause big problems."

"Sí. I know."

"But you still want to do it?"

"Sí."

"Would it matter if I told you I thought it was the wrong thing to do?"

"Sí...it matters what you theenk...but I want to do eet...eet weel show dem dey can't push us around."

Cuzo rose from his perch by the tree, took his cell phone from his pocket and punched in Luis' number. "Things are moving along. I'm going to head out. I'll meet you in a few minutes."

He walked several hundred yards to his car that he had parked just off the channel road and headed away from Port Clinton. What the hell is it with me and that woman, he thought. Love was not a word in his vocabulary, so as he worked with the idea that he had become linked with Pam, his concept was that he had been captured by her, although that was not the word he used, merely the idea. He had never felt this way about a woman before and it had happened so fast. It had to be unreal, he figured, just bullshit in the scheme of things. Cuzo does not get hung up on a woman, especially not a big Anglo woman who towered over him so that when she pulled him to her, her breasts became pillows of love. There's that word love. It is not love, it is bullshit. But it is wonderful fucking.

Using back roads, some not on any map, he drove southwest away from Port Clinton around to the western end of Sandusky Bay that stretched fifteen miles inland from Lake Erie. The land was flat with rich black loam for growing, sparsely dotted with overgrown brush and scraggly trees. Here and there a willow draped itself toward the water and a few pine trees could be seen. Sandusky Bay was an ill defined body of water since marsh grasses grew along much of it, the cattails and other reeds blurring where its shoreline was. Plus, the changing wind would raise and lower the water level.

Down a dirt road more than two miles, Cuzo pulled into the yard of property reminiscent of Appalachia. There was an unpainted, ramshackle cabin of a house, two out-buildings, and a lean-to where a 1972 Chevy sat rusting into oblivion. Luis stood in the yard in the shade of a large maple tree and drank a beer.

"How's our timing," Luis asked casually as Cuzo got out of the Continental.

"It's good if you're all loaded."

"We're ready."

Cuzo walked to the shore and looked over the boat bobbing at the end of its line. Its state registration number had been covered with white tape and the seats had strange brown colored cloth covering them. There was no dock, just a narrow muddy stretch where the boat trailer had been backed to get the powerful craft into the water. Cuzo could see in the mud the signs of struggle the truck and trailer had to accomplish their mission.

"Carlos, how are you doing?" Cuzo shook the man's hand.

"Muy bien, gracías."

"Hey, amigo, speak English, we're in the United States. The land of opportunity. Here we speak English."

The man nodded with a smile. "Of course."

"This was not easy, man...getting that thing into the water right here. We almost got stuck in the mud, but we finally pulled out."

"I can see that. But you did it, Luis, and that is what matters."

"Beer?"

"No, no, not now. Maybe later, after we're through. I want to get my clothes changed..."

"On the porch," Luis pointed, "everything is there in the shopping bag."

Cuzo changed into the faded dungaree shorts, cutoff tee shirt, and beat up tennis shoes that were there for him, and left the clothes he had been wearing in the brown bag. He headed for the boat, motioning to Luis and Carlos to follow. He walked into the water almost to his waist and scrambled aboard.

"Carlos knows this area?"

"Very well," Luis assured him as he untied the line and tossed it toward the mud. "I think we could have used a couple of more guys to help us with the boat, but I felt the fewer were involved the better off we would be. This is dangerous and could mean big trouble for us."

"We delay or postpone if any of the law is out on the water. We want it to be clear. I agree...this is dangerous. But it's what Victor wanted. Not how I would have handled Frangeletti."

"How?"

"It doesn't matter now. Hey, Carlos, you know the bay and the lake well?"

"Yes, very well."

"Good. Let's find the Frangeletti boat. It will be easy to spot, it's so goddamn big."

Carlos had started the powerful speedboat, but kept that power well in check as he steered for the open water of the bay. They hoped to draw as little attention to themselves as possible and by keeping their speed down they felt this would help. Luis had brought along three fishing rods that he stood up so they leaned out over the stern. From a distance they looked like one of the many boats cruising for a spot to drop a line and fish. It was the wrong time of the day for good fishing, of course, but that didn't matter any more than it seemed to matter to the other boats on the water with fishing rods as a symbol of their purpose.

Unlike Cuzo and Luis who traced their roots to Mexico, Carlos was from Guatemala, and it had been there that he learned to handle boats. From the time he was young, being on and around the water was second nature. His family had lived near the Caribbean coast and he and his brothers swam, fished, or sailed a small boat almost every day. Carlos became part of the intricate system of bringing drugs into the U.S. that the Padillo organization used for their commerce. In Guatemala, he had gotten caught for stealing and sent to prison. It was in prison that he met a friend of a friend of someone who knew Victor. His name had been passed on to Victor and he was recruited. It didn't take much to convince him to go to the United States to escape the poverty where he had barely survived. He was a true alien with no papers. He had been smuggled in and had worked carefully for almost seven years without detection, without difficulty, functioning within the network of operatives that Victor used. He could not drive a car or truck because he could not get a license, but a boat was a different matter. And he was one of the few in the Padillo organization that carried a gun, a Glock automatic that was always with him. He was already illegal, carrying an unlicensed handgun did not matter much. He just could not afford to get caught for anything. He was good with a boat and knew the lake, so today, he was with Cuzo and Luis.

Carlos increased the boat's speed slightly as they emerged from the bay and pushed out into the lake. He had taken great pains to keep them at a distance from other boats while moving across the bay and now, once out on the lake, that task was much easier.

Cuzo and Luis were scanning the lake for the Frangeletti boat when Luis suddenly pointed to their left as he lowered his binoculars.

"There it is."

"Let's see for sure which way they head," Cuzo directed, "after that, we'll go out and beyond where they're tracking and come back at them. We want to be heading toward the bay after we make the hit. It looks right now like they're heading northwest."

As the *Francesca* plowed across the lake at three quarter speed, Nick and Nicky both stood on the flying bridge with Captain George. This was not a day when they would be meeting another boat. Today was a day just for fun and a smaller group than usual was on board. Only Tony and Frank were along with two girls they were partial to, and Karen, the young woman who was Nick's special thing. Mitzi had prepared a wonderful lunch as she normally did for these trips and was in the process of getting the table ready. Everyone was drinking beer and enjoying the sun. Out here on the water, the intense heat of the day was quite bearable.

George knew what was required for getting the boat out away from other boats so the skinny dipping could begin and accordingly set for open water. It was not difficult to quickly be alone in the middle of Lake Erie with the nearest boat more than a mile to the south. He could now cut back on the twin diesels and get ready to drop anchor. The boat bobbed somewhat from the slight prevailing breeze that came out of the southwest.

George was almost set to drop anchor when he spotted a boat approaching them dead ahead at what seemed to be a high rate of speed. He could see the water they were churning and held off dropping anchor so he could maintain his headway and have better control if he had to take evasive action. He assumed they would veer off left or right, but he wanted to be prepared. He picked up his binoculars to check out the craft that was rapidly coming at them. He relaxed a little when the boat turned slightly to the north so as to pass by them on their right side.

The sound of the oncoming boat could now be heard above the noise of their own engines; it was quickly closing the gap between the two boats. George could see three men and fishing rods, but the boat did not look like a fishing boat...too fast...he could see that there was no number at the bow and he knew in an instant that there would be trouble. He yelled to Nicky, who had by now gone down to the deck to check out Mitzi's lunch and grab another beer.

Carlos knew that if he were to continue to head directly for the cabin cruiser it would alert its captain to impending danger early on, so he changed his heading so as to appear to be going north of the boat. With less than a hundred yards between them, he headed back directly at the *Francesca*. The speedboat would pass within a few feet of where Karen was standing at the rail.

Cuzo and Luis were ready, poised for the action planned as the answer that Victor wanted. When their speedboat got alongside the *Francesca*, each of them tossed a gallon glass jug filled with gasoline, its neck stuffed with a burning rag. These were two giant Molotov cocktails that hit the Frangeletti boat almost at once. Cuzo's jug, pitched first, hit and broke on the side of the cabin below the flying bridge, plunging that side of the boat into flames almost instantly. Luis' jug hit just over the railing on the main deck and exploded in a raging mass of fire and black smoke.

Carlos had slowed somewhat to steady the speedboat for the attack, but now gave full throttle and headed for the mouth of the bay. They were soon a dot on the horizon and by the time George or Nicky had a chance to look, they were long gone.

Miraculously, none of the gasoline splattered on anyone and no one was caught in the fire that ensued. Captain George was well trained to deal with a fire on board and took charge right away.

"Get life jackets out of those compartments," he yelled, "under the seats, under the seats. Get 'em on and get in the water."

He shut down the engines as he directed the others and grabbed for a fire extinguisher beneath the wheel. He jumped down the ladder to the main deck and started to fight the fire with the extinguisher, spraying its foam at the inferno he confronted. It was a lost cause and he knew it right away. He put on his own flotation vest and checked around as best he could to see that everyone was overboard. There had been no time to get the dingy loose from on top of the cabin ahead of the flying bridge to get it over the side. The fire towards the bow that started from Cuzo's jug had burned away half of the dingy before he even thought about getting it unlashed and into the lake.

Everyone on board had responded quickly to Captain George's commands and they were all in the water a few yards away from the boat, watching it burn to the waterline. George had not even had time to send a Mayday let alone give position coordinates over the radio to the Coast Guard. Someone must have seen the fire, he hoped, the Guard will get here soon. He reassured the others that they would be all right as they watched the fire rage and the beautiful cabin cruiser crumble into itself with hissing sounds of destruction as the fire reached water.

The charred carcass of the *Francesca* slowly slipped beneath the surface of the lake and was gone. It was a shock to Captain George as he watched the last remnants of the bow cabin slide away from view. He could barely comprehend what had just happened and kept trying to cope with his vision of the burning hull. He had taken pride in his command of the *Francesca* even though it was Frangeletti property. In his heart, it was his to be responsible for, to drive, and to control. He felt sick to his stomach.

Even on such a hot day the water felt cold, the contrast a shock to the survivors thrashing about in the water, kicking and sputtering in their attempts to stay above water, and to survive the ordeal. For Nick, who was gasping for air, it was a struggle to keep his head up, floundering in his attempts to stay calm. Although it was an extremely hot day, his lips still had turned blue and he was rapidly losing the feeling in his left hand.

"Somethin's wrong, Nicky, somethin's wrong with my arm. My arm...my hand...I can't feel my hand. I'm gonna drown...Nicky, I'm gonna drown...my chest hurts, my chest hurts...Goddamn, it hurts...who were those sonsabitches...those fuckin Mexican boys, I bet...those fuckin Mexicans tried to kill me. They're gonna do it...they're gonna do it. I'm havin' a heart attack. Those bastards...I'm gonna die out here on this lake, my lake..."

"No, pop, you're okay...hang on, help will be here right away...you'll be okay. Don't splash around so much...stay calm."

"Yeah, shit, easy for you to say...you don't have this pain."

The first boat arrived within minutes of the time the charred remains of the boat went under. A second boat was almost as quick to respond.

"You guys okay," a man from the first boat asked. He threw a flotation ring out on the water. "You...grab on, we'll pull you aboard." He pointed at Nick because he had heard the man's complaints.

"Thank God you got here so fast," Nicky yelled, feeling that now they would all be okay.

Several more boats arrived on the scene and in short order everyone who had been on the *Francesca* was pulled out of the water. Everyone was accounted for but Mitzi. She was not with them.

Nicky stood at the bow of the boat that rescued him and scanned the water around them. She was gone, she was not with them.

"Those bastards killed Mitzi," he screamed. He turned to the owner of the boat he was on and pleaded his directions. "Get this thing to Port Clinton now...now!"

The boat owner obliged without responding. He knew the old man lying on the deck was in bad shape and had to get to a hospital fast. The Coast Guard station at Marblehead had already been called, but they could not respond fast enough to get out on the lake and get Nick. But what they did do was arrange for Life Flight to head out from St. Vincent Medical Center in Toledo. By the time they got back in to Port Clinton, the chopper was there waiting and soon whisked Nick away.

"Those Goddamn Mexicans will pay for this," Nicky said quietly to Karen as he got into the helicopter to go with Nick to the hospital. "They will pay. Big time."

Cuzo knew that Victor's plan to fire bomb the boat was more retaliation than was needed to give an answer for running him off the road. That had been a minor event and even Victor knew that they could have easily killed him if they had wanted. Burning their big boat, making its remains sink, jeopardizing all of those on board - that was not warranted. It would escalate a situation with the Frangelettis they did not want. He knew that big trouble was ahead.

Carlos had piloted the boat back into the bay and to the property where their action had begun. He ran the boat directly and hard onto the mud at relatively low speed, but with enough velocity to take the bow onto the mucky slime. Luis jumped off across the bow, got the line they had left behind, fashioning it to a bow cleat, and yanked on the boat to bring it farther onto the shore.

"Don't strain," Carlos yelled, "we geet it. Okay?"

It took the strength of the three of them to pull the boat closer to the trailer. They hand cranked with the winch to haul the boat onto the trailer. Once the boat was secure, Carlos got in the truck and started the process of pulling the trailer out of the mud. It took jockeying the trailer backward and forward with a series of herky-jerky shifts, until the trailer was freed and could be pulled onto solid ground.

Carlos drove away without acknowledgment, without goodbye, without looking back. He was gone.

"Where's you car?" Cuzo asked Luis.

"In the shed over there," he pointed, as he walked towards one of the out buildings. "See you tomorrow at Victor's."

Cuzo stood there alone, looking out at the calm water of the bay, soaking up the bright sunlight, wondering what was next. He knew it would not be pleasant. The Frangelettis would now come back hard and Los Tigres would have to make some adjustments. He thought about Pam and decided to get with her as quickly as he could. This day was history. Bad history and they would pay. He made a note to himself that this was the last time he would follow a plan of Victor's. Victor had shown that he could not be the leader. But, maybe no one could and maybe their business here was over. To continue, he felt, was certain death for all of them. He wanted to see Pam and he knew, somehow, he needed to see that guy she knew - Butch. He needed to see Butch. This all had to be sorted out.

In less than forty eight hours, the power boat they used would be in Louisiana, on a remote farm, covered by a tarp, sitting in an unused barn. It would not be in water again for almost a year. Cuzo knew that the boat was a small part of what happened. What happened was because of them. They would pay the price, the boat didn't matter. Oh, its disappearance took the Coast Guard and State police out of the equation, that's for sure, in terms of getting caught and getting prosecuted, but it didn't help with the Frangelettis. Cuzo knew their reaction was to come.

18.

Nick had a heart attack all right, but it was a mild one. Although not severe, his condition still was cause for concern and the medical staff in the emergency room had acted accordingly. Not long after he arrived at St. Vincent, Nick was yelling at Nicky to get him out of there.

"Did you get a look at those guys? Who were they?"

"Calm down, pop, they want to check you out. Just try to relax."

"Get me out of here," the older man growled. "Now, goddamnit, I mean right now."

So Nick's stay at St. Vincent did not last more than a few hours. During that time, Nicky tried to keep his father under control. He also sent Eddie Majeski off to get a hospital bed and a nurse arranged for his father's house. There would be no up and down stairs for awhile and Nick had to rest. Ben Colangelo, Nick's doctor, would have to see him there at the house.

Nicky knew that the hospital gave his father first rate attention. They assigned a team to his immediate care and made sure he was comfortable. But for Nick what they did for him did not matter and he would not quit complaining until he was home. He was a non-stop succession of directives and expletives which were completely ignored by staff, shushed and mollified by Nicky, and with behavior that made him a grossly obnoxious patient of cartoon proportions. The hospital staff breathed a sigh of relief when the ambulance pulled away with Nick inside.

The hospital bed was set up in the family room of the huge house that Nick occupied by himself along with several servants and his bodyguard. The house was located in the village of Ottawa Hills, an exclusive section of Toledo, where the wealthy, both new and old money, had palatial homes. The family room was very spacious with a big television set in one corner. Nick's bed was near the window wall so he could see outside and the bird feeder. He was fond of the birds and was fascinated watching them come to feed.

"Kari, doll, you are so great. What would I do without you? You been great to me. I love ya."

She smiled as she plumped his pillow and stroked his forehead. She was a dutiful and attentive nurse for Nick. He had grown very fond of her in only a few days and acquiesced to the way she ministered to him.

"Pop you've got a phone call," Nicky yelled from the hall, "it's that Mexican sonofabitch Padillo. You want to talk or should I tell him to kiss off?"

"Nicky, Nicky, what's the matter with you? He wants to talk. Why shouldn't we talk to him? After all, we are the injured, we should be able to make a case for apology. Of course I talk to him, of course."

Nicky brought the portable phone to his father, lying in his family room, comfortable, at ease, but ready for retaliation.

"Listen, you sonofabitch, how come yer calling me? I hope it's to plead that you want to get on yer knees and beg for mercy. We'll put you assholes in purgatory. You'll wish you never crossed us, never got in our way. We let Buddy's thing go by because we knew that maybe you had a beef, but this shit...you could have killed us all. Only by the grace of God did we survive. You shithead, what were you thinking? Have you no sense?' When have...?"

"Neek, Neek, Neek. Easy up, we dun't want to harm you, but sheet man, your guys could have killed me...and my friend. She was very upset...I was upset. But leesen, I admit I over reacted to your message to me. I was pissed. I should not have reacted like I deed. I am calling to say I am sorry...to ask for you to forgeeve. Believe me, I crossed myself many times when I found out no one was killed. It was a meestake. My meestake. Look, dare is enough beezness here for everyone and I no wish to take your beezness, I just want to do mine. Dat Buddy, he made eet tough on us...he deed not understand dat we are entitled to our beezness. We should be able to do our theeng."

"Who the fuck do you think you are?" Nick asked gruffly, knowing full well that he had Victor by the throat.

"Veektor Padeeyo," Victor said slowly, "a man who knows he is at fault, a man who does not want war with you, a man who wants peace, a man who weel buy you a new boat."

"That boat cost a million bucks. You Mexicans got that kinda money?"

"We are but poor Mexican immigrants who have struggled for existence, but we weel scrape together the money for a new boat. We weel do dat to keep peace and to show our good faith. We just ask to be able to do our beezness."

"What a lotta shit. Mexicans, eh, is that right, Mexicans? You can be Goddamn thankful you Mexicans didn't kill our cook. For your information Mitzi is worth a lot. She's worth more than all you fucking Mexicans put together. What you don't understand, you goddamn wetback, is that you can always buy another goddamn boat...you know that...do you know that...you can always buy another boat. However, shithead, what you may not know is that a good Japanese cook is priceless."

"Yes, dat is true, I understand your concern and I am so glad she is not harmed."

"Scared shitless...she thought she was going to die...we all did, goddamnit, we all did...but she's okay. Fortunately for you she's okay. Hey, listen...you listen to me. You scrape together a million and a quarter and have someone deliver it to our office and we'll call it square. No war, no hard feelings, we'll say it's even. A million and a quarter in big bills...hundreds, fifties...put it in one of those sport bags and have someone bring it to our office. Is a week enough time to get your hands on the money?"

"Ten days would be better. Eet weel take son doin'. But we do eet to make peace with you 'cause we are sorry."

"Okay, ten days it is. Use a messenger service if you want, but to our office."

"That is good. Many thanks. You weel geet eet. Is true for sure you weel geet eet."

Nick punched off the portable phone and looked at Nicky who had been standing there listening to his father's side of the conversation.

"It will never happen," Nick laughed, "and who cares. Find out where all of their carwash places are and kick the shit out them. Who the hell does that fuckin' Mexican think he is? Calling here to say he's sorry. Don't hurt anybody, but smash every one of them you can find. I want to know more about their operation. We're gonna put them out of business for good. Car washes, my ass. Get someone working on it now. I want them to be out of business in a week. Buy us a boat...that shitass...he can be damn glad Mitzi didn't die. We would have capped all of them...all of them. I gotta think about it. Maybe we should still nail this Victor, that Mexican shitass. Get going."

For his part, Victor was enraged. He pushed the TALK button on his portable phone and threw it across the room. The phone hit a lamp, bounced on a chair, and fell onto the carpeted floor, spinning so that its short antenna became a pointer for some unknown prize. He had been clenching his teeth throughout the conversation with Nick and, now, he was ready to vent his anger, to rampage throughout his house, and to flail at the windmills of his frustration. He was, Cuzo speculated, angrier than he had ever before witnessed.

Cuzo waited for Victor to rage with anger once he had thrown the phone, but Victor did not, he merely paced the room. For Victor, his anger came not only from putting himself in the subservient role of apology, but from being put down about being Mexican. He heard it in Nick's voice when he had said the word "Mexicans." There was the note of derision, contempt, and disregard by being called a wetback. It was the disregard that was dangerous for the Padillo boys, because Nick had no fear of them. He would strike back without waiting for the money, he would gain his sense of retribution for what they had done to him, a personal affront that transcended the cost of the boat, that superseded the indignity of being hauled out of the water. It was the idea that anyone would dare to bring any kind of attack on the Frangelettis. It was the daring that so bothered Nick. He would strike back quickly, severely, and in a way that would cost the Padillo group a great deal. Victor knew this and thus he could not speak.

"Praly da washes," he said, almost as if he were thinking out loud, "dey geet da washes.

For Cuzo, the drug operation was over, it was time to move on. There would never be peace with the Frangeletti, there would always be the conflict, always the danger. He knew the boat thing was wrong, now the price had to be paid. It wasn't just with the Frangelettis, it was now with the law. There would be an investigation by the Coast Guard. There would be speculation by any other Feds involved by the Coast Guard and the Feds who might already be after them who figured that this was a Padillo retaliation. In any case, focus would be on them. Shit...how could Victor be so stupid?

Victor finally threw himself into a chair and hung his head into his hands. He asked for Cuzo's thoughts without looking up. He knew they were in trouble and he had only himself to blame.

Cuzo sat down across from Victor, leaned back in the chair, and watched him shaking his head back and forth. He probed within himself for an answer, but he knew that now the danger was at the highest point since they came to Ohio.

"Get rid of any paper records you have here right away. Save only what is truly important on a disk. Trash the computer. I mean trash it so its hard drive cannot be checked for hidden information. Make sure this house is clean...clean like driven snow, clean like river rocks. I believe the DEA will come...sooner rather than later. I believe we are done...you might not want to believe it...there's so much Goddamn money at stake, but I think it's over. I think we should pull in, pack up, and go back to Mexico for awhile. That's what I think. I also think you fucked up big time and I'm not sure I want to be part of this any more. What do you say? How do we get out of this? Regroup, move? Stay and get erased...by either the Feds or the Frangelettis. Let's take our money and make a calculated retreat."

"Let me theenk," Victor said calmly. "you boys go...relax...I theenk. But Cuzo..."

Cuzo looked at him squarely, his eyes trying to penetrate Victor's stolid look.

"...I reespet what you say. I decide by mañana."

Cuzo and Luis went outside toward where their cars were parked side by side in the shade of one of the large trees in front of the house. Luis leaned against his car and waited for Cuzo to say something.

"We're screwed and it's over. I'm going to meet Pam. I'd appreciate it if you'd keep track of my tail."

"Sure," Luis answered, "will do."

Before Victor had ever decided to make the phone call, Cuzo had arranged to meet Pam at her place. She had wanted him for lunch, but he knew that would never work, so now she would be making dinner. His sense was that every move, every action was dangerous, and as he drove to Pam's he tried to sort out what needed to be done. Some projects had already been set in motion and could not be recalled. There were shipments that had to be accounted for and sales contracts that had to be fulfilled. The Padillo organization had been put in motion over a period of years and it would not be easy to slow its momentum and bring it to a halt in a few hours, let alone a few days. It was too complicated and he grew sweaty hot with the frustration of trying to work it out mentally. He would have to look at the schedules, check with their operatives, and begin to give specific instructions in order to bring the machine to a stop. And this would be only after Victor made a decision. Shit, this is bad.

He drove by Pam's house slowly, but not so slowly that he would draw attention. He wanted to check out the parked cars on the street and satisfy himself that it would be safe to go in, so he circled the block. On the second cruise around, he cut down the alley running parallel to her street and parked next to the garage behind her house. He called her on the cellular phone.

"Hi, I'm parked out by the garage. I didn't want to scare you by coming up to the back door without warning, but that's what I'm going to do. Things are a little crazy right now, but they're going to be okay. Trust me, they're going to be okay."

She hugged him with all her might and pressed his face into her breasts. He enjoyed the affection and did not resist her exuberant expression, now fully accustomed to the height disparity, fully accepting of her towering presence. She was gorgeous and he rather liked being enveloped in her emotion. He could hardly contain himself with the anticipation of her being naked. She liked being naked and was quick to undress at the slightest encouragement from Cuzo. He had never been really comfortable with his nakedness, but she was getting him to like it more and more. She would strip down and entice him to do likewise. They would spend hours together that way and when darkness set in, would keep the lights off so they could prolong the naked romp. On Pam's part, she relished his muscular body and the darker skin, and when he was on tight to her, inside of her, she felt a heady wholeness to her body and a quality of euphoria she had never before experienced.

They made love without ever lying down: while they were standing, sometimes sitting, and even leaning against a wall. There was something usual or ordinary about lying down and they stayed away from that position, preferring instead, to couple themselves in various ways that seemed more ongoing and renewable, not caught in the tradition of prone positioning.

Eventually lying down became probable because of exhaustion and was their final condition of the coupling event, spread eagle on the living room floor, panting for air, sucking in new life, wondering what was next.

Cuzo watched the ceiling whirling overhead, struggled for stability, and gathered himself into a coordinated, thoughtful posture. He sure loved fucking this woman. Maybe he loved her.

"Do you own this place?" he asked somewhat tentatively, trying to be careful in the calm way he posed the question.

"No." She waited some long time before she went on. "Why do you ask?"

Cuzo was relieved. Not owning the house was a barrier he could now put aside as he worked out what they would do. The house could have been a stumbling block for how things would progress for them. Now, that was not an issue.

"I may have to...I probably will have to leave. On short notice. I want..."

"You want me to go with you?"

"Yes. Yes...I want that. I want to believe that if there is an emergency, and I have to get the hell out, you will come with me. It is important to me. It is..."

"Do you love me?"

"Yes...I love you." He recognized the words he had just said, but wasn't sure if he knew what they meant. He had used those before as a convenience, as the password for getting more sex from a woman. They had not meant anything to him when he had used them before. Now, said out loud, they rang in his ears, making him feel as if some giant hand had squeezed his head so that his brain was compressed and his thoughts ran together in bunches. Maybe I am in love, was the thought he managed to salvage from this process.

She crawled over on top of him and kissed him wildly, passionately, as if she had never before tasted him. She bit at his nipples without truly biting them, kissed him again, clinging to him with her legs as someone might who were climbing a tree. The afternoon passed into darkness that found Cuzo and Pam wrapped in a light blanket, their bodies still entwined, now rolled up on the living room sofa.

Cuzo's cell phone shocked them awake. It was still black night as Cuzo moved in the darkness to the sound of the phone in his pants across the room. He punched it on.

"We been heet. Dat sonabitch lied. He not give us chance to bring money, he strike. Señor Cuzo we must talk. We must figure out how to get out...now."

Cuzo checked his watch lying on the table that told him it was four in the morning,

"The car washes?" he asked somberly, figuring the worst had happened.

"Si, da washes. Eight or ten, maybe more."

Although Nick had asked Nicky to find out about the Padillo car washes so they could be targeted, Nicky already knew where they were and had previously developed a plan to put them out of business. All it took was for Nick to trigger what was known and set. Nicky got every available Frangeletti operative into action in short order and by evening they were ready to sweep across the Padillo carwash empire to disable most of the facilities.

Nicky put together five groups of four men each and had them meet in the main Frangeletti warehouse located on the north side of Toledo. He appointed a captain for each group. Most of the men were Frangeletti guys, but a few were free lance thugs Nicky used for odd jobs when some muscle was needed. Each team was given a list of four targets and they were to begin the hits simultaneously at two in the morning. The washes should be pretty well empty at that hour so the men would have few customers to get out of the way. Nicky had maps for each team that indicated the location of the car washes. The men studied these for several hours and talked about how they would make each hit.

"Hit hard and fast, get out and move on to the next wash. When yer done get back here...there'll be a bonus for everybody. Make sure yer not followed. Avoid the cops. You team captains...bring the maps and tools back here. Yer responsible." Nicky's voice was harsh as he barked the orders to these men. "Work fast, you won't have a problem. If the cops show up by accident, just remember: yer workin' for the black boys...Chet Washington...tell the cops you think Chet Washington hired you through a third party you don't know. I'll take care of the rest. But don't get caught. Check the area, make sure it's clear, get the job done fast. We want these Goddamn Mexicans to know we mean business. So, let's get goin'."

All of the tools and equipment they needed were assembled and each team got its car loaded and ready. They all checked their watches and headed out for their first assigned target.

At each car wash they cut all of the hoses and scattered them around the building, smashed and emptied the bill changing machines and coin operated washers, destroyed the hot water and wash and wax tanks, cut any phone lines, destroyed and emptied any vending machines, and destroyed any of the other equipment like the vacuum cleaners. They smashed all of the garage doors to the stalls with sledge hammers, and broke every fixture of any kind whether it be handle or knob, lever or bracket.

The twenty targeted car washes were treated to this baptism of mayhem and destruction in less than four hours. Miraculously, only five customers were encountered and four were easily chased away. The fifth initially resisted, wanting to finish washing his car, but confronted with the possibility of having his car bashed in by four men with sledge hammers, he quickly left.

There was one problem with the operation, an operation that otherwise went very smoothly. It happened in Tiffin. It was a fluke that Angel Partencíon would be at the car wash in that town at that time of night, but he was and he was there to confront the Frangeletti team that showed up for the hit on the place. When the first car arrived, he thought it was just another customer, but when the second car pulled in right behind and all the muscle jumped out, he knew there was trouble. He ducked behind the cinder block wall of the stall next to where he was standing, hoping they had not seen him as he moved away. But they had and spread out from the two cars in quick order as his furtive movement was spotted. Angel had pulled out his automatic when he made his first move, but kept it to his side to limit the target size for the attackers. He pressed himself against the wall and edged toward the front to see what was happening. He was shot twice without ever seeing any of those who were there that he instinctively knew were dangerous. He never had a chance to raise the automatic from his side, never even saw a vision of what he should be defending himself against, never knew that someone unknown had drawn down on him. He was dead before his body sprawled onto the floor. Angel had stopped by to wash his own car after he left his favorite late night hangout. He was saving time from his morning routine. Better to wash the car tonight, rather than waste time tomorrow when much had to get done. It was a matter of circumstance as death often is in the scheme of things. As his blood ran down the floor drain, the destruction of the car wash proceeded around him.

The attack on the car washes was swift, decisive, and convincing, and from Nick's point of view, not the final word in how the Frangelettis would respond to nearly being killed out on the lake.

"Get dressed," Cuzo ordered Pam as he pulled on his clothes. "You're gonna stay with me from now on. It will be safer."

She stumbled through the darkness pulling on her panties, stabilizing herself against him. She pushed her bare breasts to him as she clung to his body and shivered. It was a reaction to the nighttime chill and the anxiety that the call had brought to Cuzo, anxiety that was relayed to her. The call had been a message of fear and she well perceived that fear was now warranted.

19.

The Crider truck yard just off I-40 on the northeast outskirts of Knoxville was jammed with parked semi rigs across its gravel expanse. In the background, the sound of a straining switch engine could be heard working in the nearby railroad yard, grinding against the weight of three dozen loaded rail cars, each designated for somewhere in the south. The cars were being moved from siding to siding, hooked and unhooked, assembled and reassembled as each freight train was put together for its proper destination. The noise of the engine and the cars slamming together were muffled somewhat by a gentle rain that was beginning to sift through the evening sky. It had been a hot day, so when the first sprinkles of warm rain came down, they dried and were gone almost as soon as they hit the ground; but eventually the gravel glistened wet.

Crider's operation was not very busy this evening, which seemed contrary to the mass of trailers and tractor rigs that sat waiting for use. The orange glow of the overhead lights revealed several trucks near ready to pull out and a few more rigs getting checked for the road. The maintenance garage was working a second shift with a skeleton crew that struggled at several emergency repair jobs. A boom box blared through the open doors of the garage, so depending where you were standing at Crider's, it was either the sounds of the rail yard or country rock to be heard in the background.

Ron Andrews pulled his pickup close to the fence near the entrance to Crider's, shifted into PARK, and let the engine idle while he looked out over the yard. He checked to determine if he would be seen. His assessment was that he could walk onto the yard without being noticed. He quickly kissed the young woman who was sitting alongside before getting out of the truck. She slid behind the wheel, pulled the shift lever to DRIVE, and slowly eased away, giving a little wave as she guided the truck over the curb and onto the road in front of Crider's.

Ron walked through the open gate and started looking for the rig he wanted. He ducked in and out of the shadows and stayed away from the office building next to the maintenance garage. He cut an angled course through the yard toward the area where he had been told the truck would be, carefully moving from trailer to trailer. Slowly, surely, one after another, he eased by their bulk crouched low behind the huge tires, waited, watched, pressed against clammy metal, poised for each step in the quiet progression through the seemingly endless field of trailers. The deliberate way he conducted the search made him feel as if it were taking a long time as he edged toward the rig he knew was there. In reality, the search didn't take him much more than fifteen minutes or so to reach the Peterbilt rig he had been hired to drive.

Once he recognized the rig he was after, he snuck around the trailer that was along side, scooted under the trailer, and was quickly where he needed to be. Most of the trailers did not have a tractor truck already hitched, but the one he wanted did. He unlocked the cab of the big truck with the key he had been given. He fired up the powerful diesel engine and adjusted the seat to suit himself better as he looked around to check out if he were being noticed. He waited until the engine came up to temperature before he put it into gear. No one paid any attention as he rolled out of the yard.

Andrews was a member of Alan Sidrow's operation, a part-timer, hired on occasion to drive a tractor trailer rig as directed, a man who had spent more years in prison than he wanted to remember, a man who could be trusted to do his job and do it to the letter. As was the case with the way Alan built his enterprise, Andrews was a friend of a friend, recommended for the job, recommend because he could fit in with the purpose of the business. Alan did not care why Andrews had been in prison, he simply wanted a certain level of performance, a strong measure of dedicated loyalty, and the knowledge that the man would do what he said he would do. Ron had fulfilled each of those requirements and felt indebted to whomever it was that hired him for the chance to earn some extra money.

His friend, the friend who knew Alan, had made the suggestion about these part time assignments over coffee as the two of them finished their after-breakfast cigarettes. It would be easy Bobby had said, stress free and good extra money in your pocket that the Government wouldn't know about. His services would be highly appreciated, he would be well paid.

Ron knew that nothing you got paid quick money for was easy and seldom was any job stress free. However, he could not pass on the money. Ex-cons never fair well, so the money was a blessing for him as Alan figured it would be. Ron agreed to make the drives and that was the last time he and Bobby ever talked about it.

About two weeks later, he received a phone call. "Glad yer on board," the muffled voice said, "in a few days you'll get an envelope with directions and a key...and cash. Do exactly as it says and everything will be okay. Got it?"

"Yeah."

"We won't talk on the phone again," the voice went on, "just look for the envelope."

The first envelope, one of those protected with plastic bubbles, came with complete directions printed on plain white paper and the key to a semi rig. Another smaller envelope inside contained the cash. This process had continued until now he was on his eighteenth run. They were easy to do, but the stress did not go away. Ron felt the stress worrying about getting caught. He knew that he must be doing something illegal, he just didn't know what it was.

Once he got out of the yard, Andrews carefully maneuvered the rig from stop light to stop light as he worked his way on surface streets until he got to the I-40 entrance ramp. Coming down the westbound ramp, he jockeyed through the gears, pushing hard on the accelerator as he finally shifted into top gear. The scream of the engine pulsated toward high speed as he further adjusted the seat to get comfortable for the ride north. He had no idea who he was working for and no idea what the truck was carrying. All he knew was that he was to drive the rig to a parking lot in Florence, Kentucky. He would ride a Greyhound back to Knoxville. Yes, Ron thought, this was easy money with no complications so far. He figured he didn't want to know any more than he did anyway. Safer that way. He figured it must be the cargo that wasn't legal, but the money was too good and too easy to pass up. His hands were sweaty and he wiped them alternately on his pants as he commanded the rig toward the I-75 interchange.

He had not noticed the bag at first, but soon became aware of it on the floor in front of the passenger seat. He never touched it, didn't want to know anything about it. Once he realized that it was there near him, he tried to put it out of his mind, but continued to wonder what it might be. Better to not know, he thought.

The rain came harder as he rolled through the interchange onto northbound I-75 and settled into the drive with the cadence of the windshield wipers beating a steady rhythm into his consciousness. It was a sound he liked, it was a feeling that comforted him. And he had already been paid.

Ron pushed the rig northward, handling the mountain passes with respect for the slippery pavement and the steep grades the truck had to tolerate, and held a steady track for his destination. He had made sure he was well rested and did not need to stop. He had a small sack with him that contained a sandwich and a plastic bottle of water to tide him over until he got to Florence. This is a little tricky in the constant rain, he thought, but I'll be back in Knoxville tomorrow.

It was still dark when he approached the outskirts south of Florence. He had made one stop he had not planned on to relieve himself, but still made good time. The rain continued to fall straight down, the drops glistened in the headlights, and bounced light in odd patterns of glare across the windshield.

Ron pulled the rig off I-75 and followed the instructions he had been given until he reached the parking lot of a strip mall about a mile from the expressway. He parked the rig away from the stores and locked the keys inside. He stood surveying where he was, orienting himself before heading down the road back to the expressway and across to the other side. He knew it wasn't much of a distance, but the persistent rain took away from his comfort and in particular, made it out of the question for getting a smoke while he walked. There was a pay phone at the Amoco gas station where he called a cab that would take him downtown to the bus station. He had done his job and now as he stood waiting for the cab out of the rain beneath the pump canopy, he still wondered what was in the bag.

The rig Ron Andrews left behind in the strip mall sat for several hours alone in the steady rain. Eventually, toward sunrise, the rain tapered off, and stopped altogether. The sun pushed its way over the landscape, the orange ball of energy threatening another day of humid heat. It was an hour or so after sunrise that a well worn sedan, an older Chevrolet Malibu, eased by the rig as two men in the car carefully reviewed the situation. They went on slowly and parked in front of the mall's lone coffee shop. They went in and ordered breakfast. As they slopped toast in their runny eggs they could keep an eye on the rig. Finished with breakfast and satisfied that all was okay, they went back to the truck Ron had parked. The shorter of the two men pulled a lone key from his pocket to unlock the tractor cab. He got in and got the engine running. The other man moved back from the rig and watched as the unit slowly rolled away across the parking lot and was gone.

Neal Hampton was behind the wheel and would handle the final leg of the run with the rig. He knew this was a special deal, special handling of special cargo. He had no idea what it was. Probably not drugs, he thought, maybe cigarettes. He knew that he worked directly for a respectable businessman in Florence, but he knew also that the strings were being pulled by someone else, probably some Yankee mobsters. Detroit maybe or Cleveland. Big time money with something to protect, something important to move north. He liked the assignment because of the money and the small amount of responsibility he had. Drive the truck to Findlay, Ohio and park it in a motel parking lot just off I-75. Easy, he figured, easy money and it would only take a few hours. He could be back shooting pool in Florence before the end of the day.

He was very careful with the rig as he drove across the bridge over the Ohio River, through Cincinnati and Dayton, maintaining a speed less than the truck maximum, staying in the right hand lane. He did not take any chances as he contended with traffic. It was boring and tedious, but it was worth the money. Near Lima, his head started to bob, his eyes flickered and started to glaze over as he fought the urge to doze and, in the process, nearly ran the rig off the road. The sound of the tires pounding on the warning grooves startled him back to alertness. Other than that one incident, the drive was uneventful and he passed the time listening to rock music on the radio.

Neal slowed for the Findlay exit he wanted. He downshifted as he eased the rig onto the ramp off the freeway, got the green light at the surface street, and swung the rig to the right, headed for town. He appreciated the fact he didn't have to stop as he came off the freeway, that allowed him keep rolling to make the maneuver around the corner. It wouldn't be long before his assignment was ended. So easy, so very easy.

The pickup truck that cut him off startled him, shocked him back to reality. The pickup slowed quickly, so Neal reacted instinctively, hitting the brakes in panic mode. The huge truck and trailer tires skidded on the pavement as the smell of burned rubber filled the air. Not quickly enough. The massive chrome plated front bumper smacked the pickup with a neck rattling jolt the way a heavyweight boxer snaps his opponent's head with a sharp jab to the chin. The pickup lurched ahead from the blow it received and stopped. Neal was ready to burst into a rage. It had all gone so smoothly, now this. Stupid bastard, what the hell was he doin'.

Neal started to get out of the cab to determine what damage he caused or if anyone was injured. Before he could get his door open, a man was in the cab from the other side and beside him, an automatic pistol pressed into his ribs.

"Git out of the truck," the man hissed, "walk back to the freeway without looking back. You will be watched. Go back south without notifying anyone."

"I need..." Neal started to say.

"You need shit. Hitch a ride from someone. Don't use the phone. Git going."

Neal jumped from the rig and began a fast pace towards I-75, finally breaking into a jog when he was several hundred feet away. He would do exactly what he had been directed.

Cuzo sat with Luis in the pickup watching Neal's exit.

"Well, we'll see what this is," he said with a laugh, "maybe we got lucky."

They waited as Bob Diaz situated himself behind the wheel. After a few minutes of getting settled, he shifted into low gear and headed the rig around them. Luis directed the pickup behind the rig as the two vehicle caravan moved out of Findlay on county roads away from the freeway. When they reached US Route 30, they headed east towards Mansfield.

Cuzo could not help but reflect on the irony of the route they were taking. They would be going through Mansfield with the prison just off Route 30, on toward their destination of Ashland. He had followed the Frangeletti truck to the prison along this same road. The Frangeletti guys are everywhere, he thought, but they don't know how close by we are as we work our stuff. They'd be shocked. They don't know or we'd have been hit before we were. The biggest worry, however, for Cuzo was the DEA. No doubt they are investigating, no doubt in his mind that eventually they would get to the Tigres.

"It's just a matter of time," he said out loud.

Luis turned to look at him, but made no reply.

"The DEA is working on us right now I figure...just a matter of time before they show up."

Still silent, Luis stared straight ahead as he drove.

"We've been lucky to have someone inside the Frangeletti organization...it has given us an edge. Too bad our business has to end here. Tie up some loose ends...get a plan set to leave...be gone. Getting away will take some doing, but we'll work on it."

Luis nodded agreement.

"We couldn't pass this up," Cuzo said, gesturing to the truck, "especially since they hit us. We have to get out of here, but no reason not to check this out."

Soon after he and Cuzo got to Ohio, Victor had established a factory of sorts in an old warehouse just off the main downtown area of Ashland. Age had taken its toll on the structure, the outside weathered, with dirty red brick, a building that had been unused for several years until he came along to buy it.

Victor had been checking out small towns, looking for a spot where they could handle the shipments that arrived from Mexico. He thought Ashland might be the place because his gut feeling seemed right about the town. Ashland was the right size and the right location for what he thought would work best for part of their operation.

Once the Padillo group took over the building, they established a modest vending machine business that would provide reason for the coming and going of personnel and vehicles. Vending was a good cover as they went about the process of buying property and building several car washes in the area. The old building worked out just fine to receive the drugs that came to the Padillo organization and were repackaged for sale. It was a large building that extended a block long on the front and half a block toward the rear. It would, of course, readily accommodate a semi rig.

Bob Diaz ran the rig through the large doors, followed by the pickup with Cuzo and Luis. Cuzo had called on the cell phone when they were a few blocks away and alerted the warehouse crew they were near.

Cuzo got out of the pickup and yelled at Bob Diaz as he approached.

"You did good work, my friend, that went well. No problems. And we have what they wanted, whatever it is. We will get this unloaded right away. When it's empty, you drive it to Youngstown. Park it on a side street somewhere...you know, of course, to try not to be seen. Rent a car and drive to Columbus. Call Chico Mercali when you get there. He'll bring you back to Toledo. Nice work. But stay cool...and keep your eyes open my friend. It is very dangerous out there...and going to get worse."

Cuzo and Luis stood watching as Diaz and some of the other workers popped the lock on the trailer's rear doors. They pulled the right door wide open and shined a large flashlight inside. Not much. Several crates, six or seven cardboard boxes, that was it.

"Pull that other door open and let's get some light in there," Cuzo ordered.

Luis had already climbed into the trailer and was examining one of the crates.

"Might be M-16s," he speculated. "Something military...not fruit."

Cuzo was now beside him. "Shine it over here," he directed to the man who had pulled in the work light. Loose cloth had been over the top of each crate, covering what appeared to be melons. "Smell like they're ripe. Bring some cartons so we can get these out of here."

The men quickly pulled the melons from the crates and put them in the cartons and a couple of plastic bags. There was nothing underneath the melons. Cuzo stared into one of the crates for several seconds without saying a word. He looked at Luis, eyebrows raised.

"What are they doing with this?"

Luis did not answer right away, but rather dug into one of the cardboard boxes. He was greeted by a mass of oranges, some already beginning to spoil. He began tossing oranges into another of the plastic bags until he got near the bottom.

"Nothing here. What were they carrying?"

"You know, Cuzo," Bob Diaz explained, "there's one of those bags in the cab...you know like the sports guys use, except it's green like military...I just thought it was the driver's stuff...maybe its got something."

Luis jumped down from the truck first, with Cuzo right behind and almost ran to the front of the rig. Cuzo beat Luis to the door and pulled it open. There was the big olive drab bag. He grabbed the strap handles, brought it down to the warehouse floor, and yanked the zipper open. There were the plastic explosives and boxes of detonators.

Cuzo shook his head. "I thought we would find guns...ammunition, but this...this is something else. This stuff...this stuff right here... is why the guy...that Butch guy...asked about plastic. Come on, let's get that truck out of here."

"How bout de fruit?" one man asked.

"Leave it on the truck...was everybody wearing gloves?"

Sí, sí, came the responses from the men.

Cuzo and Luis stood looking at each other as the men stood waiting for the next task Cuzo would assign. There was an unspoken sense of trepidation among them as they silently contemplated their discovery.

"We're going to have to think about this," Cuzo finally offered, "what do we do with this stuff?"

Luis was still silent.

"I don't want to," Cuzo said, "but I will tell Victor. It is better that way, at least while we are here in this country. I don't want conflict with Victor right now. His decisions are frustrating...he goes at everything with anger, but we need to be able to leave without difficulty. No...no conflict right now."

"The Frangelettis will want this back," Luis said, pointing to the bag.

"That is true. And just maybe also we should let Mr. Butch know about it. He wanted me to tell him if I found out anything. Well, maybe he should know that the Frangeletti guys are moving plastic."

20.

There are plenty of good and bad reasons why someone would want plastic explosives and most of them are bad. Jackie Zimmerman wanted some plastic, wanted it as quickly as he could get his hands on it. He sat in his second floor office situated in a nondescript brick building on the east side of Detroit, on a side street just off Mack Avenue. The lavishly furnished room glowed from the morning sun pouring in the two large windows to the left of his imposing, richly polished mahogany desk, wiped clean of any dust, holding one neatly piled stack of papers. He was frustrated with the two men sitting across the desk from him. He had given them the assignment for getting "the stuff to blow up things" and they had not been able to do so. He did not know about plastic explosives, but he knew there was something other than sticks of dynamite to accomplish what he wanted. He knew that whatever this other stuff was, it was way more powerful than dynamite.

"We need to get some stuff to blow up things, powerful stuff. We want a big bang."

He laughed after he barked out the instructions to the two men. He used the editorial "we" rather than "I" when he really meant himself. "We" meaning "I" simply incorporated his organization as one thought process or desire that reflected his wishes. The use of "we" in place of "I" was a conscious decision he made because he thought that if he said "I" too much it would sound presumptuous or pompous even though he also knew that he called all of the shots for his company.

"You guys see what you can find. Somebody around here's gotta know where to get it."

The two men scrambled for several days, working their contacts, sourcing for the explosives, but had negative results. Somebody knew somebody who knew somebody who could get the stuff. Each somebody came up a dead end. Neither man relished the chore of reporting back to Jackie with the news of the fruitlessness of their search.

Jackie Zimmerman directed a hard core group of misfits in a tight-fisted way. This was a group he had molded into a stable organization that made money in drugs, gambling, and prostitution. To front the illegal operations, Jackie had carefully built a legitimate business in Zimmerman Concrete and Gravel. The company had concrete batch plants in Wayne, Oakland, and McComb counties of Michigan with a fleet of mixer trucks delivering to construction sites throughout the tri-county area. There was a big red Z on the mixer of each of his white trucks, in jagged form as if shaped from lightening bolts. The company also had a couple of gravel pits in rural McComb County. Over the years, he eventually bought more than two dozen bars and several restaurants. Unlike the Frangelettis, he resisted building an operation to bring in his own drugs, relying instead on others to supply his sales efforts. In turn, his organization had no one on the street selling, but rather functioned as a wholesaler through tiers that could mask his identity.

He had been an outsider to the Italian guys from Detroit and East Detroit that controlled crime in southeastern Michigan for years, able to survive and essentially left alone by them. Two factors helped him avoid the concern of the Italian guys. First of all, when they first took notice of him around 1958, he was small potatoes and did not warrant much attention. Second, he established a reputation for being vicious and they did not want a war with him while the Federal Organized Crime investigation was underway. Besides, he deliberately did not try to encroach on their action.

He grew up under the less than watchful eye of his father who had a tailor shop on Larned Street in downtown Detroit. His mother died when he was about two and his father rarely spoke of her. His father was a Jew, respectful and humble, little involved with his religious heritage, thankful to be in America. Jackie was an only child, bright, headstrong, able to dodge being bar mitzvahed, learning the thrill of crime from the Detroit streets, understanding how much easy money there was to be made. He also was able to dodge the police, keeping out of juvenile detention and jail. His father hardly knew what he was up to most of the time. He had no idea his son was being schooled the way he was. He assumed Jackie would not amount to much, was disappointed in that, and ashamed at his feelings of such disappointment. Jackie had avoided school as much as he could and at sixteen he never went back. Jackie's education was quite informal and he had learned that strength, the show of strength, the perception of strength, was the way to deal with competitors or enemies.

"You'd think someone could get us the stuff. What's the story?"

"We tried, Jackie, we thought we had it. Couple our friends tried for us. Buddies of friends worked on it. Nothing," replied one of the men in front of him, a solemn look on his face.

"Nothin," the other man offered in confirmation. "And a couple guys just didn't want to git involved with that kinda stuff."

"Connections," Jackie said flatly. "Connections. Not yer fault. Don't worry about it."

After a few minutes of silence, Jackie said, "Maybe Nick can help."

He picked up the phone and punched in the Frangeletti number.

"Lemme talk to Nick," he said to the young woman who answered the phone.

She recognized his voice, but did not use his name when she responded. "Mr. Frangeletti is not in. Would you like to speak to his son?"

"Where's Nick?"

"Mr. Frangeletti is recovering from a heart..."

"Oh, yeah, yeah, sure...that's right...lemme talk to Nicky."

"Certainly." She put him on hold and music played while he waited. It was music he did not recognize nor care about, music that was for him more annoyance than anything else as he waited impatiently.

"Can I help you?" The voice was very business like and pleasantly impersonal with the question. She had told Nicky who she thought was on the line.

"Yeah, yeah, you can. It would be good if you meet with me this afternoon. That possible?"

"Yes, I think I can arrange to do that."

Neither man knew for sure that his phone was being tapped, but it was good to be cautious. Jackie and the Frangeletis had previously agreed on a place and time of day that would be triggered by just such a phone call.

Nicky was waiting in his chauffeur-driven Mercedes sedan when Jackie pulled into the parking lot of the strip mall in Flat Rock, Michigan, just off I-75. It was almost three in the afternoon. Jackie parked alongside, got out of his car, and stepped into the Mercedes.

"How's Papa Nick?" Jackie asked as he shook Nicky's hand.

"Fine, fine. He's just fine. What do you need?"

"We need some explosives. My boys tell me they call it plastic explosives. Isn't that the damnedest thing? I tell ya, they make everything out of plastics these days. Who would believe it?"

Nicky did not laugh at Jackie's observation, rather smiled and nodded. He knew the man was not stupid. In fact, he knew how cunning Jackie was and how well he had done over the years making a lot of money, staying out of trouble with the law, and out of the reach of the Detroit Italians. Their historical connection with the Detroit Italians was no reason for the Frangelettis to not do business with Jackie Zimmerman, especially when he was so successful. Then too, they did not want him as an enemy.

"You want plastic explosives?"

"Yeah. Can ya git us some?"

"We can. How much do you want?"

Jackie thought about the question for several seconds before he answered. "I dunno...probably a bunch...we have several projects...what?...ten, twenty pounds...that oughta do it."

"That's a lot," Nicky said. "You have someone to handle it?"

"We'll get someone...don't worry."

So, the order was placed by Jackie Zimmerman for plastic explosives. Events were set in motion that reached all the way to Ft. Bragg in North Carolina and Daryl Hanlin.

When Nicky got back to Toledo, he went directly to Nick's house to review his meeting with Jackie. It irritated him to do so, but he had to check with Nick before placing the order. He found Nick on the patio behind the house, sitting in the shade, still in his bathrobe, his teeth clenching a freshly lighted cigar. He breathed out a small cloud of pale blue smoke as Nicky crossed the red brick, emphasizing the pleasure of his indiscretion with an obvious sigh. Nicky glared at him as he approached.

"What the hell are you doin'? And what is that?" He was pointing to a small glass with red liquid in it that sat on the table next to Nick.

"Red wine...good for your health. And this..." Nick said, as he held the cigar in front of him, "is a pleasure I've missed for awhile. I thought it was about time for one. I feel good...the doctor won't care."

Despite the consummate toughness Nick had shown over the years, he had always dealt with Nicky with a degree of softness. There was a solid bond between father and son that had grown even stronger with time. The son was truly concerned with his father's health and believed doctor's orders should be followed, which included no smoking, no drinking alcohol, and plenty of rest.

"Curious to know what he wants with the plastic," Nick said after being told what Jackie had wanted. "We supply him with plastic and he blows up somebody, we can be charged with accessory to murder. You know that, don't ya?"

"Yeah, I know that...he wants it, he's a big customer...we gotta deliver. I told him we would. Plastic is no worse than M-16s and ammo."

"Maybe...maybe not." The older man turned as he said, "Okay, but this one's touchy, I think. Tell Alan to be very careful."

"Don't worry, I will."

Nicky used his cell phone to call Alan Sidrow to order the plastic explosives. He made sure he was not followed as he drove from Nick's house to Ottawa Park and stopped on one of the roads along the golf course. Sidrow did not answer, so Nick left a brief, meaningless sounding message.

Alan Sidrow did not have a real office. His black leather attaché case served as his office, an office that was always with him. Nicky had tried to encourage him to have some kind of business to cover his operation, but Alan had resisted. Instead, he wanted a looser, more highly mobile condition for his business. For him, an office was tantamount to a prison cell. He had been in and out of prison several times for petty offenses and those experiences affected him profoundly. The idea of sitting in an office was chilling to him, the memories of being isolated and helpless in prison a clear signal to him to avoid feeling that way again if at all possible. So he conducted business as if he were operating a floating crap game, which, in a sense, he was.

His fear of being closeted in prison was not enough, however, to keep him engaged in any legitimate type of enterprise. That fear was outweighed by the sheer delight of operating outside the law, away from a regular business as he put it, where chumps and others with no spirit for the challenge and rewards of scamming and cheating the system plodded along. He was an entrepreneur in every sense of the word, charging after the big take, willing to assume the risks he knew existed.

Bright and capable under the usual assessments, blessed with excellent organizational skills, and with the ability to understand the totality of an operation, he nonetheless, still seemed to function like a small time hustler. It was, therefore, second nature for him to run this new business out of his leather bag. Quiet corners of hotel lobbies, selected shopping mall parking lots, secluded tables in certain restaurants all were his domain as he reigned supreme with cell phone pressed to his face.

Sidrow sat in the lobby of the Ritz-Carlton in Buckhead on Atlanta's north side. It was a favorite location where he enjoyed the cool escape from the afternoon heat amid the plush ambiance as he picked off his messages from voice mail. Nicky's message was among those he listened to, with an imbedded code that alerted him an order needed to be placed.

Waiting for the hour when he would call Nicky, he scanned the USAToday, not really reading, since nothing in particular interested him, but rather diverted his attention through the passage of time. It was so close to four o'clock, the time for the call, that he figured he would make it here in the Ritz-Carlton lobby. The lobby was not his first choice, but it would have to do. At exactly four he dialed the number of a pay phone on Alexis Road in Toledo. Nicky answered on the second ring.

"This is Alexis," Nicky said. "We'd like to place an order from the dairy."

"Yes, yes," Alan replied, "is it milk you want?"

"No, butter."

"Butter? Is that right. How much?"

"We'd like twenty pounds."

"That's a lot of butter."

"I know, I know. Our customer has a lot of baking to do. They think they need twenty pounds. Can you handle that?"

"Yes," Alan said as he made a note in a small book he held, "we can take care of that."

"Have a nice day," Nicky said, dropping the receiver on the phone hook.

The order for butter took only a few days to get arranged. Alan worked through a field operative who in turn contacted Daryl at Ft. Bragg. Every contact was made, every detail finalized for delivery. Four days after the order had been placed, Alan let Nicky know when the material would be headed north. They talked from pay phone to pay phone several times, hoping to have private conversations. What they didn't count on was the Padillo informant within the Frangeletti group.

Once the details had been worked out, the arrangements completed and set, it was a waiting game for everyone including Daryl. The situation was always tense for those concerned, but in this case, the demand was especially tense for Daryl. Daryl was the trigger for the start of a series of events that would bring delivery of the order to Toledo where final settlement would be accomplished. He knew how important his role was within the operation and he assumed that responsibility with all of the vigor he conducted any other duty. The call was money, the net result could be lifetime security. All he had to do was not get caught, survive, and ease out of the Army when the right time came.

Alan's field operative in Fayetteville notified Nicky when the plastic was on the way. Nicky knew that according to plan the stuff would be in Toledo the next day. Late afternoon of that day, Nicky called the warehouse to check on the truck. He told the warehouse manager to call him as soon as it arrived and when it got to be late evening and still no word, he called the warehouse again. The truck did not arrive that day or the next. Nicky knew there was trouble.

"We don't have the butter," Nicky said into his cell phone.

The severity of how he said the words could not begin to match the frustration and anxiety that he felt. There had been no phone call from Jackie yet, but it would come as sure as nightfall, as blistering as summer sun, a tirade of disappointment, a litany of anguish, and a parable of circumstances that contained the vision of threat.

"No idea, Nicky. As far as I know, everything went by plan. Let me do some checking...I'll get back with you. Same phones...tomorrow.

The next morning when Nicky got to the office there was a message from Jackie. He had called directly and that irritated Nicky. He knew there was not much he could do about it, but it festered within him as he stood by his desk, staring at the phone, wondering what he would say to Jackie. He sensed that the operation had gone wrong; he felt it within him as clearly as if he had received a direct message from someone. There was a vision for him, within him, that told the story.

The plastic would not be arriving...it was gone. How would he tell Jackie? How would he deal with this brutally simple man with limited understanding of the complexity of the material he had ordered and the difficulty in getting that material?

He debated not calling Jackie until he heard from Alan, but thought that might make matters worse. He walked down to the warehouse and there punched Jackie's number into his cell phone.

"What the hell...where's my stuff?"

"Easy, easy does it," Nicky said, trying to calm and restrain Jackie. "Don't get so excited. This is a delicate operation. Sometimes it takes longer than we expect..."

"Bullshit. You told me yesterday. You didn't call, I had to call..."

"Remember Jackie, we're on the phone...not face to face. Not a good idea to get too excited, not a good idea to say too much. Let's get together and talk...tomorrow. That will give me time to check out what's going on. Okay? Does that sound right to you?"

"Tomorrow," Jackie said tersely and slammed down the phone.

That afternoon, Nicky talked with Alan Sidrow to learn the bad news of the truck being taken from their man, taken from the operation, hijacked while in progress, and forced away from them. Now the stuff they were responsible for delivering to Jackie was out of their possession, gone without being contested, gone and out of their control. Nicky was stunned by the news. In one sense he felt no blame toward Alan, yet in another way he wanted to jump through space to grab the man by the throat and strangle him senseless.

"How could it happen?" Nicky screamed.

A part of his frustration was how calm Sidrow was about it, how evenly he spoke when he described what had happened, how at ease he was with presenting the bad news.

"Simple story, buddy, you've got someone on the inside of your operation who knew and fed the information to the outside. It was Latinos of some kind...my guy says probably Mexicans...they looked to him like Mexicans. Your problem, man, don't give me any shit. You've got a fuckin' leak. Leaks will kill you. Give me a call when you need me. Adios." Alan pressed his cell phone inactive.

Not long after his call with Sidrow ended, Nicky got a call from the manager of their subsidiary that owned and operated all of the Frangeletti trucks. He reported to Nicky that he had been contacted by the Youngstown police notifying him that the truck had been found parked in that city.

"Get it back here. Check it out," Nicky instructed, "but I doubt that the merchandise we were expecting is still in it."

"What am I looking for?" the man asked.

"You're looking for like an athletic bag...you know, like a tennis bag...only this one is Army issue...same kind of bag, but green. It was supposed to be in the cab. It won't be."

The next morning, Nicky went to Nick's house to have breakfast with his father and discuss how they would handle Jackie. He sat down without speaking, across from his father at the table in the room off the kitchen that was used for informal meals. The early sun streamed in through the windows as Nicky grabbed at the coffee Mitzi poured for him.

"Pop..."

"Say good morning first. You can ask about my health...tell me you hope I'm feeling better. And you can wait until we have some of Mitzi's wonderful food before you burden me with your problem. Okay?"

"Sorry, Pop...how are you..."

"Drink your coffee. Let's eat first."

They ate in silence as Nick slowly appreciated the omelet Mitzi had put before him, even if it were made with egg whites. Since his heart attack, he appreciated everything. As he had explained, 'There's not a lot of time, now.' Nicky picked at his omelet, contenting himself by chewing disinterestedly on a piece of rye toast. Nick seemed to ignore him and lavished praise on Mitzi for the quality of breakfast she had delivered to them. She smiled and bowed several times, giggling and chattering to herself in the kitchen as she went about making sure the two men were properly fed. When he finished eating, Nick finally looked at Nicky, a look of empathy, of concern for the frustration he knew was plaguing his son.

"The explosives business for Jackie went to shit...right?"

"Right."

"That happened?"

"Those goddamn Mexicans hijacked the truck...it was found in Youngstown...nothing in it, naturally."

"What's yer friend Sidrow say?"

Nicky shrugged, "Order more plastic. He's not responsible...says someone inside our organization tipped off the Mexicans."

"You trust him?"

"No reason not to...what does he have to gain by screwing with a good operation. Besides, stealing stuff from us is something those Mexicans would do, even though we're on their ass about the boat. They've got balls, no doubt about it."

"Selling the same plastics twice is what he has to gain," Nick said tersely, disregarding Nicky's explanation. "What's Jackie say?"

"He's hot...wants that damn stuff right now. He paid for it up front...he wants it...he doesn't want the money back, he wants the stuff now."

"We don't order more plastic. We negotiate with the Mexicans. I'll talk to Jackie. You better find out who the rat is that fed the Padillo boys information."

"How do we negotiate with the Mexicans?"

Nick did not respond at first, almost seemed to not hear the question, so preoccupied with the birds at his feeder in the backyard.

"Git hold of that private eye you said was snooping around about the dead State cop...the one you said made contact with the Mexican. Let's talk to him...he can negotiate for us since he knows them. Have Allie and Tony ask him to meet with you. You say Jackie is not happy. I'll bet not. I'll call him, let him scream at me."

21.

The persistent call of a mourning dove pulled at Clayton Meredith as he resisted getting out of bed to face the day. He had struggled with facing the day ever since he came home to Quincy, Illinois, a week earlier. He had been mustered out from Fort Bragg after two tours of duty, six years that, for him, were boring and restrictive. He didn't know what he wanted to do, but he did know he did not want to be in the Army. At Bragg he had never quite been able to be military, accept the regimen, function under constant authority, and perform the little daily tasks necessary to avoid criticism from other Joes and his sergeant. He chafed under the direction he thought was nagging, just damn nagging about stuff that didn't matter. He realized once he got home that here was more nagging. Different words, but still nagging. His mother asked him to clean up the kitchen after he made breakfast. His father asked whether he was looking for work. As he listened to the mourning dove, he also heard that as nagging. Nagging him to get up.

Clayton stood on the back porch drinking a cup of the coffee from the pot his mother left for him before she headed to work. The frustrations he felt were eased somewhat by the peacefulness of the backyard that was so familiar to him. He sat down in one of the wicker chairs, propped his legs on the railing, and absorbed the scene before him. It was so quiet he thought he could almost hear the pulse of the Mississippi River that surged in the distance. He remembered standing on the riverbank when he was younger, sensing the power that moved by, a steady rhythm of flowing water, a faint whisper, a mystical quality that hardly foretold the danger of its increased level that could flood and destroy. He missed seeing the river. Today was the day, he decided, to go have a look.

After breakfast of sausage and eggs, he did clean up the kitchen as his mother requested, grabbed the car keys from the table as he wiped away the crumbs and spilled coffee. There was only one car in this household, which his mother usually took to her job downtown at Bettman Insurance. She had gotten a ride to her job from another woman in the office so Clayton could have the car to look for work. His father had, for several years, been riding with his best friend and coworker to Schmidt's metal shop where he was a welder. The arrangement began when his father's '62 GMC pickup finally threw a rod. The rod and the rust signaled its end. Another truck was considered, but the arrangement with the friend seemed all right.

Clayton carefully backed the two year old Buick LeSabre from the garage. The family car had been assigned to him so that he could job hunt and in that lofty role he did not want something to happen to the car. That would surely be another source of nagging. His parents expected him get work, already had expressed concern over his lack of finding anything. They did not know that he hadn't even looked, not even checked the newspaper want ads. Damn, it's only been a week, he thought, here they are nagging me about it. But he had not yet checked in with his old friends, several of whom he had stayed in contact with while he was away. They had gotten together when he had been home on leave, yet he had not called them. He was preoccupied, wondering what he would do for a job, and worse, frustrated by the knowledge of the stealing at Bragg. Knowledge that really nagged at him.

Being by the river gave him little satisfaction or relief and he was disappointed in his reaction to its impact, so minimal on him. He sniffed at the river smells, hoping for an uplifting balm to come his way, an odor of comfort, a signal that he would be secure now that he had returned home. It was not given, that sign of okayness, that message from some unseen spirit of the river who could push away whatever might spoil his life. He was on his own and he knew it. He sniffed again, turned to walk back to the car, the simplicity of it all drawn upon him in a way that made him shudder slightly as if a cool wind had passed over him. He got in the Buick and drove away, satisfied that the river would never yield an answer to him that was not already there within him. He headed back to Tighe Construction.

Clayton had passed by Tighe on his way to the river, noticed the big sign out front that advertised for workers. Employment at Tighe, the largest construction company in the area was now a possibility. They needed workers. He figured this was a place where he could find a job.

There was a trailer out front of the main office, a crude sign noting its purpose: Now hiring. He went inside and was quickly shown to Mr. Pierce. There was no one waiting.

"Been in the Army?

Yessir."

Handle responsibility?

"Yessir."

"Take direction?"

"Yessir."

Be dependable...come to work every day?"

"Yessir, I can do that."

"Yer hired. Fill out these forms over here with this lady...she'll help you, get you squared away.'

"Thank you sir."

The man disappeared and his life was directed by an efficient young woman who handled all of the paperwork necessary to get the hiring process completed. She punched all of the required information into a computer, smiling seductively to him all the while she managed her tasks. She thanked him and told him he was now an employee of Tighe Construction.

"Report for work right here next Monday," she cautioned. She handed him her business card. "Here's my card. If you have any questions call me...I put my home phone number on it so you could contact me if you need to...for any questions you might have."

Back in his car, he looked at her card and smiled, pleased with the young woman's obvious display of interest in him. Maybe the river had given him something after all. He decided to call Jack Brier, the best friend he had in Quincy, a man he could have a beer with, someone to reconnect with in the right way. He put her card in his pocket.

Clayton's mother was ecstatic over the news of the job. She complemented him on being so industrious, so dutiful in getting this employment.

"Clayton, we'll help you buy a car if you need us to...we can do that."

"No, thanks, mom. I can handle it. Besides, I might be able to get a ride over there like dad does to the shop. Somebody must go by here to get to Tighe. We'll see. Not necessary right away, I guess. Can I use the car tonight?"

Jack was there at Shorty's with some of the old friends. They drank beer and swapped stories, the others talking way more than Clayton. They asked him questions about the Army, but he didn't have much to say, at least not much that he could tell them. As the mindless conversation about sports and girls droned on, he resolved what he was going to do about what he knew at Bragg.

Clayton was awake early the next morning, but stayed in bed until his parents had gone to work. Too nervous to eat breakfast, he sipped at his coffee on the back porch waiting until after nine o'clock. He sat with the phone book in his lap, trying to figure out who to call, finally deciding on the

FBI in Springfield. His assertions about Bragg were registered with one of the agents who listened calmly, who arranged to drive over to Quincy that afternoon. They would meet at the McDonald's on the east side. Clayton did not want them coming to the house, didn't want anyone to know what he was doing.

When the agent pulled into the McDonald's parking lot, he saw the rugged looking young man standing by the dark blue Buick, arms folded, sunglasses, a ball cap with the beak perfectly curled and pulled down somewhat to shield his face. He knew that was his man.

The agent parked his car down the row and walked back to the man by the Buick. "Clayton Meredith?" he asked casually as he approached.

"Yessir."

"Come on, I'll buy you a cup of coffee."

"A Coke would be better, sir."

"You got it."

The agent, a pleasant looking man in his late thirties, listened attentively, systematically took notes on a yellow legal pad as Clayton offered what he knew. It wasn't much of a story, but the agent understood the potential significance of what the young man was telling him even though he could not help wondering how true the information might be. Truth was always in question when seemingly outlandish information is offered to the Bureau. On the other hand, he reasoned, there was a standing armory alert in force at the Springfield office that meant keeping tabs on the Army Reserve unit. Plus, he remembered hearing about the problem of materiel disappearing from some Army bases, with Clayton's former base Ft. Bragg being one of them. So, he dutifully noted everything Clayton spoke about, and asked a question here and there for clarification.

"...and this one sergeant was in charge of moving stuff?"

"Yessir."

"Hanlin?" the agent confirmed.

"Yessir. Daryl Hanlin."

Clayton had gotten what he knew off his chest and he felt better for it. He had learned quite by accident of what Daryl and some other Joes had been doing and it had bothered him, festered at him for some time. He had wanted to let the command at Bragg know, but could not forge the courage to tell someone while he was still there on base. Now, it was out of him, he could relax somewhat, but, deep down, he still felt uncomfortable with the circumstances of what he had not done and also with what he had done in being an informer. He hoped his thoughts about it would go away. Somehow, he knew they would not soon fade.

Five days later, the ATF unit assigned to Ft. Bragg received the information Clayton Meredith had provided, including the name of Daryl Hanlin. The message was delivered in person by the FBI agent in charge, whose own unit would be again working in conjunction with the ATF to conduct surveillance and to eventually round up all of the suspects. First they wanted to watch Hanlin, then they wanted to pounce.

Daryl went about his routines, oblivious at first to the fact he was being watched. It was during the second week of surveillance that he noticed something. Although he wasn't sure of what it was that bothered him, he went on personal alert, already overflowing from the paranoia that wrenches at those not used to breaking the law. He watched as he drove to and from work, checked from the window of his office, mindful of those around him at the super market, noticed who was near, who might be observing, aware, always aware wherever he went, whatever he did.

No good for Dorothy to know right now what his fears were, what his instinct had brought to him, he figured. She'd be skittish and scared, let 'em know we're on alert by the way she acted afraid, the way she would be nervous and unsettled away from normal behavior. Sorry she even knows, wish I coulda kept her out of this deal. He had often looked at her knowing full well she did not understand the impact of what he was doing to get the extra money. So easy, so dangerous. He should have worked out the arrangement without telling her, having some explanation for being able to have a new truck. Too late now, he decided.

It finally dawned on him that the image setting off an alarm in his head was a face. A stranger, obviously not a Joe, a man, a strange face at two different locations: at the Cross Creek mall and the Exxon gas station. Both times he caught the man looking at him in a deliberate way, averting his eyes when realizing Daryl noticed him. All so subtle and potentially coincidental, but so meaningful within the paranoid alertness that kept Daryl on the ready. He was being watched, he was firmly convinced. Now what?

Daryl stood at his desk absorbing the realization that had slowly come over him. The operation was over, there would be no more orders, there would be no more easy money slipped into his hands. His face and neck reddened from the self-imposed embarrassment of getting caught, even though he was not caught, just being observed. Stupid, stupid, stupid...shit, how did I ever think I could keep doing it without something happening? Stealing...a thief...what would his mother think of her boy now?

The wonderful training that Daryl had received from the military had conditioned him to stay cool, to keep the wild ride of panic from taking place. This was simply an adversarial point in the operation that necessitated a change in plans. There were ten blocks of C-4 left under his house that he would have to get back inside or get rid of in some way. He knew that if Bragg security or the FBI came to the house they would tear it apart until they found the stuff. He also knew he needed to let Ned Byron know what was happening. If he tried to trigger the communication with Byron at an off base pay phone he would be watched. He didn't want to signal that alert, so he decided to chance making the call from the phone the Joes use at the other end of the building. His message to Byron was to call the number of that phone in two hours. It was not the usual triggering message, so he knew that Byron would know something was wrong. He went back two hours later and booted the grunt off the phone who was there talking. It rang at the appointed time.

"Someone on to you?" Byron asked calmly.

"You got it," Daryl replied.

"Thanks for the warning. Business concluded. Don't let 'em take you alive." Byron laughed. "Just kidding."

The phone line clicked dead. His arrangement with Mr. Byron was over. He now had to try to survive.

Dorothy knew something was wrong the second Daryl came through the side door. Over the years she had developed a sense for when it had been a bad day for him, attuned to an energy that seemed to precede his entrance. Her sense was reinforced by his body language, his tone of voice - if he even spoke - and the way he pulled at the laces to take off his boots. The signs were all there for her and she read them well. On this day, the intensity of his silent arrival could hardly have been missed even by one not dialed in to his moods. She guessed what the awful news would be. Her husband's pact with some unknown man created a shadow of fear that had clutched at her daily since it was arranged.

He nodded as he went straight to the frig to grab a beer. The unspoken admission was a stunning blow to their life. The ugliness of the unknown had come to them, the unknown of what happened if they were caught, the unknown of punishment that could take away everything.

Daryl could not look at Dorothy when he spoke.

"Get some things packed...I'm taking you to Massey's. I don't want you here while I get things sorted out."

He did not want her around while he figured out what to do with the plastic. He did not want her around when they came for him. He did not want her or the kids to see him get arrested. He did not want her near if there were shooting. There could be shooting. 'Don't let 'em take you alive,' Byron had said. He had said he was kidding, but it was no joke to Daryl. It probably was the way to go.

"I want to be here with you. I..."

She did not know how to finish what to say, to express what she felt. She did not want to reveal the black dread she now sensed about him, to speak the unspeakable for fear it would become reality, to uncover the abject fear that gripped her.

"No...no, you can't...it's the kids...it's the whole thing...you...everything. It's gotta be me here, just me to deal with it. You go to Massey's. They're good friends...they won't ask questions, they'll just help out. Stay there till I call. Get some stuff packed...toys, a few days clothes...you know what they need...what you need. Get goin'. I want you over there as soon as possible."

He knew their time was precious, but he didn't want to show it. He knew he might never see them again, it was as bad as going to jump action, going to combat. This could be much worse than jumping from a plane into a war zone. It could be much worse. He would be detached from the emotion of it, separated from feeling the coming separation, away from himself, a cardboard cutout for Dorothy to see. No dimension of depth, therefore no dimension of emotion. He would suspend belief that it could go wrong, he would act as if nothing unusual were happening, he would use his own calmness as a message to guide her. She would be okay.

"All right," she said and turned to the task.

He got them in the truck, put the three suitcases in back, and drove them to Massey's. It was a silent ride and when they arrived Cara Massey said nothing, simply motioning them into the house. She knew something was wrong, all answers would come later. Daryl kissed Dorothy, hugged the kids, and got back in the truck. This somber, surreal experience was excruciating for Daryl, confounded by trying to figure what he could do to salvage their life, angry with himself, frustrated and disgusted with his position in the system, his temperament now like a very tight piano wire in his consideration of what he might do to solve his problem. Turning himself in was not one of his considered options. He would react rather than act. Let's see what they do, he decided.

The attack force comprised of Bragg security, ATF officers, and FBI agents was still in the process of setting up around Daryl's house while the search of the house was just beginning when he turned the corner to the street where he lived. The task force command officer had been alerted Daryl and family had left. It was an opportunity to search while they were gone. He was told Daryl was on his way back. Daryl's quick return still caught them not totally organized. Not everyone part of the task force had arrived at the same time, so all did not have information about Daryl's going and coming.

The scenario was all too clear to Daryl as he rounded the corner. Cars, vans, men, weapons, jackets with ATF and FBI on them, all scrambled in a vision of fear that fired off automatic responses within him. Tromping on the accelerator, he pulled the .45 caliber automatic from under his seat, released the safety and cocked it as he steered with his forearms, and tried to race by his own house.

The quickness and audacity of his action startled those on the team still getting into place in his front yard, and the neighbors on either side and across the street. A Bragg security sergeant reacted first, not losing his composure much from Daryl's charge, fired his M-16 first at the truck's engine and front tires, and into the cab as the truck raced by him down the street. Both front tires were shredded within seconds and the engine lost power very quickly thereafter. The truck continued from the momentum of its burst of speed for another two hundred or so feet before careening into a yard where it was stopped by a large pine tree.

Two slugs from the security sergeant's weapon had reached Daryl. When he opened the door to get out, he fell headlong onto the ground. The .45 automatic he had grabbed with every intention of defending himself had already fallen to the floor of the truck. His face was in the sand, so he struggled to roll on his side in order to see his truck, now hissing from the pangs of being overheated, fluid of all kinds spilling out, the image of bullet holes popped through its lovely sheet metal.

He would not die, but there would be no more ordering from Daryl.

22.

The still morning air carried a trace of nighttime coolness when Butch first pushed off on his road bike, intent on the fifty miles or so that he wanted to cover for the day's workout. Normally, he would have started late afternoon, beyond the end of his work day, when he was satisfied he had enough of the office. An early riser, he figured that after 3:00 o'clock it was time to get at his training regimen. Today, however, he opted for the morning. He had agreed to meet Pam for dinner, so there would not be enough time to workout and also get together with her.

For Butch, Pam had become a curiosity. She had gone from being a potential problem for him by possibly hitting on him, to getting involved with a Mexican drug dealer. It had happened right in front of him and he almost could not believe what had occurred. No one knows the answers to these things, he assured himself. Yesterday, she called to ask him to have dinner with her and he had said yes, even though he would rather have declined. She was persuasive, teasing him some, appealing to their friendship once again. She wants to tell me something, he figured, probably something I won't like or would take issue with on principle.

The morning was heating up, but Butch stayed relatively cool for the first ten miles by merely moving quickly through the air. The wind he created slipped through the vents in his helmet and washed across his skin, a soothing balm to ease the temperature rise his body was generating from the effort. He headed west on little used country roads, moving by the acres upon acres of corn and soy beans. Experience with crop layout in this part of the countryside allowed him to select a route mostly through soybean planting, although the corn and soybeans were heavily interspersed. Corn was now reaching eight feet tall in many fields, which posed a problem for sighting cross traffic at the road intersections. The tall corn made the intersections blind where they grew close to the corners, so without a stop sign, Butch had to slow down to make sure he didn't get clipped by a car or truck coming through. Even with a stop sign it could be dangerous. The low lying soybeans, on the other hand, gave him full view of what vehicle might be heading for him.

Butch enjoyed these training rides through the farmland as he passed by the well tended houses and yards which were little islands in a sea of endless green. It was a peaceful time for him, seldom encountering traffic, occasionally meeting another biker, a solitary journey of commitment to staying tuned for competition. Part of that commitment was to knock out fifty miles of biking every couple of days, in between days of running, working with weights, or doing laps at his health club pool.

He had casually thought about working out for triathlon events before Cindy's death, but once she was gone, he had thrown himself into training for competition with a vengeance. The training was a way to escape from the pain of losing her, the discipline it required a way to keep from thinking about her all the time, a way to protect himself and yet selectively secure her memory. Each time he entered a triathlon, it was a dedication to Cindy, it was for him a reaffirmation of the bond the two of them once felt.

The track Butch traveled - twenty five miles out, twenty five miles back - ordinarily took him less than three hours without really pushing himself. He did it non-stop, drinking from the water bottle he kept on the frame cage, a bottle filled with his own hydration and juice concoction. With about five miles to go on the way back, he began to push himself, gradually bringing up his speed, intensifying his concentration, being less aware of his surroundings, charging for home as if he were closing a race. It was a ritual for him to do this, to get a vision of pressing and being pressed, of needing the acceleration in the final miles to make the trip worthwhile. It was a sense of pride to be able to make such an extended dash, a pleasure that exhilarated him. He was immersed in faux competition with himself and the phantom bikers. He was lost in the grip of exertion and the winning of some unknown prize.

Under these circumstances, it was relatively easy for the Frangeletti limousine to quietly cruise up behind him without being noticed by Butch, so intent on his rush to victory. The black Cadillac eased alongside, carefully matching Butch's accelerated pace, until its nose came into view of his peripheral vision. So deep was he into the Zen experience of his dash home, that, at first, he did not react to the black mass he perceived to his left. The limo inched forward until the passenger side window was even with Butch. It finally registered with him that this car was pacing with him, close to him, yet with enough size to hang over the yellow line. The traffic was increasing as they approached Perrysburg, so that there were more oncoming cars for the limo to contend with as it stayed alongside. A van, followed by a truck, honked at the limo to clear back on its own side of the yellow line.

Butch snuck a quick look to see who was driving the damn limo, but the darkly tinted glass kept him from seeing anyone. He assumed that whoever was driving was being cautious while getting by him. They would get by quickly, he thought, making sure he was as far right on the road as he could be and still maintain a safety margin, letting off the speed slightly so the limo would go by. When he slowed, the limo slowed, and moved even closer to him. Goddamnit, Butch thought, stay over, get that thing... It clicked: they wanted him. Frangeletti guys, he thought, probably the goddamn Frangelettis. Shit. What the hell do they want?

The limo began the process of squeezing Butch to stop by limiting the amount of road he had to work with, forcing him to slow, to finally stop completely. The window on the passenger side came down.

"We'd like to give you a ride," the man said with a smile. "The bike goes in the trunk."

Butch did not argue. Two good reasons to go along, he thought as he rode in the limo's plush rear seat, enjoying the air conditioning, delighted to let his sweat soaked body settle in, relishing the wet mess his sweat was making on the fine custom leather upholstering. First of all, I can't overpower these guys, and, second, I'm curious what the Frangelettis want. Their contact with him was not entirely unexpected. They know what is going on...they know I've had contact with the Mexicans. Considering what has been going on between these guys, I figured they might touch base. What do they want? It will be interesting to find out.

The drive to Ottawa Hills took no more than twenty minutes. The Frangeletti driver paid little attention to speed limits and voided the impact of stop signs and traffic lights where no other cars were present. This is like driving in Rome or Paris, Butch thought, no one follows the rules there either. When the limo entered the wealthy village of Ottawa Hills, the noticeable change in upscale houses would be quite obvious to even the casual observer. This was one of the most affluent areas in northwestern Ohio and the Frangeletti estate was in its midst. The irony of the Frangelettis living amid the rich and powerful of the city was not lost on Butch. The Frangelettis were rich and he conceded to himself that they had their own kind of power. The volume of their riches allowed the Frangeletti family to reach into political and business recesses, that might otherwise be inaccessible, in order to leverage and extend their power. Money bought them privilege, protection, and position through patronage. It sure helps to have lots of money, Butch concluded.

The process of picking Butch up and bringing him to Nick's house was not a strong arm event. It had been conducted dispassionately and politely. There was an unstated assumption on both sides - by the Frangeletti guys and by Butch - that he would get in the car and come with them without resisting, without complaining, as a willing participant in the exercise they had been directed to perform by Nick.

Butch marveled at the drive up to the house that covered more property than most people in the city owned, curving gracefully through the green, meticulously tended front lawn to the cobblestone parking area before the huge entry. The entry was highlighted by solid teak doors, handsomely carved with a vineyard motif showing vines and leaves, a few baubles of grapes, exquisitely represented in fine detail.

He was led through the house to the back sun parlor where Nick greeted him with an almost courtly, yet strange wave of the hand.

"Have a seat right here, Mr. Greiner," Nick offered, without rising from the stuffed chair where he was resting. "I'm Nick Frangeletti...in case you wanted to know. Would you like something...an iced tea...beer? I know you've been out exercising...you must be thirsty."

"Thanks...water will do...I know who you are."

"Yeah, most people do. I want to thank you for coming over, Mr. Greiner," Nick went on, completely ignoring the fact his boys had brought Butch there with implied force. "We need to talk."

"There's always the phone...even if its just for the invitation part...you know, ask me to come by, see what my schedule is, check to see when I'm available...you know...stuff like that...the way things are normally done. Anyway, 'we' don't need to talk...you might, but 'we' don't."

Nick was in the process of lighting a fresh cigar as Butch spoke, seemingly ignoring the jab Butch had given him. He savored the first few puffs before he spoke, carefully blowing the smoke at the nearby window, fascinated with the way it wafted against the glass and bounced into oblivion.

"Birds probably don't like that smell," he said absently, "probably kill 'em just like us. Would you like a cigar, Mr. Greiner?"

"No...no thanks. Don't smoke."

"Thought not...thought I'd ask..."

"What is it you want?" Butch pressed the old man with growing impatience that was prodded by his physical discomfort. He had ridden himself into a sweat over nearly fifty miles of biking, only to be subjected to the quick change of air conditioning with no time to stretch or cool down. "It's too damn cold in here...besides, I've got a busy day ahead of me."

"Get the man a bathrobe," Nick ordered.

At that moment, Nicky entered the room, making his presence known with a greeting to his father. "Pop, how's it goin'?"

Again, Nick gave the courtly wave, this time with a slight smile.

"We just started talking. Good timing for you...you can deal with Mr. Greiner. He seems a little pissed that he's here for a conversation...says it's us who need to talk not him"

Nicky nodded, took the cup of coffee offered to him, and addressed Butch who was putting on the robe one of the men brought to him.

"Do you know who this is?" Nicky pointed at his father, nearly exploding from anger at the affront Butch gave them. "Do you know who this is?" he repeated.

"Yes, I do, Nicky...and I don't give a shit, so back off, calm down, or we won't get anyplace. Is that clear?"

Nick chuckled as he blew more cigar smoke at the window, while Nicky turned his back on Butch. After a long pause, he turned back to Butch.

"Look, Greiner...we know you been talkin' to the Mexicans. We need you to do something for us."

"I've talked to one Mexican...hardly by choice...almost by accident, in fact..."

"A key guy..."

"I don't know..."

"Yeah, a key guy. We want you to talk to the key guy again. That would help us out."

"And say what?"

"The Mexicans took something of ours and we want it back. We want you to tell them to give it back to us."

"Why don't you ask them yourself?"

"Listen," Nicky said sharply. He had never sat down since he arrived and was now pacing the floor. "We don't have a contact point...a number, besides its awkward...very awkward...they also owe us money they promised for sinking our boat, but what we want is something they stole...outright stole from us."

"What is it?" Butch asked impatiently.

"You don't need to know...they'll know what yer talkin' about when you ask them to return to us what they stole..."

Butch started to laugh. "You think they'll give something back to you just because I ask them for it...for you...are you serious? What the hell is it?"

"You don't need to know..."

"Well maybe you ought to take care of your own damn problem."

"Mr. Greiner," Nick said, as he inserted himself back into the dialog, "we have a special situation to deal with...it's awkward...unpleasant. Not in our best interests to be seen chatting with the Mexicans...by any of the Feds that are prowling around right now...all kinds...FBI...drug guys.

They're always nosy, always checking us out, but...but there seems to be an increase in activity. Our sources tell us to be very careful. We don't want to go directly to the Mexicans. We need you to carry the message...make the request for the return of our stuff."

"Well, you're going to have to tell me what it is, what's involved if you want me to do something for you...I want to know what I'm getting into. Put yourself in my place - you wouldn't want to fly blind would you? No...hell no...you'd want to know what was in the cards...what you might be up against and how to deal with the other guys...what they might say, how you'd have to respond, what you might expect from..."

"Okay, okay, we get yer point." Nicky was back in the conversation. He looked at Nick for the nod of approval that was given ever so slowly, the quiet reverie of cigar smoke wisps circling the old man's face.

"We have a client," Nicky began, "who placed an order with us for some plastic explosives. As you can imagine he is very anxious...very anxious to get his hands on the stuff. He had reason to believe that we could deliver and we could. So we placed an order with our supplier. Next thing you know, the truck carrying the stuff is jacked by the Mexicans and now they have our stuff. We need that stuff, since we lost our source...that's right, the source dried up...the stuff comin' to us was the last from that supplier. Now, our client is crazy mad...he wants that plastic...he paid for it...he wants it. He can cause big trouble...big trouble, even to us. Like queer everything with the Feds. The slightest thing right now and the Feds will be all over us. We need our stuff back. We need you to talk to the Mexicans...get them to give it back. They owe us, they gotta give it back."

"They're Mexicans," Butch said, "not easy to deal with, I would guess...the Padillo guys."

Butch was churning inside with what he had just learned, struggling to keep calm, careful to not seem too eager to be of service. So, it was the Frangelettis who ordered the plastics. Wonder how the Mexicans knew what truck to hit?

"Who cares what they are...we want our stuff back...that's what matters." Nicky still had not sat down, continuing to pace the room.

"I don't work for free, Nicky, I get a thousand dollars a day for short assignments, longer projects get negotiated."

"Big deal," Nicky scoffed as he pulled a gold money clip from his pocket and peeled off ten one hundred dollar bills. He dropped the grand in Butch's lap. "Here's a start...let us know how much more for gettin' it done."

"I didn't say I'd do it."

"Sure you did...when you named yer price. When you name a price that means yes...otherwise there's no point in saying what yer rate is...that's the way it works."

"Really? Never heard that one."

"Yeah, really. That's the way it works for me. So...anyway...this thing needs to get done right away...the boys will take you back to yer place...get on it today. We need to get an answer from the Mexicans by tomorrow. We need to know what they're thinkin'.

Butch stood up knowing he had been dismissed. There was no point in arguing with Nicky. He had resisted enough, knowing full well that the Frangelettis were used to getting their own way, used to giving orders that got carried out without back talk, so he might as well take the money and give it a try with the Mexicans...with Cuzo, anyway. He tucked the hundred dollar bills under the elastic waistband of his pocketless cycling shorts and started to take off the bathrobe as he headed for the door.

"Naw, keep it...you'll need it with the AC in the car." Nicky handed Butch a business card. "Call me at that number tomorrow. Just tell me when we can meet...don't say anything else...anything about what yer doin'. Got it?"

Butch nodded yes as he thought to himself how much Simmons at ATF will be interested in what was going on with the plastic explosives that had come to Ohio. That would be his first report even before he tried to contact Cuzo. In fact, Cuzo would not matter until he had also called Connelly at the FBI. He would be the Frangeletti messenger and question asker, all right, but there was no way he would not make sure the Feds would be able to give them some grief. Just as he exited the room, he looked back to see Nick, slouched in his chair, still blowing smoke at the window.

23.

The quiet, well established neighborhood where Butch lived was upscale without being pretentious, well cared for without being overdone, a place where young professionals liked the feeling of genteel community they helped to inspire. Maple, oak, and beech trees lined the streets like so many maids-in-waiting, seeing the hard-working professionals off to work, welcoming them home in the evening, staunch and erect in salute for the daily effort they witnessed. This was a neighborhood for raising children, hosting backyard barbecues for friends, knowing and even caring about your neighbors, and for enjoying a good life. The neighborhood intensified Cindy's loss for Butch and he had made a mental note to look for another place, but had been too busy to act on his impulse to leave here.

Cuzo sat nervously waiting in his parked car a block from Butch's house, carefully scanning his surroundings, seeming to consult a three ring binder he held conspicuously upon the steering wheel. He knew that he could not wait too long or he would attract attention in this neighborhood. Already, a man in the yard across the way had looked him over. He was using the binder to make it appear he was in real estate or making an inspection of some kind. If he stayed there beyond a time that would seem normal, someone might call the cops. He was hoping his timing was good. He knew where Butch was and wanted to be there when Butch returned.

As the Frangeletti limo closed in on Butch, Cuzo had been a patient observer, knowing full well whose vehicle it was. He had spotted the limo trailing the bike as he was headed for Butch's house. Pam had told him where Butch lived. It was time to talk, Cuzo figured, and Butch's house might be the best place. It had still been early when Cuzo first tried to reach Butch by phone, but all he got was the answering machine at his office. He thought Butch might still be at his house and decided to go unannounced to see if he could catch him there. When Cuzo witnessed the Frangelettis nab Butch, he knew they would take him someplace, talk, bring him back to his house. A routine maneuver, he figured, one that would get them back about eleven. From ten thirty on, Cuzo was in Butch's neighborhood, cruising, trying to act as if he were looking for an address, hoping he wouldn't be noticed. Eventually, Cuzo made the decision to park in the next block, down from Butch's, consult his binder, try to look as if he belonged there, act as if he were engrossed in something, concentrate on looking busy, and ignore the man who had looked at him from the yard across the way.

His pretense of someone in real estate probably worked. The man who had checked him out went on about his own business and no one else noticed him, at least that he could view. Cuzo had been in the pretend mode for less than five minutes when he saw the limo pull up in front of Butch's house. His timing had been quite good.

Once the limo had deposited Butch and his bike and had disappeared, Cuzo drove to the house, slowly pulled into the driveway. Butch was still in the living room with his bike when Cuzo rang the door bell.

"Holá, señor," Butch said, laughing, "just the man I want to see. Saves me making a phone call...waiting for you to make up your mind to answer back. What gives?"

"We need to talk," Cuzo answered, ignoring Butch's comments, "can I come in?"

Butch opened the screen door to let Cuzo enter, puzzled by the high degree of tension that came from the man. It was a different kind of tension than before, more like a lot of anxiety, Butch thought. Before, he was tense, but a tension that came from his combative nature, not where he was nervous about something. He is very nervous. Something is wrong.

"Is Pam all right?" Butch asked.

"Yes...yes, she's fine...wants to talk to you, but she's fine...she's okay. I..."

Butch waited for Cuzo to continue. There was the ticking of a wall clock in the background, birds chirping with random notes of activity, but Cuzo was silent in the midst of a very long pause while he reckoned with what he wanted to say, should reveal.

"...she's going to do well...," Cuzo finally went on, "we're going to do well. We'll probably be leaving...not a good situation here with the Frangelettis.

"She's meeting me for dinner tonight."

"Yes."

"What's your story? You had a reason to come calling. What's wrong? What do you need? Let me have it...then I'll tell you what I need...the message. Have a seat."

Cuzo sat down in the large black leather chair near the front window. From there he could view the street in front of the house. He was always on guard, on alert for the next move from the Frangelettis.

"Want a beer? Soda?"

"No...thanks."

"Well? You first...lay it on me. You are here with a purpose...spell it out."

"I had a purpose to head me here...to find out what you knew...to find out how bad it is with the Frangelettis...or the Feds...if you would tell me. Probably not. Seeing you with the Frangelettis changed everything around. They wanted you...wanted you to do something for them is my guess. Now, it doesn't make any difference what I wanted..."

"How's that?" Butch interjected.

"Because once you meet with them, what they want and what your own purpose is...they become more important than what I want to know. And what I want to know maybe doesn't matter because of what you want."

"You're talking in circles," Butch laughed.

"You know what I mean, even if I am talking round and round. The point is: you want something...it is bigger for you than what I want."

"The Frangelettis asked me to be their messenger...to you, to the crowd you're involved with..."

"By threat...they threatened you?"

"No. No direct threat. With those guys, however, you always get the idea that there's some kind of danger behind a request they have. Just a sense, not really what they say. Besides, they paid me my day rate to talk to you."

"What do they want?"

"They want their stuff back."

Butch was curious to see what, if any, kind of reaction he would get from Cuzo when he dropped the message from the Frangelettis on him, but only the slightest movement came to the Mexican's lips as if he were about to quickly respond, but held himself in check. He blinked once, a second time, before he replied. Cuzo prided himself in control of his reactions, limiting someone's ability to read what he was thinking. Butch marveled at how the man stayed calm.

"What stuff is that?"

Butch laughed at Cuzo in a raucous way that was meant to be derisive and was clearly so to any observer, including Cuzo himself. He felt the sting of the laugh, but still did not react outwardly.

"I'm having a beer, sure you don't want something?"

"Yeah, I'll take a beer."

Butch went to the kitchen and pulled two bottles of Mexican Bohemia beer from the refrigerator, popping off the tops with two quick snaps of the opener.

"You'll like this one, I think," Butch called from the kitchen as he retrieved the beers.

Butch handed a bottle to Cuzo, who looked casually at the label, but made no comment, not even thanks, as he merely nodded in acceptance of the drink.

"We can play cat and mouse for a long time," Butch said, "I am getting paid a day rate. Keep screwing around, it just runs my bill up."

In truth, Butch had not expected Cuzo to just spill his guts right away simply because the subject had been broached to him. No, it would be a process with the man, the slow dance to reality, the level of meaning that would be true communications between the two men, a closing of the gap, Butch thought, the culture gap that makes Cuzo wary of everyone, especially an Anglo, even when he knows he should play it straight. If I spoke Spanish it would not matter. I am not from within his world and outside his world is mainly the enemy. But he will get to it, eventually.

"What did they tell you," Cuzo finally asked after several minutes of silence and several slugs of the Bohemia, "the Frangelettis...what did they say about us?"

"They said you guys hijacked one of their trucks...said there were plastic explosives on the truck and you guys now have it...their stuff. They want their stuff back. They wanted me to ask you for their stuff back...fast. Seems they have a customer for that stuff and they need to make delivery soon, real soon. Quite nervous about it, I think, but they are very serious. They want it back tomorrow. Tomorrow as in tomorrow, not tomorrow as a manner of speech. You guys are already in big trouble with the Frangelettis, why would you hijack their truck when you know they're going to be on your ass big time?"

Cuzo took another swallow from the Bohemia, exhaled a huge sigh, and leaned his head back onto the leather chair. He stared at the ceiling.

"How do they know we took their truck...?"

"Mexicans...Mexicans did it...they say Mexicans did it. How many Mexican gangs have the balls to steal from the Frangelettis? Don't be cute. They know, just like you knew who stuck Jerry. You didn't see it actually happen, but you knew. They didn't see you do it, but they know. You know damn well that's how things work...everything is not witnessed to be understood and known."

Cuzo was now struggling within himself for answers, for how to proceed with this issue. Of course the plastic could be gotten in one day, but he had to stall for time, time to think, time to consult with Victor, time to plan appropriate action. They were now totally defensive to the Frangelettis because of the money for the bombed boat, the plastic. They were back pedaling when they should be retaliating for the damage to all the car washes. They needed a plan, he needed a plan for his own sense of security, protection. His considerations were several: he could deny the accusation, trying to convince Butch how absurd it would be to steal from the Frangelettis on top of everything else; he could reveal, to some extent, what had happened; he could reveal what had happened and split right away with Pam, just the two of them; he could deny and split; he could delay the inevitable by lying about the whereabouts of the plastic; and so on and so forth through a maze of action combinations. The plain white expanse of the ceiling gave him no insight or inspiration.

"How come the Frangelettis did not contact us direct?" Cuzo asked, changing the subject for diversion, to gain time in conversation while he tried to sort out his options.

"Let me guess," Butch said, placing his right forefinger to his chin, his voice gripped with sarcasm, "one reason might be that they don't want direct contact with you because the Feds are hot on your ass and they don't want to be tainted by you...what do you think of that? And how about this: they don't like you guys...you guys are beneath them and they hold you in supreme contempt. There...a couple of damn good reasons to stay clear of you when they want back what they think is rightfully theirs."

Cuzo knew that the time had come to deal with Butch in a way that would give him a chance to talk to Victor.

"Yes, of course," Cuzo responded, after several more seconds of continued staring at the ceiling, "those are two very good reasons, both probably true, although you might be able to understand that we are used to being looked down on, and even though we know we are looked down on, we hold the Frangelettis in contempt as the filth they are, filth that is covered with an Italian silk mantilla so it is difficult for others to see what slime they are." Cuzo paused again, collecting his thoughts, ready to handle Butch. "Yes, we got their truck...we got their plastic explosives. We kept the plastic, they got their truck back. We have it...we have it in a safe place...not around here. There's no way I can have it to them by tomorrow."

"If it's anywhere in Ohio you can have it to them tomorrow," Butch said, smelling the stall. "I don't know what their plan is if you don't come up with their stuff, but it won't be nice, I would guess."

"You don't understand...tomorrow is impossible...but regardless, I must talk to Victor Padillo...it is Victor who runs the show, he is boss with our counsel, but he has the final say...he must decide what happens. I must talk to him first. However, I think I can speak for Victor in some respect. We did not know the plastics were on the truck. We have no use for that stuff...it does not fit with what we do.

We would want them to have their plastics back, but it must be arranged, Victor must decide how that happens."

"Yeah, it needs to be arranged all right. When can you talk to Victor? Call him from here? Tonight? When?"

Cuzo took out his cell phone and punched in a number. "I will try to reach him now."

As he waited for the phone to be answered, he stood up, draining the last of the Bohemia as he paced the living room. Finally, there was an answer.

"Victor? Let me talk to Victor." There was another wait. "Victor...yes, yes...we have a situation...I am with Greiner now...his place...he talked to the Frangelettis and they want their stuff...the plastics...by tomorrow. That's what I told him, but he thinks I'm stalling. Yes, yes...yes." Cuzo now did not say a word for almost two minutes as he listened to Victor. "Yes, I'll be there soon."

"So?" Butch posed.

"I will call you tomorrow morning...I will tell you what is arranged. That is the best I can do right now. You can tell the Frangelettis that they are getting their plastics back and the million dollars we promised, but it will definitely not be tomorrow."

"They probably won't be happy..."

"They should be...they get everything they want," Cuzo fired back as he went out the front door, "I'll call you tomorrow."

With the degree of anxiety the Frangelettis had exhibited when he had talked to them, they would not react well to a delay. What kind of pressure could be on them, Butch wondered, who is it that could make them want to move so fast? Someone more ruthless than they are, he figured. That wouldn't seem likely, but it is possible.

Butch pulled out Nicky's business card to call him, before realizing he was still in his biking gear. Nicky can wait. He shaved, showered, and dressed before going back to the phone to give the man a call. There were several rings before a young woman's voice answered. She was quite business-like, professional. Butch would hardly have guessed this was a girl who liked weekend boating with the Frangeletti party. There was a minute wait until Nicky came on the line.

"Can I help you?" The girl had informed him that it was Butch on the phone, so Nicky was prepared with his best phony business behavior in case the phone were tapped, which it most probably was.

"Yes, I wanted to let you know I can't meet with you tomorrow, but I will be giving you a call in the morning to schedule a meeting for later. I..."

"Not good...not good at all. We gotta meet tomorrow...that's a must."

"It's out of my control, but I can say that it's in process...there's not going to be a problem with what you want, but scheduling needs to be confirmed."

"That is a problem."

"Sorry, that's all I can do right now. Talk to you in the morning." Butch punched off the portable phone and dropped it down onto the base.

Time to call Connelly, he figured, carefully pushing the buttons to input the FBI number. In a brief conversation, Butch arranged to meet the agent at the Holiday Inn French Quarter just off I-75.

Playing it straight with the good guys was important to Butch even though he could be critical of the ineptness and bungling that often fouled up some of their operations. Once upon a time he had lived with the foul ups first hand, had seen men lose their lives as a result, had seen careers ruined, and had felt the sting of command rebuke for someone else's screw-up. Those memories of deep frustration and anger that came from those episodes still bothered him. They were the kinds of issues that sullied an otherwise excellent reputation, they were issues not easily forgotten, that clung to a man like bad breath or body odor. He knew also that information he would give Connelly - like the story about the Frangelettis, the plastics, and the Mexicans - could be a blessing for any ongoing investigation, a gift that makes things easier. There were enough hurdles in the legal system for the good guys, let alone the elements of the investigation itself, so that anything that made the operation easier was cherished. And he was thinking selfishly, considering his own personal work now that made it important to keep in the good graces of both the FBI and the ATF. In his work he never knew when those connections would come in handy. No way had he wanted to be stonewalled by those guys, or harassed for that matter. No, it was best to be on their side, their helping hand, to be appreciated, not condemned.

24.

The spacious atrium was a pleasant enough place to wait ordinarily as it was that afternoon, a quiet haven, removed from the clamor of the traffic outside and the distractions of the confined lobby space. The brightness of recent renovation was readily apparent to Butch as he walked around the area, finally depositing himself on a couch by the far wall where he could spot anyone coming from the lobby. The usual complement of green, broad-leaf tropical plants were his companions, making the most of the filtered light available from the defused skylights high above. It wasn't long before Connelly came down the corridor to the atrium, toting a cumbersome looking briefcase, faced flushed with excitement. Perspiration in large beads clung to his temples as if they were artificial and had been glued to his head. As he got closer, several of the sweat beads revealed that they were real by breaking into little rivers of moisture that ran down to his neck. He was the victim of stress that nearly consumed him.

Connelly smiled through the countenance of anguish, a toothy smile in quiet contradiction to his apparent suffering. He tossed the odd looking satchel onto the couch and stood before Butch, hands on hips. Whatever his anxiety, whatever it was making him sweat so much, he was a man pleased with himself or at least satisfied with some situation in his life. He pulled an intricately designed handkerchief from the inside left pocket of his suit coat, carefully wiped his face, and deliberately folded and re-pocketed the cloth.

"You lose about thirty pounds and you wouldn't sweat so on a day like this," Butch offered. "Surprised the Bureau doesn't get you on a weight loss regimen. You couldn't run after a suspect if your life depended on it."

"I'm within limits," he wheezed, the sweat still running, the redness still pulsing in his cheeks and neck, his brow almost matching.

"Bunk...you are way beyond the limits. Sit down here before you fall down."

"Not likely to fall down," he said, easing himself onto the couch next to Butch. "This does feel good, however, very good after the kind of day I've had."

"What's up?"

"Lots...but let's hear what you've got for me...you called...you must have had something...must have stumbled onto something...like I thought you would. I told the guys...that Greiner...he keeps messing with the Mexicans and the wops and he'll fall into something for us. I told 'em. Told Simmons at ATF...told Hargrove at DEA...Greiner would get to something eventually. Whaddaya got?"

"Big deal for Simmons, but I wanted to get to you first...thought you could pass it on. After all, you're the senior guy in this thing, you're the guy who will make things happen. I guess I felt more comfortable giving you what I know rather than the others. Certain comfort zone...trust, maybe..."

Butch was carefully posing his words, knowing full well it was the FBI he wanted to be close to, to have trust in him. The others, the ATF, the DEA were merely offshoot organizations far removed from his mindset and experience. It was the FBI he was most familiar with, the others were renegades as far as he was concerned. The DEA and the ATF were both subservient to the FBI, so for Butch, the FBI role, their specter in his business was most important.

"What did you get?"

"The Frangelettis have hired me to talk to the Mexicans to ask them to give back a batch of plastics the Mexicans hijacked from them."

"No shit? From Ft. Bragg?"

"I have no idea. I talked to the Mexicans...one Mexican...his name is Cuzo...Cuzo Mosca...he's not the leader, Victor Pad..."

"Yeah, yeah, we know. What did Mosca say when you delivered the message?"

"Said they'd give it back, but he had to work it out with Padillo. Said also that they would give the million bucks for the boat they fired."

"What was the deal? Why have you carry the message instead of making contact with the Mexicans, asking for their stuff?"

"They were afraid you might be watching or listening and find out. Didn't want to be discovered."

Connelly laughed as Butch gave the reason.

"This comes at the right time...it's uncanny..."

"How so?"

"Tomorrow, I head a task force with the DEA to raid the Padillo place out west of here. DEA has been doing their job, ready for the squeeze. We know that both the Frangelettis and the Mexicans have been dealing, but we figured it would be easier to go after the Mexicans. Not so much political flack, if you know what I mean. Going after the Mexicans...no one cares about them. On the other hand, the Frangelettis are wired. We're gonna need more time to nail them, but we will...believe me, we will."

"What do you think you'll get?"

"Don't know...Padillo, his records, any stash they might have...we'll get something. Don't worry, this operation will put them out of business."

"My guess is you won't get a thing...you won't get Padillo or Mosca, you won't get any evidence. You warranted up?"

"You bet. Judge Morse is behind this all the way. We'll have them on federal charges by tomorrow afternoon. Listen, I want to thank you about the plastics info...we'll get on that as soon as we make the bust tomorrow. I'll let Simmons know right away that we have an avenue to travel here in Ohio. The stuff is in Ohio, right?"

"That's my understanding...I think so," Butch replied, "I assume it is."

"What's your next move?"

"Tomorrow, Mosca is supposed to let me know how and when the Frangelettis get their stuff. He is talking to Padillo. Then I meet with Nicky Frangeletti someplace...he thinks the phones are tapped..."

"They are."

"I fill Nicky in on the details of getting their stuff. If you bust Mosca, makes it tough getting the word back to Nicky."

"Too bad. That's the way it goes. This operation comes first, then we deal with the other thing. The first order of business is to collar Padillo and Mosca, then we go from there. Nicky will have to wait."

"My guess is Padillo and Mosca won't be there tomorrow when you arrive."

"What do you know?"

"Just a guess...they're not stupid. Besides, Mosca showed all the signs of flight when I talked to him. Ready to bail...operation over, money made, go home to Mexico."

"I doubt it. They're so goddamn cocky...think they can get away with anything. They can't resist going after more money. They'll be there...fat and sassy...asleep and vulnerable when we hit at dawn. Watch us."

There it was, Butch thought, the arrogance that stupefies, that allows only the privileged thoughts of the anointed to be of value. It was this inability to think in the terms of the bad guys that stiffed the operations of federal agencies charted with the responsibility of getting after the law breakers. The law breakers were creative, had no rules, would break the rules even if they had any, knowing only that they must survive, knowing also that the agencies that pursued them lived and worked in little mazes that they ran around in assuring themselves that they were gaining on the bad guys. The bad guys sat outside the mazes laughing at the effort, the futile, energy-stressed exercises to do their job. Their job in a box, a box in which only they functioned.

"Good luck tomorrow," Butch offered, as he and Connelly parted company in the parking lot.

Connelly merely gave a wave of his hand and charged off towards his car, the weird looking briefcase slapping at his knees as he walked.

It took only a matter of minutes for Butch to negotiate the traffic and signal lights on the short drive from the Holiday Inn to Harry's Supper Club where he had arranged to meet Pam. He marveled at the audacity and confidence Connelly had, calmly moving ahead with his business without ever fully understanding the reality of what was happening in the darker world of crime he probed, unheeding its subtleties, caught in an historic concept of being right no matter what. This was the fundamental weakness of any governmental investigative agency, regardless of what laws they had been chartered to enforce.

His thoughts turned to Pam as he approached Harry's . Pam, the distraught widow, who got him started and into the middle of this mess. Pam, not long the distraught widow, whom he had not talked to for days. Pam, who was now the lover of one of the bad guys. How the hell do these things work out like this, he wondered?

She was already seated at a table when he got there. His greeting as he sat down was affable enough, but certainly not as warm and friendly as it might once have been. She didn't seem to notice, kissed the tips of the fingers of her right hand, and placed them on his folded hands that were pushed out in front of him rested on the table.

"You look so serious," she smiled, "what's the matter?"

She was dressed in one of the tailored suits she wore for work, looking properly professional. Even as she sat back in her chair, legs crossed, her tall, angular body made her posture seem odd, not relaxed, uncomfortable. The smile she had flashed him as she asked the question was an effort for her to produce, but it was the image she wanted to give him. He was not fooled.

"When you got me started looking into Jerry's killing I didn't realize it would take on a life of its own. It's now a career challenge..."

"Oh, it can't be that bad."

"It's that bad...I'm in the middle of stuff I don't want to be in the middle of. There's the Frangelettis, the Feds, your buddy Cuzo, and the Mexicans. It's more than I bargained for when you asked for help. And now you're out of it...off with the Mexican. Jerry is long forgotten in this and..."

"Life goes on and as I've thought about it, I'm not sure our marriage was going to go on...anyway, he's dead and I can't change that...what I have to do is go on with my life."

"Not much of a mourning period, if you ask me."

"It's relative...a matter of perspective...not for you to judge..."

"You're right. It's not up to me to judge. So what's your plan...what's next for you? You wanted to talk to me. What's up?"

She smiled at him without answering at first, shifting in her chair with the awkwardness her uncoordinated long body dictated, fidgeting with the expensive gold watch on her left wrist. The waitress who descended on their table prevented an immediate reply.

"Can I start you off with a cocktail...glass of wine?" The middle-aged woman posed the question with a flatness in her voice that comes from repeating its words day after day, year after year, and with considerable disregard as to what the answer might be.

Butch nodded deference to Pam who ordered a very dry vodka martini on the rocks.

"House Chardonnay," Butch said, without looking at the woman, not losing his focus on Pam. His piercing stare was unnerving for her and she again changed her posture in the chair.

"Yes, I did want to talk to you," she finally said.

"Yeah, I figured it was important. You've been so busy with Cuzo it would have to be something important to tear yourself away from...from his, shall we say, company."

He knew now that she wanted to tell him that she was leaving, but he was not going to make it easy for her by broaching the subject or jumping out with it. She would have to bring it up. Say what she had to say. He would not help.

"Butch," she said, looking into her lap, "things are very different."

"Yes, they are."

"My life is different."

"Yes, I'm sure it is."

"Dammit, Butch," she snapped, "this isn't easy...it's...it's that..."

She was not looking at him, her eyes wandering around the room, hoping for some help that she would get from something she saw that would make the telling easier.

The waitress appeared from nowhere, deftly placing napkin and martini in front of her, the wine by Butch.

"You folks ready to order?"

"We haven't even looked at the menu yet...give us a few minutes," Butch directed.

"Take your time," the waitress countered.

"Butch...I...I'm in love with Cuzo..."

"Is he in love with you?"

"Yes, I think so."

"You think so? What does that mean?"

"He hasn't said it in so many words, but I know he does. He...he shows all the signs."

"That's nice. Is he communicating with you in sign language?"

"You know what I mean...he's nice, he's wonderful, and thoughtful, and..."

"And great in the sack."

"That too." She looked directly at him when she said it, this time with a smile more real than before.

"Okay. Now what?"

"We're leaving," she blurted, "we're leaving...soon. I'm going with him. He has to leave here..."

"No kidding. Do you understand the concept - fugitive from justice?"

"Yes."

"You were married to a cop and you are going to run off with a Mexican drug dealer?"

"Does it matter he's Mexican?"

"The operative words here, my dear, are drug dealer...not Mexican. Don't get confused with the reality of the situation, don't let's muddle it up. If he has to leave it's because the law is after him. If you go with him, the law will be after you, also. Do you get it?"

"I get it. I love him and..."

"And he's exciting?

"Yes."

"Being on the run will sure be exciting. Where are you going?"

She looked away.

"Where?"

"To Mexico...I think. You won't tell...please, Butch, don't tell anyone."

"If you run to Mexico with him I won't have to tell anyone...the law will already know about it. And you'll be a fugitive just like Cuzo and the rest of those Mexicans he works with...forever, until caught or you die. Is that what you want?"

She didn't answer and no wonder. He had given her a concept she hadn't considered - being a fugitive. Not a pretty role to play. It'll take time to sink in, Butch figured. She's twirled around by him, dazzled with the sex, the excitement the little shit has offered her; she can't get anything straight. The waitress came back and took their order, so it was time she could use to avoid answering him, try to collect her thoughts, and wonder if she were doing the right thing.

"No, I wouldn't choose to be a fugitive, but if that is what happens...if it happens as you say it will, that's how it will be. You probably didn't know that I spoke some Spanish. I do even better now. I think I'm going to like Mexico. Cuzo has told me a lot about Guadalajara, the family, the kind of lifestyle we'll have. I can get used to being rich very quickly, enjoy a side of life I've never had...only thought about. I've seen pictures of where we'll live. It's a gorgeous hacienda. I'll be very comfortable there."

She had stiffened in her resolve and he had pushed her to it. No doubt when she came in here to talk to me, he figured, she wasn't sure if she should leave. Now, she was sure, set in what to do, and he had helped her along.

"What was it I said that made you decide for sure that you would leave?"

She looked at him quizzically.

"When you came in here you weren't sure. You thought so, but you weren't set with it."

"I guess it was your damn attitude that I was doing something wrong. I've done a lot of the so called quote unquote right things in my life and not been very happy. Now, I guess I'm doing something wrong to be happy. It's as simple as that, I guess."

"It's not simple at all."

"I hope you'll come visit us." She smiled her easy, natural smile again, content with what was to happen.

They were nearly finished eating when Cuzo approached their table. He moved quickly, but with a grace and manner of someone with good breeding, used to the elements of a finer life. He was no common drug dealer. Butch now had a new appreciation for Cuzo. He had known Cuzo was smart, but now he knew the level of sophistication on which the man operated. Cuzo might defer to Padillo, but the real brains rested with Cuzo.

Pam beamed when she saw him, more alive with his presence, relieved at being rescued, in a sense, from the pressure of dealing with Butch. Cuzo kissed her neck, a lingering kiss of intense familiarity, a sure sign they were more than just friends.

"May I?" he asked, looking directly at Butch.

"Sure, why not. There won't be more special occasions like this."

"You told him?" he asked, turning to Pam.

"Yes."

"Not right away...eventually, after we get things taken care of. I haven't sat down with Victor yet, but I will tonight. I will get an answer to you tomorrow. We will get this thing squared away with the Frangelettis. Everything will work out."

"Maybe. I've talked to Nicky and he's pissed. He doesn't want a stall...he figures it's a stall. Or maybe I'm pulling something. Anyway, I'm in the middle...I don't like it. He's looking for an arrangement to happen quickly or I get the idea he's going to come looking for you guys."

"Like I said before...you'll hear from me tomorrow. Okay?" Cuzo laid a one hundred dollar bill on the table. "This is for dinner...should cover most of it. Come on," he turned to Pam, "we've got to get going. We have another commitment."

Pam gracelessly arose from the jumble her body had been in as she rode the tension of the men's interchange and lurched somewhat toward Butch to kiss his cheek.

"I might not see you again before we leave," she whispered to him, "this has to be good-bye." She kissed him again and rubbed the back of her hand across his cheek. "Good-bye."

"Pam..."

She stopped and turned to him.

"Vaya con diós."

"Graciás," she laughed, and was gone.

25.

The soft light of pre-dawn, a salmon-colored sky that spread up and away from the northeastern horizon, edged over Tim Connelly as he let his car roll to a stop a couple hundred yards down the road from Victor's house. He had the lights off for almost a mile, wary of letting the Mexicans know they were coming. It was a kind of pseudo-precaution since a lot of cars passed on this rural road at all hours of the night. Somehow in his mind he believed that his lights alone would warn them of the team's approach. This was another example of the lack of reality the Bureau had that would have driven Butch crazy with frustration. In fact, those left in the Padillo house were sound asleep as were most of the rest of northwestern Ohio, save those unrelenting farmers who had enough sleep and were already on the move. Even at that, those farmers moved quietly through unlighted houses, not willing to arouse still sleeping wives, silently dressing, moving outside to catch the smells, sense the air that would tell them of what to expect from the day's weather.

Connelly slipped into his bullet-proof vest and pulled on the dark blue vinyl wind breaker with the letters F•B•I stenciled on the back. He pulled a 12-gauge shotgun from the case in the trunk and pressed in the shells to get it fully loaded. He tried to muffle the sound believing that any sound at all would signal their arrival. He motioned to the other agents who have ridden with him to move up the road.

The way the raid had been set up called for the DEA agents to come overland from the farm behind the Padillo place so that the rear of the compound was completely covered. The other agents from Connelly's office assigned to the raid, six in all, would come up the road opposite from where Connelly approached. They all had two-way radios for contact and coordination.

Connelly and the three men with him moved to within a hundred yards or so of the place and stopped at his silent command of holding up his right arm, much like the military column halt. He wanted to take a position behind a large oak tree and some shrubbery a few yards farther on at the edge of the field next to the Padillo property. A large drainage ditch was between them and the position he wanted.

"Cross this ditch," he whispered, "and get behind that tree over there." He pressed the send switch on his 2-way and notified the others where he was by the tree as landmark. It was still too dark to see much more than outlines and dark shapes.

They started down into the ditch single file with Connelly in the lead. Suddenly, something moved, quickly running across their path, a bounding blur, an animal of some sort, big as a dog, and a bullish determination that startled the men.

"Jesus Christ!" the man behind Connelly hissed.

"What the hell was that?" asked another, using a throaty whisper that disguised his fear.

"Probably a raccoon," Connelly answered, "nothing that will bother us. Doesn't want to get near us, I imagine. Anyway, relax, he's gone."

They continued their descent down the side of the ditch, which was about six feet deep, and found themselves in a slurry of ill smelling brackish water that soaked them to their knees.

"Jesus Christ!" the man behind Connelly uttered again. "Goddamn, I'm all wet."

Connelly hissed a shush to the men, all of whom were now grumbling about their water soaked shoes and pants.

"Keep moving up the other side," he said with a curt, subdued direction that was more than a whisper, yet not a full voice, "When you get up the other side, move on down behind the tree and those bushes."

This was a miserable way to the get the operation started, he thought, not a good omen for the work ahead.

While Connelly and his men where moving down the road at the front of the Padillo property, ten DEA agents were moving through the corn field at the rear. The tall corn provided sufficient cover for the men as they crouched over and hustled along the rows toward the Padillo house. Their test was not one of water as the FBI agents had in front, but of enduring the searing slashes of the corn stalk leaves, the edges a fine rasp that cut at the men's cheeks.

Duane Hargrove led the way through the corn until the DEA agents were less than twenty five yards from the fence that surrounded Padillo's place. He held up his men as he got on the two-way.

"Tim?" There was static, but no answer. "Tim, we're almost to the fence...twenty five yards, maybe...you hear me?"

"I read," the voice crackled in reply. "We're ready...let's move in."

On Hargrove's command, a simply whistled move out, the DEA agents struck to the fence. One of the men had a heavy-duty wire cutter and snapped out a section of the fence in a matter of seconds. Still in the shadows and low visibility of early dawn, the men had not seen the Doberman guard dogs that had approached. The dogs had first sensed the men as they crept through the corn field from the west, their scent wafted ahead on the soft prevailing breeze, a light movement of air, but enough to alert the dogs. The dogs silently watched as the fence was cut and the men scrambled through. The dogs attacked in fang-bared rage with all the fury their heritage and reputation ascribed to them. It was a stunning fury, with slashing teeth, a bloody, ripping attack.

One agent would later report how shocked he was, caught by its unexpected suddenness, worse than any shoot out he had experienced.

The reflex action of the men to the dogs' attack was to defend by opening fire. No thought was given to blowing their surprise raid, their only thought now was to keep from getting chewed up by these dogs. Hargrove did not fire first, but he was second, emptying his automatic with a rapid burst of shots in several directions intended for the bounding, slashing dogs.

There had been four guard dogs on the attack, now three dead and one crawling away from the men, fatally shot, trying to seek some form of safety it did not know. Three agents were severely lacerated from the vicious bites, bleeding profusely, moaning in wounded agony. Another agent had somewhat deflected a dog's attack, wrestling the animal to the ground. Unfortunately, the shots from the other agents and Hargrove were not as selective as they would have wanted. Three of the four agents attacked were also shot by their own men. None of the wounds turned out to be really serious, but a tremendous amount of blood was being shed. It was a mess and it already smelled of death to those who had experienced death.

Three men sleeping in the Padillo house were awakened by the loud buzz of the security alarm and moved rapidly into action with the sound of shots. Ramon was the first man out the door, half dressed, headed for the sounds at the rear of the compound. In the now expanding light, he picked out a target and fired one shot that hit the agent next to Hargrove just above the bullet-proof vest. The bullet was a hollow nose that expanded into a missile that took away the left side of the agent's neck at the shoulder. Ramon emptied his gun as he was nailed with two blasts from a 12-gauge by one of the FBI agents moving in from the front. Ramon died almost at the same time as the agent he shot. One of Ramon's last wild shots hit Hargrove in the thigh just above the knee and shattered the bone. The scene had gotten bloodier and the operation had just started.

The two other men had come out of the house behind Ramon and opened fire on the DEA agents toward the rear. The second man, with an automatic rifle, realized the attack was from two directions and turned to face the FBI force coming at him. He opened fire with the weapon almost as if using a hose to water the lawn and sprayed a fan of bullets at the advancing agents. Their protective vests were some help as they dived for cover, but many of the slugs tore at flesh. For one of Connelly's men, hit three times, his vest was no help. He died several minutes after being shot.

Although he was severely wounded, Hargrove kept his composure, slipped a new clip in his automatic, dropped to his knees and crawled forward as best he could towards the Mexican shooters. With the increasing light and his lowered position, he could see the man firing at them. He squeezed off two rounds from his automatic that killed the man instantly. Hargrove saw the man fall before slumping to the ground in a semi-conscious state.

Several agents fired at the man with the automatic rifle, hitting him almost simultaneously. His bloodied body crashed into a small maple tree and fell solidly to the ground as his spasming finger still pulled at the trigger, sending a wild array of bullets into the air, shattering tree limbs and windows in the side of the house.

This was terrible carnage for what had been a fairly simple drug raid and the disaster was caused mostly by four dogs. Without the dogs, it would have been an easier, straightforward bust. Now, there were two dead agents, eight men wounded and dog bitten, and the suspects all dead.

Connelly moved toward the house, the light now full so that the battle scene was revealed.

"Check the house," he directed to one of the agents still standing, "see what's in there. We gotta search the house thoroughly, so let's get at it. Jimmy," he said to the agent next to him, who was holding his arm where he had been shot, "get on the horn and get medical help out here...notify the sheriff we'll need some help and keep those goddamn reporters back at the road."

As terrible as the operation had gone, with casualties and wounded, there was an equally distressing situation for Connelly. It was the close presence of the news media as witness to the disaster. He had sensed some good publicity for the Bureau, so he had notified a contact he had at the Toledo Blade, and at channels 11 and 13 television that there might be a good story out in the country this morning. Channel 11 had sent their helicopter as soon as there was good light and it now circled overhead, with its camera zooming in on the bodies. Now, he would have to contend with all their questions, all their judgments.

Word got to Connelly quickly that Hargrove had been hit and he made his way to the spot where the DEA agent in charge had collapsed. He knelt down to offer his support.

"What happened back here?" he asked Hargrove.

"Jesus Christ, it was the dogs...they never barked, they just attacked. We shot in self defense...we shot our own guys..."

"Shh, shh, don't say any more. We've got paramedics on the way...just stay tough...don't say any more...nothing. We'll get you taken care of."

It wasn't long before the scream of sirens from emergency medical vehicles could be heard as they raced along country roads, hurrying to bring the aid that was needed.

"Get the wounded...at least those who can move...right up here by the house," Connelly instructed, "try to help the others as best you can. Get 'em covered, keep 'em comfortable. Help is on the way...you can hear the sirens..."

"Nothing on the dead Mexicans," offered one of Connelly's Special Agents, "no wallet, no identification, nothing...but I don't think any them is Padillo or Mosca."

"Call the county dog warden, we need these dead dogs to be taken care of. Must have had their throats fixed so that they couldn't bark," Connelly said to his second in command Ed Raymer, "they wanted to make sure the dogs had a real advantage in the dark..."

"A silent attack," Raymer answered, "maybe they got their alert from some kind of security system."

"They got their alert from shots being fired," Connelly answered, sarcastically.

"They have a system," one of the other agents said, "video cameras and motion sensors. There's a control center in the house. You can take a look Tim, but there's not much else in there."

When Connelly went in the house the lights had already been turned on and much of the search had been completed. He walked from the living room to the master bedroom. There were no clothes, no personal effects of any kind that were obvious. The kitchen looked used because of the three who had still been in the house. All in all, there was nothing. It was clean. No computers, no drugs, nothing. Padillo and Mosca were long gone.

"Get the lab guys on this right away, there's got to be something here even if we can't see it."

When Connelly walked back outside, he noticed his wet and muddied pants and shoes for the first time. They smelled from walking through the ditch slop. Higher up on his pants were blood stains. He went over to the garden hose attached to the spigot on the side of the house, turned the handle with an angry, very deliberate twist, and proceeded to carefully spray cold water on his pants and shoes until he thought they were clean. He wished he could wash away the misery of the situation as easily.

Connelly did not like thinking about the score for the operation's work. Of the sixteen FBI and DEA agents used, two agents were dead, eight agents were wounded. There would be an investigation, there would be finger pointing, and there would be nasty, nasty blame for what had occurred. No doubt about it, this was the scene of a first class debacle. And Connelly still had the news media to deal with, before he could even think about getting home to clean up and change or of retreating to his office to sort out how he would defend himself against the onslaught of criticism from others who had not lived through the ordeal.

Three EMS trucks arrived almost at once, but were kept from entering the compound by the locked front gate. The first truck sounded its emergency horn, a worthy attention getter to match with already screaming sirens.

"Damn," Connelly yelled, "get someone to the front gate and get it open."

The order he gave was much easier pronounced than executed. The gate was chained and no one had or could find a tool like a wrecking bar that could be used to break it away.

"Drive one of the damn cars through it," Connelly screamed, "we've got shot guys in here who need help...run that goddamn gate down."

They waited while one of the agents hurried along the road to where they left their cars and drove back to the driveway in front of the house. The first EMS truck had to back up and the agent directed the sedan into the gate. The gate broke loose, but snapped up and away from its hinges in a way that flipped it at the sedan's windshield. The gate crashed through the windshield hitting the agent in the face. Three of his front teeth were knocked out right away and two others would need to be removed later. His nose was broken and severe lacerations were inflicted in five places around his face and forehead that would require over a hundred stitches and subsequent plastic surgery. However, now the EMS trucks could enter the Padillo compound.

Connelly watched with horror as the gate crashed in on his man. The event seemed to him to be taking place in slow motion and he was caught with an overwhelming feeling of nausea He vomited uncontrollably onto his pants and shoes as he doubled over convulsed with a powerful retching. His reaction the culmination of his revulsion for what had gone so terribly wrong.

Raymer rushed over to give his boss some comfort.

"Let me use the hose again," Connelly said as he spit.

Again he sprayed water over his pants and shoes. He threw the hose aside, walked over to a sidewalk area, and stamped his feet to shake off some of the water.

"We're having a hard time with the reporters," Raymer said.

"I'll talk to them, but wait until we get things squared away."

Four more EMS trucks arrived to join the others. The emergency personnel worked quickly to stop the bleeding of the wounded agents before they got them into the trucks. One by one, they left the compound headed for St. Lukes Hospital in Maumee. The five dead men would wait for the lab guys and the county coroner.

"All of the wounded will be okay, the paramedics said," Raymer offered, as if this would make Connelly feel better, "and Purtis is on his way to..."

"Why didn't DEA surveillance have this scoped out?" Connelly asked abruptly, "Padillo moved out of here at least a couple days ago. Why didn't we know he wasn't here? Mosca, I'm not surprised wasn't here...didn't live here anyway. But to have the place clean? They sure knew it was time to get the hell on the move."

"You'll have to ask Hargrove about that, Tim, they were supposed to be watching the Mexicans."

"Damn, that's why we have to control these things. Okay, so now we need to get flight warrants for those two and for some John Does. They're on the move, it's just a matter of time before we get them. Better call Cleveland and see if we can get some help over here."

"Hey boss," one of Connelly's other agents called to him, "the dog warden is here."

Connelly sighed, shaking his head. "Jesus, the dogs are going to be taken care of before our guys."

26.

News coverage of the tragedy at the Padillo compound was on every television station. The full impact and meaning of the story was intensified by dramatic views from the Channel 11 chopper that showed the dead FBI and DEA agents, and the Mexicans, still lying on the ground. Even CNN had a stringer crew on the scene eventually, to offer continuous updates nationwide on what was happening. Tim Connelly was interviewed once and shown repeatedly, trying to explain what had happened, telling why the operation had been such a disaster. He was somewhat testy initially responding to the piercing questions the reporters fired at him, but battled with himself to keep his composure. For him, it was almost worse than being fired at by the Mexicans. He stood up to the television cameras and microphones, however, projecting a sense of assurance that he knew he had to portray if he wanted to survive this ordeal. He tried to stay calm and low-keyed, controlling his voice so as to not betray the anger and frustration that churned within him. He was an impressive spokesman on television.

"...they seemed intent on defending themselves without surrendering," Connelly tried to explain, "we had no choice but to return their fire..."

"Did you identify yourselves when you advanced on the house?" asked one of the reporters.

"No, this was a routine drug bust where we do not identify ourselves until we are in position and ask for entry into the premises. The shooting started by the suspects before that could take place. We were merely defending ourselves against their fire. We had..."

"How were the dogs involved in this, Agent Connelly?" interjected another reporter.

"Did you have a search warrant?" asked still another, not waiting for the previous question to be answered.

"Yes, we did." Connelly jumped on the second question first, hoping against hope that somehow the previous question could be avoided. "We had a search warrant duly executed with a Federal judge. It is, I might add, standard procedure to not notify the suspects well in advance in a drug raid. With notice, evidence can be destroyed. I think you folks realize that potential, then, too, other actions can..."

"What about the dogs?" the reporter persisted.

There was a pinched, very pained look on Connelly's face as he started to answer. "The dogs were used as..."

Victor pressed the mute button on the TV remote control when Connelly started his explanation. There was silence in the room except for the slurping noise Luis made as he sucked on a can of beer. Cuzo looked at him, shaking his head no, and the slurping stopped. Pam sat next to Cuzo with one gangly leg thrown over the armrest, leaning her body against him, hugging his leg with her right arm.

"Doze dogs cause heem lots of trouble, dat meester FBI smartass," Victor stated, "hees having hard time talking hees way out of dat shit. Doze reporters all over heem." He looked at Cuzo, raising his eyebrows as he spoke. "You were right again, Cuzo, we deed not leave any too soon." He tossed the remote onto the table next to where he sat.

"How long are we going to be here in this dump?"

Gloria asked him from the doorway between the living room where they were watching television and the kitchen. She, too, was drinking a beer, but she had hers in a tall plastic glass. She had not dressed yet and her robe, left open, revealed her pink silk pajamas. Without slippers, she pressed one bare foot against the other as if to keep them warm.

"Not long, my sweet," Victor answered in a way uncharacteristic of him, "not very long at all. We jes need to make some arrangements, a few phone calls and we move on. We will go to a nicer place for a few days den...den...who knows...we need to figure that out right now. You ladies, you go upstairs while we figure out what we do. Go on...go on...everything be okay, you see...go on."

He waved his hand at them as he spoke and they quickly left the room. As she left, Pam gave a look to Cuzo who nodded his head up and down in affirmation of her departure.

Victor, Cuzo, and Luis sat in the living room of a two-story farm house on the outskirts of Elmore, Ohio, that Luis had found the year before. The house had been established as a way station in the event they had to hide or had to be on the move to get away. It was kept loaded with food so that no trips to the market were necessary for days and, as a farm, had gasoline at the ready to fill their cars so they did not have to stop at a gas station. The cars had been pulled into the large barn that sat about fifty feet from the house. There, the vehicles would be out of sight and ready to move when the time came.

Establishing the house had been the subject of much discussion over a period of several months. It had been Luis' idea and Cuzo had supported his suggestion, recognizing at once how valuable it could be in case of emergency. Victor was not so sure and dragged his feet about giving the order to get it done. He was not opposed, necessarily, but at the time things were going well and he didn't sense the need. Luis and Cuzo, on the other hand, did sense the need. They were closer to the street action and already felt the pressure from the Frangelettis. Plus, the black guys weren't making things any easier. The black guys were willing to shoot anyone that was competition. At least the Frangelettis showed some restraint. Except for the now-crippled Buddy Cappeletti.

Luis also found Manuel and Judy Gonzalez, a middle-age Mexican-American couple, to live in the house and work the small acreage, establishing a legitimacy to the place. The property was in a semi-rural area, where several other Mexican families lived nearby, so that Manuel and Judy were not conspicuous. Luis explained to them that sometime maybe they would have a few visitors for a short stay. Several days, and the visitors would be gone. This was their limited knowledge of what might happen if the house were needed as a haven. The couple was supported by the Padillo organization without really knowing the full extent of why they were being taken care of or who their benefactor was. They had figured they probably did not want to know.

As the men sat in the living room, the Gonzalez couple sat quietly in the kitchen, slowly drinking their coffee. They could hear little of the news report or what the men and two women had been saying. The five had arrived the afternoon of the day before, the visitors Luis had said might come. The five had gone to bed early and gotten up early. Judy had prepared food for the visitors the night before with the meal highlighted by a big platter of fried rabbit. The table conversation had been jovial and relaxed. This morning, they thought it somewhat strange that Luis and the one woman would drink beer for breakfast, but it was not their business.

Victor came to the doorway to the kitchen to address them.

"You've done well, Manny...Judy, we'll be gone in a couple days and you can have de house to yourself again. While we are here...you just go on like normal. Do da farm stuff, you know, work da garden, you know what I mean...jes go on like we're not here...'cept for meals. Judy, dat was good food last night. I have not had rabbit in a long time. Tonight, maybe steaks, eh?"

Victor was in a good mood at a time when Luis and Cuzo thought he would be petulant and demanding as he most often was when things did not go well for him. Thanks to Cuzo, their maneuver - pulling up stakes and bailing out - was not a last-minute arrangement, but rather a well-planned retreat. Victor had resigned himself to the fact that they were out of the drug business in northwestern Ohio. He was now ready, actually looking forward to moving on to new things.

He was not ready to leave, however, without gaining some satisfaction of knowing that he had inflicted one last hurt on the Frangelettis. He wanted the last word in retaliation for having been put out of business here. It had not been necessary for them to get after our business, he reasoned, they could have ignored us and gone along with their thing and not lost customers or money and everything would have been okay. Everything would have been okay if they had just taken care of their own business, worried only about the black guys who did cut into their action, and left us alone.

As Victor thought about retaliation, he figured that it should take dramatic form so as to cast a broad stroke of pain that would touch as many of their enemies as possible. He felt he had the answer of how it could be done, but they would need some help and a few days to get ready.

"We got to stall for a day or so," he told Cuzo. "Time to geet dees theeng set."

"What thing are you talking about," Cuzo asked with a quizzical expression, "I'm not following you."

"Oh, of course. I have been theenking of what to do. One last theeng to show how tough we can be...to say adiós in a way dey remember."

Cuzo was frustrated. He had worked diligently to make all of the arrangements for their retreat, a plan that had been carefully scheduled, but that would not allow for much to go wrong. If he knew Victor, the man would have some idea that could make the plan fail. Cuzo was well aware that Victor's ego was making it difficult for him to simply leave, to get away, without wanting to strike back somehow.

"Let's not complicate things," Cuzo offered, "we have arrangements. We leave. We keep it neat and simple. To try to do something now that retaliates...well, it only complicates matters. Not a good idea."

"I know how you feel, Meester Cuzo. What I have in mind we can do and steel geet going with no trouble. There might be some danger, I spose, but that eez the way with dees things, there can always be danger. Some reesk, but we make eet work."

"What did you have in mind?" Cuzo asked, dreading to hear what it might be.

"We going to throw a party at dee warehouse in Ashland. Good place for a party. We going to eenvite Frangelettis and we going to eenvite doze boys from DEA and FBI. We have dem all at dee same party. Frangelettis, doze bastards, dey want da money and da plastic stuff. Da Fed guys want us. And dey want to catch a beeg sale tween us and Frangeletti. You, Cuzo, you get word dees morning to Meester private investigator, dat Frangeletti can geet der money and plastic in two days. Tell heem you don't know where yet. Tell heem you call heem tomorrow."

"Greiner won't buy it. He'll know it's a stall. How about I tell him we need to move the stuff to a safe place for the transfer. That'll take another day at least."

"That's okay," Victor confirmed.

Cuzo punched Butch's office number into his cell phone, got the answering machine. He did not leave a message. He tried on and off for about an hour before Butch finally was live.

"Good morning."

"Let's hope so," Cuzo said, a tinge of something in his voice that Butch recognized, but couldn't identify. "You can tell the Frangelettis that we will be all set in two days. We're moving the stuff to a safe place where we can make the transfer and the cash pay off. I'll call you tomorrow and let you know where."

"You guys are in deep trouble, now," Butch said, ignoring the message Cuzo had given him. He was more concerned about Pam. "You're on the run...with Pam. They'll catch up with you sooner or later. Pam will do time just like you guys...just for being along on the run. Is she there with you?"

"Did you hear my message?"

"Let me talk to her."

"Did you hear my message for the Frangelettis?"

"Yes, it's a bullshit stall. They won't believe it. Put Pam on."

"You can help them believe. Besides, it's true. Two days...we'll be all set. They get paid, they get their stuff. Pam will call you at home tonight. We're too busy now."

The phone connection went dead and Butch muttered 'dammit' as he punched in the number to get Nicky.

While Cuzo talked to Butch, Victor was busy with his own cell phone, calling Houston. In the years he had operated with Cuzo in northwestern Ohio, there had been several times when he needed his former employer's help. The help had been extended without question and when occasion came to reciprocate, Victor did so unfailingly, with a sense of loyalty that was heightened by the thought it might pay off for him some day. Keeping open the line of communication with the Houston syndicate had been a good decision, Victor reasoned, beneficial for both organizations. Again he needed their help. It took several minutes on hold, but eventually he heard the voice of the head man himself, Carlos Angel. This was not his real name. No one knew his real name or where he was from, only that he had come from Mexico. He was ruthless and clever, and had survived in the drug dealing world for a long time. Carlos never did time, never was nailed by the opposition, although the changing faces of the competition in Houston had tried over the years.

The clarity and articulation of Carlos' English had been another point of respect that Victor had for him. Just hearing Carlos speak had been intimidating to Victor, impressed also with the man's bearing and extreme self-confidence. Although Victor became less intimidated over time, he knew that Carlos' anger could reach anyone, anywhere. He truly believed that and, consequently, knew that he never wanted Carlos angry with him.

"Vic...tor," Carlos greeted jovially, saying the name in a slow, exaggerated manner. "How are you? Even here in Houston, you are on the news. You know, I thoroughly enjoyed how the dogs disrupted the raid. That was a good trick I taught you, don't you think?"

"We are good. We are safe. Thank you." Victor concentrated on his English, conscious of what Carlos would think if there were too much accent.

"How can we help Victor? I think that you probably need some help right about now."

"We are okay. We move again tomorrow. We do not need help like you might theenk."

"No. What is it then?"

"We need a man who knows plastic explosives and we need heem tomorrow."

"Really? And that quickly. Well, you must have something important in mind."

"Yes, yes, we do. We are going to give a party for some people. A going away party."

"It can be done I believe," Carlos confirmed, "but let me check on it. Where would he be flying to...Cleveland?"

Cuzo's cell phone rang, so he lost the end of Victor's conversation with Carlos.

"Yes?" Cuzo answered warily.

"Greiner. Listen, Cuzo, Nicky is jacked. He says he's got big time pressure after him...dangerous pressure. Screw the money, he says, but he needs the stuff now."

"Not possible for two days," Cuzo responded. "You can assure Frangeletti that we have the money. They will get the money we promised. And they will get their stuff. I'll call you tomorrow with the place and time. We can't do any better than that."

Cuzo punched off his cell phone as he walked up the stairs to the bedroom where Pam was seated on the bed, her long legs pulled up to her chest, her arms wrapped around them, hugging them tightly, her chin dug into the cleft between her knees. He went to her and softly kissed her forehead, brushing back her hair as he did so.

"You okay?" he asked quietly.

She smiled and nodded yes.

"We leave here tonight...as soon as it gets dark. We've got a nice house to go to...we'll be there another day, then we'll take a trip."

She patted the bed for him to sit and when he did she reached for him, holding his cheeks, pulling his face to her, kissing him passionately. She put her arms tightly around him, clutching, pulling, twisting until she had him on the bed along side her. She bit his chin, kissed him fervently.

"Take your clothes off," she whispered.

"I can't right now," he said as he pulled away and got off the bed. "Later...this afternoon."

"Promise."

"Yes," he said, as he drew his finger across his chest in the sign of a cross.

Victor was standing, looking out the large window that viewed the back yard, the barn, and the fields beyond. He held a coffee mug.

"Look at them," he said, pointing with the mug.

Cuzo saw Judy hoeing in the garden, carefully pulling at the ground, tending to the plot that provided daily vegetables. Beyond, Manuel was setting out feed for their pigs.

"They are good, simple people," Cuzo said, "they have no idea why we are here."

"Yes, dey are good. It is good dey know little about us." Victor put the mug on a nearby table. "Carlos will help us. He weel be calling soon, I theenk."

"The Frangelettis are upset about waiting for their stuff. I told Greiner we talk tomorrow."

"Yes, yes. You will tell heem where and when. Dey will come to our party."

Victor's cell phone chirped and he grabbed for his pocket to punch it active.

"Victor?" the voice asked.

"Yes, Carlos. We have been patiently waiting."

"I know you, Victor, you are not patient. No more than I."

"It is true, I confess."

Carlos laughed and said, "I have your man. He goes by the name of Jason Dillard. He flies to Cleveland tonight. He will take a car to the place you told me. He is your man. Victor..."

"Yes..."

"This is an expensive arrangement. We will work that out when you get settled. Agreed?"

"Yes, of course."

Victor turned off the cell phone and faced Cuzo.

"Dees weel be a wonderful party for doze bastards."

27.

Butch sat in his office staring out the window. What did those Mexicans have planned? They were heading for Mexico, he was sure of that; the talk about it not merely idle conversation. He propped his legs on the small table that sat before the window and wrapped his hands behind his head. His meditating posture. Several folders that had been on the table slipped off as his feet pushed into place, but he ignored the scattered papers that slid across the floor. He was too deeply engrossed in the puzzle of what the Mexicans had in store to be concerned with their disarray.

The crazy events that had occurred over the past few weeks made a jumble of his rational thoughts as he tried to piece together what had happened and to make some sense of the events in a context he could understand. Being drawn into and a part of the world of Frangelettis and Padillo by Pam had diverted him from his business, from several commitments he needed to fulfill. He felt a certain helplessness about the circumstances of what had transpired, not being able to sort out some answer, to figure out where things were going. If Pam did call him tonight, he decided, he would try to work her for some more info, something he could use to figure out what Victor and Cuzo had in mind.

Along the way, Jerry had been forgotten, Butch lamented, his death the beginning element, his death a faded memory for Pam, who was enraptured in a new world of excitement and thrills she did not understand. At least I don't think she understands, he ventured silently. If she does, I would be surprised. Jerry had been forgotten by me, too...until right now. How easy it is to forget someone. He thought about Cindy for the first time in several days and kicked at the table, knocking the rest of the file folders to the floor.

It is certainly true that day to day life is easier when the memory of someone you miss terribly is not festering within you. Few of us have the strength to deal with those memories daily, long term. There is a sadness that comes as a result, that over time we will eventually lose the memory, lose the thought contact that lets us remember. Fading, ever fading, Butch thought. He pulled open the center drawer of his desk and pulled out a framed color portrait of Cindy. He pushed aside a stack of papers and sat the eight by ten photograph in front of him. He adjusted it slightly to minimize the glare from the light coming through the window. Photographs can stop the fading, he thought. Why have I kept them all hidden? Afraid of remembering, not wanting the pain? He did not want that to be the truth, but maybe it was so. He made a mental note that when he got home he would get out as many photos of Cindy as there was space to put them. He was determined to not let her memory fade.

The door opened and Tim Connelly pushed through, his bulk crowded the small space Butch used as an office. He swatted at the door with his briefcase and the door slammed closed behind him. The ever-present beads of sweat were poised on his forehead just waiting for enough mass to cascade across his face. He sighed a large throaty sigh and sat down in the chair across from Butch.

"You used the elevator," Butch accused, disdainful of the man's hefty condition, his puffy neck.

Connelly nodded yes.

"I heard the elevator working...hardly thought it would be you coming in here. What's going on?"

"I needed a place to land for awhile, someplace where I wouldn't be spotted. Besides, I wanted to find out if you've got anything new. "

"I thought about you. You must need some relief...Bureau after you, the press. Your little operation turned to shit fast didn't it?"

"Yeah, it sure did. Jesus, what an abortion that was. And it all started with those damned dogs. Silent dogs, just waiting for the DEA guys to move through the fence. Two agents dead as a result. Boy is the Bureau on my ass. It's going to be tough to survive this fiasco."

"I told you Victor and Cuzo would not be there."

"Yeah, I know. I didn't believe it."

"The big guys up the chain don't understand or have forgotten stuff like that happens. Operations can go bad through no fault of anyone. Or was there fault?"

Butch was half sympathetic, half sarcastic. He knew what happened when an operation went bad, but he also knew there could be mitigating circumstances when the agents brought on problems by sins of omissions or commissions. Either way, the sins were suffered by everyone involved, as was the case this time.

"For one, truth be known, the DEA guys should have been aware those two were gone." Connelly wiped a handkerchief across his brow. "DEA was supposed to have the place covered. Somehow Padillo and his woman slipped out. Don't know where Mosca was. Regardless who was or was not in the place, there should have been some evidence somewhere...drugs, money, records...something. There was nothing. It was clean."

"You have other evidence don't you?"

"Some, and a couple of minor members of the gang...runners who know little. But Padillo is now a fugitive and we have arrest warrants, we've got them on the wire across the country. It's just a matter of time before we have them in custody. Until that happens, my life is hell."

"Well, I have Cuzo's cell phone number for you...whatever help that is and I know they plan to head for Mexico. They make it out of the country...they're gone. You won't get them back."

"The cell phone doesn't help much, since they're on the move. Have you talked to Frangeletti?"

"Yeah, I've given Nicky the messages Cuzo wanted him to have and he's pissed. You know, Tim, they're stalling. Had me tell Nicky they had to move the stuff to a good spot for the transfer. I think that's bullshit. I think they have it right where they took the truck and unloaded it. A warehouse someplace...someplace where they could drive a semi into and not be noticed..."

"Hell, that could be anywhere...a big barn, any kind of building."

"But not around here."

"You know," Connelly paused, trying to remember, "I think I read something in a report that Padillo had something going east of here...south of Cleveland. I better check on that."

"They've got something cooking or there wouldn't be the stall. Anyway, Cuzo is supposed to let me know yet today where and when the transfer will be made. I've got to relay that to Nicky."

Connelly pushed himself up out of the chair with a groan. He reached in his pocket, pulled out a business card, and handed it to Butch. "Call me as soon as you know...as soon, regardless of the time. My cell phone number is there, also."

He pointed at the card.

"I'm surprised it hasn't been ringing while you've been here," Butch laughed.

"I turned it off so I could get some peace," Connelly said, and reached in the old briefcase, retrieved the small black phone to click it active, and dropped it back in the case. He threw open the door and was gone.

Butch pushed the door closed as he surveyed his office. He quickly picked up the folders and papers he had kicked to the floor. He needed to get back to the cases he was committed to and to prioritize what needed to be done. His eyes blurred, a sense of numbness overcame him as he sorted through the files, placing each paper in the proper folder, barely able to comprehend what they meant. He would start fresh tomorrow, less preoccupied by thoughts of what would happen to Pam. She was an issue he had to get out of his mind. She was on her own. She may or may not, probably not, call tonight. At this point, what was there to say? He could not change what was going to be, only live with her decision, accept it and go on with his life. Pam would be a friend that once was, departed, yet not dead, out of his life, but more than likely, out of contact. In Mexico, with Cuzo, transported on the edge of excitement. I've got to get out of here and go do some running. I'll feel better.

The jarring sound of his phone snapped him back to focus. It was Cuzo.

"Here it is. In Ashland, a warehouse at the end of 14th street south of downtown...986. Nine o'clock tomorrow. We'll be there, we'll have the money and the plastic. Greiner...?"

"What?"

"We have things covered...no double crosses...no funny stuff...make sure the Frangelettis understand that. It won't be good for them if they try anything. Not good at all. Got the message?"

"You bet," Butch said, and he repeated the address and time to Cuzo. "No funny stuff. I think they know that...I don't imagine they want anything queer from you guys, either."

Cuzo did not reply and the connection was dead. Nothing said about Pam calling later.

It was a sense developed over the years, so that when Butch approached the back door of his house from the garage, he had an awareness of someone inside. He had often wondered what triggered the perception. Was it a smell? A sound? An aura? Whatever it was, he had mastered reading the perception as an alert, the faint signal that another human was near and present.

Butch tried the door knob. It was unlocked. Of course it was, knowing full well he had locked it when he had left that morning. He braced himself for whoever was inside, ready for the possibility of an assault, but at the least the probability of confrontation. He moved through the kitchen and dinning room, the pungent odor of cigar smoke sharp in his nostrils. There in the living room sat Nicky Frangeletti along with his two goons Allie and Tony. They each had a dark-colored, expensive cigar that they were puffing on, filling the room with gray-blue clouds of stench. Butch quickly pulled open the front door and several windows to try to air out the place. Nicky and the other two said nothing while Butch went about ventilating the room.

"No wonder you weren't in the office when I called." Butch was more than irritated with their intrusions. "Weren't we supposed to meet somewhere...so we wouldn't be spotted? Don't you think this place is being watched?"

"I decided in person...now," Nicky said, "there's not a lot of time. I wanted to see your face...see if you were playing straight or screwin' around with us. This whole thing is a stall...you know it, we know it. Our client has given us an ultimatum..."

"Mosca called a little while ago and I tried to get you at your office. He says to meet them in Ashland tomorrow at nine...in the morning. It's a warehouse. Here's the address." Butch handed Nicky a slip of paper with the address carefully penciled. "Says no funny stuff or the whole thing goes in the dumper. My guess is they won't be there before the time, anyway, so there wouldn't be much sense of going early. Besides their boys have the place secured, my guess."

Nicky looked for a minute or so at the slip of paper Butch had handed him. There was confusion on his face as he blew more smoke into the room and contemplated the information he had been given. He was far from satisfied with what he had just learned.

"Where the hell is Ashland? Nicky grunted. "What the hell they doin' in Ashland?"

"East of here, boss," Allie offered, "couple hours drive. Middle of nowhere, other side of Mansfield."

"It's not a town we're in?"

"No," Allie concurred, "closest place we run anything is the prison at Mansfield."

"Don't mention that goddamn place," Nicky snapped.

"I don't know if I'll talk to Mosca again, but if I do, what do you want me to tell him?"

"Tell that little bastard we'll be there." Nicky got up and headed for the front door. "You'll get the rest of yer money next week. Cash. Someone will bring it by."

The three men were gone.

Butch shook his head as he headed upstairs where he changed into running shorts and singlet. He pulled on and tied his running shoes, debating with himself whether or not to call Connelly now or after he ran. He decided the call could wait until he had re-infused himself with life through the long, sweat-bursting run he planned to take. He would be alone with that energy for awhile, at least. He measured his strides, concentrating on form and steady rate, not running at race speed, but rather a notch or so below, still quite fast, a crushing pace in the summer heat for someone else with lesser skill and conditioning.

After the run, after he had cooled somewhat, after Gatorade, after a lone Bohemia, Butch was ready to ease back into the mental struggle for what the Mexicans had planned. He knew they had something planned for the Frangelettis and it still bothered him that he had not figured what it was about.

As long as it didn't involve Pam, it probably doesn't matter. His phone interrupted the mental gymnastics.

"Butch? It was Pam's voice. "Cuzo said you wanted to talk to me. Why? We already said good-bye."

"Yes, that's right. When I talked to him earlier I asked him if I could talk to you, but he said later. I guess this is the later."

Butch grabbed a pen and pulled a notepad closer to the phone. He wanted to be able to doodle and make notes to himself as he talked to her. Perhaps she would reveal something, anything that could give him a glimpse at what was to come.

"I wanted to make sure you were okay...and...well, I wanted to see if I could change your mind. Get you to stay." Butch was groping for words. "Maybe I could pick you up, bring..."

"Are you crazy? she said, testily, "I've sold or donated all of my things, only have clothes with me...there's nothing here for me anymore. Butch...Butch, thank you. For everything. You know I appreciate your help. I know you think I'm leaving you in the lurch. I am and I'm sorry. I know you think I'm forgetting Jerry, but I'm not. It's just that my life has to move on...Jerry is gone...I'm alive and I have to live my life. I'm going to do it with Cuzo. Can you please understand?"

"I'll try," Butch said, sadly with a sigh. "But its difficult...I'm concerned because...well, I think you're in over your head and..."

"Look, I've got to go. We're on the move and..."

"How are you getting to Mexico? You have airline tickets? When do you head out?"

"I don't know what Cuzo has arranged, Butch, so I can't help you. He said we would be on our way tomorrow. I don't know the plans, but I'm sure Cuzo has everything set. He always seems to have everything under control."

"Just wondered. Hey, listen, tell Cuzo Nicky said they would be there tomorrow."

"Oh...okay," she said, sounding puzzled, "whatever. Goodbye, Butch."

She was gone and he hadn't learned anything. He already knew Cuzo had things under control. Cuzo was clever, that's for sure.

Butch punched in Connelly's cell phone number and waited for the connection to be made. The recorded message came on to inform that the cell phone was not operating at this time. Hiding again, Butch thought.

He went to the hall closet and took out a cardboard box that he placed on a chair in the living room. He slowly pulled up the flaps of the box. The box was jammed with several large photo albums and more than a dozen framed pictures. They were pictures of Cindy, of him with Cindy, Cindy with her parents, her college graduation picture so formally posed, and those with several close friends. Butch began placing them on tables, the mantel, the counter in the kitchen, until he had all of the framed photos to view wherever he stood on the first floor. He took their wedding picture upstairs and placed it on the table near the bed they had shared. Memories bring joy and sadness, the two emotions bound together irrevocably in the pattern of remembering. Through his sadness as he positioned each photo was the comforting joy that he would not forget her.

Once Butch completed his mission with the pictures, Butch tried Connelly's cell phone. This time the connection was made.

"Took a little rest again, I guess?" Butch teased, although he knew that such prodding was not appropriate for Connelly about now. He couldn't resist, however.

"Nap, needed a nap. What have you got?"

"I've got what you need. Something to get you off the hook. But I didn't find out much else about what they have planned to split. I do know they're headed for Mexico tomorrow. It's probably right after they meet with Nicky. Anyway, they're meeting tomorrow at nine A.M. in Ashland..."

"Shit, that's Cleveland. Why the hell in Ashland?"

"I would guess so they feel they have total control over what happens. I think their concern right now is the Frangelettis, not you guys. Besides, you still get credit for the info and it's big. Frangelettis will be there, the Mexicans...don't mean to tell you about your job, but you better get the ATF involved. Plastic explosives, remember. This could be real big for you Tim, big for the Bureau."

"I knew they had something going on over there. I should have checked that out sooner. Where in Ashland?"

Butch felt sorry for the man: career in disarray, potentially left out of the big operation, his fate was not blessed. He gave Connelly the address of the warehouse.

28.

Jason Dillard had inspected every inch of the Padillo warehouse in Ashland. He stood, hands on hips, in the large open area surveying the setting he had to work with, reviewing within himself what he must do to accomplish what Victor wanted. Nearby, Cuzo sagged his left shoulder against a support column with arms folded across his chest; watched as the man took command of his surroundings. He is to be admired, Cuzo thought, he is a man of skill who can be counted on for special assignments, a man who knows where he contributes to an organization. He has special knowledge that few others possess. He has established a reputation that takes him where Carlos Angel wants him to be, that brings him here to help us. His work will make the party complete for Victor.

Jason Dillard was in truth Juan Quintero. Born in the barrio of Los Angeles to parents who had come across the border into California with the hopes and dreams of finding work and a better life as many thousands of Mexicans had done over the years. For Teresa and Ricardo Quintero it was the classic story of wanting so much, but finding so little in the United States. Menial jobs, poor living conditions, scurrying, always scurrying to stay ahead of the Immigration Service, they hid and worked and survived.

Juan Quintero had watched the suffering of his parents who struggled to care for him, his younger sister and baby brother. He learned English from other children and from listening. Listening first to the television which was his friend and informer, his teachers in school, and listening carefully to what he heard on the street. He was the pseudo-child of a widow woman with a green card so he could go to school and not have his parents discovered as illegal aliens.

By the time he was ready for the seventh grade, he decided he had enough of school and moved to the streets for a different kind of education. He moved as a loner, weaving through the tough gangs that dominated his neighborhood. He wanted to be alone, to trust only himself for himself.

A turning point for Juan came one afternoon when he spent several hours with his uncle Albert - Alberto Tapacio - an uncle who had been to Viet Nam and who had lost a leg. Uncle Albert had not lost the leg in Nam. It happened after he was back home at Fort Campbell, an accident falling off the back of a truck, with the truck backing over his legs. They took the right leg at the knee. He could have had an artificial leg, but chose not to, and hobbled sufficiently on crutches the rest of his life.

Uncle Albert had seen Juan on the street this time, asked Juan to go to the nearby bar with him, to sustain his drunkenness already established, and to orchestrate the boy's life. It was not the first occasion the boy had the pleasure of beer, but still he sipped at the bottle carefully as if he were one who had never experienced its heady impact. There had been some trouble with the bartender at first, but eventually a bottle was brought to the table for Juan. Albert and Juan sat in the shade at the sidewalk table beside the bar and discussed Juan's future. Or, at least, Albert discussed Juan's future. Juan merely listened, nodding once in awhile to show his uncle that he was listening.

"You need to get off the streets," Uncle Albert intoned, his speech slurred to some degree by several days of steady drinking, "get in the Army like I did so you can make something of yourself."

"I don't want to lose a leg," Juan had said, knowing full well his remark was one of jest to a man too drunk to be anything but serious.

"Hell, I didn't lose the leg in Nam. Could have. Shot at enough. Dumb bastards tellin' us what to do didn't know shit. Coulda got us killed. We didn't put up with too much, though. Got 'em to lay back by fraggin' the shit out of 'em. That made the young bucks think twice about sendin' us inta too much crap. So, we come home. Just like that, we come home. And I fell off a truck, not bein' careful. You be careful. You be careful and git off the streets. Git in the Army where you can learn somethin', be somethin'."

That afternoon and those words, hung with Juan for days. Oh, Uncle Albert said a lot more, a lot more, but the admonition to get off the streets and get in the Army stuck with him and he used them as a guidepost. He managed to keep clear of the gangs and when he turned eighteen, he signed up with the Army. There was no record of his birth and he claimed to be an orphan. The true record of his existence in the United States was begun with and documented by the Army. He was now an official person, whereas before, he was only the drifting, foraging, child of aliens, hoping to stay alive long enough to see what life might be about and to grope for some means for continuing to stay alive. He was off the streets.

Juan spent ten years in the Army. Not a distinguished career, but as an average Joe who did his job and kept his nose clean. At least in the eyes of the Army that took scant notice of his low profile. His performance met standards, nothing exceptional, and he stayed out of trouble. What else he had going for him was another matter. Life on the streets had made him worldly-wise beyond the understanding of most of the other Joes around him. He could deftly steal almost anything he wanted to get. Not for himself, but to sell. For Juan, it was a business that he easily managed and one from which he derived a lot of money.

After he had completed basic training, he was shipped to Germany where he spent three years. Back stateside, he was assigned to Fort Campbell, Kentucky, where he stayed until he mustered out of the Army, only gaining the rank of E-4. It was during his second tour of duty at Ft. Campbell that he met Geraldo Mendoza, who was from Houston. It was a relationship that began slowly, as Juan warily sized up Geraldo, tried to determine if and how much he could be trusted.

"You are good, very good," Geraldo had said the first time they had talked.

Before this time, they had only exchanged nods or a brief acknowledgment of the other, a quick perfunctory greeting, or a communed blast at Army bullshit.

"Yeah? Meaning? Juan countered.

"Meaning you steal good," Geraldo had laughed at him.

Juan's expression did not change and he silently, stoically looked at Geraldo.

"I can make it really pay for you, man," Geraldo continued, "I have connections. Some people in Houston. They could be big help to you."

"If you have such good connection, what the hell are you doing in the Army?"

"A judge made that call for me. He said, 'you can go in the Army or you can do hard time, like two to five years in state prison.' It made sense to me, man, get in the Army, do a few years easy, and get out. No way, man, you want to get inside a prison in Texas. Nooo way."

That was how it started with Geraldo and that was how Juan got to know Carlos Angel and his organization in Houston. Little did Juan know that in a few short years he would quietly kill Geraldo at Carlos' direction.

Although short and slight of build, Juan was deceptively strong and extremely adept in handling a knife. He had used a knife on the streets of L.A. to protect himself, so the use of a knife was an acquired skill that the Army helped him refine and perfect. He had killed Geraldo with a very common hunting knife that he had stolen and that he left in the man, sure it would not be traced. He also had become trained and highly proficient in the use of explosives. This skill he would also practice for Carlos.

With reenlistment time pressing in near the end of his second tour at Ft. Campbell, Juan's Captain let him know what was expected of him. The Captain told him that his name had come up for Korea. Reenlist and go to Korea for a year, or get discharged. There were no other options for Juan.

"Bullshit, man, get out now," Geraldo had said, shaking his head in disgust, "time to go to Houston. Time to work in Carlos' army. Six months I join you. I'm goin' back to work for Carlos. You go now. You see...you make really big money."

With honorable discharge in hand, Juan went to Houston. Carlos liked him almost immediately and established him within the organization handling special projects. There would be no routine work for this special boy, Carlos had said. This special boy will be very important to us. Juan appreciated the recognition that he was special to Carlos, although he did not know why it was so. There became a silent, intense bond between the two men that created within Juan a feeling of deep loyalty. Within Carlos, was a sense of trust, not something he felt about many men.

Juan thought about Geraldo fleetingly as he sat on the airplane headed for Cleveland. Knowing the plastic he would be handling for Padillo was from Bragg had triggered memories of Army service. All those years, meeting Geraldo who got him to Carlos. Too bad Geraldo had cheated the organization, something Carlos would not condone. Juan had followed Geraldo from Houston as the man fled blindly, knowing his indiscretion had been discovered, knowing the consequences of cheating Carlos. He had tracked Geraldo to Colorado Springs, where he caught him in a King Soopers parking lot late at night. Geraldo never knew who his killer was.

It was indeed an execution, Juan pondered, the sentence imposed by the benefactor Carlos. Nothing exceptional or extreme about the penalty, for it was one that could be expected in dealing with those who defy his authority or take advantage of the organization. Geraldo took advantage, believing that he was smart enough to fool the benefactor. It was the matter of age that Geraldo misread. Carlos was old, so Carlos would not notice. Geraldo did not understand that age is often perceived by those younger in relation to their own youth, not understanding that a man of fifty is not really old in life terms. At fifty, Carlos was strong, quick of mind, and missed nothing that went on within his organization. He was truly sad when he told Juan what he wanted him to do, but he was firm in delivering the order for execution.

Carlos had called Juan in Kansas City after he had talked with Victor. He explained to Juan what Victor wanted, where Juan had to go to get the job done.

"Have you completed your work there? I wanted to make sure I reached you and determined your status before I committed your services to Victor."

"I'm done here."

"Good, good. I assume all went well?"

"Yes, perfectly."

"I would suggest you go as Jason Dillard. Do you have that package?"

"Yes. I have it with me."

"Good. You will meet Victor at the warehouse. I told him the things you would need and he assured me he would have those items for you when you arrived. You will be Jason Dillard to him. He has no need to know your real name. There will be a Cuzo Mosca with him. Pay heed to what this Mosca says, what he thinks. He is the one who has taken care of their departure. Confirm with him that they will be leaving the country. They must leave the country. This thing will make all hell break loose."

"Of course," Juan confirmed.

"Don't come back to Houston for awhile. I suggest you stay in L.A. for a couple of months. Or Phoenix. Maybe Phoenix is better."

"I'll go to Phoenix...as Ron Thomas. I have that package also."

Juan had established several identities that he could use when he was on assignment for Carlos. Each identity was a package of drivers license, credit card, social security number, and five hundred dollars in cash. With Carlos' help and direction, these identities had taken many months to create and finalize. When an identity was no longer needed, the entire package was destroyed, less any cash that was not used.

Before the plane landed at Cleveland's Hopkins Airport, Juan removed his current identification for Tad Bricker from his wallet and put those items in his brief case. Before closing the case, he opened a hidden panel and pulled out an envelope marked JD. He placed the pieces of Jason Dillard identification in his wallet and put the empty envelope back in the case.

He was nonchalant, very casual as he moved off the airplane to the baggage claim area. He was dressed in a charcoal gray two-button summer weight wool suit, white shirt, pleasant and nondescript necktie. His clothes, even his shoes, presented a total ensemble that fit in nicely with the other business travelers getting off his flight. Once he had retrieved his single executive overnighter, he went directly to the Avis counter to get his rental car. He had called from Kansas City to reserve a mid-size sedan, so when he presented the Jason Dillard drivers license and VISA card, it was short order for the paper work to be completed and receive the car keys.

After he left the Avis parking lot, he drove into the nearest gas station he could find, a BP station close to the airport. He bought an Ohio map, a cold 20-ounce bottle of diet Pepsi, and a large bag of potato chips. He studied the map for several minutes to get his bearings, quickly finding Ashland. He folded the map in such a way so that he could easily refer to the route he needed as he drove. He pulled open the chips, placing them on the seat next to him, twisted the cap off the Pepsi, and started the drive to Ashland.

It was dark when Juan first drove by the Padillo warehouse. He continued on for three blocks, turned into the unlighted parking lot of a small factory, and positioned the rental car in the shadows beneath a scrawny maple tree at the back edge. Light from the sodium vapor street lamp at the corner lost most of its power by the time it reached the parking lot, its eerie orangeness making gloomier an already dingy neighborhood.

He popped the latch for the trunk, got out, opened his executive overnighter, and pulled out a small package that he pressed open with his thumb. Inside, was a black belt holster with a Glock automatic nestled into it, fully loaded, ready to be cocked. Juan slipped the holster onto his belt at his right side and buttoned his suit jacket. There was no bulge, no indication that he was armed. He closed the trunk, pulled his briefcase from the back seat, and headed up the street to the warehouse.

Next to the large main door that pulled up overhead to allow vehicles to enter the warehouse was a regular entry door. A doorbell with a black button was at eye level on the door jamb, beneath which was a small card with neatly spaced lettering that said 'Press for Service.' Juan pressed the bell once and he could hear inside, in the distance, the hollow ringing of a buzzer. Cuzo opened the door about six inches to make the contact and identification.

"What is it?" Cuzo asked, a certain surliness to his tone that surprised him.

It was a stupid question and when he heard the tone of his voice, he was angry with himself. Who the hell would it be? What else could he have said? It was of no matter, because the business man who stood there did not react to the stupidity, merely responded properly to an improperly asked question.

"Jason Dillard. I've been asked to give you a hand. May I come in?"

"Sure...right...come on in."

Juan stepped into the building.

"Cuzo Mosca." Cuzo offered his name as he offered to shake the man's hand. He closed the door and bolted it secure.

Juan looked at Cuzo carefully as he entered, not immediately responding to Cuzo's offered hand. It was instantaneous and instinctive, the visceral reaction Juan had to Cuzo, a reaction of dislike, a reaction of contempt. After that momentary hesitation he stuck out his hand to meet Cuzo's in a vigorous grip and shake. Cuzo sensed the man's reaction. His take of the man came from more than the hesitation to the gesture of civility, it was in his eyes. Cuzo looked into the eyes and saw something wild, something glowing as if there were pin pricks of fire that could just barely be seen from the outside. Cuzo knew this was a man he did not want working with the enemy. This was a man who fortunately is helping us. Why does this man dislike me, Cuzo wondered, he knows nothing of me.

"Cuzo," Juan said slowly, "Yes, I was told to expect you."

"Come on, I want you to meet Victor."

They walked across the open expanse of the warehouse to a small office to one side. The office had two large glass windows, so Victor and Luis were clearly visible as Cuzo and Juan approached.

"Victor Padillo, yes...Jason Dillard. Glad to be of service," Juan said as he shook hands with Victor.

"This is Luis," Victor said, as he pointed to Luis in the far corner of the room.

Luis nodded, without attempting to move forward to shake Juan's hand. Juan nodded in return.

"We have all of the things we were told you needed."

Victor pointed to two bulging nylon athletic bags on the office floor beneath its windows that looked out on the open warehouse.

"I suppose you want to look around?"

"Yes, I do, but first tell me what you want to achieve."

Victor nodded to Cuzo to handle the reply.

"We will have Jesús bring the Frangelettis in here and tell them to wait while we are summoned. Jesús will go to get us and leave by another door down that hall and on the other side of the building. We figured it would be best in here. Soon after that, the Feds should break in for their raid. Once they are in, it should happen."

"Let's see how much plastic you have," Juan said.

"Right here." Cuzo moved out of the office to the mound of blue vinyl tarp nearby at the warehouse wall. He pulled the tarp away to reveal the pile of plastic explosives and detonators.

"Impressive. This will do what you want." He went back inside the office and zipped open the nylon bags, surveying their contents with obvious approval, mumbling, nodding, smiling at Victor. "It is marvelous how Radio Shack is so helpful in these matters."

Juan began the process of inspecting the warehouse as the three other men watched him. No one had said a word as he moved about, measuring by stepping off distances, checking electrical outlets, pressing on walls, and otherwise thoroughly surveying the building on the inside. When he had completed his inspection, he stood, hands on hips, in the large open area.

"Victor...I understand what you want. It can be done very nicely. With the amount of plastic we have to work with, it will take the whole building. Make sure Jesús gets out quickly. There won't be much time after the others come in to join your party."

"Perfecto!" Victor exclaimed. "That will be good. And you will be the trigger?"

"Yes."

"How will you do that?" Cuzo asked.

"Don't worry...I will take care of it."

"I ask because Victor wants to see it happen."

"Really? Victor, you want to see your warehouse disappear?"

Victor chuckled, "It is a pleasure I want."

"Okay. We'll be outside and a distance away. You can see it."

Juan spoke with quiet assurance and he went about his business of getting the party ready.

29.

Butch was entangled in a web of sleep that trapped his mind and twisted its processes into a weird, distorted world. He woke with a start, his body in a tremor, an involuntary contraction of his leg muscles, part of the ending sequence of a very confusing, very frustrating dream. He had been running after someone - maybe it was Pam - the long legged person able to stay just ahead of him as they ran across a long, high railroad trestle. Below was the white water of a surging river. In the background were fake mountains like some bad movie set. The person he was chasing looked over their shoulder. It was not Pam, it was some strange man, a man that looked like a woman, a man that metamorphosed into a huge elk with fourteen-point rack, an elk that became a man again, a man that evaporated into a blinding flash of orange as the trestle exploded, the bits and pieces flying about, disappearing away and into a trapdoor that, in turn, diminished to a vanishing point.

He jumped out of bed in the dark, smashing his left big toe into one of the legs of the dresser. He yelled 'dammit' to the darkness as he frantically tried to get his bearings through blurred eyes and check the time on the glowing numerals of the alarm clock. He steadied himself on one leg as he rubbed the throbbing toe. It was six thirty in the morning.

The meaning for his dream had come to him as he passed through the never-never land of half-sleep, that place where one softly drifted towards consciousness right before being awake. The meaning was the answer, the answer for what was in store for the Frangelettis and the Feds. The picture of the future had come to him through the distressing images of his convoluted dream. Death stalked all of them, Butch realized, death at the hands of Victor Padillo.

Why hadn't the answer come to him before? Why get the Frangelettis to their warehouse in Ashland? Padillo probably even counted on my feeding the information to the Feds. Cuzo kept track of everything, no doubt they knew about my connection. Victor wanted his shot at the Feds, also. The reason was so clear, now that he thought about it. Each time something was done against Victor, he retaliated. He was not going to quietly, submissively give back the plastic explosives, hand over a big chunk of money and fade away to Mexico. Oh, no, not Victor. Victor was going to have a payback big time and get all the offenders that he could. Catch his enemies in one spot. Victor was going to use the plastic explosives to blow up all of them. It was to be his master stroke of retaliation, his final signature of revenge for those who had been a part of taking away his business.

Butch chided himself for being so slow to realize what was going to happen. He should have seen it before now, but maybe it wasn't too late to intervene. Victor was certainly the man for such treachery. Not as sophisticated as Cuzo, but with all the viciousness necessary to want final, consuming revenge. That's why the stall. They needed time to get everything set, get the plastic in place in the warehouse and wired so that it could be remotely detonated. Victor likes the danger of it letting go, the realization that he strikes back with force. Bastard! On to Mexico without another thought and Pam goes with him. And Cuzo. Cuzo probably doesn't want this, but he has no choice.

Butch stood at the sink in the bathroom, the light on, trying to get himself awake and fully functioning. It was not as easy as it used to be. He splashed cold water on his face as he waited for the water to get warm, held a hot washcloth to his eyes, rubbed his face, and dared to look in the mirror. He dressed quickly and went into the other bedroom he used as an office. He stared at Tim Connelly's card lying on the desk. He wondered which number to call, finally deciding on the man's home phone. After a few rings, a woman answered.

"Hello," she said hesitantly.

"This is Butch Greiner. I'm a private investigator who knows Tim. Is he home?"

"I...he...he..."

"Look, Tim is in danger. If he's not home, he must be headed to Ashland. They're probably going to raid a warehouse down there and it's going to explode. He's in danger."

"I don't know," she said, "he's not here."

"Sorry I bothered you." He punched the line dead.

Butch dialed the man's cell phone number, but got the recording that said the phone was not in service.

"You dumb shit," Butch muttered. "Turn on your goddamn phone."

He called information to get the number for the Ashland Police. It was a struggle with the information operator, but eventually he got the number.

"Ashland Police, this is Charise." The woman's voice sounded very young, so young, in fact, that it startled Butch for a moment.

"Yes, Charise, this is Butch Greiner from the Toledo area. I'm a private investigator. I've got a problem...I need to make contact with the FBI in your town...they're there on assignment..."

"Your name again please."

"Greiner...G-R-E-I-N-E-R. Butch. I need..."

"Your phone number, Mr. Greiner?"

"Look, there's not a lot of time here...let me talk to a command officer...please." Butch emphasized the word 'please' and raised his voice as he said the word.

The line was silent for several seconds before Butch looked at his watch to begin timing the delay. The young woman must have been trying to find the watch commander and not been able to reach him right away. There was a click and the line was open.

"Captain Brooks...can I help you?"

"Captain Brooks, this is Butch Greiner...I'm up in the Toledo area. I am aware of...I least I think there's going to be a Federal raid on a warehouse in your town and..."

"Greiner? What's your connection?"

"I've been working with...or...or...providing Tim Connelly, the FBI agent in charge here in Toledo, with certain information about some bad guys. I think the bad guys..."

"What kind of raid?"

"Well, it's probably a combination of FBI, DEA, and ATF. Have you guys been notified of a stakeout or a raid there?"

The line was silent for several seconds. Again came a click.

"Brooks? Brooks...are you there?"

"Yeah, sorry. Nothing. We haven't had any contact with the FBI or any other Fed Agency for some time that I'm aware of. About a year ago the DEA was doing an investiga..."

"Great. Now listen to me please. There's a Mexican gang that has a warehouse in your town. Some guys are coming there from Toledo to meet the Mexicans. The FBI is aware of the meeting and is probably going to raid the meeting. I think it's a setup to blow up the guys coming from Toledo and the Feds. The Mexicans have big time plastic explosives...they mean business, believe me. This is a very bad situation."

"How do you know this?"

"Never mind that right now. Just get to the warehouse..."

"On your say so?"

"Try to think of me as a good informant...get..."

"We get crank calls all the time trying to get us to do one thing or another."

"Wanting you to get hold of the FBI? Wanting you to check out a..."

"Well, no, not the FBI thing, but we get bomb threats on a regular basis."

"You're wasting time. Check it out...just check it out."

"Okay. Umm, what's your name and telephone number?"

Exasperation was beginning to set in with Butch, but he contained himself. The truth was, the Captain did not know who he was, did not know if it were a prank or some off-balance personality trying to give the cops a hard time. As calmly as he could, he gave Captain Brooks his name and telephone number, and the address of the warehouse.

"Right, right, I know that building," Brooks muttered, more to himself than to Butch, "legitimate business there, if I recall. I'll...I'll have...ah, umm, I'll have someone check it out. Are you at this number right now?"

"Yes," Butch answered through clenched teeth.

"Okay," Captain Brooks said and the line went dead.

Butch put down the receiver and stared at the phone, shaking his head in frustration. Before he could do anything else, the phone rang.

"Greiner," Butch snapped.

"Yeah, Captain Brooks, Ashland Police. Wanted to check this number you gave. I'll have someone look into this." Again, he was gone without another word.

"Shit," Butch said, "he could have just as easily checked with his operator's caller ID.'

Butch sat there in his bedroom office trying to decide what to do next. What would be the best way to get this thing stopped? He punched in Connelly's cell phone number again and this time he got the busy signal. At least he has his phone on, Butch thought.

He hated the idea that he might not be able to do something to head off Connelly and the others from being caught in a trap. He could do so if he got to Ashland in time, but time and distance were against him. If he left immediately, there was not enough time to drive to Ashland before nine. With a helicopter it could be done. But where would he get one? It came to him: the Channel 11 news chopper. He grabbed the phone book, looked up the Channel 11 number, and punched in the one for the news room.

"Eleven news. Lassiter," the tired voice answered.

"Who's in charge?" Butch demanded.

"Right now it's Jack Porter. Why, waddaya need?"

"I need to talk to Jack...this is an emergency and a big story...related to the drug bust you guys covered."

"Hang on."

Assistant news director Jack Porter came on the line after what seemed like forever to Butch, who was drumming his fingers on the desk in front of him, at the same time doodling furiously.

"Porter, waddaya got?"

"My name is Butch Greiner, I'm a private investigator working out of Perrysburg. I have had recent connections with the FBI in relation to the Mexicans...the Mexican gang that was hit with the drug raid that went bad. I think the Mexicans have set a trap over in Ashland for the Feds and some guys from Toledo that they're set to meet this morning. I think they're going to blow them up, in fact, I know they're going to blow them up."

"Who is going to blow up whom? I'm not following you."

The Mexicans are going to blow up the Feds who are going to raid a meeting between the Mexicans and someone, probably Nicky Frangeletti..."

"Frangeletti?"

"Right, it's a deal between the Mexicans and the Frangelettis. The Feds are going to raid the deal, but it's a trap for all of them."

"Is it the guy Victor Padillo that the Feds are after?"

"Yes, yes..."

"So waddaya want, waddaya need?"

"I need your helicopter to get down there and warn the Feds...Tim Connelly of..."

"Yeah, the FBI..."

"Yes. I've tried to get through to him, but can't. I've tried to notify the Ashland Police, but I'm not sure that's any help. I want to get down there. You guys can get me there and get one hell of a story besides."

"Sounds like a story all right," Porter said calmly, "I'll get a reporter and camera guy on it and notify the chopper guy. You head for Metcalf. You know where Metcalf Field is?"

"Yes," Butch yelled and hung up the phone.

Butch checked his watch as he headed for his car, realizing he had been screwing around for almost an hour trying to get something done on the phone. He knew the general location of Metcalf Field without knowing exactly how to reach the airport. He figured he would get close, ask for directions. As he drove, he pulled apart the glove box looking for a map of the Toledo area that he thought he kept there. It was not. Trying to keep his eyes on the road, he dug through a pile of notes, folders, newspapers, receipts, and an occasional map that had collected on the rear seat. The search was awkward as he reached back to sort through the mess. There was no map he needed.

At the major intersections he was forced to stop by the flow of morning traffic, but at lesser cross streets, where there was a light or stop sign, he slowed somewhat, checked to make sure it was clear, and rolled onward. After twenty minutes or so of plunging toward Metcalf, only vaguely knowing where he was going, he pulled into an Amoco gas station to get directions. He found out that he was less than ten minutes away.

When Butch arrived at the airport, the Channel 11 chopper had been moved out of its hanger, but had not been started. He parked and ran towards the chopper. A young man inspecting the craft greeted Butch as he approached.

"Morning. TV guys aren't here yet. You the investigator Porter mentioned?"

"Yes, I..."

"Can I see some ID?"

"This isn't a commercial flight."

"Porter said to make sure it was Greiner. Just doing what I was told."

Butch took out his wallet, pulled his drivers license from one of the pockets, and showed the man.

"Great. That's all I needed.

A vehicle braking to a stop interrupted the men. The Channel 11 Jeep Cherokee had arrived. Two men jumped out, one of whom went to the rear of the Jeep and pulled out a video camera. They walked quickly towards the chopper. The young man without the camera spoke first.

"Jack Stewert. You Greiner?"

"Yeah."

"Good morning. Good to meet you." The two shook hands. "This is Tom Novak, my camera man. You already met Pat Dailey, I guess."

Butch nodded and shook hands with the other two men.

"I didn't actually meet Pat, but he did check out my ID."

Stewert laughed, "Yeah. Good."

"Let's get going," Butch insisted, "we don't have a lot of time."

They climbed aboard and Dailey began his preflight routine. After completing the checklist, the engine was fired, it whirred alive, and screamed into action as the blades responded to the jet power.

"What's the flying time to Ashland?" Butch asked the pilot over the engine and air noise.

"About an hour."

"That might just do it," Butch said. It'll be close, though."

As Dailey ran up the RPMs, vibration intensity increased, sending a shiver through Butch. The noise, the sound of the blades grabbing at the air, the force of yanking all of the weight off the ground, formed a totality of sensation that resurrected composite forms of memories within him. Each piece of each vision linked with fear, interlocked with the inherent danger of being in this machine, and dangers beyond, those dangers he had once experienced. This would now be a Zen tribute to mind control and a zone of infinity that brings internal peace to allay fear, that takes away the stubborn agony of anxiety. He would not close his eyes, but he wanted to shut them tightly. He looked out the side window as the ground moved away, the sensation of moving barely perceptible at first, the distance expanding rapidly. He had used the Zen tribute before, on assignment, when there was no control over what was happening, no chance to be somewhere else except in his own mind.

"Jack," Butch yelled over the noise, "you have a cell phone?"

"You bet." The young man handed his cell phone to Butch.

Butch punched in Connelly's number. Busy. Dammit, busy. He's probably there already in position. He looked at his watch. Yeah, he's already in place. Damn!

Dailey brought the chopper to forward level flight at about twelve hundred feet and the ground started to move by rapidly as he gained speed. Below, farms and fields moved pass the window as Butch looked out over the countryside. For the most part the land was green with a house here and there, barns and out buildings, and landmark factory buildings. He settled back as best he could, handling the fear that shadowed him, poked at him, and he hoped the time would pass quickly. He knew, however, it never did in these situations.

"Great fun in the chopper, isn't it?" Stewert was enjoying the ride. He might as well be at Cedar Point or Six Flags. "You don't seem to like it."

"Best way to get someplace," Butch countered, dodging the question, avoiding a discussion on his state of anxiety.

"What makes you think the Mexicans are going to blow up this meeting?"

Butch did not answer right away.

"Porter told me what you thought was going to happen."

"It came to me in a dream," Butch finally responded, "it was very clear when I woke up...I should have figured it out before, but somehow...I just didn't put it together."

"If it's true, I hope they wait 'til we get there. That would be great on tape."

Butch looked at Stewert in amazement. The young man had no concept of what this mission was all about, he only wanted a hot story, with hot footage.

"Yeah, right," Butch mumbled.

On the ground and far ahead of the chopper, Nicky Frangeletti was resting quietly in the front passenger seat of his big

Mercedes as Allie drove, drawing on his first cigar of the day, outwardly calm and inwardly nervous about what the day held in store for him. He wondered if they were headed for some kind of trap, but he was ready for that circumstance. The rest of his boys were in the van that followed, well armed, primed for a fight with the Mexicans if something strange happened. Nicky was not willing to share his concerns with Allie. He wanted to appear fearless. Allie was fooled.

30.

Nicky never wanted to get up when he had been sleeping, no matter what time it was, no matter what day of the week. For Nicky, sleep was a divine experience, likened to being at a Pavarotti concert when the singer was in his prime or reveling in the pleasures of a fine Tuscan red wine. To be wakened at five thirty in the morning was a monumental task for Nick's valet, a struggle almost without measure for Nicky. His groans, moans, protestations and cursing belied the severity of what was occurring to him. His struggle to bring himself to consciousness came from some long forgotten happenstance in his childhood that persisted, was condoned and uncorrected, and plagued him still. His inability to rise from sleep in a somewhat normal manner did not bother Nicky. Nor was he concerned that this whispered-about affliction within the Frangeletti organization meant his reputation would always be that of problem child and lazy. In truth, he was far from lazy and once awake and alert, his energy and devotion to the business was without question. He never could shake the label, however.

As much as he resisted the call, as much as he protested, as much as he longed to linger in the pleasure of sleep, Nicky still knew what this day meant for him even as his mind grappled with the desire to remain asleep. It would be a day fundamentally important to him because of how it would be viewed in the eyes of the rest of the organization. He had been chosen to represent the Frangelettis in the meeting with the Mexicans, although he had manipulated his father's decision. This was no small occasion, an impending confrontation not to be taken lightly.

Once the Frangelettis received Cuzo's message from Butch, it became a matter of determining who would go to deal with the Mexicans, considering who would lead and how many would be included. The discussion was intense as were most decision-making conferences within the Frangeletti organization.

"As long as I feel good, I must meet with this Mexican, Padillo, face to face...let him see that I am not weak. Let him see that he is still dealing with a strong man who will not take any of his shit," Nick said quietly.

He spoke the words with self-assessed conviction, but others participating in the meeting were not secure with his words. His face was pre-death gray, the skin hanging loosely at his cheeks, a lifeless mask to pain that nagged at him. Nick's strength and energy could not begin to match his ambition for the leader's role.

"No way, boss," Allie spoke the words that Nicky had prompted, "this is no time to git inta this kinda thing...yer still gittin' better...no time to take chances with your health."

"Oh, bullshit, I'm fine, just fine. I ride down there in the car, meet with the Mexicans, get the stuff, ride home. Now, what's so tough about an assignment like that? I can handle it."

"No, Pop, Allie's right, this is no time to screw with yer health. This is one of those times when I need to step up to the plate and take care of it. You need to relax and wait for my call. After that, you can call Jackie Zimmerman to tell him we have the merchandise. You..."

"Yeah, he's pissed, big time. That Jackie can get mean. If he ever thinks we're pulling something on him, there will be war with Jackie. That would be a war we don't want, even though he's in Detroit and we're here. Bad, real bad."

Nick did not seem altogether unhappy that the others were overruling his declaration of leading their delegation to Ashland.

"You could be right," Nick hedged, waiting for the final punctuation to insist that he stay behind for his own health.

"Damn right," Nicky said, "yer doctor would yell bloody murder. You know it doesn't make sense."

Allie and the others nodded agreement, a silent chorus of bobbing heads that made it easy for Nick to back away from his position.

"All right, all right, but let me say this if I'm not going...you guys listening? Those goddamn Mexicans might have something up their sleeve for you guys. I don't mean just be careful, I mean be real careful. Everybody goes, not just Nicky and Allie. Take the..."

"Pop, Allie and I can handle it. Padillo is not stupid. He knows if he pulls somethin' he'll git his ass kicked. He knows..."

"Everybody goes...Tony, Jack, Eddie, Frank, Willie, Phil..." Nick gestured in an arc around the room to the men seated there, a gesture that was a wave to ordain their service for this mission. "This is your protection, Nicky, this is your assurance the Mexicans will keep it straight. Our guys follow in the van. That's a must. Gotta be that way. Understand?"

Once awake and dressed, Nicky had walked through his father's house, a cup of hot coffee in hand, rousing the other men who would be going. After the previous night's meeting, none of them had left the house. They slept on sofas, the floor, and in the extra bedrooms; most had slept in their clothes. Mitzi had a huge breakfast of scrambled eggs, Italian sausage, and toast ready for them, and they were on the road.

Nicky and Allie had silently watched the dawn sky brighten into daylight as they headed east, the faint sounds of rushing air and tires on pavement the only intrusion to their otherwise quiet ride.

"Gonna be hot again," Allie offered, trying to stay calm as his anxiety increased with each passing mile.

Nicky nodded agreement.

"Hope this thing doesn't take long. Don't wanta hang around in a warehouse when it's hot. 'Course early morning shouldn't be so bad. Later in the day would be a bitch."

He looked at Nicky for some sign that he concurred with the assessment about the temperature and for some indication as to whether Nicky had fear. Allie saw no fear in Nicky and he felt somewhat more at ease.

Nothing was said for several more minutes.

"We'll be early," Allie said, looking at his watch to compare the time with the car's digital clock, "we're only about a half hour away."

"Early is good," Nicky responded, "the Mexicans will be ready, we're comin' ready...don't worry about it. It'll go off fine."

Indeed the Mexicans were ready and so were the Federal agencies poised to take advantage of a situation they considered to be of great fortune that fallen into their laps. They had moved into position from their rendezvous point, now waiting to pounce on the warehouse once their targets were all inside. Tim Connelly was part of this contingent.

Connelly had gotten word to Hal Barton, Special Agent in Charge of the Cleveland FBI office about the meeting of the Frangelettis and the Mexicans. Barton had coordinated everything necessary for a force from his office and units from the DEA and ATF. They assembled outside of Ashland, ready to move into place at the warehouse. He had, at Connelly's insistence and after heated discussion, authorized Connelly and two of Tim's men to be included.

Mary Connelly had held a hot wash cloth to her husband's flushed face, trying to soothe and comfort this man so dear to her who was racked with frustration. She also knew her husband was filled with trepidation about the impending action with the other agencies. There were so many things that could go wrong, he had said earlier in the evening - just look at what happened in a simple operation out at Padillo's. This is a lot more complicated, more important. So many things to get screwed up.

Connelly never went to bed. There was no way he could have slept, anyway. He checked and rechecked his automatic, his shotgun, his bullet-proof vest, the amount of reserve ammunition he would take, and the map and notes of directions he would use to meet the others. He fidgeted and paced. He sat stoically as Mary applied the hot cloth, which she tried to do periodically when he would land in a chair for a few minutes. It was fruitless to tell him to relax. Being at ease was not in the cards for Connelly at this point.

"That goddamn Greiner is right," he said grimacing as he spoke the words.

Mary smiled at him, waiting for the explanation.

"Get the weight off, he said, get the weight off. I gotta get the weight off. After we clear the decks on this thing tomorrow, I'm going on a diet. Gotta get the weight off."

Mary rubbed his shoulders. "Try to relax," she had told him, it's almost time to leave." If he were not going to get some sleep, neither was she. She would wait until he was gone.

"Agents Kennedy and Binkert are meeting me here. Then we'll go on and meet Dale Royce and the rest of the DEA guys...ATF, they'll be there. Royce is leading the way for Duane Hargrove...he's still in the hospital getting that leg healed. Nasty...it was nasty the wound he got out at Padillo's. Just a fluke, a stray from one of the Mexicans who had already been taken down by Kennedy. Damn shame. He's out of commission for awhile."

Mary stood there listening to her husband rattle off the names, wondering about these men who put their life on the line for the law to be upheld. The randomness of agents' death that they had experienced tore at her. Who's turn would it be this time?

"They're here," Connelly said, and he began to get his gear.

She kissed him good-bye with neither of them saying a word. He went out the front door carrying his shotgun and bulletproof vest and walked through the darkness to the car where the two agents were waiting. He had not turned on the porch light so as to not draw attention to their activity at this odd hour. No sense in rousing the neighbors. He put the shotgun and vest in the trunk and got in the car, exchanging minimal, subdued greetings. The three agents headed east for the assembly point to meet with the other groups of the operation.

"What's our timeline on this deal?" asked Agent Kennedy.

"Meet by seven at the contact point just outside Ashland," Connelly explained, "get assignments from Barton and move in on the warehouse so that we're in place no later than eight. Royce is handling the DEA team, Simmons ATF."

"Damn shame about Hargrove," said Kennedy.

"Yeah," Connelly said slowly.

"Royce any good?"

"Yeah, he'll do fine."

Dale Royce had assembled his men at their office in downtown Cleveland. They would make the drive to Ashland in two vans, the rear section of each crowded with the equipment and extra ammunition they would need.

None of the DEA agents spoke about Hargrove as they put their gear in the vans and climbed aboard. They each wanted to say something about him, to express something of comfort to each other to ease the tension. His absence was a terse comment about the danger of their work. The shocking account of how the recent move on the Mexicans went so badly was fresh with them and now, here they were, going after the Mexicans again. There was an ominous tinge to this operation that they sensed, that was intensified by having someone new in charge. Hargrove had been a man they trusted, relied on through one successful drug bust after another. Then the episode at the Padillo compound. Hargrove out of action, an agent dead. The unspoken question each of them had was whether Royce could handle being in charge.

As the vans headed out of the downtown area, one of the agents in the van Royce was riding could not contain himself any longer and broke the silence.

"Hey, Royce, try not to get shot on this bust. Okay?"

Royce smiled and responded without turning to the man who was sitting behind him. "That was my intention."

In Middleburg Heights, south of Cleveland, two ATF vans sat in the parking lot near the building that housed the agency's offices. With Ralph Simmons leading the way, he and his men marched out of the building in single file, each man with weapons and protective gear. In the predawn darkness, the quiet was only occasionally jarred by a passing car or truck on the nearby freeway. Moisture from heavy dew dripped off the vans. Few other vehicles were around at that time of morning, except for those the agents had used to reach their office.

Simmons had thoroughly briefed his men about the next morning's assignment. They would be going in as a surprise with the FBI and DEA, they would locate and secure the plastic explosives, they would take the plastic into custody for examination and identification, and they would withdraw. They would be prepared to return fire, if necessary, and they would shoot to kill. This could be, he warned them emphatically, a true combat zone. They must be prepared for the worst, a heavy retaliation for coming in on the meeting of these two groups of suspects.

These were men well aware of what had happened to fellow agents at other operations, where their men were killed by not being ready enough for what might come at them. These men vowed among themselves to not let that occur to them tomorrow morning. They would indeed be ready. Such was their certainty as they discussed the upcoming action on the ride to Ashland.

Hal Barton arrived at the rendezvous point just outside of Ashland a little after six thirty. He was in command of the operation and, feeling the pressure of that role, he believed he should be first, that being first was part of command decision, a factor for showing leadership, and a means of instilling morale. The overriding burden of coordinating the raid weighed heavily with him. He carefully reviewed his notes as he sipped a cup of coffee. He held the several sheets of paper with both hands, scanning the words he had produced on his computer, line after line of single-spaced directions for the procedures he wanted to be followed and the actions he wanted taken by the men who would be assembled with him. Next to him were the kits his secretary had prepared that would be handed out to everyone. The kits, labeled for each respective team, contained maps, street directions to the warehouse, descriptions of the suspects, and actions for each agency.

Barton had intended to be as thorough as he possibly could under the short time constraints he had since being informed of the meeting between the Frangelettis and the Mexicans. He believed that the problems Connelly encountered on the Padillo raid were from lack of preparation. He did not want that to be the case for this situation, he did not want to command a disaster. Only time would tell how Connelly's career would go after what happened at Padillo's, but the way things looked now, Connelly probably wasn't ever going to be promoted again.

Not long after Barton had arrived, the cars of other members of his team pulled into the parking lot. They parked near their leader, got out and stood in a group behind his. One agent stood apart from the others to light a cigarette. No one said anything, but they did not want him close and he knew it. His action was not of respect for them, he just didn't want to hear their complaints.

"Spence, give me a hand here if you will," Barton said as he emerged from his car, quickly stuffing his folded note sheets into his jacket pocket, "grab those folders on the front seat. Give everybody here one and pass 'em out to the others when they get here."

"Okay," the agent responded, and went to Barton's car.

"All right, now, we all set on radios?"

There were nods and random words of 'yes' from the agents attesting to their radio readiness.

Barton looked over his men as each of them was handed a folder and they began to review its contents. He was waiting for a reaction, a sign of approval for the thoroughness of his leadership. None came, so he prompted a response.

"Any comments? Did we miss anything?"

He carefully used the editorial 'we,' thinking this sounded more team oriented, less conceited. He believed this was another part of the command role.

There was some head shaking, but no one spoke.

At that point, the car with Connelly and agents Kennedy and Binkert arrived, followed within minutes by the ATF guys. These agents had just started to review the info folder they had been handed, when the DEA vans came into the lot. The men, many of whom knew each other, milled about to greet and make some introductions.

"Okay, men, let me get your attention. We don't have time to socialize." Barton was now in command leadership mode. "We need to get some things straight, here. Believe me, this is going to be one touchy operation. These Mexicans are clever...they can be treacherous. Just ask Special Agent Connelly over there. He found out how treacherous these bastards are." Barton had not planned on pointing out

Connelly's failed effort, but when the thought came to him while speaking, he didn't pass up the chance to take a jab at the man. "Check your packet...maps show where you will be around the warehouse, maps show how to get to the warehouse from here. We will be in constant radio contact right up to the time we go in. I'll give that order. The Frangelettis from Toledo will be going in to meet with the Mexicans. At least, that's how we get the story of what is going down. The Mexicans are supposed to turn over some plastic explosives to them as well as some cash for some reason, some kind of payback for something. You guys in ATF are responsible for the plastic and I'm assuming that you know what you're going to do. Am I right on that?"

"Right, Hal, we're all set," Simmons replied without looking up from the folder he had in his hands.

Barton continued reviewing the details of the plans until everything had been covered. He checked his watch before directing the agents into action to their coverage of the warehouse. Quickly, all of the vehicles were gone from the lot. It was twenty minutes before eight.

In this entire group of men, ready to do battle with bad guys, there was not one ounce of cynicism for what they were about to do. They were dedicated and believed they were with good purpose. They could wait patiently, yet anxiously, for the time to come when the trap would be fulfilled and they could move into action. They could wait because they were used to such waiting, an uneasy sense among them as they watched the warehouse.

Perhaps some measure of redemption can come to me, Connelly thought as he sat at his assigned position near the warehouse with Kennedy and Binkert. *Maybe if this goes well, some of the stigma gets minimized. Thanks to Greiner we all get this chance to nail the Mexicans and the Frangelettis. Too bad he's not here to see it happen.*

Meanwhile, Butch sat stiffly, steeling himself against the noise of the chopper blades, wondering where Connelly might be, who else might be involved, wondering if he could get there in time, wondering if he got there in time would they even listen to him considering their collective sense of ego and self-righteous purpose. I might not, he thought, turn out to be a very good savior.

31.

Jesús watched the Federal agencies move into position over a period of fifteen to twenty minutes just as Victor had said they would do. They didn't seem to him to try to hide their approach, their movement, as they got close to the warehouse. He had no way of identifying the affiliation of the men he witnessed, but he knew they were FBI and DEA for sure. Cuzo had told him there also would be men from an agency with which he had no knowledge called the ATF. He wondered which was which as he saw the cars and vans that looked like the law. Some drove by slowly and parked nearby; others appeared from side streets to find their parking spot. Funny how these law men always have cars and vans and trucks that look like the law. Their wheels don't look those that regular people have. How could they not think that someone who should be noticing would not notice them?

Jesús knew that what was about to take place was not a party. He shook his head back and forth as he watched, the audacity of Victor a puzzle to him. There was a craziness of Victor that he had often perceived, but that craziness had always translated into more and more money for all of them. It was hard to deny Victor's motivation even though his methods could be unusual. Victor had used the word party over and over. For Jesús, it was the wrong word to use. He knew better than to even suggest to Victor that there was word usage that needed to be changed.

Jesús moved through the warehouse from one peephole to another, places that had been determined and produced for assessing their security. These viewpoints had the sole purpose of checking on what was going on outside and allowed him to track the progress of the raiding force. Sweat came to the palms of his hands and to his armpits even as he stood stock still watching. It was the tension of anticipation. He believed that he would be able to escape, but he would have the narrowest of margins with which to execute that escape.

He had checked and rechecked how he would move, how he would walk, every action calculated to get him out of the warehouse as quickly as possible. At the end of the back hallway was a steel door that opened into a stairwell that contained a short flight of steel steps leading down to another steel door at the bottom. The second steel door led to a narrow tunnel that ran under the alley behind the warehouse. The tunnel ended at a third steel door that allowed access to an area beneath the loading docks of the building across the alley. At the end of the area under the loading docks was a flight of concrete steps that went up to the outside. His car would be parked there. He had practiced in the dark, with a flashlight, and the move to his car took an average of thirty seven seconds once he closed the first steel door to the hallway. He figured it would be enough time to get away safely.

It was almost eight o'clock when Jesús determined that the law seemed to be in place. Only an occasional truck rolled by, headed for one of the other nearby warehouses or small machine shops. He must wait for the Frangelettis. Waiting was something he did well. He had overseen the operations of the warehouse almost from the time that Victor had begun using the building for the vending business. Mainly, that meant making sure the warehouse was secure, to keep the others who worked for Victor from stealing from the large supply of vending products, and to see to it that no undo attention would be drawn to the building. Jesús made sure the city permits were in order and was, in effect, the front man for the Ashland operation. He tried to be alert under the usual circumstances, but with the impending meeting, he had heightened his vigil for the situation, constantly monitoring what went on around the building. He had seen the law car roll by slowly the day before. He knew the warehouse was being checked out for the raid. That was good, he thought, they will come into what Victor has planned for them.

When Hal Barton got word from Connelly about the meeting in Ashland he knew he didn't have a lot of time to mobilize the forces that were required, that should be part of the operation. He had made the appropriate phone calls to the other agencies and selected the group from his own office that would take part. He wanted to see the meeting spot for himself before getting the task force there and drove to Ashland soon after receiving Connelly's call.

It was not an imposing structure, he thought, as he drove by the warehouse, there should be no difficulty getting inside quickly. He turned at the first corner and went along the side of the building to the back. There was a door that could be used from the side street and another large double door at the rear. The building did not appear to be occupied and there were no vehicles parked near it. He had noted the numerals 9-8-6 over the front entry. It was the right building, but it sure looked dead.

He punched the Cleveland office number into his cell phone and got through to the agent he had assigned to get information on the building.

"Jack...waddaya have for me on this warehouse in Ashland? I'm sitting here now and it looks pretty quiet."

"Leased to a man named Jesús Colon, Hal, rent's been paid regular as clockwork since the lease was signed. Landlord says there's been no problems...says it's a bunch of Mexicans with a vending business...says he's been in the building several times since they moved in and it looked legit to him. That's all we know so far."

"Thanks, Jack. From the way this place looks, I don't think we'll have any problem getting in. We should be able to take care of this even on such short notice. I don't think they would realize we knew about the meeting or were right on top of them. Surprise will be our advantage. I'm heading back...have the guys get their gear ready so we can move out early tomorrow."

Hal Barton had, as did Jesús, considerable tenacity when it came to waiting. He had waited in situations like this many times over the years. Waiting for the moment to strike. Those waits had always ended with productive results: arrests and prosecutions. He watched and waited, somewhat satisfied with the force he had assembled and gotten into place around the warehouse. He had assigned the ATF group the side entrance and the DEA team the rear. He would lead his own force of FBI agents in the front door of the building as the main strike after the Frangelettis got inside. He had given Connelly and his two men the task of covering the two large truck doors that opened to the street in front of the warehouse. He figured they could prevent any escape attempt that might be tried by running a vehicle out those doors.

For Connelly, the minor assignment for him and his men was an insult, but he accepted Barton's terse directive on the matter without complaint. They took up their position in an alley directly across from the warehouse and would move their car close to the overhead doors on Barton's command.

"How's it looking over there, Ralph?" Barton asked of Agent Simmons, using his two-way radio. "Have you got a clear signal?"

"Yeah, I can hear you loud and clear," Simmons responded. "Nothing going on at the side. We're all set in position...we can get to the door in seconds...we can break through pretty quickly it looks like."

"Good. Just wait for my command. We'll give the Frangelettis time to get inside, then we'll hit. Royce, how's it look where you are in back?"

"We're all set," Royce answered with no elaboration.

Another thirty minutes went by before one of Burton's agents came on the two-way.

"Two vehicles approaching slowly...might be them...Mercedes and a van right behind. Got the binocs on the car...looks like Nicky...looks like his photo...another guy driving...must be the rest of his goons in the van. He wasn't coming to this meeting without protection that's for sure."

"Everyone on alert," Burton snapped into his radio, "get ready, they've arrived."

Jesús saw the Mercedes pull up in front, a van pulled up right behind the big sedan. The waiting was over, he thought, we are now in action.

Nicky looked at the warehouse with disdain wondering why they had to meet the Mexicans in a place like this.

"I suppose this dump is appropriate considering it's a bunch of lousy wetbacks we gotta deal with."

"Yeah, right," Allie laughed.

"You know, Allie, it was a big mistake the old man made letting these guys get started in the vending business here. He talked with the Cleveland boys and they all decided to leave 'em alone. After all, it was only Mexicans, what kind of trouble could they give us. They shoulda known. Now, it's come back to haunt us."

"Yeah, right." Allie did not laugh.

Nicky got out of the car, stretched, swung his arms around, and pulled at the seat of his pants to adjust them. He stood waiting until Allie came around the car next to him and the others from the van were standing close. He led the way to the door where he waited while Allie knocked and pressed the small button over the jamb.

The door opened almost immediately.

"Mr. Frangeletti?" Jesús asked politely.

"Yeah, Nicky Frangeletti. We're early, but I figured you wouldn't mind."

"No, not at all. Mr. Padillo is getting some work done in his office, but I'm sure he won't be more than a few minutes to finish up. You can wait over here...there's some comfortable chairs...although we didn't expect so many of you to come."

Jesús led the way to an area in the center of the warehouse where a table and cushioned chairs had been placed. On one end of the table were a coffee server and cups, cream, sugar, spoons, a tray with soda pop and juice, and another tray with doughnuts, cookies and bagels. At the other end of the table were several cardboard boxes.

"Have a coffee, jelly doughnut, or whatever...You can sit right there and I'll let Mr. Padillo know that you've gotten here a little early. He'll be right with you, I'm sure."

Nicky watched Jesús walk across the warehouse and down a hallway towards the back. He poured a cup of coffee, picked up one of the jelly doughnuts, and took several bites. Suddenly a wave of terror ran through him. He had not sensed it until now, but the realization swept over him with crushing pain almost as if he were having a heart attack. This was a setup, a trap. It had been too easy, the Mexican too polite, and there was no one else around, no muscle, nothing. He set down the cup and tossed the rest of the doughnut back onto the tray. His throat was choked with so much fear that he could hardly speak. He turned to Allie, but at first, no words came out, only the guttural sounds of an attempt at saying something.

Allie assumed Nicky was choking on the doughnut and slapped his back vigorously to dislodge the particles causing the problem. Nicky pushed him away, finally released from the panic that had made him react so.

"No, goddamnit, I'm not choking. This is a setup."

"How? Where's his guys if it's a setup?" Allie asked.

"It's a setup, I'm tellin' you." Nicky pulled his automatic from its shoulder holster and almost in unison the others did likewise.

Nicky, Allie, and the other six men stood in the quiet, dimly lighted warehouse, guns drawn, looking around for the trap to be sprung. There was no sound, other than the metal to metal clatter of rounds being chambered in their automatics. No noise, no rustle, no stir from within the warehouse save their own heavy breathing. A minute went by. Still nothing happen.

"Shouldn't that Mexican be coming out of his office by now?" Allie whispered.

Nicky didn't respond because he didn't know what to make of the situation.

"This is the FBI. This is a Federal raid," Hal Barton said as he came through the front door, "maintain your position and get your hands up where we can see them."

Barton was prepared to break in the front door, but he tried opening it first on the chance it was not locked. Indeed, it was not locked and he moved inside quickly followed by the rest of his men. He and his men were ready to return fire, but assumed their surprise would prevail and there would not be shots fired. He did not realize, of course, that Nicky and his men already had their weapons drawn. However, he quickly saw the glint of steel and knew what it meant.

"Don't try to use your weapons...drop them now...we have a lot more firepower..."

Nicky had his back to the front door when Barton came in and was startled when the agent had yelled his identification. Was the trap getting us busted? It was a fleeting thought he had as he turned and fired three shots in a reflexive, almost programmed manner. One of the slugs hit Barton's vest at the sternum, a second tore through his right arm, and the third hit the wall behind. As those shots resounded, the other agents from the DEA and ATF stormed into the warehouse, on edge from the sound or gunfire, ready to open fire in return.

No more shots were fired. The time had arrived for Victor's party to have its surprise event, a surprise he wanted all of those attending to experience. It was for the lousy Frangelettis and the lousy Feds. Good-bye. It was retribution for the death of Angel Partencíon. And good-bye, again.

Victor, Cuzo, and Juan had watched the warehouse from the roof of a nearby building. They too had seen the Feds move into position, had watched with anticipation as Nicky and his gang pulled up and went inside.

"You should not be here," Juan had cautioned, "you should be on your way to the airport or, better yet, your plane should already be gone."

"No, no, amigo," Victor said, "I want to see eet happen. I need to be here. I don't want to be told about eet."

Cuzo shook his head in dismay, but knew there was nothing to be done to dissuade Victor from relishing the moment by being here to see the results. They would have to be careful, be swift, be sure about getting over to the airport. There was not a lot of time to avoid what would surely be a horrendous manhunt and the closing down of escape routes.

Victor folded his arms, his face stern with the intensity of the anger that boiled within him. He nodded slightly as the Federal agents moved into the warehouse. Everything had occurred just as he had told Cuzo that it would. He waited for Juan to use his magic box.

Juan held a small instrument in his hand, slightly larger than a garage door opener. This would trigger the explosion about to take place. He waited for ten seconds to elapse from the time the agents went inside before pushing the button on the side of the controller. The blast let go with a jarring force they could sense there on the roof top even before part of the shock wave pushed at them.

Juan had placed the plastic explosive charges to create maximum effect within the warehouse. He was trying to kill everyone inside, not blow up a building. His goal was almost achieved. Two DEA agents near the back of the building and an ATF agent covering the side door were all spared the full force of the explosion. The three men were severely injured from flying debris, but they would in time recover, although the ATF man lost the sight in his left eye.

Juan had assumed the greatest number of men to be near the table that Jesús had prepared - certainly the Frangeletti gang, which was the prime target - so he had made sure that area would be devastated. That was the way it worked: Nicky, Allie, and the six other Frangeletti goons did take the full force of the explosion, their remains scattered about the warehouse and through all the openings in the walls and roof blown apart from the blast. Later that day, the FBI lab team was hard pressed to locate much of them for examination. Nicky's automatic was found later on the street in front of the warehouse, although with all identification removed, the FBI had no way of knowing it was his. His gun was just one of many that were present in the warehouse that morning.

Butch was looking forward, scanning the oncoming buildings of Ashland, when the plastic let go. The chopper pilot yelled: "Wow. See that?"

"Damn. Yeah." Butch knew for sure that he was too late. How many died, he wondered?

Although some distance ahead, the blast that took off part of the warehouse roof was clearly visible. All manner of debris flew up and out in all directions, while a cloud of dust and smoke quickly formed. They were too far away yet to feel the shock of the blast, but its effects were clearly apparent.

News reporter Jack Stewert, sitting next to Butch, sat in stunned silence. Finally, he said, "You were right...God, you were right...I mean...shit, look at that." He turned to his camera man sitting forward next to the pilot. "You get that by chance?"

"Naw, camera wouldn't pick that up, it's too far away. We'll get it when we get closer. Anyway, it probably's still gonna be smokin' and burnin'. We'll get some good stuff, don't worry."

Butch wanted to say something to the two young men so unconcerned with what really happened, who blithely ignored the loss of life, the shattering of families, the crushing of hopes and dreams of the agents caught in the explosion. Their concern was for the story that would boost their careers. What could he say that would mean anything to them about what had just happened? Nothing, he decided, nothing he said to them would matter.

Smoke continued to rise from the warehouse as the chopper closed the distance. What would Pam think if she knew this happened, Butch wondered. He closed his eyes and hoped that somehow, some way, fate had intervened, and he hoped that, indeed, Pam had not known it was going to happen.

32.

Cuzo was justifiably nervous as he handled the car that took him and Victor to the airport in Mansfield. He drove fast, but carefully, not willing to take chances with the speed limit, although pressing just over the edge every time there was an opening in traffic. Eventually, they were on a little used two-lane rural road and he pressed even more.

Since he had worked with Victor he had constantly been concerned that something would go wrong with their operation. So many reasons for screw ups, so many ways to be tripped up by the law, so many men involved who could turn on them for a buck. He had known his concerns were justified. They had gotten this far with Victor's crazy scheme, yet there was plenty of opportunity to have something go wrong. There was still the distance to cover to get to the plane. Anything could happen. His anxiety made him grind his teeth and shift uncomfortably on the leather seat as sweat began to saturate his shirt and the back of his pants.

"I don't want you to say anything to Pam about what just happened," Cuzo said without looking at Victor.

"Of course not. And Luis? Have you warned Luis?"

"He already knows not to say anything."

"She will know sooner or later. You know eet."

"I'll deal with it...when we're in Mexico. Time and distance will make it easier. She will understand once we're there."

"You must admit, eet was very good wasn't eet? My party was very good. Eet was justice for Angel and Ramon. I like we could do eet for dem. Beautiful eet ees, dees revenge. Very nice."

Cuzo did not answer, concentrating on the truck he wanted to pass.

The explosion had been a shock to Cuzo even though he expected it. He had stood on the roof with Victor as Juan sent the signal, knowing full well what would happen, but not knowing really what would take place. Seeing, feeling, and hearing the blast at close range had been beyond his experience. He had never been near an explosion before. The full impact of the results were difficult to comprehend, even as an eye witness. He remembered listening to Juan in the immediate aftermath of the onrushing force of the explosion describing the concussion and what it would do. Juan was talking to no one in particular, merely giving a narrative account much like a play by play announcer would do at a sports event. Juan noted how the concussion would kill everyone in the primary zone, how anyone in the secondary zone would sustain such severe injuries that they would be life-threatening, that little evidence of the Frangelettis would be found.

Cuzo recalled the projectiles flying by them, a mess of odd-sized shrapnel, the whizzing sound they made zooming unseen through the air, the rattle of pieces that hit the wall of the building below them, and the warehouse seeming to come apart belching smoke and dust, and eventually the licks and snaps of flames. The warehouse had paint, paint thinner, gasoline, and kerosene stored there, all of which helped produce a conflagration after the explosion of devilish proportions that would burn the building to the ground.

Much of the building was still standing right after the explosion, creating for Victor a sense of disappointment. In his mind was the visualization that the warehouse would totally disintegrate. But with Juan's casual discourse about the results, with bits and pieces of the building flying by and hitting around them, he was satisfied the trap had been a success. He was more smug than gleeful in his reaction once he was sure how devastating the event was. Smugness that came from his own arrogance, his challenge to overcome the insecurity of dealing with Cuzo's assuredness and education, from the advantages of background on which Cuzo relied. He knew full well that Cuzo did want him to do this thing. It was dangerous, it created a greater reason for the Feds to pursue them for a lifetime, and it made it more difficult for them to get out of the country quickly and efficiently.

Juan was quietly delighted with his handiwork, but gave little indication to Victor and Cuzo of how he felt. He was the dispassionate professional. Of course the outcome would be as he dictated.

Cuzo pointed to the car in front of the warehouse that had gone unnoticed at first.

"They must have been part of the raid," Cuzo offered, "looks like they took a hell of a hit...badly damaged in front...whoever was inside might have survived."

It was the car with Connelly and agents Kennedy and Binkert. As instructed by Hal Barton, with Kennedy driving, the car was headed up to the large truck doors to prevent escape. It was parked, motor running, facing the warehouse when the explosion came. The shock force tore open both of the building's overhead doors allowing material hurled from inside to bombard the car with a stream of deadly fragments. The doors still dangled from their cables after the explosion, like victims clinging to some semblance of order, waiting helplessly for aid to arrive.

The three agents were not killed, but Kennedy and Binkert in the front seat were seriously injured, miraculously not losing their eyesight. Connelly was hit once by a small piece of steel of some kind that tore at his head right at the scalp line. It would take twenty five stitches to close the wound, but he would consider himself to be very lucky. He sat stunned in the back seat trying to figure out what had happened. Stupefied by the shock of the blast, he could not factor events for several minutes. By the time paramedics arrived, he kept mumbling about a 'trap'. He said the word 'trap' over and over as blood and tears washed over his face until he passed out in the emergency van.

With the fire raging in the shell of the warehouse, Victor and Juan shook hands. They needed to move quickly. Through the roof service door and down the back stairs they went, two steps at a time, and exited onto the alley. Juan was into his rental car off to Hopkins Airport in Cleveland, gone before Victor and Cuzo were in their car. By late afternoon he was in Phoenix as Ron Thomas. Jason Dillard had vanished and Ron Thomas would live in a modest apartment near the University for several months until he was needed for a new assignment.

Cuzo slid behind the wheel and calmly, with deliberate urgency guided the car down the alley, not wanting to draw any attention to their departure. They could hear sirens, but as they moved away from the grisly scene, no police or fire squads had yet arrived. Cuzo's last picture of what they had done was in the rear view mirror. Flames jumped and lashed at what was left of the warehouse, already progressing to the building next to it. It would be a severe test for the Ashland Fire Department.

Butch and the others in the chopper could clearly view the inferno beneath them. Pilot Dailey curled the craft around the site only several hundred feet above ground so the cameraman could get the best shots. Stewert chattered incessantly into the tape recorder he clutched with both hands, totally engrossed in the scene below. Butch was silent, wishing Stewert would shut up, wishing he could do more than just watch from this suspended perch, so close, yet a world away in relative safety. They had witnessed secondary bursts leap from the main fire, which Butch had attributed to containers of flammables of some kind. Two other nearby buildings were now also on fire, compounding the problem for those that had to fight and contain the blaze.

It was pretty easy to guess, Butch figured, what happened to the Frangelettis and any of the Federal agents inside the warehouse when the plastic explosives let go. Poof, they were evaporated. Just like Victor wanted. That sonofabitch. He had counted on everything working out just the way he thought it would. Once he had the Frangelettis committed it was easy to assume the Feds would get there if they were tipped off to what was going down. He used me through Cuzo. He had me figured, also. He knew I wouldn't let the meeting go by without trying to help the Feds by feeding them info. What a sucker I was. Pulled right into his bullshit scheme.

The chopper circled the warehouse slowly giving Novak a chance to get video coverage of the scene from every direction. Dailey took the chopper as low as he could and still have a measure of safety from the heat and smoke. It wasn't long before the billowing smoke obscured their view of the debris and Dailey took them up higher to keep clear.

Butch saw the first pumper company arrive, get their hoses connected to hydrants, and begin the staggering battle with the flames. Other fire trucks quickly arrived, their crews spilling out to join in the struggle to get the fire under control. Right behind the fire trucks were several emergency vans with paramedics.

Butch sat back in his seat aboard the chopper and quit looking at the spectacle below. He was overcome with his own frustration from his inability to get word to someone that would have prevented the explosion from taking place. Of all the agents, he only knew Connelly personally, but he knew the rest were all good men. Dedicated men who should not have died that way. He didn't care about the Frangeletti guys, although they probably didn't deserve to die like that any more than the Feds. In a sense, though, he supposed, they asked for it. They didn't want Jerry dead, specifically, but weren't concerned when he was killed and it was their guy that did it. Bad boy, Buddy, shame, shame. Buddy would have gone relatively unpunished if it hadn't been for the Mexicans.

Butch knew that his thoughts were crazy, caught and twisted by what happened to all those men. Crazy from the rage that seeped into his feelings. Crazy from the frustration. He fought within himself to regain control of his thoughts.

The next step was to get Victor and Cuzo, he reckoned. No time can be lost because they can't be out of the country yet. They are long gone though, he figured, on a private jet, most likely, well away from here. They probably had some stooge set off the blast, someone expendable, so they could escape without difficulty. They'll go to Mexico, no doubt, and the Feds will have to hunt them down and get them back.

The drive to the Mansfield Lahm Municipal Airport had started to take its toll on Victor. He became as ill at ease as Cuzo, beads of sweat showing on his forehead, the constant rubbing of the palms of his hands on his pants.

"How much longer?" Victor asked.

Cuzo did not answer immediately, his pause a reflection of the anger he had for being needlessly put in this position, anger at Victor's prideful step at retaliation, anger at the tension that gripped him.

"We are in this spot because of your decision," Cuzo finally said, his voice controlled and quiet, "otherwise we would already be in Mexico."

"How much longer?" Victor repeated, ignoring Cuzo's accusation and subtle condemnation. "Eet can't be too far, eh?"

"No, we're close."

"You know, amígo, there ees such a thing to be considered...eet ees that revenge is sweet..."

"Revenge can also get you caught...or killed. Revenge can sometimes be stupid."

"You are angry, amígo, but I am happy...very pleased with my revenge, very satisfied..."

"And the wet hands?" Cuzo pointed at Victor's hands rubbing his pants.

"Certain plans are dangerous, verdad, but they are worth eet."

Cuzo was quiet again and eased the accelerator down a bit, wanting more speed in his effort to get there quickly, yet not be radar bait. There was no point arguing with Victor. After all, there was a long plane ride ahead of them and no point having such tension in front of Pam. The flight to Mexico would be touchy enough, so it would be most unpleasant, an added burden to have argument and contention as companions on the plane. Besides, once they were in Mexico, he, Pam, and Luis would split with Victor. The partnership would be over. Cuzo could tolerate the trip with Victor to reach that end. He had been edgy about his relationship with Victor for months and to perceive that relationship ending made Cuzo relax, somewhat.

The first road sign of direction to the airport appeared and Victor pointed to it without speaking, but he turned to Cuzo with a smile and nod as if to say: We are close, no? Shortly, another sign showed. They were almost there.

Luis stood by the General Aviation hanger at Lahm field casually drinking a beer that he held behind him when not sucking in strong gulps with the usual slurping sound. Nearby, Jesús sat on a bench shaking. He had been all right dealing with Nicky and his men, getting through the run from the warehouse, suffering the drive to the airport, but once he arrived and reported to Luis, he had gone to pieces. He understood what had taken place, nearly a victim. He had gotten in his car and was almost out of the alley that extended from the back of the warehouse, when the explosion let go. Pieces of concrete, brick, and metal sprayed his car as he turned onto the next street. Unlike Cuzo, and unlike how he had been instructed, he drove as fast as he could to the airport. His teeth chattered, he was so shaken.

Cuzo had entrusted Luis with the responsibility of getting Pam to the airport and making sure she was on the jet that had been arranged. Cuzo working through a friend in Guadalajara, had contracted for the Cessna Citation to be in Mansfield on this day. Through a complicated series of maneuvers, the jet had arrived in the US at Albuquerque, moved to Omaha, and settled at the Mansfield airport the night before. Cuzo had met with the pilot, making sure he knew where their destination was, assuring himself they would leave the country with no difficulty. The pilot, Jorgé Habrigas, had laughed as he confirmed how simple their trip would be. They would fly in accordance with Air Traffic Control directions until they were in little used air space in southern New Mexico. They would be across the border with slight notice. He said they would refuel at a prearranged airport in northern Mexico, so they could make Guadalajara with ease.

The debate between Cuzo and Victor about where they would land in Mexico had been tense, but short. Victor, who wanted to head for an airport near Mexico City, relented because Cuzo could make the connection work with friends in Guadalajara. Besides, Cuzo argued, too close to the capitol puts us too close to the government and the higher necessary bribes we would have to pay. By going to Guadalajara, it is safer and costs us less. Even going to Guadalajara will cost us plenty.

After talking with Jorgé, Cuzo gave Luis, who went out to the jet with him, instructions for the following day: take Pam and Gloria to the plane, make sure they were on board and comfortable, and all of our belongings are stowed. When Victor and I get there, he had said, we won't want to waste any time. Luis' biggest responsibility, what showed Cuzo's immense trust in the man, was to have charge of the four travel bags with cash. This was Cuzo's money. Victor's money, in larger denomination bills, was always with him. With everything else illegal that they had done, what matter was it to take such amounts out of the country? Electronic transfers could be traced.

Luis had gotten Pam and Gloria on board and settled. He waited for Jesús, satisfied he was ready, pacifying himself by sucking on one of the beers from his briefcase.

"They will hunt us down like dogs," Jesús said, his voice trembling as he tried to regain his composure.

"They will never touch us," Luis said calmly.

"I didn't know it would be so...so powerful. You can't believe the sound. Did you see the car? It got hit with all kinds of shit...dents everywhere. What if I had not gotten out?"

"But you did, Jesús, you did. And now you are safe. Relax, everything is okay. Soon you will be home...we'll have lots of money...women...a nice life. You will see. So relax...enjoy the plane ride."

"Mexico is not my home. I have never been to Mexico. My home is here in this country."

"Where was your father born?"

"Monterey."

"In Mexico?"

"Yes, but..."

"No, my friend, Mexico is your home whether you want it to be or not. Here in this country you are a segment, Hispanic, Chicano, Beaner, Wetback...I've told you before...you are a name of a kind, not just a man. In Mexico, you will be a man...a man with money...a better standard of living, and you will not be a racial segment. The money you have earned with us means nothing in this country. Where and how could you spend it as a criminal? Few ways, few places. There's more to having money than getting drunk and whoring. In Mexico, you will have respect, you will be somebody. That, my friend, is worth a great deal. Ahh...they are here. We shall soon be on our way."

Cuzo sprang from the car. He stood waiting with his arms folded as Victor pulled the two large travel bags from the trunk. He did not offer to help carry them, but Victor waved to Luis for assistance.

"Luis, all ees well, sí? Of course. And Jesús, you courageous one, such valor to be so close to the action. Your contribution will not go unrewarded. Let's geet on the jet. Now we leave."

Before Victor boarded the plane, he dramatically waved a hand from right to left with bombastic sweep to precede his proclamation of pleasure. "Dees ees a great country. We made a lotta money here. God bless America. Adíos." He jumped up the steps and onto the Cessna.

Pam and Cuzo were already in deep embrace when Victor entered the main cabin.

"What took you so long to complete your deal?" Pam asked, unknowing of events.

"Eet always takes longer when there ees a big payoff," Victor replied, "but you were comfortable, no?"

Cuzo settled into a seat across from Pam at one of the tables and they held hands over its small surface. The interior of the plane had been outfitted to look much like a hotel cocktail lounge, a pleasure and relaxing jet, rather than one for business. The others also took seats and nervously peered out the windows just as the Captain came back from the cockpit.

"We are buttoned up, ready to go" Jorgé said, now the man in charge, "get your seat belts fastened. We'll soon be off and to cruising altitude quite quickly. There is plenty of food and drink on board for you to enjoy. Sit back, relax. Soon we are gone."

"Captain, can you head east after you takeoff?" Victor asked.

"No, Meester Padillo, we cannot...not without causing problems for us. It would draw attention we don't want. We takeoff southwest with a westerly heading. We want limited contact with Traffic Control, so it is not a good idea."

"Too bad," Victor sighed, "I would have liked one more look at our party."

33.

The fluid, easy motion Butch usually had as he ran was missing, replaced by oddly mechanical, graceless strides. He was forcing himself to run, pressing to keep at it through the tension that dominated him. Although he was running on the softer dirt trail through the Fallen Timbers Metropark along the Maumee River, his knees still ached. The ache he was trying to run off persisted because he could not relax and slip into the running style that was ordinarily his. Each step was very deliberate, with a consciousness about it that was required to keep moving. Each step seemed to Butch as if he were squeezing something away, the way a smoker steps on a cigarette butt to press it lifeless, pushing and twisting the foot to make sure.

Concentrating so on his running style had taken away the enjoyment of the view as he passed by the river. The curious delight Butch had normally experienced when he was running was gone. His ability to take in the sights and sounds and smells as he moved along had always been an added motivator to keep going with a training regimen that allowed him to be a competitive triathlete. At least in his age group he was competitive, usually finishing in the top three in his group, more often than not gaining the first or second slot. On this day, as with the last several days, running was merely an ordeal to be coped with, an exercise in aggravation. Knees hurt, socks weren't right, it was hot, too many bugs, callous rubbing against the shoe on the left foot - this was his litany of distractions for this day. There was no pleasure, there was no view, no promise of feeling better, merely the burning desire to quit and walk to his car in the parking lot near the shelter house.

He stopped and stared out at the river, lost within himself, caught in his own frustration, trying to determine if the view he absorbed would make him feel better. Unfortunately, it did not and he continued his forced run for nearly an hour more before he doubled back towards the parking lot and his car. He drove back to his house soaked with sweat and still unsatisfied with how he ran and how he felt. Neither running nor biking, nor any of the other physical exercises had been helpful to change his mood.

Butch had worked for days trying to rid himself of the anger and frustration imbedded in him. They were still with him. He kicked at his back door when it didn't open quite quickly enough for him, cursing the door and his own lack of patience. Once inside, he pulled a pitcher from the refrigerator that contained his own concoction of fruit juices and supplements that he periodically mixed in his blender. He poured a glass that he quickly drank, then poured another.

He walked to the living room to see who and what was parked out front, expecting a television or radio truck, or someone else from the news media wanting his time. There was no one and he was relieved. Ever since the bombing, he had been hounded by the media clamoring for interviews, wanting to get his story about what had happened to young Frangeletti, asking questions about Pam and the Mexicans. Channel 11 had played up the story of how Butch had commandeered their chopper to try to stop the explosion.

The incident had made a news celebrity of Jack Stewert, who had conducted several interviews with Butch. Plus, there was the on-the-scene footage shot from the chopper that was shown over and over for days. He had given brief interviews to national TV guys, but they all wanted more. Several of the cable news talk shows tried to get Butch, but he had refused their requests. He wanted to maintain a low profile, not talk openly about something so horrendous, that bothered him so much. He did not like having his motives or his psyche probed on national television or anywhere else. He had rebuffed the additional requests for interviews enough times that maybe the media would leave him alone. Some of these guys are persistent, though, you never know when they might turn up for another try.

The three Federal agencies involved also had taken up a lot of Butch's time. They each had interrogated him several times extensively, finally convinced he knew no more than what he told them. Eventually, each agency formally thanked him in writing for making the attempt to save their men.

In the meantime, he stayed away from his office and his business suffered as a result. He had accomplished little for his clients since returning from Ashland.

The phone rang and he waited for more rings, trying to decide if he would answer. When he did answer, the voice startled him. It was Pam.

"Wanted to let you know that...that I'm okay."

Her voice was huskier than he had remembered, but otherwise the same.

"What is it you want me to say?" he snapped.

"I thought you might..."

"Thought what? Thought that I might care?"

"I guess I was wrong by the way you sound."

"Tell me," Butch pressed, "do you know what happened in Ashland?"

"That was not..."

"Do you know?" he yelled.

"Yes, but that was Victor's doing..."

"Bullshit."

"Cuzo did not..."

"Don't give me that. It wouldn't have happened without Cuzo. Cuzo the arranger. Besides, Cuzo fed me the information that got everyone there."

She did not respond.

"Well?" Butch spoke the word with such force into the phone his hand shook. "Are you satisfied with that...satisfied with what you've gotten into?"

"I didn't call for a lecture, I called to let you know I'm all right...I'm happy with Cuzo...we're going to have a nice life here...it's beautiful and the people are wonderful. I..."

"Jesus...that's nice Pam. Enjoy it while you can because it's not going to last long. It's only a matter of time. It will be a race now between the Feds and the hit man Nick Frangeletti has hired to get Cuzo and Victor and anyone else in that gang that is down there with you. It's a toss up as to which of them gets to you first. My bet goes to Nick's guy. The Feds will try to do it legally and that will take longer. Yeah, Cuzo and Victor have to watch their step now...always on guard, watch their movements, keep in seclusion...otherwise they will get nailed. And believe it or not, more than likely, Pam, you'll get nailed right along with them."

"We've separated from Victor...we're on our own...with another man, Luis. Victor is gone. It was his doing, Butch, Cuzo would never have wanted to kill all those men."

"Oh really? Well, they're still dead...and there are a lot of distraught families trying to recover...some of those families are in financial trouble as a result. None of the survivors will ever be the same, as a matter of fact. Yeah, those guys are very dead. You're a part of it whether you want to be or not, whether you think you are or not. The stain of it reaches you...you who were off somewhere, blithely dreaming about soaring off to Mexico and the bliss with your lover. While you were waiting to leave, Cuzo and Victor were killing more than two dozen good men..."

"I know. I saw it on CNN. But that doesn't mean..."

"You shouldn't have bothered to call Pam because I wasn't really worrying about you. My concern has been with the families of those men Cuzo murdered."

"Thanks a lot...and don't worry," Pam said, her voice taut with sarcasm, "I won't ever bother you again. Have a nice life."

There was the distinctive click as the phone connection ended.

Butch, in a rage, threw the empty plastic juice glass he still had in his hand through the doorway into the kitchen. The glass hit a corner of the refrigerator, clattered off a wall onto the floor. It skidded to a stop under the table. The fact that she hung up on him when he wanted to hang up on her was a flash point for his anger.

He stormed about his house in a fury as he showered and dressed, and left for Murray's in downtown Toledo. He gripped the steering wheel tightly and clenched his jaw. He knew he had to be careful so his rage did not come forth on the drive. He had called Tom Wachoviak the day before to arrange meeting for lunch. As usual, Butch wanted answers he thought Tom could provide.

The regular crowd was already in place when Butch got to Murray's, except there was no one representing the Frangeletti bunch. Those guys were low profile right now since Nick had pulled the string on just about everything in their operation. The Frangeletti organization was reeling from the loss of Nicky and the other slugs that were in the warehouse with him, and also doing a dance to keep the Feds at bay, mainly the DEA. Nick had always been successful handling such matters, but with his bad health and the loss of his son, it would be questionable how effective his efforts might be. It had only been a few days since Nick had phoned him and Butch could still hear the strain in the old man's voice as he thanked Butch for trying to help prevent what happened to his son and his men. Nick ended up getting rather maudlin, very sentimental, finally ending the conversation in tears.

Tom found his way to Butch's table and sat down without being greeted by Butch. Tom didn't speak right away. They had not seen each other in weeks, but the simplicity of this contact now was because, as is often the case with men, they did not need to speak a greeting. There was the implicit understanding of how each man felt. They shook hands and that was all they needed to connect.

"Would you ever have thought it would turn out this way?" Tom asked.

"Never," Butch said, sadly shaking his head, "not at all."

"There's not a lot for me to tell you," Wachoviak said, wishing there were some way he could soothe the anguish he saw in Butch. "Connelly's okay, but the other two guys with him got pretty beaten up from flying debris. Tough career thing for him, though...two disastrous raids back to back in short order. That's a career that has crashed and burned...big time."

"Yeah, I've talked to his wife. He hasn't left the house since he was released from the hospital. Won't talk to anyone, she says...not even the Bureau. Won't see anyone. She says it's going to take him awhile. My guess is he'll leave the FBI soon and get into something else like...oh, say...corporate security or something like that. None of it was his fault, but you are so right...he's going to take the fall. Too bad."

"Seems the FBI honchos have a different take on whether or not it was his fault. I hear they have a short list of mistakes...or rules violations. They may just be real or they may be manufactured...I haven't heard the particulars. In any case, it's not good for him."

"I was afraid they would do that to him."

"He'll be okay. You're right, though, he'll get out of the FBI, but he'll be all right. At least he wasn't in the warehouse.

The man who kept him out of the action - Hal Burton - wasn't so lucky."

"That's true. Very true."

"Jerry's wife went with them?" Tom knew the answer, of course, but he was probing Butch to find out what he thought.

"She called me this morning...right before I came down here. Can you believe it? I don't know what she was thinking...or what she really wanted. She's in dreamland. She thinks they're rid of Padillo and everything is going to be okay. She thinks Cuzo wasn't really involved, that it was Victor...Victor's idea, Victor's doing...her Cuzo would never want to hurt anybody. Jesus, what detachment from reality."

"Word is that Nick has a hit man on the move to Mexico with orders to get everyone involved. Everyone...including what's her name..."

"Pam."

"Pam. Yeah, she gets it, too."

"That's what I told her. The Feds or a hit man. No way was there going to be a long happy life in Mexico."

"Fact is, the word I hear is that the Feds are going to back off right now just so Nick's man can take care of things. If he can't or doesn't, they'll move on it. I don't think the Feds will need to get involved. You talk to Nick? That how you knew?"

"He called to offer me his thanks. He got pretty emotional. He said he was going to take care of things. I knew what he meant."

"It's already started. They found two of the Padillo guys early this morning...down in Hancock County. You figure whoever didn't have the privilege of going to Mexico made a run for it. Two, so far, haven't made it."

"What's the word on the explosion?"

"They don't know a whole lot yet. No doubt, of course, that it was plastic explosives. Story is that the plastic was stolen from Ft. Bragg for the Frangelettis. The Mexicans hijacked the truck carrying the stuff, used it to blast everybody. ATF says a pro was involved...the Mexicans didn't do it themselves...they brought in hired help...someone who knew explosives...someone who knew how to get the maximum effect from what they had to work with. All of the signs point to a pro. They sure got the results they wanted. Man, there was nothing left and three other buildings also burned down. It was quite the sight there in Ashland, I guess."

"Yes, it was," Butch said absently, "I can vouch for that."

"You know, it's really funny," Wachoviak went on, "we haven't been able to find one lick of evidence relating to the Mexican's business operations. No records, no files...nothing. They left clean."

"Thanks to our man Cuzo, I imagine," Butch laughed, "he would know how to do that. Victor would have forgotten something...not Cuzo."

The men were silent for several minutes, sipping their beers, before Butch spoke again.

"The Feds must be all over the Frangelettis, I would imagine?"

"Yeah, and we're working with them on it so I can't say too much. I can tell you that it's probably over for Nick's operation. It isn't likely that he'll do time because of his age and the heart condition, but you never know...he might join his cousin in Mansfield."

They finished their lunch and said their good-byes in front of Murray's. As they shook hands, Tom gave Butch a pat on the shoulder.

"It all ended a long way from where it started. A long way. You were just along for the ride. There wasn't anything you could do about anything. Don't spend a lot of time second guessing yourself."

"You may be right," Butch nodded, "but it sure doesn't feel good in my spot."

"You were helpless, but you didn't know it. That's the way it is sometimes. Anyway, it's been a strange few weeks...sorry what's happened to you...you got mixed up in a goofy mess. It didn't turn out right for you...I'm sorry about that. Take care...I'll talk to you soon."

"Thanks," Butch said quietly.

Butch drove back to his office in Perrysburg, trying to lose himself along the way listening to the play-by-play of an Indians game. He found himself not staying with it, not even caring about the score.

He stood in the middle of the stuffy room staring at the messy desk scattered with file folders and papers, the blinking light on the answering machine a pulsing plea for attention, and the stack of faxes that had accumulated. Where to start? How do I get going again? He wished Cindy were here now. She would be able to comfort him and help him sort out his feelings. He missed her terribly.

Butch poked about at the papers and files on his desk as he tried to structure some perspective in his mind for what had happened. He was caught in the emotions of what had occurred and knew that he needed to put some reason to it. In his mind it had to have meaning. Cindy could always do that for him. He stacked the files on the right side of his desk in alphabetical order according to their tab name. He pulled the loose sheets of paper into one pile in the center of the desk, and adjusted the stapler and paper clip dispenser so they were aligned in front of him. He sat with folded hands and looked about the room. None of this helped. It was merely action without purpose. It was inside his head that needed rearranging, he reckoned. He didn't want to be there, wondering if he could ever get started on another case again.

And that was ridiculous, it was what he did, what he had done for a long time. What had happened to those men would not really change anything for him. But right now it mattered.

He couldn't push away what was eating at him. The impact of all those men dying weighed heavily upon him, an emotional burden he was trying to shake. He knew that their deaths were not his fault, but still, there was an edge, a sliver of responsibility within him that was troubling. He had felt this way twice before when assignments were bungled or circumstances twisted fate and men died. It was not his fault those times anymore than now, but the sense of responsibility clung to him. There was that feeling: I should have been able to do something to save them. But it wasn't true then, not true now. All of the men who died were trying to accomplish something. The truth for Butch was that it was death without meaning. It was very sad.

Printed by Libri Plureos GmbH in Hamburg, Germany